Here Comes Your Man

a novel by derek gentry

Here Comes Your Man

a novel by derek gentry

**hysterical
publishing**

Here Comes Your Man: A Novel
Copyright © 2010 by Derek Gentry

Published in the United States by Hysterical Publishing.

Library of Congress Control Number: 2010901976

ISBN: 978-0-9826455-0-5

1

Hopefully Nowhere
07.28.1999

After surrendering my ID at the security desk, I turned back to Marco. He smiled and stuck out his hand.

"Thanks again, Garrett," he said. "And give my best to Leonard. Do you know where he's sending you next?"

"Hopefully nowhere," I said. "After this, I'm supposed to stay in Seattle for a while."

"Well, if you ever get back to Boston, be sure to give us a call."

"Thanks, Marco. Bye."

With that, I pushed through Genosys's revolving front doors and headed for my rented Lumina. To the parking lot security cameras, it probably appeared that I had someplace important to be, but I didn't. It was 5:40 p.m. on Tuesday, the database project that had consumed me for the last fourteen weeks was now complete, and I wasn't flying home until the next morning.

Of course I did have a plan. Over three years of near-constant travel, I'd become skilled at disposing of solitary evenings in strange cities. After a stop back at my room, I'd have a Mushroom-Swiss Burger (medium-rare) at the hotel bar, watching the 6:00 p.m. *Friends* rerun while I ate (no matter what city you're in, *Friends* is on sometime). After dinner, I'd head to Cambridge for a movie.

The Brattle Theater, a single-screen art cinema in Harvard Square, had been my salvation throughout this assignment. The Brattle had a different theme for each day of the week—Film Noir Mondays, Hong Kong Tuesdays, Frankenheimer Fridays—so I could just show up and see something that I'd never even heard of. The Brattle's audiences, cheering and applauding as if at a live performance, were as entertaining as the films themselves. Even if I didn't speak to a single person, I never left feeling like I'd spent the evening alone.

After the movie though, I'd enter the most treacherous part of any night on the road. I'd get back to my tomb-silent hotel room with nothing more to do, and I'd be gripped by the need to call someone. Specifically, I'd want to recline on my bed (television on, but muted), and talk for ninety minutes with somebody who already knew my deepest, darkest secrets, but who for some reason still liked me anyway.

My work schedule with Cavanaugh Associates—a month in one place, two months somewhere else—pretty much precluded dating, and I was usually too busy to mind being unattached. It was just in these odd, idle moments that I'd become aware of my aloneness. I'd run through my mental phone list—my best friend Bella, my sister Karen, Kevin Lanier, my ex-girlfriend Christina, various college and high-school friends I hadn't contacted in far too long. But I knew without even picking up the receiver that none of these calls would satisfy this particular craving. Sometimes I'd call anyway. Sometimes I'd call everyone I knew (except Christina), one after another.

In these moments, I often decided that it was time to quit my ridiculous job and try staying in one place long enough to have a real relationship. It always sounded like a great idea at midnight, but it just never happened. I'd fall asleep with the television on, and in the morning, I'd get up and go back to work.

After thirty years on planet Earth, I've begun to realize that I'm just not the kind of guy who *does* things. I'm more like the proverbial object that, whether in motion or at rest, tends to remain that way until acted on by an outside force. Like my ex-girlfriend Christina. Or my boss Leonard. Or the woman I met at the airport the very next day.

೧

At 8:30 on Wednesday morning, I was waiting at my gate at Logan, playing solitaire on my laptop and hazily watching other travelers shuffle past. I'd started to space-out a little—trying to guess who was leaving home, who was going home, and who was somewhere in between—when I realized that someone was speaking to me.

"Is anybody sitting here?"

It was a tall-ish woman, roughly my age, with pale, un-freckled skin, and wheat-blonde hair pulled back in a po-nytail. Her face reminded me of a girl I'd had a crush on in second grade—grey-blue eyes and a gently upturned nose. She wore a black t-shirt and blue jeans, and a messenger bag hung heavily off one shoulder, tilting her lanky frame to that side.

"Hm? No, I don't think so," I mumbled, looking down. Her steady, arched-brow gaze was more than I'd been pre-pared for at that hour. "I think someone just abandoned this here," I said, gathering up the *USA Today* that was spread over the seat in question. Glancing around, I noticed that the gate area had filled up considerably over the last half-hour—she'd had to sit next to *somebody*.

"Thanks," she said, dropping her bag to the floor with a thump.

She took out a book, and I went back to solitaire, doing my best to demonstrate that I was utterly unfazed by her presence and had no plans to harass her.

I'd often daydreamed about stumbling upon the love of my life at the airport. I imagined that I'd spot her in the check-in line, or the newsstand, or the duty-free shop, and with some disarmingly witty remark, I'd strike up a conversation. By boarding time, things would be going so swimmingly that we'd ask to be re-seated together. In-flight, we'd take turns making each other laugh, and for whatever reason—be it jet lag, dehydration, or altitude-induced hypoxia—she'd fall hopelessly in love with me before we returned the real world, before she had a chance to realize how unextraordinary I actually was.

Of course none of this even crossed my mind when Ms. Messenger Bag sat down beside me. The daydream was so disconnected from my reality—I hadn't been on a legitimate date in more than three years—that I no longer even recognized an opportunity when one presented itself. For the fifteen minutes that we sat there—she reading her book, me pretending not to notice her—I never considered speaking to her.

❧

For the Boston-to-Chicago leg of my trip home, I was ticketed to seat 27B, the middle seat in the rear exit row of a 727-200. Being so far back, mine was among the first rows called for boarding. The messenger-bag woman and I actually stood up simultaneously, and then we both hesitated, each waiting for the other to go.

"Sorry," I said, waving her ahead.

"Thanks," she said, with a smirk so adorable that it nearly floored me. *That's* when I knew that I was in trouble. In that moment, I realized that she was, for me, the very definition of suffering: hopelessly out of my league, but irresistible nonetheless.

Not that I'm totally unattractive. When I look in the mirror, I see a symmetrical, pleasantly boyish face (I'll be carded until I'm fifty), and I see bright blue eyes, neatly-trimmed blonde hair, and a wide, friendly smile. But at 5′ 10″ and 205 pounds, I also see someone who is pudgy—I have an all-over softness that deters women from taking me seriously. I do exercise from time to time, but I have little restraint when it comes to pizza and dessert.

On the positive side, I have excellent posture, and I do try to dress well. My job requires me to wear business suits, so I buy nice ones, all of them selected by my friend Bella. Hugo Boss and Calvin Klein seem to be her favorites, and I have a closetful of them in an inky rainbow of slimming blacks.

As Ms. Messenger Bag and I made our way through the vacuum-cleaner tube of the jetway, I couldn't resist checking her out a little—the sway of her golden ponytail, the tomboy shift of her hips—but I did try to be respectful about it. Which is to say that her giant bag was blocking my view of her butt.

Once on the plane, our progress was slowed considerably by early-boarders who clogged the aisle while stowing their carry-ons. As we inched aftward—row 19, row 20, row 21—I fully expected Ms. Messenger Bag to turn off somewhere and exit my life forever. But she just kept going, and when she reached row 27, she side-stepped over to the window seat and plopped herself down.

I was more than a little flustered by this development. I actually double-checked my boarding pass, even though I knew I was in the right place. After spending too much time adjusting the position of my garment-bag in the overhead, I finally sat down beside her. She smiled as I was stowing my laptop case under the seat in front of me.

"Serious leg room, huh?"

"Oh...yeah, it's nice," I agreed. The gap between rows 26 and 27 on a 727 is positively cavernous.

"All I need now is an ottoman," she said, kicking her feet out to illustrate the concept.

"That *would* be nice."

"Although, I guess that would interfere with the whole emergency exit thing—three ottomans blocking the door. Otto*mans*? Otto*men*? Seems like it should be otto*men*, huh?"

"I actually prefer otto*persons*, if you don't mind."

She laughed, a surprisingly dorky little nose-explosion.

"Well it wasn't *that* funny," I said.

"No, you're right...I think I'm just giddy not to be sitting next to Rasputin back there."

"The aromatic one?"

"Oh my God—all I did was walk past him and I thought I was going to pass out."

"I could switch with him," I offered.

"No, that's okay...really. That would be the one flight where I'd be praying for the oxygen masks to drop."

The seat to my right remained empty for a while, but it was eventually claimed by a gaunt gentleman in a red golf shirt. The shirt had some kind of country club crest on its pocket, and the name "Art" was stitched onto the sleeve. Art nodded to me as he sat down, his toothbrushy white crew-cut standing in stark contrast to his deeply tanned skin.

The flight attendants waved half-heartedly through the departure liturgy: seat belts, oxygen masks, lavatory smoke detectors, water landings. During this process, I studied my emergency information card, feigning interest in my exit-row responsibilities and resisting the temptation to initiate further conversation with Ms. Ottomen, who was blinking into the morning brightness of her window. Occasionally, she would reach back and take hold of her ponytail, as if to make sure it was still there.

As we started to pull away from the gate, she turned to me and spoke again.

"So how do you like your Dell?"

"Hm?" I tried to sound surprised, as if I'd been so un-lecherously unaware of her presence that I hadn't heard her question. "Oh, my laptop? Yeah, it's nice. I just got it, actually."

"I'm thinking about getting a new notebook. I have a new-ish Dell workstation that I like, but my laptop is ancient."

I nodded as we paused to consider this, both of us staring down at the dark shape of my laptop case as if it held the answer to something. What *I* wanted to know was why this woman owned two computers and was thinking about buying a third.

"So, what do you do for a living?" I asked.

"I work for a company called Amphibian Software?"

"Sure, I know Amphibian—WebFoot Pro, right?"

"Right! Wow…most people I meet have never even heard of us."

"Well, I'm an IT consultant, and I do some web development. What do you do at Amphibian?"

"Well, normally I'm a developer, but this week they had

me here in Boston working our booth at the WEBTEC show. They wanted someone 'technical' to chaperone the marketing ditz, and I was the lucky winner."

"You didn't enjoy yourself?"

"Not really. After sitting at a table for two days straight with Wendy yakking my ear off about the guy she just broke up with, I'll be glad to get back to the office."

"That's in San Francisco, right?"

"Yeah, I'm just making a connection in Chicago."

"San Francisco's great. I almost took a job there a few years ago."

"So where are you headed now?"

"Seattle."

"Is that home?"

"That's where they send my credit card bills anyway. I haven't spent much time there lately, but I'm hoping to get reacquainted with it."

"I'm surprised you need to travel that much, doing web development."

"Well, I do other stuff too. I just finished a big database project for a biotech firm here—that was something I kind of had to be on-site for. But you're right—practically speaking, I could do 90% of my work from my living-room. But for some reason, most of our clients would rather have someone physically present in their office for a few weeks or months...so I go."

ᘐ

We chatted right through takeoff, pausing only at the loudest moments. I was probably talking too much, but I so enjoyed the way she listened that I couldn't help myself. After three months alone, it was intoxicating to feel that someone was right there with me, completely engaged in what I was saying. I felt like I'd just been released from a vow of silence.

After a while though, I did manage to shut myself up and ask her more about herself. Mostly she told me about her experiences with the aforementioned "marketing ditz."

"It started on the flight out. She was like a freaking fountain, a never-ending stream of personal, slightly disgusting information."

"Such as?"

"Oh, you know, chronic medical conditions, preferred methods of birth control..."

"Wow."

"Yeah. I'm a naturally nosy person, but Wendy cured me. By the time we landed in Boston, I knew more about her than I ever wanted to know about anyone. And *then* I had to spend two entire days with her: sitting at the booth, eating with her, rooming with her."

"You shared a room?"

"Yeah, Amphibian was too cheap to spring for separate rooms. I'm sure that was the thinking in sending me instead of one of the guys."

"I have very few coworkers I'd want to room with."

"Oh, I was absolutely horrible to Wendy, disappearing every chance I got. But it seemed like the more I abused her, the more sickly-sweet she got. By last night, she was calling me 'honey' all the time. You know, 'Let me get the door for you, honey.' Or, 'Try some of my moisturizer, honey—your skin looks so dry.' I just wanted to slap her."

"She might've enjoyed it."

"The thought crossed my mind. But anyway, I just couldn't spend another second with her, so when she was in the shower this morning, I bolted. I was supposed to be on an 11:30 nonstop with her, but there was one seat available on this flight, so I grabbed it."

"You just *ditched* her?"

"Well, I left her a note saying there was an emergency at home. Which is half true, because if we'd flown together, I might've been forced to kill her. I just hope she doesn't show up at my apartment tonight because she's so concerned."

It was hard to say which I was feeling more strongly at this point—attraction or admiration. Ditching Wendy was the kind of decisive act that I would merely fantasize about, and I loved her for having done it. I also loved the fact that, for the moment anyway, I was the only person in the world who knew about it.

ॐ

Just as I was starting to think something might be happening between us, our conversation hit a patch of dead air. It was just after the beverage-and-pretzel service. We'd been getting along wonderfully, and we had so much in common that I knew there must be a thousand things we could talk about. But somehow, not one presented itself.

And so we sat: she gazing out her window, crunching on the ice from her Diet Coke, and me silently spiraling into panic, convinced that at any moment she would return to her book and not speak to me for the rest of the flight. As the silence lengthened, my feelings of hopelessness grew into full-blown terror. Finally, I couldn't stand it any longer.

"You know, my boss played golf with Bill Clinton."

I immediately regretted saying it. It was so obviously an act of desperation that, even more than silence itself, it emphasized the fact that I had nothing to say. But to my relief, she accepted my blurted announcement as a humorous/ intriguing thing, as opposed to the show-and-tell/attention-seeking thing that it really was.

"Oh yeah?" she said, rolling an ice-cube from one cheek to the other. "Who won?"

"I don't know. Probably Leonard, my boss. He plays about five times a week, so I think he's pretty good by now."

"You don't think he'd let the president win?"

"No, Leonard usually votes Republican. During the whole impeachment thing, he ranted and raved about how Clinton was such a liar, and how he'd permanently damaged the presidency. But of course when he got chance to play golf with the man, he jumped at it. After that, he switched to making fun of Clinton's golf swing."

"Now *there's* a reason to impeach," she said. "I mean, as far as the other stuff goes, it doesn't strike me that Clinton is really any *more* of a liar than anybody else in Washington— he's just had less success at it."

"Maybe he just needs a private tutor," I suggested. "Someone from the Reagan administration perhaps?"

"Exactly! I mean, I've heard so many people say, *If he'd just told the truth from the beginning, blah blah blah.* But give me a break, even if he'd been totally honest, they still would've eaten him alive…in a manner of speaking."

Having just taken a big, fizzing gulp of Diet Coke, it was all I could do to keep from spraying it out my nostrils.

"Sorry," she chuckled, scrunching her nose, "was that disgusting?"

"No," I said, when I'd finally managed to swallow. "Well, I mean, a *little*, but…I just wish I'd thought of it first."

Setting down my soda, I glanced over at Art, wondering if he could hear us well enough to be offended. He was already asleep though, his bristled head slumped toward the aisle.

"Wendy would've turned red and ducked under the seat if I'd said something like that to her. Although somehow she had no problem telling me about her latex allergy..."

"Wonderful."

"After a few days with her, you have *no idea* how good it is to talk to a normal human being," she said, tugging emphatically on my forearm.

I'd been attracted to her before, but it was in this laughing, Coke-choking moment that I fell in love. I wondered: *Could I really ask her out?* I'd been out of the dating world so long that I could hardly remember how it worked normally, let alone when you lived 800 miles apart. *If I asked her to dinner, would I offer to fly to San Francisco, or invite her to Seattle? Or would we perhaps meet in a neutral city in Oregon?*

While I was mulling this, she turned to me suddenly, porcelain brow furrowed.

"What's your name?" she asked, a friendly demand.

"Garrett," I said, unsure if this was a situation where last names mattered. Sometimes my first name alone is enough of a mouthful. I can't seem to pronounce it clearly enough for anyone, especially when ordering takeout. "Garrick? Gehrig? Carrot?" For those situations, I've adopted the pseudonym "Bob"—everybody can say Bob.

"Dana," she reciprocated, shaking my hand across the armrest.

"Anderson," I added, deciding late that last names *did* matter. "Garrett Anderson."

"Burns," she smiled, as if her own name suddenly sounded strange to her.

☙

Dana had been holding a book on her lap since takeoff, and after the name exchange, I finally recognized it. It was a book of poetry called *The Summer of Black Widows.*

"Sherman Alexie," I said, nodding toward the book. "He lives in Seattle."

I said this like it meant something, as if I was always bumping into him at QFC. In truth, Mr. Alexie could live in Budapest and I would see him just as often as I do now.

"Have you read it?" she asked.

"No, but I read *The Business of Fancydancing* and another one, a book of short stories."

"How did a four-star computer geek like you end up reading poetry?" she asked, only half-kidding.

"I was actually an English major in college, thank you very much."

"No shit."

"*Totally* shit."

"So how did you wind up as a computer-consultant guy?"

"Well, coming out of school, I discovered that the most lucrative job my English degree earned me was working the drive-thru at McDonald's..."

"Mmmm."

"But I'd always had a kind of geek-streak in me, and I eventually stumbled onto a company that was so desperate for technical help that they were willing to train me. Sometimes I wonder why I went to college at all."

"Oh, but it gave you *depth*," she said in a wide-eyed guidance counselor voice. "I'm sure you're a much better developer for having read *The Sound and The Fury* and *Ulysses.*"

"Is that why I never understood Joyce? Was he writing in COBOL or something?"

"He was, actually. Compiled properly, *Finnegan's Wake* is just a mainframe version of 'Pong.' The man was *way* ahead of his time."

As we were chuckling about this, Dana reached down and tugged her messenger bag toward her. Flipping it open, she raked around until she found a stick of lip balm, in the process revealing an array of other items—a banana, a CD walkman, a spiral notebook, a half-eaten sleeve of Girl Scout cookies, a tiny screwdriver set, and an umbrella.

Her CDs were what really caught my attention though. The three that I could see were all by the Pixies, my favorite band, and the one on top—*Doolittle*—was something I'd listened to almost every day while in Boston.

"That's a great CD," I said, laboring to appear casual about this discovery.

"Yeah," she said, pausing in the middle of her Chapstick application. "I kind of wonder why I brought the others with me, because *Doolittle* never came out of the player."

That was it for me. As soon as I saw those CDs, I knew I had to do something. I thought: *If she'll go out with me, I'll just quit my job and move to San Francisco.* And the thing was, I was dead serious—she was too perfect to be true, and I knew I couldn't let her get away.

❧

Ten minutes later—this was about 11:00 a.m. Boston time, 10:00 a.m. in Chicago—the flight attendants handed out tiny blue boxes containing our one-size-fits-all "lunch": a miniature ham sandwich, a red apple the size of a golf ball, and a single butterscotch-chip cookie. I usually decline such pseudo-meals served at strange hours, but I was so giddy from the Pixies discovery that I took one. I did, however, feel the idiot need to comment on the selection.

"Ham and cheese. Very daring, don't you think? A lot of people don't eat pork."

"Yeah, you're right."

"And what did they give us for condiments? Yellow mustard, and 'lite' mayo."

"I'm sticking to the mustard," Dana said.

"Yeah, I'm not a fan of fake mayo."

"My husband actually puts maple syrup on his ham sandwiches, if you can believe that. Spreads it right on the bread."

Initially, I didn't hear anything after the H-word. *My husband...* My mind froze right there, trying to figure out how that word had snuck into our conversation. *My husband...* Luckily, after I'd recovered slightly, I was able to have the rest of the sentence read back to me by whichever lobe of your brain keeps listening after everything else has seized.

I felt like I'd been clubbed with a three-hundred pound pillow. With one breath, Dana had shattered all the fantasies I'd been nurturing since takeoff. But I was more than just disappointed—suddenly, I was looking at a stranger. Dana Burns was not at all the person I'd thought she was. I had to accept that there was another whole part of her (that I didn't know and could never really access) that was a wife to some syrup-abusing freak in San Francisco.

Part of me wanted to end the conversation right there—snatch up a towel and run screaming from the proverbial hot-tub—but I did my best to stifle any visible reaction. Physically, I was still sitting there with her, our faces no more than 12 inches apart in the forced intimacy of Coach. I continued talking and making jokes and smiling like a jackass, but inside, I was already cutting my losses, packing up and retreating, re-vaulting the secrets that just moments before I'd been prepared to reveal. Above all, I was resisting the urge to look down at the ring I knew must be there, but which I hadn't thought to check for until now.

We talked about her husband, Brian. He was the *sous chef* at "Portobello," a San Francisco restaurant that I had actually visited and enjoyed. From there, I did my best to shift the conversation to Brian-free topics: the best meals we'd had, the worst meals we'd had, our mutual dislike of lobster, and of course, vermin larvae we'd discovered in packaged foods.

To an outsider like "Art," awake since lunch, it must've appeared that we were getting along famously. Even Dana seemed oblivious to the rift that had opened between us— she acted like I'd already forgiven and forgotten the husband thing. But I was the whole time holding myself back a little, depriving her of my funniest and most honest observations, just as she had deprived me of part of herself by marrying this Brian character. All I could think was: *How dare she make me like her so much when she was already married?*

∽

At this point, I should probably mention that landings terrify me. I don't mind takeoffs, and I actually think turbulence is sort of fun, but for me, landing is always a near-death experience.

One might think that after 300 carnage-free touchdowns, I'd overcome my landing panic, but I haven't. Every single time, I go through the same exhausting existential crisis, convinced that *this* will be the last day of my life. Every single time, I mentally say goodbye to all the people I'll never see again, and somehow, I come to terms with my own imminent death. And then of course the plane doesn't crash and I forget all about it until my next flight.

On that day with Dana Burns, I felt the panic awaken as we began our descent to O'Hare, the jet slowing perceptibly and seeming to pitch downhill. As the seat-belt sign bonged to life, I looked over at Dana peering out her window, and I thought: *I am utterly alone in this world. No one knows me, not the way Dana and her husband know each other. I am going to die alone, and it will be as if I was never even here.*

This "alone" business was a new wrinkle that I attributed directly to Dana. She'd given me a glimpse of the intimacy and connectedness I might've had, and now all I could feel was its absence. What had I been doing for the last three years? What had I been so afraid of? Why had I wasted so much time?

While stricken with these thoughts, I was still attempting to appear composed by chatting with Dana about Lake Michigan: its dimensions, its depth, its contents. I tried, by looking directly into Dana's eyes, to avoid noticing that the ground was lurching closer and closer, but I was only somewhat successful.

"You know," I quavered, "I think somebody told me there are actually whales in the Great Lakes."

"*Really?*"

"I thought that's what I heard. Who was it that told me that? Maybe I saw it on the web somewhere. Humpback whales? They're kind of small as whales go, right?"

"How would they get there though?"

"Through the St. Lawrence, maybe? It's a big river, right? Although I guess it is hard to imagine...you'd think there would be dams or something..."

"Aren't the Great Lakes *fresh* water?"

"Mm...I think you're right. And whales live in salt water, right? So that's definitely wrong. I must be thinking... maybe I'm thinking of someplace—"

The plane struck pavement and I froze, unable to finish

my thought. As the jet careened along the runway, leaning ever-so-slightly to its right, I was caught there, waiting for the moment when we would finally tilt all the way over. The wing-tip would catch the asphalt, and the plane would cartwheel, tearing itself to pieces with its own weight. Tons and tons of flaming *stuff*—engines and luggage and shrieking passengers—would be sent hurtling in every direction.

Dana waited attentively, as if I might still complete my sentence.

"Are you all right?" she asked, concern crinkling her brow. She put her hand reassuringly on my arm.

I still couldn't speak, but as my terror passed to resignation, my mind became clearer. I thought: *She really is a nice person. I've probably been too hard on her. It's not her fault that I'm so psychotic that I was ready to move to San Francisco just because we like the same defunct rock band. She didn't have to spend the whole flight talking to me, but she did.* Looking at it that way, I started to feel guilty for having been angry with her about the whole husband thing.

Staring into Dana's worried squint, certain that I was witnessing the last moment of my life, I recognized a simple truth, one that my ridiculous job—constantly switching cities, offices, and coworkers—had been pointing me toward for the past thirty-nine months: All human relationships are finite. Despite what we might like to think, *all* relationships end, and in that sense, they're all equal. Why should we discriminate on the basis of time? Five minutes with the right person might change the course of your life.

When the plane finally slowed, now taxiing across the tarmac, docile as a city bus, I was able to speak again. My catatonia had lasted only five or ten seconds, but it had seemed much longer.

"I'm sorry," I said finally.

"You scared me for a minute there. I thought you were having a stroke or something."

"I'm just not fond of landings."

"Well, I'm with you on that, but then again, I don't travel for a living. Barf bag?"

"No, I'm good. Thanks."

The plane rocked to a stop at the gate, setting off a frenzy of belt-unbuckling and bin-popping that quickly proved pointless, since no one could move yet. While we all waited for the doors to open—many people standing in the aisle, others stooped awkwardly under the overheads—Dana played at identifying the smokers in the crowd by the degree of tension in their faces. I smiled as she pointed out a twitch here and a grimace there, but I was really only half-listening. She'd mentioned having a two-hour layover at O'Hare, and I knew that unless I did something, we'd probably part ways at the arrival gate. I couldn't let that happen though—married or not, I wasn't ready to say goodbye to her yet.

Unfortunately, my only idea was to suggest that we have lunch. This was absurd considering that it was still so early, and doubly absurd considering that they'd allegedly served us lunch on the flight.

When it was finally our turn to move, Dana and I filed quietly down the aisle and out through the sloping, snaking jetway. Once in the terminal, we drifted—still loosely tethered—toward a bank of blue screens.

"Okay," she said, scanning the monitors. "I'm looking for San Francisco, flight 1164..."

"There it is."

"Ah. Okay, so it's gate number...C22?"

"It's down that way, to the right, on the other concourse," I said.

"Okay, cool. Did you find your flight?"

"Have you ever been to Albuquerque?" I asked, pretending I hadn't heard her question.

"No…why?"

"It's just a strange looking name. Al-bu-kwer-kee. What's in Albuquerque, anyway?"

"I don't know. Isn't it near Santa Fe?"

"Yeah, I think you're right. Santa Fe…someplace else I've never been. I've been to Wausau, Wisconsin three times, but I've never been to Santa Fe. That's pretty sad, huh?"

"Well, I've never been there either, so…I guess I'm pretty sad too."

"I guess so," I nodded, now looking down at my toes.

Silence.

"Well, this was great," she said finally. "I really enjoyed this."

"Yeah, me too." I nodded, realizing that I was running out of time. "And you know, actually, I was just thinking… we were talking about places we've never been and things we've never done…well, we weren't actually *talking* about things we've never done, but I was thinking that *one* thing I've never done is have lunch with the same person twice in the same day."

"*Really*," she smirked, crossing her arms skeptically.

"Yeah, it seems like such a simple thing, but I've never done it. Just like, you know, I live in Seattle, but I've never been to the top of the Space Needle. I mean, in that case, I don't think I'm missing much, but this lunch thing is something I'd really like to try before I die, and where I'm getting on another plane soon, it might be a good idea to cross it off the list now, you know…seize the day."

"I see," she said, still smiling.

"So what do you think? Do you have any big plans for the next hour or so?"

"Not really."

"Are you up for a second lunch?"

"Sure."

"I mean, you don't have to eat if you aren't hungry. Personally, I seem to be able to eat anytime, especially when I'm at the airport."

"I could eat," she said. "That ham sandwich was pretty unsatisfying."

"Okay, good. This'll be good then."

"So when's your flight to Seattle?"

"Oh…it's a while yet. I have pretty long layover here."

It wasn't exactly smooth, but it did the trick.

As we walked the terminal surveying our dining options, I felt elated for having taken that step, for having delayed Dana's departure from my life, if only briefly. In the end, we chose a generic snack bar that wasn't too crowded. We each got a large Diet Coke and two slices of cheese pizza.

"So what do you suppose Wendy is doing now?" I asked at one point.

"Oh God…"

"You do realize that you're going to Hell for abandoning her."

"I can accept that, as long as Wendy isn't there with me."

"What are you going to tell her? What was the big emergency?"

"Well, the one thing I'd thought of was that Brian cut off a finger at work or something."

"Which finger?"

"I was thinking thumb..."

"That's good. Will they be able to reattach it?"

"Oh yeah. It's amazing what they can do these days."

Sitting in that snack bar with Dana, I began to realize that this was a Moment in my life, a scene I would rerun again and again in memory. And so, while we talked and ate our floppy airport pizza, I did my best to take everything in, collecting all of the details I might otherwise forget: the glossy turquoise tabletop swirled with tiny scratches; the rhythmic jangle escaping from the headphones of the guy at the next table; the way the light, streaming through the windows behind Dana's head, made a glowing corona of her stray hairs.

Soaking in this scene and recognizing that it was likely my last with Dana, it occurred to me that I still had a chance to improve this memory-to-be, to go the one place I hadn't gone and thus banish any possible (future) regret.

"Okay," I said, "we've known each other for what...nearly four hours, right?"

"I guess so, yeah."

"I feel like I want to tell you a secret. Can I tell you a secret?"

"I'm only interested in secrets," she smiled.

"You're sure? It's pretty personal."

"Absolutely."

"So I should just come out with it then."

"Yes, you should."

"Okay, so this is it. This is the thing. Remember, back on the plane, when we were talking and they brought us lunch?"

"Yeah..."

"Well, we were talking about ham sandwiches, and you mentioned your husband likes his with maple syrup, and I know I may have *seemed* pretty cool about it, but I was actually rather stunned. Stunned and disappointed."

"That my husband likes maple syrup on his ham sandwiches?"

"Uh, *no*...that you *had* a husband...that—"

"I know…I was just, you know..."

"Making fun of me at this very vulnerable moment?"

"Sorry," she said. "So you hadn't noticed the ring?"

"Nope."

"Yeah, I wasn't sure. I never thought to look for them before I got one myself. I never know if I should say something..."

"Like, *Hi, I'm Dana Burns, and you can forget about it, buddy, because I'm married...*"

"Well, maybe something a *little* subtler than that."

"Like mentioning that your husband likes maple syrup on his ham sandwiches."

"Right. But I mean, if I say something right away, it can sour the whole conversation, you know? Now you're not just talking to me, you're talking to me *and* my husband. But then if I wait too long, no matter how subtly I mention it, it comes out like a bombshell. Like I was somehow concealing it."

"That's very true."

"But anyway," Dana said, now looking me directly in the eye. "About what you were saying...you were stunned and disappointed?"

"Yes."

"So what am I supposed to do with this information?"

"What are you supposed to do with it?"

"Yeah." She was smiling, but somehow that didn't make her question any easier.

"Uh, well...I'm not sure. I mean, I wasn't, you know..."

"Take your time..."

"Well, you don't actually have to *do* anything with it," I said finally.

"Then why did you tell me?"

"I don't know...I just thought, you know...I just felt like I ought to."

"Uh-huh..."

"I felt like it would be false of me *not* to tell you...and I didn't want to fly back to Seattle feeling like I'd been false with you. I would've been disappointed with myself."

"Okay," she said, taking another bite of her pizza.

"Okay...? Okay what?"

"Okay, that's a good answer. It was a hard question. I didn't necessarily expect you to come up with anything, but you handled it pretty well. I'm impressed."

"Well...good, I guess."

"I can be a real pain in the ass sometimes."

"I see that now."

"So I take it you aren't seeing anyone?"

"That's correct."

"Who was the last person you dated?"

"I guess that would be Christina."

"Why'd you break up?"

"I don't know, really. We dated for nine months, but she was always kind of lukewarm about us. From day one, I always felt like she was about to break up with me. But I was also convinced I could turn her around."

"How did it end?"

"The breakup itself was actually very sudden. We were

supposed to go to Victoria for a long weekend."

"Up in British Columbia?"

"Right. It was for my birthday, actually. We'd planned to take the ferry over on Saturday, but on Friday night, Christina left a message on my machine saying that she'd changed her mind, she didn't want to go to Victoria. Oh, and she really didn't think it was working out with us, so maybe we should just stop seeing each other."

"On your answering machine?"

"Yeah, and for whatever reason, I didn't notice the message when I got home on Friday night. So I got up Saturday morning, saw the light flashing, and played the message. I hadn't even had any caffeine yet, you know, so I was standing there in my boxers listening to Christina cancel my birthday trip and dump me, all on a 12-hour tape-delay. "

"Ughhh..."

"Yeah, it was not a high point for me."

"How long ago was this?"

"About three years. Actually, it was just a few weeks after I'd turned down that San Francisco job."

"Because of her?"

"Mm. What an idiot, huh? When I'd mentioned the job, she'd told me she wasn't interested in a long-distance relationship. All in all, it would've been a lot easier if she'd just come out and said that she wasn't terribly interested in *any* sort of relationship, long-distance or local..."

"Seriously."

"So...how long did you say you've been married?"

"Eleven months."

"And how long did you and Brian date before that?"

"Three years or so."

"So even if I'd met you, say, two years ago, I'd be looking

at pretty much the same situation."

"Pretty much."

"Okay, but let me ask you this. For future reference, you know, in case on my next flight I meet a Pixie-loving, poetry-reading, software developer who *isn't* married..."

"Okay."

"So imagine you're that woman, okay? Basically, it's like you, but without the husband. No fiancé, no boyfriend... not even a really close male friend you're on hugging-terms with."

"Okay."

"No laughing now—this is serious."

"Okay."

"All right, are you in character?"

"Yup."

"So you've met me on the plane, and we've talked and had a good time. We get off here at O'Hare, we're eating our midmorning pizza, and at some devastatingly perfect moment, I suggest that instead of going our separate ways, we have dinner together in Santa Fe or someplace semi-exotic like that. What would you say?"

"I'd say you're obsessed with mealtime."

"A simple yes or no answer will do, thank you."

"Hmmm..."

"Take your time. Oh, and if it helps, I've got scads of frequent-flyer miles, so we can go First Class for nothing."

"First Class?"

"Yup. Oh, and would it matter if I mentioned that I'd already missed my flight home just so I could spend an extra hour with you?"

"You *missed* your flight?"

"Well, no...not *really*—but if I *had*, would that be a

good thing to mention...or not?"

"Well, that *is* kind of sweet I guess, but...only if things are going really well. Otherwise it might be a little creepy."

"Okay, noted. So...what do you think?"

"Sure. Why not? Dinner in Santa Fe sounds cool."

"Really?"

"Sure."

"Well...thanks. I mean, given the situation, my putting you on the spot like that, you really didn't have much of a choice, but still...it's nice of you to actually say it. Thanks."

"No problem, Garrett."

With that last word, I realized that she'd given me what I needed: I'd been instantiated. She'd spoken my name, and thus her experience of reality officially included me. It might sound like a silly thing to want, but at that moment, it seemed like the only thing that mattered. It was also the thing that made it possible for me to say goodbye an hour later when it was time for her to leave. We shook hands and walked off in opposite directions—she to her plane, and me to arrange for a new flight home.

∽

Thankfully, my replacement flight was half empty. I dozed, slumped beside my window, all the way to Seattle. Normally, I wouldn't have bothered closing my eyes—the unsatisfying unconsciousness of plane-sleep just leaves me groggy—but I really needed to turn myself off for a while.

And even though I was only half-asleep, I dreamt. In this bleak, skipping-record of a dream, I was back at O'Hare with our former row-mate, Art. We were marching single-file through an endless airport terminal, passing gate after hazy gate. Art, with a huge cow-spotted golf bag slung across his back, was plodding along, always two steps in front of me. I could muster neither the energy to pass him, nor the willpower to stop walking. It was exhausting.

When I felt the plane dropping toward Sea-Tac, I opened my eyes. Directly before me, rising through the otherwise unbroken undercast, was the startling, ice-crusted brow of Mount Rainier. In a dozen years of living in Seattle, I'd never had such an intimidatingly unobstructed view of the mountain—it seemed close enough to touch. I felt a sinking hollowness in my gut, a sensation that might've been hunger or nausea, but wasn't quite either one.

Staring out my window, hypnotized by Rainier's incomprehensible enormousness, I made a resolution. *In the unlikely event of a successful landing,* I whispered prayerfully, *I will take some vacation time next week and try to figure some things out. Maybe even take the whole week—see how it goes from there.*

As the jet slipped down through the clouds, I gradually became aware of a voice off to my right. It was vaguely familiar, and for a moment, I thought it belonged to someone I knew. After looking, I realized that the voice was only familiar because, in my obliverie, I had been hearing it throughout the entire flight.

Across the aisle from me sat a little girl, maybe four years old. She was barefoot, and had her legs pulled up underneath her on the seat. She was wearing a pair of those prehistoric airline headsets, the ones that literally blow the in-flight movie soundtrack into your ear canal. In her best pilot-voice, she spoke into the unplugged end of the headset tube as if it were a microphone. Again and again, she announced:

"This is me, over. This is me, over."

❧

I was dead serious about taking a few days off, but waiting at the baggage carousel, watching unclaimed suitcases jerk forlornly past on the conveyor, I knew I wouldn't follow through with it. The odds weren't good: in thirty-nine months with Cavanaugh Associates, I'd taken exactly four vacation days. I'd made other attempts, but somehow, I'd always let work creep back in. In that light, my desperate little resolution seemed about as meaningful as a lifelong smoker saying "I should really quit" as he lights another cigarette.

It's not that I'm a workaholic—I consider myself a supremely lazy person, slavishly following the path of least resistance. It just so happened that, given my dam-burst workload at Cavanaugh, the easiest thing was to keep bailing, all the time.

I knew a big part of it was just habit. I've recently come to the sad conclusion that Habit is everything. We humans like to think that we have free will, that we choose to do what we do. And while that may be true in some respects, I can now see that the main reason that we "choose" to do anything is the fact we did it yesterday, or last Saturday, or last year.

2

Macrina Bakery

If I had to marry a restaurant and eat every meal there for the rest of my life, I would marry Macrina Bakery. Which is really saying something when you consider the fact that I don't drink coffee, and they don't serve dinner. What Macrina *does* do is make the most fantastic breads, muffins, pastries, and sandwiches in Seattle, and on the weekends, they offer a full brunch menu with table service. In that regard, I'm particularly fond of their Brioche French Toast, topped with warm fruit compote and powdered sugar. The Fried Egg Sandwich with spicy tomato sauce and Muenster cheese is also an excellent choice, especially if you've just had the French Toast the day before.

On the bright, breezy Thursday morning after my return from Boston, I walked the three blocks from my apartment to Macrina Bakery in a kind of foggy anticipation. I hadn't slept well—a combination of jet-lag and Dana Burns hangover—but I was happy to be home, and happier still to be on my way to Macrina. Stepping in from the sidewalk, I paused just inside Macrina's open front door, submerging myself in the familiar din of voices, clinking spoons, and frothing milk. I felt a warm wave of relief standing there, as if this arrival—and not my subdued landing at Sea-Tac the night before—truly marked the end of my trip.

The café was a small, high-ceilinged space, painted in earthy shades of olive green and maroon, and hung all around with blackboards declaring the day's selections in the parallel universes of bread, sandwiches, and hot beverages. The entry was busy with people—some peering into the pastry case, a few in line at the register, and others waiting for coffees or soy-chais already in progress. Off to the left was the seating area—just seven small tables and some stools at a counter, all of it washed in morning light by the wide First Ave windows.

April was working the register, and when she spotted me in line, her eyes widened cartoonishly and she grabbed her heart in mock shock. She recovered quickly though, jabbing her tongue out at me while she made change for the woman in front of me (who gave me a suspicious look as she left).

Over the course of my roughly eight hundred visits to Macrina Bakery, April and I had developed a certain strange rapport. I say "strange" because April was peculiar all by herself, but also because our relationship was comprised almost entirely of two-minute exchanges that were heavy with phrases like, "I think I'll have a the French Toast today," and "Do you want a bag for your muffin?" After two years of this, I still didn't know April's last name, and yet she acted as if we were old friends. Usually I decided that April acted just as familiar with everyone, but in certain moods, I could convince myself that there really was something meaningful between us. After all, if you packed all of our little moments together, we'd probably been standing at that register chit-chatting for two days straight.

"Hey Garrett," April chirped when I finally reached the counter. "How was Boston?"

April was in her early twenties, about 5′4″, and hyperactive-skinny. As usual, she wore a black t-shirt and blue jeans under her Macrina apron, and her dirty-blonde hair (streaked with fading fire-engine red) was tied back in a brief little fountain. The silver hoop in her right eyebrow stood in sharp contrast to the otherwise innocent, elfin quality of her face—her round cheekbones and bright blue eyes, which often seemed ready to pop out of her head. I couldn't identify any one thing that was singularly attractive about April, but there was just something magnetic about her, something gravitational in her radiant gaze and up-to-something smile that made you want to be part of her solar system.

"Boston was fine," I said, surprised that she had remembered where I'd gone. "It's good to be back though."

"Because you missed us so desperately?"

"Definitely."

"Garrett missed us," April said, playfully hip-checking Noreen, another longtime Macrina employee, as she attempted to squeeze past April on her way to the pastry case.

"Of course he did," Noreen said, glancing up and smiling. "Hi Garrett. Nice suit."

"Yes, yes," April said, "but the question is, does he own any that aren't black?"

"Well, I have two that are charcoal grey."

"You *must* let me help you get some variety into your wardrobe," April said. "Actually, I saw this jacket at a vintage store yesterday that would look great on you. It was this cool three-button cut, narrow lapels…not far from the one you're wearing really, but in purple velvet."

"Purple velvet?"

"Yeah, it was gorgeous. Interested?"

April grinned at me, and it was hard to tell whether she

was merely making fun of me, or if she was a little bit serious.

"Well…obviously it sounds fabulous to me, but I'm not sure my boss would be as enthusiastic. We've got a pretty strict no-velvet policy in our office."

"All right," April said, eyes narrowing. "I guess you're just not ready to be helped yet."

"I guess not."

"So what's it going to be today? I saw you ogling the tartlettes."

April was right—I'd been teetering between a pseudo-healthy low-fat banana-ginger muffin and an openly decadent apple tartlette. But just as I opened my mouth to announce my decision, April held up one finger to stop me.

"Oh…wait!" she said, eyes wide again. "Can you hold on for one minute?"

"Sure."

"Just one minute. I'll be right back," she said, stumbling through the door that led back into the bakery itself. A moment later, she returned and, with a theatrical flourish, handed me a flyer for an art exhibition.

"Some friends of mine and I are having a show at the Seattle Art Academy on Friday night, mostly sculpture and 3D art."

"The Seattle Art Academy?"

"Yeah, it's a little art school up in the U District. I'm in a workshop program there."

"Cool."

"You should come if you're going to be around. I think you'd like it."

"Okay, yeah. I'll try to make it."

"Great. Okay…well, I think that's enough harassment

for today. What'll it be?"

℘

With my banana-ginger muffin secured, I set off down First Ave toward work. As I walked, I examined the flyer for April's show, trying to guess why in the world she thought I might enjoy it. The flyer, dominated by an illustration of a nervous eyeball peering through a keyhole, offered no details beyond the event's date and the artists' names. In the end, I concluded that April's "I think you'd like it" was probably just something she'd said because it was shorter than, "I'm going to invite you even though I know you won't come," much in the way that my "I'll try to make it," could be loosely translated to, "This looks like an event at which I'd feel enormously uncomfortable and out of place." Regardless, the flyer delivered one shocking revelation about April—her last name was "Franklin."

My purpose in going to the office on this day was unclear, even to me. If my goal had been to accomplish something meaningful, I probably would've worked from home, but it seemed important to show my face in the office after such a long absence. And though I'm loath to admit it, there was a social need driving me there as well—even if I was ambivalent about most of my coworkers, they all knew who I was, and they didn't make me walk around wearing a "VISITOR" badge all day, a relief after being a stranger for so long.

Cavanaugh's offices were on First Ave in downtown Seattle, a dozen blocks from my apartment in Belltown. When I'd first started with the company three years before, Cavanaugh Associates had been an abstraction—seven consultants working from dens and living-rooms and client offices. Back then, each of us had kept in regular contact with

Leonard, but unless we were collaborating on a project, we hardly saw each other. Cavanaugh had subleased a small space downtown, but it was really a glorified storage room, just big enough for a half-dozen servers and a swivel-chair.

Personally, I'd liked working for an abstraction, but right around Leonard's 59th birthday, he decided that we needed a real office, with windows and furniture and bland photos on the walls. He had all kinds of reasons: with the Internet booming, Cavanaugh had doubled in size, and he insisted that having an office would facilitate communication, "making us all better consultants" (Leonard himself hardly even used a computer). He also said that an office would give our clients a comfortable place to visit (which, to my knowledge, none ever have).

All in all, it seemed far more plausible that Leonard's office-lust was just part of the impulse that drove him to buy a new Jaguar XK8 around that same time. In his career, Leonard had held a series of semi-high-profile jobs at big corporations, and although he was probably making more money than ever, being the owner of Cavanaugh Associates just didn't have the glamour of his past positions or (perhaps more importantly) the positions still held by his golf buddies at various Fortune 500 companies. In the end, I think Leonard just wanted some tangible evidence of his success, and in the wake of his second divorce, in which his wife had taken their house on Mercer Island, Cavanaugh was all that Leonard had left.

So Leonard got his office—a glassy space on the top floor of a downtown mid-rise—but with so many of us traveling or working from home, there were never more than four or five people present on a given day. Leonard was always there though, and he couldn't seem to stop adjusting the office geography and décor. Every time I returned from a trip, I'd find that something had changed. Coming back from San Diego once, I'd discovered that every stick of our minimalist Scandinavian furniture had been swapped for pieces with an Art Deco look. The next time, everything had been swapped back. I'd had no less that four different chairs in the new office, one of which was replaced while I was at lunch.

So as I was riding the elevator up to the sixth floor on the morning after my Boston trip, I was already wondering what might've changed in my absence. New paint? New carpeting? New productivity-enhancing light fixtures? Given how long I'd been gone, anything was possible.

When the elevator doors finally opened though, I almost didn't get off because I thought I was in the wrong place. Filling what should've been an expanse of beige carpet was a curving reception station, an enormous, flared fruit bowl in tongue-and-groove maple. The desk itself was so overwhelming—lit from all angles and trimmed in a forest of exotic greenery—that it took me a moment to realize that there was a woman sitting in the middle of it all, already smiling at me hesitantly.

"Um, hi…can I help you?"

She had straight brown hair to her shoulders, and her face had the oft-blinking look of someone who had only recently traded her glasses for contact lenses.

"Is this still Cavanaugh Associates?" I asked.

"Yes, can I help you?"

"Oh…hi, I'm Garrett," I said, finally stepping off the elevator. "I work here."

"I'm Gwen. I'm the new receptionist." She half-stood to shake my hand across the desk, self-consciously smoothing the front of her knee-grazing Ann Taylor skirt. She was girl-ishly gangly, and she moved stiffly, as if she were wearing her mother's clothes. She looked about 19.

"Nice to meet you, Gwen. Is this your first day?"

"No, I started last week," she said. "Why...is this *your* first day?"

"Oh, no...no, I've just been on the road for a while."

"I see," she nodded, unconvinced.

"Okay. Well...nice to meet you, Gwen."

"Nice to meet you too, Gary."

ॐ

My encounter with Gwen left me with many questions: Why would a company that never has visitors need a re-ceptionist? Which had come first, Gwen or her humongous desk? Was Leonard now trawling high-school proms for new employees? And most importantly, *How could anyone ever think of me as a "Gary"?*

As usual, there weren't many people in the office. Mak-ing my way down the glass-walled hall, I nodded to Wal-ter Rubens (the Y2K guy), waved to Vincent Carter (the database guy), and saluted Bill Greenough (the mainframe guy). I'd been hoping to see Kevin Lanier, my one legiti-mate friend at Cavanaugh, but judging from the dearth of food wrappers and coffee cups on his desk, I guessed that he hadn't been in Seattle for at least a week.

My own office was as anonymous as all of the hotel rooms I stayed in, partly because I was never around, and partly because I had a neurosis about leaving personal items at work. My fear was that something cataclysmic would happen—World War III, or an eruption of Mount Rain-ier—and I'd be unable to get to the office to retrieve my stuff. Leonard compensated for my knickknacklessness by relentlessly accessorizing my office for me—two sepia-toned photographs of Pioneer Square had appeared on my wall one day, joined a week later by an antique coat rack. Upon my return from Boston, I discovered a pair of six-foot jungle plants huddled by my window, apparent refugees from the reception area arboretum.

Thankfully, my desk was just as I'd left it. While my laptop was booting, I took out the muffin from Macrina and cracked a Pepsi One, hoping to banish the grogginess that seemed to have been worsening all morning. I'd hardly had a sip of my soda when I looked up to see Leonard leaning in my doorway, a sly smile warping his kinglike face.

"Welcome back, Garrett."

Leonard was a young sixty, with wispy grey hair that receded sharply at the corners of his hairline. He always dressed impeccably, and on this day he was wearing a grey Brooks Brothers suit with a cheery yellow tie.

"Hi, Leonard. How're you?"

"Excellent. I got a message from Marco. He absolutely raved about your work for them."

"Well, I'm glad he's happy."

"Marco's done pretty well for himself, eh?"

"Marco? Oh…yeah, I guess."

"You know, I was the one who got him in the door there."

"Yeah, you mentioned that."

"Of course they showed *me* the door soon afterwards," Leonard chuckled, "but Marco really stuck."

I just smiled. Leonard took an odd pride in his extensive resume of terminations, but I was never sure what to say when he brought them up. Of course, there was one gigantic upside to Leonard's long and winding career—he'd made friends everywhere he'd worked, and those friends had become Cavanaugh's most profitable clients.

Leonard had two permanent brow furrows directly above his nose that, depending upon the situation, could make him appear either demandingly skeptical, or slightly disoriented. As he was chuckling about getting fired from GenoSys, he lapsed into the latter for a long, Reagan-like moment. A second later though, a flash of recognition rejuvenated his regal features—he'd remembered why he came to see me in the first place.

"You haven't heard from Brendan in the last 24 hours, have you?"

"No, but that's not unusual. Is he missing?" I asked, trying not to sound too hopeful.

"Not exactly," Leonard murmured, drifting back into thought.

"Can I help with something?"

"Hm? No, it should be fine," he said, mustering another smile. "Say—did you meet Gwen?"

"Yeah, I did...on my way in."

"Isn't she fantastic?"

"She seems great," I said. I had no idea what Leonard was talking about, but I knew the conversation would be shorter if I agreed.

"She might be the best hire I've ever made," Leonard said, waggling one thick finger in the air as he sauntered off down the hall. "Except for you, Garrett. Except for you."

❧

I'd met Leonard in 1996, at a party thrown by Olympic Internet, the now-defunct Seattle ISP that I was working for at the time. My boss Jerry, who had worked with Leonard in another life, introduced us. I was part of Olympic's "Web

Presence" group, creating websites for small businesses who didn't have the expertise to do it themselves.

Leonard seemed inordinately interested in my job, grilling me on the sites I'd built and the technical certifications I'd earned. This struck me as an oddly focused line of questioning from someone I'd just met, especially at a party. It made a lot more sense later, when I realized that our conversation had actually been an interview.

Before leaving that night, Leonard offered me a job making nearly twice what I was making at Olympic. He explained that one of his consultants had come down with appendicitis, and he needed someone to step in and lead a two-month West Coast seminar tour on the topic "Building Dynamic Websites with Microsoft Tools." He'd already squared things with Jerry, and if I accepted the offer, I'd leave in three days.

"Well, I'm flattered, Mr. Cavanaugh, but I don't know if I'm really qualified..."

"Oh, you'll do fine. From what I can tell, you know more about this crap than the guy I was going to send."

"Still, it's not much time to prepare..."

"There's nothing to prepare. The whole presentation is done—the outline, the slides, the bad jokes. I just need someone to deliver it. And of course if you happen to be so impressive that the attendees want to hire *you* to build their damn websites for them, so much the better."

I searched for reasons not to do it, but I couldn't find any. Tiring of Olympic, I'd already started looking around for another job, something I think Jerry knew. Even more importantly, Christina had dumped me via answering machine just two weeks before, and I'd done little since but decompose in front of the TV. Two months of travel sounded like a perfect chance to escape my apartment and go some-place where I wouldn't run into Christina.

When I took the position at Cavanaugh, I'd told Leonard that I'd do it for a year—I just couldn't picture myself staying in such a burnout job any longer. I'd save some money and figure things out from there—maybe I'd even go back to school. Leonard had accepted my pronouncement without argument, probably thinking he'd be able to change my mind when the time came. And he was right—my one- and two-year anniversaries had passed without incident. I'd *considered* quitting almost every day, but inertia had won out. Leonard also had an uncanny ability to sense dissatis-faction and preempt it with money—nobody at Cavanaugh ever seemed ecstatically happy, but nobody ever left.

೮෨

After Leonard departed my office, I decided to call Bella to see if she wanted to meet me for lunch. I dialed her num-ber, but instead of Bella's voice, I got a recording: *"The num-ber you have reached has been disconnected..."*

Very slowly, it all came back to me: Bella had moved. While I was in Boston, she'd moved in with her boyfriend Joel in Bellingham. And given that she now lived ninety miles north of Seattle, there was very little chance that she'd want to meet me for lunch today. Or any other day, for that matter.

Of course I'd known that Bella was moving; I was orig-inally supposed to be home in time to help, but I'd got-ten so wrapped up with my project that I'd forgotten. Sit-ting there at my desk, I absorbed the disappointment all over again: No longer could I just show up unannounced at Bella's apartment in Ravenna. There would be no more spontaneous brunches at Macrina, or last-minute movies at the Cinerama. Suddenly, Seattle felt very empty, and for a moment, I wished I'd just stayed in Boston—at least there, I'd had a system.

❧

Bella Marcellino and I graduated from the same high school in Portland, Maine, and unbeknownst to each other, we'd each made the oddball decision to attend the University of Washington on the opposite side of the continent. Two days after arriving in Seattle, with all of my belongings still jammed into my '84 Jetta, I spotted Bella in the campus bookstore, her head cocked sideways as she scanned the spines in the Fine Arts section.

Bella was about 5'6", and on that day, she was wearing a baggy UMaine sweatshirt and jeans. She had brown eyes and sharp, delicate features, but the thing that really jumped out at you was her rampantly curly brown hair. In a desperate attempt to maintain order, Bella always had it pinned or clipped somehow, but it was forever on the verge of bursting loose anyway.

I hadn't known Bella very well in high school, but I was so glad to see a familiar face in the bookstore that day that I marched right over to her. Back home, we'd probably exchanged less than a dozen words, but in Seattle, we became instant friends. I think we'd each come to UW looking for a change from our lives in Portland, but we ended up spending most of our time together. By junior year, we'd become roommates, renting an apartment off campus.

Whenever anyone asks about it, I say that romantic attraction has never been an issue between Bella and I. But of course that's a big fat lie—our friendship nearly ended one Sunday during that first October at UW, and it was all my fault.

We'd been head-down studying all weekend, and by Sunday afternoon, we were both completely fried. We were in Bella's room—she was doodling on her Art History notes, and I was nodding off under one of the Norton Anthologies—when she suddenly came up with the idea that we should try to "find" the ocean.

"Find it?" I parroted, mostly trying to conceal the fact that I'd been unconscious.

"You know, go see it. Not Lake Washington, or the Bay, or the Sound...the honest-to-goodness, wide-open Pacific Ocean. Have you ever seen it in person?"

"No."

"Well, me neither. We should go—it'd be good for us."

After conferring with Bella's Seattle-native roommate Kara, we learned that it would be a three-hour drive to the ocean, much longer than either of us had expected. I assumed that this would kill Bella's enthusiasm for the plan, but she was undaunted.

"Come on, Garrett. Is there something else you'd *rather* do?"

"But three hours each way? It'll be dark by the time we get there."

"I'm telling you, we need some time away from this place. When was the last time you actually left campus?"

We got in my car and started driving. At Kara's suggestion, we were headed for a town called Pacific Beach, about 30 miles up the coast from Aberdeen. Just getting out of the U District was a great relief though—with each mile we drove, I could feel the muscles in my neck loosening. And for the first time in a week, Bella and I didn't talk about exams, or how many papers we still had to write.

"So is your father still lobstering?" Bella asked at one

point.

"Yeah, although he's been threatening to sell the boat for ages."

"Well, he should talk to my brother Pete—he keeps talking about *buying* a boat. Although I keep telling him it's a bad time to become a lobsterman."

"Pete's the next-youngest, right?"

"No, Theresa is closest to me in age. Pete's a year older than her. And Paul's the oldest."

"Right," I nodded, as if that explanation had crystallized my understanding of Bella's family tree once and for all. "And they're all still in Portland, right? I'm surprised they let you leave the state."

"I got some resistance when I first brought it up, but after following them all through school, I had to go somewhere else for college. My aunt has lived out here for a while, and I'd spent a couple weeks with her one summer, so...here I am."

"Well, at least you'd visited. My college research consisted of reading a postcard in which my sister declared that Seattle was cool."

"Karen lived here?"

"Briefly, before moving to San Diego."

"Well, I think she's got you beat distance-wise—that's probably further from Maine than Seattle is."

"Yeah, but there are fewer earthquakes here."

It was dark by the time we rolled into Pacific Beach, a tiny town that on that fall night had a certain edge-of-the-world feeling to it. As soon as we were out of the car, we could hear the waves, a gentle but unceasing sound that was unlike anything in Seattle's aural landscape. We walked toward the beach, the waves' shushing becoming more enveloping with each step. It was a sound that I'd grown up with, and yet I felt like I was hearing it again for the first time.

For a while, we just sat in the sand without speaking. The moon was up, washing everything in blue and throwing sharp shadows off the dark clusters of driftwood. So wide and sandy, this place was nothing like the rugged beaches we'd known in Maine. Even the water seemed different, the waves moving in slow-motion compared to the chaos of the Atlantic. When it got too cold to sit any longer, Bella and I got up and walked, still not saying much.

Since our first meeting in the bookstore, we'd spent a lot of time together—meals, studying, movies, and generally hanging out. There was never any question about the fact that we were just friends, but in the weeks before this trip, I had nonetheless begun to feel the tug of something more. Mostly I tried to ignore it, knowing that it could only mean trouble, but sometimes that was difficult. Walking along a deserted, moonlit beach with Bella was one such time—the whole way, I had to resist the impulse to take her hand.

After a while, Bella stopped and sat down on a washed-up tree trunk, facing out at the black water. I sat down beside her.

"I'm glad we came," Bella said, glancing over at me and smiling, blue light slanting across the crisp features of her face.

I really meant to answer her—the words "Me too" actually floated through my head—but instead of speaking, I leaned over and kissed her softly on the lips. For me, it was the natural consequence of an unbearably romantic moment, the climax of all our time together. Foolishly, I had assumed that Bella was in the same moment.

Bella didn't pull away so much as she just *waited*. It was

obvious from her lack of participation that I'd made a mistake; it only remained to be seen how bad a mistake it was.

As I retreated, my shadow drew itself down off her face, unveiling an expression that to this day I wish I could forget. Traces of her smile remained, but they were awash in disbelief. Bella blinked as if she'd suffered a disorienting blow to the head.

"I—I'm sorry," I said. "That was—"

"No," she said, still recovering, "it's okay."

"That was so stupid...I—I don't know what—"

"Don't worry about it," she smiled. She rubbed my shoulder, presumably to comfort me, but it had no such effect—I just wished that I could be anywhere else, with anyone else. We just sat there for a long moment, the waves reasserting themselves in our silence.

"Come on," she said finally, pulling me up off the log. "Let's head back."

We walked back to the car, Bella holding tight to my hand and pulling me along. It wasn't just being rejected that stung so badly—it was Bella's shock. Clearly she didn't have romantic feelings for me, but apparently it had also never crossed her mind that I might have such feelings for her. Her reaction had made me feel sexless and absurd, but at the same time, I was grateful to her for not holding my own clumsy stupidity against me.

Left in my childish hands, relations between us would've remained awkward after that night at Pacific Beach, but Bella wouldn't allow it. She just kept showing up at my door and grinding away at me until all of my sharp edges had been worn smooth. By spring semester, it was a non-issue—Bella's reaction that night had cured me of any romantic feelings that I'd had for her, and her persistence had lightened my lingering embarrassment.

For our last two years at UW and two more after we graduated, Bella and I shared an apartment in Ravenna, only separating when Bella decided to shack-up with her then-boyfriend Jon. That move hadn't been a big deal—I'd been happy to get my own place, and we saw almost as much of each other as before (particularly after Bella evicted Jon six months later). Her move to Bellingham felt much different though, and not just because of the distance.

Bella met Joel at her food co-op. I knew that she was serious about him the day that she asked my opinion of her hairstyle. We were at her apartment, about to go pick up her groceries, but Bella got stuck in front of the mirror and couldn't stop fussing with her hair.

"What do you think?" she asked, holding the bushy tangle up on top of her head. "Should I wear it like this, or should I wear it down?"

"Wear it down."

"You think it looks better down?"

"I think it would be *easier* to wear it down. Could you even get it to stay up like that?"

"I could clip it up, or tie it with something."

"Seems like too much effort to me."

"But does it look better?"

"No."

"So you like it down."

"Yes."

"Okay, I'll wear it down."

Bella had little patience for her appearance, least of all her hair. Her frustration was understandable—I've never known anyone with a bushier, more uncompliant mane. She grew it to her shoulders because at that length—or really, at that *weight*—it would sort of hang down like ordinary hair. Her hair battles had always been more practical than vain though, so this sudden concern with its attractiveness was baffling. That is, until we "accidentally" ran into Joel at the co-op.

At that time, Joel was doing his Masters in Education at UW. After a few weeks of flirting over organic dairy products, they'd started dating. When Joel finally finished his program, he was offered a job teaching fourth grade up in Bellingham. It was the job he'd been hoping for, but he considered not taking it because of Bella. She wouldn't hear of it though, and so he moved, and they started commuting to see each other on weekends.

I certainly couldn't hold it against Bella for moving—Joel loved his job, and Bella could continue her graphic design work anywhere she could plug in her Mac. Really, it was a wonder that they hadn't done this sooner.

ↁ

Once I'd gathered myself, I found Joel's number and dialed again. This time, Bella answered.

"Hello?"

"Hello, Ms. Marcellino, I'm calling from the Seattle Police Department. Did you file a missing persons report for a Garrett Anderson?"

"Oh, yes, do you need me to identify the body?"

"Well, no…actually, we think he *may* be alive. I just need to ask you some questions for verification purposes."

"Okay."

"So you indicated that the man that you're looking for is male, correct?"

"Usually, yes."

"And does he prefer boxers, or briefs?"

"Well, he *wears* boxers, but only because he can't admit to himself that, deep down, he actually prefers briefs."

"Excellent. And one last question: does he play center field for the Anaheim Angels?"

"Oh, no…I'm sorry—the Garrett I lost has absolutely no athletic ability whatsoever."

"Hey now…"

"I'm sorry," Bella laughed, "He has *very little* athletic ability."

"Okay…I can live with that."

"When did you get back? Wait—you *are* back, right?"

"Yeah, I flew in last night."

"Everything go okay in Boston?"

"Yeah, it took a little longer than I expected, but it eventually came together. Sorry I didn't make it back for the big move."

"Oh, don't sweat it—we had plenty of help. Joel's brother was here, and another teacher from Joel's school. It went pretty quickly."

"Great…well, it sounds like I've officially achieved obsolescence in this relationship. Do you need anything else from me before I toss myself off the Space Needle?"

"Actually, I've been having some computer problems I was going to ask you about…"

"Thank *God*. So how are the new living arrangements?"

"Pretty good. I'm still not completely unpacked, but it's coming along."

"And you aren't at each other's throats yet?"

"No…not *exactly*," Bella said, a slightly odd tone entering her voice. "Actually, we, ah…Joel and I got engaged, if you can believe that."

"Holy crap!"

"Yeah, seriously, huh?"

"Wow, that's great, Bella…congratulations!"

"Thanks."

"So when did this all happen?"

"Last weekend. I thought about calling or e-mailing or something, but I really wanted to tell you in person. At least now you're in the same time zone."

"Wow. So have you picked a date yet?"

"Not a specific date, but we're thinking next June, after Joel's done for the summer. Do you think you'll be in town then?"

"I'll make sure I am."

"Because I was actually hoping that you'd be my Maid of Honor."

I started to laugh, but stopped when I realized that Bella wasn't laughing with me.

"Wait—you're serious?"

"Absolutely."

"Can you do that?"

"It's *my* damn wedding; I can do whatever I want."

"Well, okay then. In that case, I'd be honored. But I would like to have some input on the dress—I don't want something that's going to make me look like a house."

"Actually, I'd prefer that you wore a tux."

"Could I at least wear a sash that says, 'Maid of Honor'?"

"You can wear a tiara if you want, just as long as you don't schedule any trips or let yourself get dragged away at the last minute."

"Okay, deal…June is officially a no-fly month for me. So, is Joel's Best Man going to be male or female?"

"It's his brother, Will. Sorry."

"Will I at least have a little harem of bridesmaids to

order around?"

"Sorry, no bridesmaids either. It's going to be a small ceremony. But you can bring a date if you want."

"Oh, swell. Maybe I can find a tux place that rents those too."

"So I take it you didn't meet the love of your life in Boston?"

"No exactly," I said, deciding that my Dana Burns encounter was too much of a had-to-be-there experience for this conversation. "I spent most of my time with a balding guy named Marco. It was all I could do to resist yelling out 'Polo!' every time someone said his name."

"Was he at least single?"

"Alas, no. Story of my life."

"Well, I think you've just got to get back on the horse. At three years, it starts being something that you have to explain."

"Yeah, I know."

"Has there been *nobody* you've been interested in? You must've met a few women in your travels, right?"

"Yeah, I guess. I kind of liked that woman Liz...you know, in San Diego?"

"The one with the weak stomach?"

"Yeah...I guess I can't really call her after that..."

"What about that girl at Macrina, the one who had the dream about you?"

"April?" I said, the hairs on the back of my neck lifting as I spoke her name.

"Yeah, April. She's cute, and she's always had a thing for you—you should ask her out."

"You think she has a *thing* for me?" I really wasn't being coy here—I just thought Bella must be confused.

"Is it so inconceivable?"

"Well, I don't know...I just never...I guess I just thought she was a little goofy."

"Well, there's no question about that, but she also happens to like you."

"I actually just saw her this morning..."

"Now there's a surprise."

"She invited me to some kind of art show thing on Friday night."

"See, that's a sign—you have to go."

"I mean, she wasn't inviting me to go as her date or anything...she just gave me a flyer. I'm sure she gave them to everyone she knows."

"She *likes* you Garrett...I've seen it. No woman would recount an entire dream she had about you if she wasn't at least interested. But I guess the question is, are you interested in her?"

"Well, sure...yeah, I guess."

"Well, you should give it some thought. And when you're finished thinking, you should get yourself to that show."

ও

Before hanging up, Bella and I made plans to get together on Saturday—I'd drive up to Bellingham for dinner with her and Joel. For the most part, I felt only warm and fuzzy things about their engagement—Joel was a great guy, and they'd always seemed really happy together. If any two people should get married, I thought, it's them.

There was, however, a tiny voice in my head screaming, *BUT WHAT'S GOING TO HAPPEN TO ME!?!?* My closest friend had moved to the boonies, and now she was getting married. Children were undoubtedly right around the corner, putting me on the fast track to being that sad "uncle" who comes to all the family parties but who isn't actually related to anyone. "He seems nice enough," everyone whispers, "but what *happened* to him?"

It was that image of myself—pudgy and alone at a succession of Disney-themed birthday parties—that made me think seriously about what Bella had said. I'd always been attracted to April; the profound disappointment I felt on the days she wasn't working sometimes made me wonder whether I was addicted to Macrina's food or April's attention. Still, I never would've thought to ask her out—she was just so energetic and off-the-wall, I couldn't imagine her being interested in a computer programmer who'd graduated from college around the time she was boycotting her junior prom because it was lame.

On the other hand, Bella's instincts about these things were always better than mine. The more I thought about it, the more I suspected she might have a point about April's dream.

This is how it went:

Bella and I met for brunch at Macrina one Saturday morning. It was busy, so Bella wrote our names on the waiting-list clipboard that hung by the door. April was refilling someone's coffee at the back counter, but she saw me and frantically waved me over with this big goofy smile on her face, a kind of pantomime giddiness. I made my way back to her warily, and April leaned across the counter as if to tell me a secret, her voice low but excited.

"Hey, I was hoping I'd see you today! You were in a dream I had last night."

"Oh...really?"

"Yeah, I dreamt that there was this race with these

teams, you know, like there were these teams racing each other, carrying stuff, and you were on my team."

"Carrying stuff?"

"Yeah, each team had to carry a canoe that was loaded with stuff—backpacks and tents and cases of Snapple. You had to get the canoe across the finish line to win."

"That sounds…heavy."

"Well, there were like six of us carrying it, kind of like pallbearers, so it wasn't *that* bad."

"So what happened?"

"Well, we were racing, and the race went everywhere—through the woods, through office buildings, through Westlake Center—and I was invisible, and my clothes were invisible too, and at some point, I got hot from carrying the canoe, so I took off this invisible jacket that I was wearing and I set it down someplace, and then right away I couldn't find it again."

"Because it was invisible."

"Right! So I was crawling around on the ground, feeling around for this invisible jacket, and I knew we were losing valuable time, but for some reason I didn't want to go off and leave it behind. And everybody on the team was all irritated with me and they wouldn't help look, except for you. You were crawling around trying to help me find it."

"Was I invisible too?"

"No, I was the only one."

"Did we ever find the jacket?"

"I don't think so. We were looking for a really long time, but then the dream changed to something totally different…I don't even remember what happened next. Isn't that *so* weird?"

"Yeah, that's…yeah. Very weird."

Just thinking of April and her invisible jacket made me smile. And to be honest, I was so preoccupied with the whole April question that I didn't accomplish much at the office that morning, beyond reading every story on the Seattle Times website and sending Kevin Lanier a "Where are you?" e-mail. By 11:30, exhausted from fake-working and watching Leonard pace up and down the hall—he still hadn't located Brendan—I decided to get out for some lunch.

On my way to the elevator, I passed Gwen watering a ficus in front of her desk. I slowed for a step or two, wondering if I should mention that the tree was artificial, but I elected to tiptoe away silently—it just wasn't worth the risk of being called "Gary" again.

The wind had kicked up since the morning, and it played havoc with my tie as I walked down First Ave. On another day, I might've headed back to Macrina for lunch, but I needed to think, and I couldn't do it around April.

Cutting through Pike Place Market, I had to negotiate the dense little mob surrounding Pike Place Fish, the world-famous seafood stand where the fishmongers toss whole salmon around like infielders celebrating a strikeout. At this particular moment though, nobody was buying fish, so the crush of camera-wielding tourists was stuck watching these guys in orange PVC overalls haul ice and mop the floor. It was a tense little standoff, and I could tell by their impatient looks that a few foreigners in the crowd didn't grasp that this was an actual business, and not some kind of city-sponsored performance art. I sensed that violence might erupt if the fish didn't fly soon.

At a café down on Western Ave, I ordered a sandwich and sat down to give April's flyer another look. The fact that, before Bella's badgering, I hadn't even considered attending this show seemed like an almost genetic part of my identity, as fundamental to who I was as the fact that I always slept on the right side of the bed, or that broccoli made me gag. I assumed that April had intuited this—that she was the kind of person who invited people to things, and I was the type who politely declined (or just didn't show up).

But why was I like that, reflexively rebuffing people and things that lay outside my comfortably airless cocoon? Was I, despite a decade in laid-back Seattle, still just a frosty New Englander at heart? I'd convinced myself that April's show just wasn't my kind of thing, but maybe that was just some kind of adolescent social fear talking. How many other connections had I missed because of this timidity masquerading as discretion?

With this question in my mind, I flashed on the image of a woman I had passed on the steps of my building about a year before. It had happened as I was returning from a particularly draining business trip, capped off by a seven-hour delay in Denver. Exhausted and feeling quite sorry for myself, I stumbled out of the cab in front of my building and started laboriously up the front steps. As I trudged upward—head hung melodramatically, suitcase dragging behind me—a woman came out the front door and started down the steps.

"Hi," she said politely as the distance between us closed.

"Hi," I echoed, glancing up without really looking at her.

But just as she slipped past me, I heard her footfalls stop.

"Hey...are you okay?"

I turned back and stared at her for a moment, not fully comprehending her question. She had brown, bobbed hair and eyes the color of apple cider. Her expression was uncertain, as if hoping that my problems weren't actually as serious as my body language suggested.

"Oh, I'm...yeah, I'm fine," I mumbled, feeling both warmed and foolish for having inspired such concern in a stranger.

"Oh. Okay," she nodded.

"Thanks though," I said, suddenly wanting to keep talking to her but unable to think of anything else to say.

"Sure," she said, continuing down the steps. "Seeya."

"Bye," I said, frozen in place, already knowing it was a mistake to let her keep walking, but also knowing that with each passing second it was less and less likely that I'd drop my bags and run after her. Only when she was around the corner and out of sight could I move again. For weeks afterward, I'd watched for her around the building, but I never saw her again, and I was never able to determine which lucky neighbor of mine she'd been visiting.

As I replayed this scene sitting in the café, it occurred to me that my tendency to retreat might be more habitual than genetic, each new withdrawal making the next one all the more certain. Bella had often called me "a creature of habit," which I'd accepted as a quasi-compliment because I had an image of myself as steady and reliable. But now a different image came to mind: an Irish Setter we'd had briefly back in Portland who'd obsessively licked one spot on her leg until it was hairless and raw. Mom had treated the spot with bitter apple and even athletic tape, but Maggie had licked on mindlessly, undaunted by all obstacles. So was it "steadiness" that had kept me from ever taking a vacation, or from chasing that woman down the street? From here, it looked more like helplessness in the face of overpowering habit.

But I'd overcome my habitual way of being with Dana Burns, and I was glad, even if the result had been disappointing. Maybe the best way to honor that day with Dana, I thought, was to go to April's show and see what happened… to break my hiding habit, if only for the sake of breaking it.

I felt a rush at making this decision—it was so unlike me, and it felt like progress. Maybe April and I were meant to be, or maybe we weren't, but at least I was going to find out.

I practically floated back to work, and as I passed back through Pike Place, it seemed as if my euphoric mood was rippling through everything around me. The fish were flying again, and it was easy to imagine that the tourists' applause was really for me.

❧

Gwen was back in the fruit bowl when I got off the elevator after lunch. By this time, I was feeling so good that I gave her a confident "Hey Gwen" as I passed, looking her squarely in the eye and practically daring her to mangle my name. She didn't say anything initially—she just blinked a few times and smiled queasily—but just as I was about to disappear down the hall, she cleared her throat.

"Um…I think maybe Leonard was looking for you?"

"Oh…okay, thanks," I said, cheerfully reversing course toward Leonard's office.

"Actually, I think maybe he's in the kitchen?" she added with an uncertain squint. "He said something about cleaning the refrigerator?"

"Right. Thanks."

I found Leonard standing before the open refrigerator, with the kitchen garbage can standing headless beside him. With his shirt-sleeves rolled neatly to his elbows, he was peering apprehensively into a damp-bottomed paper bag.

"Hey Leonard. Gwen said you were looking for me?"

"Hm? Oh yes, Garrett…" he said, barely glancing up. Giving the bag one sniff, he dropped it heavily into the trash. "I was hoping you could help me out with something."

"I'll try."

"As you may know," he said, now turning his attention to a Tupperware container filled with a chunky green liquid, "we've just finished up a project for an online sporting goods retailer in Atlanta."

"Brendan's project."

"Right," Leonard said, holding the Tupperware up to the light for a viscosity check. "And while the client has been thrilled with most of the work we've done, apparently they are now experiencing a small problem with part of the system. Some kind of 'exemption' I believe?"

"A fatal *exception* maybe?"

"Yes!" he said, emphatically chucking the whole Tupperware container and looking directly at me for the first time. "See—I knew you'd be on top of this. Apparently this exception is tripping things up from time to time. I was hoping you could take a look at it this afternoon—you know, lend your expertise to the project."

"Sure. Who should I talk to? Were you able to find Brendan?"

"No, Brendan left for some R&R, and I haven't been able to raise him on his cell. As you might imagine though, the client is anxious to get this resolved as quickly as possible."

I'd always been impressed by Leonard's ability to make the direst of situations sound rosy (although the fact that he often had no idea what he was talking about undoubtedly made it easier). Knowing his tendencies, I could guess at the real details of the situation: the e-commerce system was dumping orders left and right, the client was screaming, and Leonard had been trying with increasing desperation to locate Brendan, who was passed-out on a Bermudan beach, getting sun-poisoning with his cell phone buried at the bottom of his suitcase.

"Well, if you can put me in touch with someone in Atlanta, I'll see what I can do."

"Okay, I'll call them now. Do you think you can get it working this afternoon?"

"Honestly, I won't have any idea until I dig into it."

"Okay, well, I'll get you that contact," Leonard said, hauling an armload of takeout containers out of the fridge and dropping them *en masse* into the trash. "Thanks, Garrett."

"No problem," I said, heading back to my office. Before I was out of earshot though, I heard another load of something heavy go into the trash.

"Savages," Leonard muttered.

∾

Being dragged into someone else's mess normally inspired much passive-aggressive grumbling on my part—these cleanup jobs had become a bigger and bigger part of my workload as Cavanaugh had grown, adding less capable developers along the way. But on this day, it would've taken more than Brendan's latest botch-job to unhinge my happy-go-lucky mood: I was going to April's show. A girl might like me. Life was good.

In truth, I was glad to have something to immerse myself in briefly, a kind of rebound project after my long-term relationship with GenoSys. Otherwise, I would've had to start planning my next big projects, and I was finding it difficult to think about scheduling a trip to Oregon or Minnesota or wherever when all I wanted to do was stay home for a while.

As promised, Leonard put me in contact with the systems administrator in Atlanta who was able to describe the problem in detail and send me the relevant files. At first, it looked like a simple fix: I discovered two hard-coded references to databases on a development server that Brendan had forgotten, the programming equivalent of leaving a clamp in a patient's abdomen. Once the application moved to the production server, these references no longer made sense, creating a half-dozen scenarios that would crash everything—scenarios that Brendan obviously hadn't tested before scooting off to wherever.

Beyond that blatant error though, Brendan's code was just ugly. I found three more ticking bombs while looking for the source of the original problem, and even when his code worked, it was alarmingly inefficient—I quickly identified a dozen places where small changes would either speed things up or save precious server resources.

Knowing that it would all end up back in my lap if anything broke, I spent the next several hours simplifying and streamlining Brendan's pages, defusing potential landmines before they could go off. And despite the time it took, it felt good. I celebrated each bit of junky code that I banished, feeling as if I was making the world a better place one line at a time.

By the time I'd finished my work and FTP'd the final code back to Atlanta, it was almost 8:00 p.m. in Seattle; Leonard, Gwen, and the rest of the Cavanaugh crew had been gone for hours. Sitting at my desk, waiting to hear back from the systems administrator, my thoughts drifted back to April.

I was remembering the last time I'd had brunch at Macrina, right before leaving for Boston. I'd sat at the far end of the back counter, and April had stopped by to chat. She was telling me about a concert she'd been to, and right in the middle of a sentence, she'd farted—a round little muted-trumpet *ferp*. It obviously took her by surprise, because she stopped talking, mouth open.

"Do you think anybody heard that?" April whispered.

"I don't think so," I said reassuringly.

"Okay, wait," she said, closing her eyes in concentration.

A beat later, April produced a note that seemed to go on forever and actually rose in pitch—more slide-trombone than trumpet. This time, all heads at the counter spun in her direction. When it was over, April took two elaborate bows, blew a few kisses to her confused public, and refilled everyone's coffee.

At the time, I'd been both mortified and awed by her fearlessness. April was fun and easygoing in a way that I had *never* been, and I thought I could use some of that in my life. She was also pretty darn cute, which was something else I definitely had room for. I'd never felt so drawn to someone who could make me so uncomfortable.

I felt an optimistic tingle down the back of my neck just thinking about going to April's show. Of course there were still plenty of potential obstacles—she might have a boyfriend, or she might not even be interested—but in my increasingly optimistic/delusional state, I just knew that none of those things would be true: April and I were destined to be together.

When my cell phone finally rang, I'd gotten so lost in thought that I actually jumped.

"Hi, this is Garrett."

"Hey big boy, what're you wearing?"

For just a second, I wondered if my contact in Atlanta had started drinking. After all, it was pretty late on the East Coast. Then I recognized the voice.

"Um…Kevin?"

"Were you expecting somebody else?"

"Well, yeah, actually…I was waiting for call back from Atlanta."

"Oh, Spanky…please tell me you're not still working at this hour…"

"Sadly, I am."

"Well, so am I, but at least I've got an excuse—I'm trying to get out of this godforsaken city tomorrow."

"And which godforsaken city would that be?"

"Sacramento, again. Wait—did you say *Atlanta*?"

"Yeah."

"My. God. You know, if Leonard himself had to clean up after Brendan, that little shit would've been gone long ago."

"I'm sure. So you're coming back tomorrow?"

"That's the plan. Feel like buying me dinner? Ingrid's got me on probation again…I'm not even sure what for."

"Well, believe it or not, I'm actually busy tomorrow night. With a girl, sort of."

"Like Sherrie and Lorna sort-of, or…?"

"No, she's legitimately female…she just doesn't know we have plans."

"So you're stalking her."

"Yeah, although I do have some inkling that she wants

me to stalk her…as all stalkers do, I guess."

"Well, I certainly wouldn't want to intrude on *that*. And, truth be told, it might actually be in my best interest to catch up with Ingrid anyway—you know, make a show of contrition for whatever it was that I did."

"Or didn't do…"

"Yeah. But I'll be in the office all next week—will you be around?"

"Yes, thankfully, I don't have any travel planned for the next few weeks."

"Okay, well, I'll see you then, Spanky."

"Oh, Kevin, I meant to ask—have you met Gwen?"

"Stefani?"

"No, our new receptionist."

"We have a receptionist?"

"Yup."

"Well, I guess it was only a matter of time once that Amish flying saucer landed in our lobby. Somebody has to keep Leonard company, right?"

☙

My plan for Friday was to make a brief appearance at the office, staying just long enough to connect with Leonard and ensure that everything was still humming in Atlanta. With any luck, I'd be out by eleven and could spend the rest of the day preparing for April's show.

In that regard, the biggest challenge was figuring out what to wear. My years with Cavanaugh had left my wardrobe without much middle ground—I could wear a business suit and wingtips, or a t-shirt and Tevas. It looked like a shopping trip might be necessary, something that I knew could take a while without Bella's help.

Gwen was reading a paperback when I stepped off the

elevator on Friday morning. She closed the book as I approached and started into her receptionist routine.

"Hi, can I help y—oh…hi."

"Hi, Gwen. Is Leonard in yet?"

"Yeah, but he's on a conference call," she said, already returning to her book. The disappointment in Gwen's voice suggested that she was beginning to realize how little Cavanaugh really needed a receptionist.

The crew from Thursday was back again—Walter Y2K, DB Vincent, and Mainframe Bill—but Friday also brought Roger ASP, who did a lot of the web-database integration work that Kevin and I also did. I'd collaborated with Roger on two projects during my first year at Cavanaugh, but I hadn't seen much of him recently. He and his wife had had their first child in the spring, and since then, his office appearances had become even rarer than mine.

I chatted briefly with Roger on my way in, dutifully asking him about "the baby," a term I resorted to because I couldn't remember the child's name or sex (and the photos on Roger's desk were inconclusive). I actually liked Roger— he was a talented, modest guy—but we'd never developed much of a bond. He was only three years older than me, but the gap felt more like a decade. Kevin Lanier, on the other hand, was a full *five* years older than me, but managed to make me feel comparatively mature.

After my Roger-conversation ran out of steam, I went back to my office to wait for Leonard to get off his call. I spent some time browsing for outfit ideas online but, uninspired by everything I saw, I began to wonder if I should just wear one of my countless black suits after all. No matter what I wore, April would give me shit about it, so what did it matter, right?

Unless, of course, I arrived in that crazy velvet jacket she'd been raving about. That would be pretty funny, I thought, if I could track the thing down in whatever vintage store she'd visited. It also seemed like an idea that Garrett Anderson would never in a million years follow through with.

But still, if I was already breaking habits, why not one more? Just for laughs, I ran a search for vintage clothing stores in Seattle. I'd just found a promising place on Capitol Hill—their website actually featured a photo of one such jacket—when Leonard appeared in my doorway, scaring the crap out of me.

"Oh...Leonard, hi."

"Am I interrupting?"

"Not at all. What's up?"

Leonard sat down in the chair opposite my desk and gave me his patented fatherly smile. I actually had to stifle a grin—although I had no proof, I'd long suspected that Leonard regularly practiced this expression in the mirror. Once he spoke though, I had no problem keeping a straight face.

"I need you to go to Atlanta," he said. "The client is still having problems, and they've asked that we send someone back immediately. There's a noon flight that I think you can make if you leave now."

I felt myself slump under the weight of Leonard's words. It was the worst thing he could've said, and yet part of me had suspected it was coming all along.

"There are problems with the pages I worked on?"

"No, apparently there are other issues...I'm not even sure what. I just need you to go out there and get it resolved. This client has a lot more work coming up, and we can't afford to have them unhappy."

I'd been floating all morning, but now I felt too heavy to move, watching all my hopes of the last 24 hours shrink into the distance. It all seemed so silly now, my daydreams of April and how going to this stupid art show would somehow redeem me and right all the wrong-turns I'd taken over the last few years. What had I been thinking? I wasn't going to April's show tonight, and I wasn't even going to visit Bella tomorrow—I was getting on another freaking plane.

"What about Brendan?" I asked, mostly out of spite. "Maybe we should track him down and send him back. Let him clean up his own mess."

"The client specifically requested that we send someone *other* than Brendan."

"Smart people," I said, just fishing for a reaction from Leonard, some small acknowledgement of his own culpability in this. Leonard just gazed back at me with his stupid smile, and I sunk even further into my chair.

"How long would I be there?" I asked.

"Hard to say. Even if it's a quick fix, I'd still want you to take a few days to be sure everything is settled."

It was more than just missing April's show that was bothering me. I'd *just* gotten back to Seattle, I'd been looking forward to some downtime at home, and already Leonard was sending me away again. Which made me ask myself: *Why am I even considering this?* For three years, I'd been Leonard's dutiful soldier, and he had rewarded my hard work with harder work, cleaning up after clowns like Brendan. Didn't I deserve a break once in a while?

"Isn't there anyone else you could send?" I asked.

"Uh, well…hmmm," Leonard fumbled, surprised by the question. "I'm not sure…"

"What about Roger? He's great with this stuff, probably better than I am."

"Well, *perhaps*...but..."

"But what?" I said, beginning to lose my patience with Leonard.

"Well, Roger's married, and he's got an infant at home... and where it's so last minute..."

"Uh-huh..."

"You understand, right Garrett?" Leonard said, once again pressing the fatherly smile. "You're just in a place in your life where this kind of thing is easier for you. Your life-style is more...flexible."

"Yeah, I know." My annoyance was actually fading, but I was feeling something else now, something new. I just wanted Leonard to be quiet for a second so I could think.

"I wouldn't ask on such short notice if it wasn't an emergency," he added.

For a long moment, I just sat there looking down at my keyboard. I sensed Leonard squirming in the silence, but I wasn't trying to make him suffer—I just wanted to work out what I was feeling, to identify this thing that had just surfaced. Eventually, I saw that it was just a question, one that I'd returned to in different forms recently.

"Do you think it's possible, Leonard," I finally said, "that this job is actually the reason I'm still in this 'place in my life'?"

I hadn't raised my voice, but Leonard was clearly taken aback. He just blinked at me wordlessly, his regal face confused.

"Well...uh...I..."

"I'm sorry, Leonard, that wasn't fair. You don't have to answer that...I just have to quit this job."

"Oh."

"I just can't do this anymore."

"Well, we can talk about Atlanta…maybe there's another way to approach it. And I've actually been thinking that we need to review your compensation…"

"It's not just Atlanta. I should've quit two years ago, but I've just been in denial, or too afraid, or whatever. I just have to go…it's time."

"Oh."

We both sat there quietly for a moment—me looking at Leonard, Leonard looking at the floor. My feet were tingling and I desperately wanted to get up and dance, but I remained seated out of respect for Leonard.

"I'm not sure what to say," he said eventually.

"Well, you *could* just say, *Okay, Garrett, if that's what you have to do.*"

"Okay, Garrett. If that's what you have to do…"

"It is. Thanks, Leonard," I said, standing up to shake his hand across the desk.

"So you're leaving today then?" he asked, taking my hand but still looking bewildered. I would've liked to have given him more notice, but I knew that if I waited another two weeks, I might forget to leave altogether.

"Yeah," I said. "I think it makes sense to do it now, before I dig into any new projects."

"Okay. If that's what you think is best."

"I'll stop by your office before I leave."

⌘

Ten minutes later, I delivered my laptop to Leonard. I found him sitting quietly in his office, his hands lying flat on the surface of his desk as if trying to prevent it from floating away.

"This is yours," I said, setting the laptop on his desk.

"Oh, right. Thanks." Leonard looked down at the computer as if he'd never seen one before.

"I also e-mailed you a list of all the projects I had upcoming...I assume you'll want to contact the clients and spread them around to the other guys."

"Right. Good thinking," he said, hardly looking up at me. Leonard was so abstracted and silent, I began to feel guilty about leaving. I knew it would inconvenience him, but I'd hadn't considered the possibility that Leonard might be *hurt* by my departure. Seeing the effect it was having on him made me realize that this man, about whom I felt such extreme ambivalence, probably considered me something of a friend.

"Well, I guess this is it then," I said. "Thanks again, Leonard."

"Okay, well, good luck, Garrett." Leonard stood and absently shook my hand again. Then he looked me in the eye, a little worried. "It wasn't Gwen, was it?"

"No, not at all." I smiled. "Gwen seems very nice."

"Are you angry with me about something else?"

"No, I'm not angry. I just need to not work here anymore."

"Fair enough," he said with relief, smiling a little now. "Well, good luck."

"I'll see you around."

"Good, yes." he said, brightening further. "Give me a call—we'll play some golf."

☙

As I turned and walked empty-handed out of Leonard's office, two thoughts went through my head: 1. Despite myself, I was finally going to take a few days off. 2. Not personalizing my office really had paid off in the end.

I did feel weird about leaving without telling Kevin La-nier, but given that he was probably already on his way back from Sacramento, there was nothing to be done. I figured that I would just call him at home on Saturday.

Gwen was still reading her book when I passed back through the lobby. She didn't look up even as the elevator doors dinged opened.

"Bye Gwen," I waved.

"See you later, Gary," she said, flashing me a reflex smile.

"I hope not!" I said, as the elevator doors closed. But Gwen hadn't even heard me.

3

The Rest of Friday

Emerging onto the First Ave sidewalk, it struck me: as many times as I'd considered quitting my job, I'd never given much thought to what I would do next.

It was a beautiful day in Seattle, it was barely 9:30, and April's show was still ten hours away. Standing in front of Cavanaugh's building, I weighed my options. Should I call Bella and give her the good news, or go to Macrina for breakfast? Should I check my net worth at an ATM, or or maybe just run naked through Pike Place Market?

Each of these ideas had obvious merits, but I really wanted to find the perfect way to celebrate this momentous occasion. And then it came to me: I would march straight back to my apartment, plant myself on the couch, and watch *The Price is Right*.

&

I'd moved to Belltown six months after starting with Cavanaugh. After a few years in sleepy Ravenna, I wanted to try living downtown, thinking I might leave my apartment more often if I could walk to cool stuff. I liked Belltown's low-key mix of incongruous elements—hoity-toity restaurants like the Dahlia Lounge sharing the neighborhood with laundromats, union halls, and hip music hangouts like the

Crocodile Cafe. The population was an equally varied collection of the artistic, the academic, and the homeless.

I looked at several different buildings and ended up choosing the oldest and most amenity-free of the bunch—a worn, three-story brick place on Second Ave near the corner of Battery. The 85-year-old building had no elevator, and its lobby was really more like an oversized phone booth paneled with dented mailboxes. You probably wouldn't say that the place looked neglected, but it had obviously been allowed to age.

I found the old building's shabbiness welcoming though, in part because I'd finally accepted what my dry cleaner and my late mother had always known: I was a spaz and slob. This was the kind of place where I could be myself; nobody would even notice if I gouged the woodwork moving furniture or dumped an entire bowl of pasta with red sauce on the 20-year-old wall-to-wall carpet.

My building's official name, according to the plaque bolted to its exterior, was "The Regent at the Regrade." This was a reference to the Denny Regrade, the district created in the early 1900s when Denny Hill was liquefied and sluiced into Elliott Bay. As amazing a feat as that must've been, it was even more amazing to me that anyone would brand anything with a word like "Regrade"; I could only assume that it had been the work of the same unpoetic individual who had named the "Sanitary Public Market" at Pike Place.

Regardless of the plaque, the inhabitants of 2208 Second Ave never referred to the building by its official name. Within its steadily deteriorating walls, the building was known simply as "The Retrograde."

ᄋᄼᄀ

My apartment was a nondescript one-bedroom on the

second floor. From the hallway, you stepped into a tiny foyer, identifiable as such by the nautically themed "Welcome Aboard!" mat left by the previous tenant. Following the front hall back into the apartment, you passed the narrow kitchen on your left, a short hall leading to the bedroom and bathroom on your right, and finally arrived in the living room, which had windows looking onto Second Ave.

When I arrived home after my shortest-ever day at Cavanaugh, I was still too wound-up to sit right down in front of the TV, so I put on The Pixies' *Doolittle* and thrash-danced around my living room, whirling faster and tossing off more clothing with each passing bar. I finally collapsed onto the couch, now half-naked and completely out of breath, as the final chords of "Wave of Mutilation" buzzed the Retrograde's brittle brick walls.

In the end, I wasn't able to make myself watch *The Price is Right*; its Technicolor reality was just too much of a downer. I'd only thought of the show—a background-noise favorite of my grandmother's—because it was the highest form of indolence I could imagine: you've really got nothing to do if you have time to watch *The Price is Right*. But after fifteen minutes with Bob Barker and the Beauties, I was up off the couch again, too wired to sit still any longer.

☙

At 6:30, I left for April's show wearing the velvet jacket that I'd spent the afternoon hunting for in Seattle's vintage-store jungle. I was 99% certain that I'd found the one April had mentioned, and it actually seemed to fit pretty well, but of course that hadn't stopped me from scrutinizing it in the mirror for an hour, trying to decide if it looked too much like something from the Willy Wonka Goodwill collection. I flip-flopped about wearing it roughly ten times, finally rushing myself out the door before I could change my mind again.

As my door thudded shut behind me, I saw my new across-the-hall neighbor ambling down the corridor in my direction. He'd moved in while I was away, and although we'd nodded in passing once or twice, we'd yet to have a conversation. At that moment, already feeling some butterflies about April's show, my first impulse was to duck back inside before I was forced to interact with him. I would've followed through with this plan, but I quickly realized that the door was locked, and that my keys—including the car key I'd need to go anywhere—were still on my kitchen counter. Thus trapped, I turned to face him.

"Hi there," he said, with a crooked smile. "I guess we're neighbors. I'm Clay."

Until that moment, he'd seemed imposing. He was about 6′4″ and lanky, his hair buzzed to a smooth shadow. But he had serene brown eyes, and he was more soft-spoken than I'd expected. He wore a grey REI t-shirt, and he had a computer bag slung over one shoulder.

"Oh, hey…I'm Garrett," I said, as if just noticing him.

"Nice to meet you. Have you lived here long?"

"Yeah, a while I guess…almost three years?"

"So I guess you must like it?"

"Yeah, I do. I like it."

Clay smiled as if expecting me to elaborate; I just smiled back.

"Okay, well, it was great to meet you, Garrett. I guess I'll see you around?"

"Yeah. Okay. Great."

We shook hands and I headed down the hall as if to leave. Once Clay was safely inside his apartment though, I hustled back to my door, dug the spare key out of my wallet—this wasn't the first time I'd locked myself out—and went back in for my car keys. I felt bad that I hadn't been friendlier, but I told myself that I'd make it up to Clay the next time our paths crossed.

 භ

My car, a green '91 Jetta that replaced the '84 I'd driven out from Maine, had been on its last legs for years, probably not helped by sitting undriven for weeks on end in a cramped U-Park lot three blocks from my building. It needed a new clutch and there was a widening hole in the exhaust, but the car just kept going, always ready for more punishment.

Which is another way of saying that I'm an awful driver. Flooded with visual information, I'm easily flustered and distracted behind the wheel. I cut people off without realizing, and I often have to swerve or stop short to avoid pedestrians, cyclists, and parking barriers. It's just a matter of time before I kill someone; hopefully it will only be myself.

It was on the drive to the Seattle Art Academy that all of the day's stress and excitement finally began to catch up with me. *Did I really quit my job without any kind of plan?* The palpitations kicked in while I was parallel-parking—*What if I never, ever find another job?*—but it wasn't until I was walking up the sidewalk toward the brick Academy building that the panic finally consumed me. *What if Bella was wrong and April has no interest in me? I look like a fricking fool in this jacket. Have I completely lost my mind?*

I was frozen on the sidewalk, paralyzed by these thoughts, when my phone started buzzing in my pocket. The Caller ID said "Number Unavailable," but I answered anyway.

"Hello?"

"You *asshole*."

"Excuse me?"

"Guess where I am right now."

"Oh, Kevin, hey...I think we've got a bad connection. Are you at Sea-Tac?"

"Nope. I'm on a fucking flight to fucking Atlanta."

"Nooooooooo..."

"Oh yeah."

"Oh, Kevin...I'm so sorry. I can't believe you got stuck with that."

"Well, once Leonard fired Brendan, he didn't have many options," Kevin said, barely concealing his glee.

"He fired Brendan?"

"Yes, sir. Tracked the fucker down in Aruba and told him not to come back."

"Wow...I can't believe he finally did it."

"Well, the little prick had it coming. But you're officially my hero, man. Who would've guessed you'd quit before me, huh? I just wish I'd known—I could've been there to throw confetti or something."

"Well, it was a kind of spur-of-the-moment thing..."

"Clearly. Oh, and Ingrid sends her congratulations. Of course now she's all over me to do the same thing, so... thanks for that."

"Well, maybe someday I'll actually meet this Ingrid."

"Who knows—I guess anything's possible. Maybe we'll all have dinner when I get back. That is, if I'm still speaking to you."

"That would be great."

"Okay, well, this is costing Leonard about a buck a second, so I should probably go."

"Okay. Well, call me from Atlanta if you need a hand."

"Yeah, right. Later, Spanky."

ɞ

I'd first met Kevin Lanier in San Francisco, during week six of the seminar tour Leonard had hired me for. It was a Friday, and after ten hours of lecturing and schmoozing, I staggered back to my room and flopped face-first onto the bed. The tour—changing cities and hotels every second night but always delivering the same inane presentation—was wearing on me more than I'd expected. Lying there on the coarse hotel comforter, I searched for the motivation to get up.

I'm not sure how long I'd been unconscious when the phone rang. I reacted slowly, dragging myself across the bed until I could just reach the nightstand.

"Hello?"

"Hey, is this Garrett?"

"It is."

"Hey, this is Kevin Lanier. From Cavanaugh."

"Oh hi, Kevin." (I had no idea who he was—at that point, Leonard was still the only Cavanerd I'd actually met.)

"So how's it going?"

"Good. How're you?" (Whoever you are.)

"Great. Hey, a client gave me two tickets to the ballgame tonight, and I was thinking you might want to come along."

"Well, that sounds great," I said, "but I'm actually in San Francisco right now."

"Well that's a relief, because so am I."

"Oh, you're not—?"

"I'm standing in the lobby of your hotel."

"Oh, sorry," I said, amazed at my own confusion. Somehow, I hadn't noticed that I was holding my room phone rather than my cell. "I've just had a really long day."

"I'm familiar with that feeling, man—I did the tour last year."

"So you're down in the lobby?"

"Yeah, I've been in San Francisco for a while, and I saw on the schedule that you were in town. I actually sent you a message last night, but I'm guessing that you haven't had time to take a dump let alone check your e-mail today."

"That sounds about right."

Ten minutes later, I was strapped into the passenger seat of Kevin's rented Corsica, which he tossed around the road with only passing regard for other cars. He'd race up to somebody's bumper—the whole time telling a story and gesturing with at least one hand—and then at the very last second, he'd swerve around them with a casual tug on the wheel. Kevin also liked to play the radio at a brain-jamming volume, so everything we said had to be shouted.

"You have a girlfriend, Garrett?" he barked over at me.

"Uh, no…do you?"

"Sometimes. It depends on Ingrid's mood," he said, grinning through his bristly brown moustache and goatee.

"What's that?"

"IT DEPENDS ON INGRID'S MOOD."

"Oh."

"Periodically, she throws a fit about my traveling, and she breaks up with me."

"So what's the current status?"

"Right now, we're on. But honestly, it's hard to tell the difference, on or off. We still have sex either way; it's just a matter of whether or not she talks to me afterwards."

From anyone else, this would've been way too much

information, but just fifteen minutes into our relationship, I was already beginning to expect such revelations from Kevin. I didn't feel confident that it was true, but it didn't seem to matter.

"Seriously though," he continued, "I can't walk this line forever...she's going to reach her limit eventually."

"So what're you going to do?"

"I've got a couple things brewing," he said, steering with his knees while searching for a better radio station. "I shouldn't be at Cavanaugh for that much longer. Although I've been saying that for a year now."

"*Jesusmother!*" I howled, bursting into nervous, tittering laughter at one of Kevin's more thrilling maneuvers, a left-right two-car avoidance that chirped the Corsica's tires.

Kevin just grinned. "Okay, okay..." he said, "*that* was kinda close."

Despite Kevin's sprint-and-swerve driving style, I was never *too* worried that we would actually crash—he was always just attentive enough to avoid catastrophe. While my own erratic driving instills no such confidence, riding with Kevin was a lot like being on an amusement-park ride: the loud music, the suggestion of danger, and the underlying (and perhaps unrealistic) expectation of safety.

At the time, I remember being surprised that a personality as big as Kevin's could be contained in such an insubstantial body. Kevin was roughly my height, but he was easily forty pounds lighter. Something about the slightness of his build and the pouf of his chestnut hair made me think of a matchstick. If it hadn't been for the facial hair, I might've guessed that he was closer to 15 than 35.

ᔅ

The tickets that Kevin had been given, it turned out,

were in the front row of 3Com Park's altitudinous upper deck. Kevin and I were both disappointed by this, but for very different reasons—he because we were so far from the action, and me because we were so far from the ground. Thankfully, my torment was short-lived—after five innings of hanging himself over the edge in search of better seats to sneak into, Kevin got bored and suggested we head to Chinatown for a late dinner. I didn't argue.

Kevin parked the Corsica on Columbus, and as we were walking to the restaurant, I asked him about the post-Cavanaugh plans he'd mentioned earlier.

"Well, I've put away a chunk of change to start my own business; I just haven't decided what I want to do yet."

"You have some ideas though?"

"Yeah, I've got tons of ideas, but it's something different every week. I'll probably be fifty before I figure it all out," Kevin said, his voice trailing off as he squinted at something up the block. Finally he just stopped on the sidewalk and stared.

"What the hell do you suppose is going on there?" he grinned.

Just ahead of us in the dark, two middle-aged women were rather indiscreetly trying to break into a beige Corolla. One of the women—wavy blonde hair, white slacks, tropical-print smock—had an untwisted coat hanger fished through the weather-stripping at the top of the passenger-side window. The other one—slightly thicker-set, straight brown hair, chocolate brown knee-length dress—had her hands cupped goggle-like against the glass, and was attempting to talk the blonde through the operation.

"A little to the right...no, left...back further...back...back—ohhhhhh..."

"Shit."

"You almost had them."

Eventually, Kevin spoke up.

"You ladies need some help?"

The women swung around to look at us, and I finally realized what Kevin had already seen—these women were actually middle-aged men.

"Oh, we just locked the keys inside," the brunette said, shaking her head.

"*She* locked the keys in it," the blonde corrected. "She can be such a ditz."

I'd been fooled, not because they actually *looked* like women—they were too tall, their shoulders too big—but because they were so casual about it. And based purely on their outfits and hairdos, they could've been any two of my aunts coming home from Las Vegas Night at the VFW Hall.

"Well, I knew you weren't trying to *steal* the car," Kevin teased, "because an actual thief would've been gone by now. My real question is, what are you hoping to accomplish with that coat hanger?"

"Well, I can see the keys in there, they're *right there,*" the brunette said, tapping the glass. "I almost had them a second ago too, but then they slipped off onto the floor."

"I could take a crack at it, if you like," Kevin offered, peering in the window.

"Be my guest," the brunette said, stepping aside.

Kevin solemnly extracted the hanger from the passenger window and, bracing it against his thigh, began shaping it expertly, the three of us watching him, rapt. After four or five bends, he had created a perfect pair of bunny ears.

The blonde started giggling. "What the—"

Donning said ears, Kevin walked around the car and

pulled open the rear driver-side door, which had apparently been unlocked all along. Standing by the open door, with the traffic whooshing past behind him, Kevin took a couple quick bows. Then, with all of us laughing and applauding, Kevin *locked* the door and closed it, leaving the keys inside.

The blonde laughed even harder, but the brunette looked concerned. I was pretty confused myself.

"Did you just...? Did he just...??" the brunette stammered.

"He locked the door!" the blonde cackled, "Now we're *really* screwed!"

"We were *in*! What the hell are you doing?"

"Well, if I just let you in that way," Kevin said, coming back to the sidewalk and unbending the bunny ears, "what would you have done the next time? You have to at least let me show you the proper way to open a Corolla with a coat hanger."

The brunette didn't seem amused.

"Come on," Kevin said, "it'll just take a second. Just step over here and observe."

"Go on, Lorna," the blonde said, "you could use the practice."

Reluctantly, Lorna went and stood beside Kevin as he bent the end of the hanger into a U, which he then he fed down into the door, between the window and the lower weather-stripping, directly above the lock.

"Basically, you just fish around here until the lock starts to wiggle...see that?"

"Oh yeah...look at that," Lorna said, actually intrigued now.

"And then you just yank the hanger straight up and the lock should...oh...the hook must've unbent. Let me try that again."

Three times, Kevin reshaped the hook, fished it down in the door, and yanked it up only to find that it had completely straightened itself. Kevin chuckled nervously.

"Don't worry," he said, "I can totally get this—it's just a flimsy coat-hanger. Here, I'll double it over this time."

While Kevin and Lorna fiddled with the hanger, the blonde woman and I stood off to the side watching. After a moment, she introduced herself.

"My name's Sherrie," she said, offering a meaty but hairless hand.

"Garrett," I said. "And that's Kevin over there."

Upon hearing his name, Kevin flashed us an uneasy smile.

"Don't worry, hon," Sherrie said, "We're in no hurry—if you hadn't come along, Lorna would still be trying to snag that key-ring."

Now Lorna glared at Sherrie, who seemed completely unfazed.

"So hon," she said, turning back to me, "do you have a girlfriend?"

"Uh, no," I said, slightly bewildered at having been asked that question twice in the same night. "Not at the moment."

"I didn't think so. No offense, but you look recently dumped."

"I *look* dumped?"

"Big time."

"How exactly can a person *look* dumped? I mean, maybe this is just what I look like."

"Well, first of all, am I right?"

"Well, sort of, but it wasn't all that recent. It was like

three months ago." I was exaggerating—it had only been two months.

"Hon, some people could get dumped on Wednesday and be free of it by Friday, but for you, three months is recent. You're holding onto it for some reason."

"Well, I don't *think* I am, but..." Part of me couldn't believe that I was having this conversation with a stranger—a transvestite no less—but most of me really wanted to hear what she/he had to say about it.

"Did she cheat on you?"

"No, not that I'm aware of anyway."

"She must've done *something* to you."

"Well, she did kind of string me along for nine months..."

"There you go..."

"And then when it didn't suit her to have me around, she broke it off like it was nothing."

"Like she was returning a sweater that didn't match her bag?"

"Exactly!"

"So she used you then. Good-looking woman?"

"Yeah, she was attractive. She knew it too. I think she always felt that I was beneath her somehow, but I made decent money and I was willing to spend it on her, so..."

"What was her name?"

"Christina."

"Oooh, I never liked that name. She sounds like a real bitch to me, hon."

"Oh, she's *definitely* a bitch," I spat, surprising even myself.

"There you go! See, you look a teensy bit less dumped already. You just need to let it out."

"You think?"

"Oh yeah. You just have to let yourself get a little pissed-off and you'll lose this whole wounded-puppy thing in no time. Life's too short. Speaking of which, I hope they figure this out soon. I'm so hungry I could eat my own arm."

"Well, Kevin and I were just on our way to some Chinese place up the street."

"House of Nanking?"

"Yeah, have you been?"

"Oh sure, they have fantastic dumplings."

"Well, you're welcome to join us...if you want."

Somehow, inviting this cross-dressed stranger to dinner felt utterly right. At that point, even Kevin was barely more than a stranger to me, so what was a couple more?

"Well that's sweet of you," Sherrie said, playfully pinching my arm. "Actually, Nanking does sound pretty good right now—"

Just then, Kevin finally popped the lock on the Corolla.

"Thank *God*," he sighed, extracting the hanger and opening the door. Lorna ducked inside and grabbed the keys off the floor.

"Damn cheap coat-hanger," Kevin said, "I'm really sorry about that."

"All that counts is you got us in," Lorna said. "You ready to go, Sherrie?"

"Actually, Garrett here invited us to House of Nanking—how about walking over there instead?"

Kevin looked over at me in bug-eyed amusement. I avoided looking back at him because I was afraid that he'd make me laugh.

"Oh definitely, Lorna," Kevin said, "come to dinner with us. You have to let me make it up to you for locking you out of your car."

Lorna shrugged. "Okay. Just let me lock the car again."

House of Nanking was a bright little dive, possessing the loud, sweaty ambiance of a subway car at rush hour. It was after ten when we arrived, but the place was still jammed with diners. When it was finally our turn, the waiter/host/chef led us to a tiny table wedged so inaccessibly into a corner that he had to lift it completely over his head to allow Sherrie and Lorna to squeeze in.

No more than a minute after we'd been seated, food started arriving. First to land was a huge bowl of hot-and-sour soup, dropped so unceremoniously on the table that some of it sloshed out onto the chipped Formica. Three minutes later, a plate of pot-stickers was balanced across the top of the soup bowl. Then came the scallion pancakes, a scallop dish, the spicy green beans, and the Nanking Chicken.

The food was simple but good, and we gobbled it down in a futile attempt to keep up with the onslaught of dishes. Throughout the meal, Kevin kept us all laughing—me, Sherrie and Lorna, and even the couple from Cincinnati at the next table. Surrounded by strangers, he seemed utterly in his element, as comfortable as a man in his own living room.

While we were eating, I recalled how exhausted I'd been before Kevin's call, lying on my hotel bed wondering how I could possibly last another two weeks on the road. But six hours and two transvestites later, I felt like I'd caught a second wind.

It was a strange and unexpected little gathering, and I'd played a small role in making it happen. Kevin walked through the world as if he owned it, as if nothing were off-limits to him. In Kevin's world, everything was interesting, and all problems had solutions. I thought that my world could probably be a little more like that.

ೞ

Reenergized by Kevin's profane Airfone pep-talk, I pocketed my cell and pushed through the front doors of the Seattle Art Academy. Inside, I followed a series of hand-markered "Sculpture Show–>" signs down the main hall to the gallery itself, which was already quite crowded, echoing with laughter and the music of the jazz trio thrumming in the back corner.

For a while, I just drifted through the bright, high-ceil-inged space, scanning the unexpectedly lively crowd for any sign of April. It quickly became clear that I needn't have worried about my outfit—all manners of dress were on dis-play here, from cargo shorts to business suits to costume-like ensembles that would've been appropriate for Mardi Gras. Having braced myself for a much more strenuously artistic gathering, the actual event's joviality was quite a relief.

The art itself was also more fun than I'd expected—bold and colorful and absurd. The show's centerpiece, towering over everything, was a vibrant recreation of Michelangelo's "David." It was identical to the original in most ways—same slouch, same bushy hairdo, same snarky expression—but this David was constructed entirely of Froot Loops, and sported a colossal, zucchini-like erection. When I got close enough to read the tiny title card, dangling provocatively from David's up-curving manhood, I discovered that the piece was actually called "David and Goliath" and that it was the work of none other than April Franklin.

It was while I was standing there, squinting up at Da-vid's day-glo boner, that I heard April's voice behind me.

"Oh my God, Garrett! Hey!"

I turned around and April was practically on top of me, wiry limbs pulling me into an unexpected hug.

"I can't believe you're here! Thank you so much for coming!"

"My pleasure."

As she slid back out of my arms, I saw April's gaze catch on my jacket before looking up at me. It was the first time I'd ever seen her at a loss for words.

"What the…? Is this the…? From the place? From Capitol Hill?"

"I think so."

"How did you…? I mean…are you *okay*? Do you have a fever? Do you need to sit down? How do you feel?"

"Actually, I feel pretty good."

"Well, you *look* fantastic!" she said, stepping back for a better view. "I mean, I was totally right, right? That jacket is the *bomb* on you. Don't you love it?"

"Yeah, I think so…it's definitely growing on me."

April herself was wearing a threadbare Violent Femmes t-shirt, a black miniskirt, red fishnets, and (of course) knee-high purple galoshes. Her red-streaked hair, usually tied up behind her head, was down for once, falling just shy of her shoulders.

"Come on," she grinned, taking my hand. "I want you to meet some people."

Over the next hour, I think April introduced me to everyone in the gallery—a pair of high-school friends from Fremont (where April had starred in the drama club, mostly because she was the loudest one on stage), her mother's thirty-something boyfriend Dean (Mom was on a Whidbey Island yoga retreat), a trio of college roommates (Melissa, Megan, and Maya, all from different colleges), two of her instructors from the Academy (married to each other, both quite buzzed), a friend of her brother Josh (who was the original owner of the Femmes t-shirt, and now an actor in New York), three other artists with pieces in the show (including "Boyfriendectomy," "Kama ShoeTra," and "Illegal Alien Autopsy"), and a half-dozen other "friends" whose precise connection to April I couldn't discern or immediately forgot.

All of April's friends seemed nice enough, but I soon started to wonder if she could possibly have room in her life for anyone new. The one hopeful sign was the fact that I was the only person April kept by her side the whole time, pulling me along with her as she zigzagged through the crowded room. She was also obviously having a good time, gleefully trying new identities on me with each new introduction.

"This is my friend Garrett. He's a hair stylist for *Buffy the Vampire Slayer*."

"Garrett actually went to clown college with my brother, but now he's a VP at Microsoft."

"Garrett was my model for 'David and Goliath.' Well... the penis part anyway."

"Garrett's a dance instructor on Alaskan Cruise Lines."

"Garrett's in charge of large-mammal reproduction at the Woodland Park Zoo."

"Garrett's a park ranger on Mount Rainier. Unfortunately, he's also agoraphobic, so he's out on disability."

April's friends accepted her fantastic pronouncements in stride, apparently knowing her well enough not to be surprised by anything she might say (although I did get some sidelong glances from another couple who overheard the "penis model" intro).

At first, I assumed that April was merely entertaining

herself with these stories, continuing her long-standing tradition of trying to make me blush. But I also noticed that she seemed to be reading my reaction to each new fabrication as if it were some kind of test, her own peculiar way of figuring me out. Seeing this, I did my best to follow April's lead through this odd little dance, embellishing her lies with new details and anecdotes. It took me a while to get comfortable with the idea, but I eventually started to enjoy myself.

"Bill Gates is not nearly as serious and buttoned-down as people think. But he does have an absolutely enormous ass—that rumor is 100% true."

"It used to bother me when the older women wanted me to pretend to be the guy from *Dirty Dancing*, but, you know…now I kind of like it."

"The hippos are really the biggest challenge. If they're not in the mood, no amount of Barry White is going to help."

The funny thing was that, through a half-dozen of these performances in which neither of us uttered a single word of truth, April and I seemed to forge a more intimate connection than we had in two years of chit-chat across the counter at Macrina Bakery. Of course, that also might've been because April kept grabbing me inappropriately in an attempt to make me laugh.

The last person I met that night was Kate Bridges, one of April's roommates. Kate was thirtyish and tall with cropped brown hair and dark, narrow eyes. Compared to April, she was dressed conservatively—a black t-shirt and jeans—and she projected a friendly poise that reminded me of a Marketing Director I'd once worked with in Tacoma.

My introduction to Kate was the first truthful one of

the night, and April delivered it with a "game-over" grin that made it clear that I was now under oath.

"This is my friend Garrett, the infamous French Toast Fiend of Macrina Bakery."

"Hey Garrett," Kate smiled, shaking my hand. "Nice to finally meet you."

"Yeah, you too."

"If I remember correctly, you do something with computers, right?"

"Yeah, I'm an IT consultant," I said, suddenly realizing that even this was now a lie. "Or…at least I was until this morning."

"Oh?" Kate said, flashing April a quizzical look, "What happened this morning?"

I opened my mouth to answer, but discovered that this was actually a difficult question—what *had* happened, anyway? And before I could find the right words to explain the past few days, April suddenly slumped against me—her head dropping onto my shoulder—and began snoring loudly.

Once I'd regained my balance, it dawned on me that April probably assumed I was launching yet another lie, and that faking a narcoleptic fit was just her means of protest. Part of me wanted to wake her and explain that I was actually telling the truth this time, but Kate seemed so intent on ignoring April's sudden unconsciousness that I decided to do the same. I also resolved to answer Kate's question as simply and honestly as I could—as it was, I still needed to figure it out for myself.

"Well," I began, brushing a stray clump of April's hair away from my mouth, "my boss really wanted me to make this last-minute trip to Atlanta this morning…"

"Okay," Kate nodded seriously.

"But I really wanted to come to April's show tonight..."

"Okay..."

"So, in the end, I guess you could say that we compromised: I quit, and he sent somebody else."

April snorted dramatically, but then settled back to sleep on my shoulder.

"Wow," Kate said, seeming as surprised by April's non-reaction as she was by the information itself. "So, do you have any idea what you're going to do next?"

"Not really. I've been feeling pretty burned-out though, so, just off the top of my head, I'm thinking I should take some time off and decompress."

"But you'll probably stick with IT in some form, right?"

"Who knows...I guess anything's possible."

At this point, April's head finally snapped up off my shoulder.

"Wait...you're serious? You really quit your job?"

"I did."

"Just so you could come to my show?" April asked, almost breathless. I got the distinct impression that her excitement had more to do with my burgeoning potential for erratic behavior than it did with anything meaningful that might be implied by said behavior.

"Well, I mean, my job *had* been sucking the life from me for the last three years, and I was really only still working there because I was too lazy and afraid to quit, but, yeah... other than that, it was all about tonight."

"Cool!"

After a brief discussion of my next career move—April was adamant that I should apply for this private investigator's assistant job she'd seen advertised in *The Stranger*—Kate stepped outside to call their other roommate, Neil, who had said he was coming to the show but who had never actually surfaced. This left me and April alone (as much as that was possible in the middle of a crowded gallery) for the first time since I'd arrived.

"I really like your piece," I said. "I didn't get a chance to tell you that."

"Thanks."

"I do have one question about it though…"

"Okay…"

"Is it wrong that it's making me hungry?"

"Not at all," April grinned. "There are no incorrect responses."

"Well that's a relief, because at this point, I'm going to need a gallon of milk and an entire box of Froot Loops before I'll be able to sleep tonight."

April just laughed.

"See, this is another one of those situations where you *think* I'm kidding, but I'm actually being totally serious."

"So you're really unemployed?" she asked, eyes narrowing in mock-suspicion.

"Completely."

"Well, in that case, we have to do something to celebrate."

"Definitely."

"Ooh—we should stay up all night!" she blurted, an ecstatic whisper.

"Okay."

"Sorry, I don't know why I said that—it just popped out."

"I'm game if you are."

"It's not, you know, too high-school?"

"Well, I never stayed up all night in high school so…

no."

"Do you have a car?"

"Sort of. It's out front."

"Okay, well, give me like, five minutes and I'll be ready to go?"

I meandered around the room once more while April said her goodbyes. A few minutes later, I saw Kate return from her phone call. Pretending to be engrossed by an interactive piece called "Celebrity Gene Swapper," I watched out of the corner of my eye as she and April chatted briefly. Before parting, April gave Kate hug and, somewhat surprisingly, a quick kiss on the lips.

A moment later, April appeared by my side, one eyebrow raised.

"Are you ready?"

❦

In the Jetta, 50ᵗʰ Street NE. 10:04 p.m.

"So did Kate track down your roommate?"

"Yeah—he just overslept. It's a good thing she called, because otherwise he might've missed work again."

"He works nights?"

"Yeah, he's a security guard at the Seattle Art Museum."

"That actually sounds kind of cool."

"He could probably get you a job there if you're interested."

"Would I have to carry a gun?"

"God, no. I think Neil mostly reads comic books and jerks off in the bathroom."

"Hmmm…suddenly that sounds much less cool."

"I don't think the jerking off is *required*…"

"How do you know Neil again?"

"He's Kate's cousin. We moved in with him when his

last roommates moved out last year."

"And how did you meet Kate?"

"She was in a band with a guy I dated like, four years ago."

"Kate was in a band?"

"Yeah, she still is. I mean, it's a different band now, but…she plays bass."

"Wow…I would never have guessed that."

"She's really good. We should go see her play sometime."

"Definitely."

"And then afterwards, we should get matching tattoos…"

"Obviously."

"And mohawks."

"*You read my mind…*"

"See…I knew you weren't well when you showed up tonight."

"Speaking of which, where are we headed exactly?"

"Don't you want it to be a surprise?"

"You're right—I do. So don't tell me, no matter how much I beg. Actually, maybe you should blindfold me now."

"Oh, I think we want this exit. Yeah—Union Street—this is the one."

"Okay…we're exiting."

"And you're picking the next activity, so start thinking."

"Okay…cool. Do you suppose the zoo is already closed?"

Neighbours, 1509 Broadway, Capitol Hill, 10:50 p.m.

"I don't have a philosophical objection to alcohol or anything—I've just never liked it that much. Plus, it just makes me sleepy, which seems pointless. Although, my parents probably would've liked to have given me the occasional drink when I was little."

"Were you just as hyper back then?"

"Um, are you suggesting that I'm hyper *now*?"

"Yeah, a little. But in a good way of course."

"Well, according to my Mom, I just wouldn't sleep at night. I even remember being in like, kindergarten, and staying awake in my room doing little projects until midnight. In the morning, my parents would usually find me passed out on my bedroom floor."

"What kind of projects?"

"Usually some kind of art project. There was one period where I was totally obsessed with just cutting shapes out of colored construction paper. I'd do it for hours on end, trying to come up with new and amazing shapes that nobody had ever seen."

"And did you succeed?"

"Not really. I could never quite create what I was seeing in my head. But for six months, my room was littered with these trippy snowflakes."

"Do you still have any of them?"

"No, Mom cleaned them all out one day while I was at school. Thinking about it now, it's amazing that my parents never tried to medicate me…I'll have to thank them for that."

Neighbours, 1509 Broadway, Capitol Hill. 11:37 p.m.

"I don't think I've ever seen your hair down before…it looks nice."

"Thanks."

"Do you wear it up at work because you have to, or…?"

"Mostly it's just easier."

"Ah."

"So…how long have you been in love with me?"

"Excuse me?"

"I mean, I'm just curious…what's this all about?"

"What's what all about?"

"You know…buying that jacket, showing up tonight, announcing that you quit your job…"

"Well…"

"We've been flirting for like, two years, and now all of the sudden, it's like, *Heeeere's Garrett!* I mean, I've been through like, seventeen relationships since we met. I officially wrote you off several eons ago."

"Well, in my own defense, I didn't actually realize that we were flirting until yesterday."

"What???"

"I didn't fully realize that we were flirting until my friend Bella clued me in."

"So what exactly did you think was going on?"

"I just thought you were really friendly."

"Well, I'm definitely a friendly person, but I don't recall showing any other customers my Cat-in-the-Hat tattoo…"

"You're right…that should've—"

"I mean, I do have some exhibitionist tendencies, but still…"

"I don't know…I guess it just never seemed completely plausible that you might be interested in me."

"Because of your overpowering B.O.?"

"Hey—it's *really* warm in here."

"I know, seriously, huh? Anyway, I'm sure I smell ten times worse than you do—I think I forgot to put on deodorant today."

"You *think* you forgot, or…?"

"No, I'm sure…I actually ran out yesterday. Is it really bad?"

Neighbours, 1509 Broadway, Capitol Hill. 12:01 p.m.

"Well…"

"Well?"

"I just wasn't…I mean, you just surprised me…"

"Well…having learned that subtlety is completely lost on you, I just thought…"

"No, definitely…good thinking. In fact, is that Isaac guy still around? Maybe if he saw us he'd finally believe that I'm not gay."

"He'd probably just say that you were overcompensating."

"That's true…I might be. But I have to say, I do enjoy overcompensating."

"Sorry I was gone for so long. I can't seem to stop running into people I know."

"Well, you know a lot of people."

"She's really more a friend of a friend. She just wouldn't stop talking, even after I like, closed the stall door. I think she was on something…"

"Maybe she met Isaac—I think he offered me some crystal meth."

"And you didn't take it?"

"Well, I was going to, but…"

"But…?"

"But…I remembered that I still had your wallet in my jacket pocket, and that if I got all high and ended up on a ferry to Vancouver or something, you'd be left here with no money and no identification, which would really kind of suck. For you, I mean…"

"Thanks for thinking of me."

"No problem."

"And thanks for being such a good sport about coming here."

"Are you kidding? This place is great."

"Really? You actually like it?"

"Yeah, I think it's officially my second favorite place to dance in Seattle."

"Your first being…?

"My apartment…just because it has better music."

"Well, we should come back on a Thursday sometime—it's 80s night."

"Cool."

"So are you ready to get back out there?"

"Sure."

"Now if Isaac had only seen you dancing…"

"Excuse me?"

"I mean, personally, I think it's fantastic…very energetic. But it's just not something a gay man would be seen doing…ever."

"Well, I'll try to be more careful."

"Just watch the elbows—with the lights in here, I don't always see them coming."

QFC, 1401 Broadway, Capitol Hill. 1:30 a.m.

"So this is seriously our next activity?"

"But don't you think it was destiny, given that we were so close to a 24-hour QFC?"

"I guess so."

"And really, you have no one to blame but yourself. As an artist, you have to consider the effect your work is going to have on your audience."

"Uh-huh."

"I bet half the people who were in the gallery tonight are out doing the very same thing. You probably could've made a fortune selling Froot Loops at the door."

"Well, we're definitely taking these back to your place. I want to see where you live."

"Really? It's not that exciting."

"Well, we've still got like, five hours to kill—they probably aren't *all* going to be as exciting as this."

The Retrograde, Apartment 2D. 2:12 a.m.

"Does he have any idea?"

"No, I've never said more than hello to him. But I figure that's what he gets for always leaving his trash in the hall."

"Do you have a title for it yet?"

"I've alternately been calling it either "Garbage Man," or "You Are What You Eat, Apartment 4C," but it's still kind of taking shape, so…I'm not sure."

"I've always wished I had an outlet like that, something creative. I've just never found anything I had any talent for."

"Well, programming must be kind of creative, right?"

"I guess you could call it creative, but I'm not somebody who'd say that code ever rises to the level of beauty. And in the end, it still doesn't express anything."

"Well, you've got some free time now…you could take a class at the Academy. Or you could even take a pottery class with my Mom—she's got her own studio in Fremont."

"How long has she done that?"

"Pretty much forever. As long as I can remember anyway."

"Is your Dad around?"

"Yup—he lives in Fremont too, down the street from

Mom. They're actually really close, and Mom's good friends with my Dad's wife Connie."

"That sounds…unusual."

"Yeah, I think it's one of those situations where getting divorced was totally the best thing they could've done for their relationship. Connie's always telling my father, *I hope our divorce is as good as your first.*"

"What does your Dad do?"

"He teaches math at Garfield High."

"So both of your parents are teachers then."

"Yup. And I'll probably end up teaching eventually. Actually, I'd love to be a high-school art teacher."

"You don't want to be a professional artist?"

"I don't think so. I mean, I love what I do, but I'm not sure I'd ever want to have to pay the rent with it, you know? I'd rather be free to make whatever I feel like making without worrying about whether or not somebody would ever buy it."

"I'd buy your stuff."

"You've only seen one piece."

"I'd still buy it. You sure you don't want a bowl?"

"I'm good."

The Retrograde, Apartment 2D. 3:06 a.m.

"I thought we were leaving…"

"Well, we were, but…this suddenly seemed like a better idea."

"I see."

"I mean, we can go now if you want…"

"Well…hold on for a minute."

"Okay…should I close the door?"

"Are you worried what your neighbors will think?"

"Actually, I don't really know any of my neighbors. Well, except this new guy across the hall. Actually, I just met him tonight, on my way over to your show."

"Uh-huh."

"Sorry…I'll just close the door."

"Good idea."

Alki Beach, 5:00 a.m.

"I can't believe you've never even heard of it. It wasn't a big hit or anything, but still…"

"Sorry, Garrett—I just don't see many movies."

"You don't like them, or…?"

"No, I like movies okay. It's just that sometimes when I'm actually watching them, I get kind of anxious."

"Anxious?"

"Well, maybe more like antsy. I feel like I should be doing something more productive."

"Hm."

"What?"

"Well…I guess I've always sort of felt that watching a movie, even a crappy one really, was pretty much the most productive thing I could be doing at any given moment."

"How about now?"

"Now what?"

"Would you rather be watching a movie right now?"

"No…but this hasn't usually been one of my options."

"Are you sure?"

Kerry Park, 6:23 a.m. (sunrise).

"You don't have to work today, do you?"

"No, I took the day off."

"On the off chance you decided to stay up all night?"

"Well, I was originally supposed to go to this party a guy in Kate's band is having, but…something more interesting came up."

"Mm."

"How about you? What are you going to do with the first day of the rest of your life?"

"You mean after I sleep?"

"Yeah."

"I'm supposed to drive up to Bellingham for dinner tonight."

"Who's in Bellingham?"

"My friend Bella? She moved there a couple weeks ago."

"Wow…that kinda sucks. You guys were pretty close, right?"

"Yeah."

"You know, for a while, I assumed you were a couple."

"That's understandable…I made the same mistake once myself."

"Somehow that doesn't surprise me. So are you going to tell her all about your big date?"

"Is that what this was?"

"I'm pretty sure."

"Honestly, I have no idea what I'm going to tell her…I haven't even told her I quit my job yet. She'll probably think I've lost my mind."

"Well, you have. But in a good way."

4

April in August

I'd originally had mixed feelings about visiting Bella and Joel at their new apartment. While I was looking forward to seeing them again, I couldn't help regarding this first trip to Bellingham as a ceremonial acknowledgement of the fact that things would never be the same. We were establishing a depressing new world order, but I was still mourning the old one.

But after eleven hours with April, my attitude had improved dramatically. I awoke Saturday afternoon feeling renewed, and instead of brooding through the 90-mile drive up I-5, I couldn't seem to wipe the grin off my face. Yes, the daydreams were occasionally problematic—I briefly drifted into the path of an 18-wheeler while bantering with the imaginary April in my passenger seat—but my mood was so stubbornly buoyant that not even a brush with death could trouble me for long.

I'd been to Joel's old apartment in Bellingham a few times, but he and Bella had rented a bigger place together, the left half of a two-story duplex not far from Joel's school. I'd always liked Bellingham, a tidy little port-city-turned-college-town, but given its location twenty miles from Canada (and convenient to very little), I'd never been able to imagine myself living there. When she'd first told me she was moving, Bella had offhandedly mentioned that she thought Western was looking for IT help, but even then, I'd had doubts about the long-term wisdom of following Bella from one zip code to another.

Just as I was about to pass Bella and Joel's house for the third time (I'd forgotten to write down the street number), Bella stepped out onto the front porch and waved. I tried to make my last-second swerve into their driveway appear playful rather than panicked, but the fact that my front wheel hopped the curb undermined my efforts.

"Hey stranger," Bella smiled, meeting me with a hug halfway across their small square of lawn. "Long time, no see."

"Yeah, it's been a while."

"Not quite long enough for your muffler to heal itself though, huh? Honestly, I think I heard you coming off I-5."

By this time, Joel had shambled outside as well. He was no more than 5'10", but he'd always seemed bigger to me. With his tree-trunk limbs and auburn curls, he reminded me of a Viking, albeit a clean-shaven, vegetarian Viking with a compulsion to hug everyone he met.

"Hey Garrett," he grinned, matter-of-factly crushing the air out of my chest cavity. "Welcome back."

"Thanks." I wheezed. "It's good to be home."

It was a little overwhelming, seeing them again; the eye-moistening impact of the moment caught me off-guard. After three months on the road, I think I'd started to forget what it was like to have real, flesh-and-bone friends. Or rather, I think I'd *forced* myself to forget, an act of self-preservation that I was now optimistic I wouldn't have to repeat.

I'd been worried about how Bella, practical as she was,

might react to the news that I'd quit my job without any real plan for the future. As I retold the story sitting in their living room (already infinitely homier than my own), I decided not to mention any role that going to April's show might've played in my decision. Instead, I emphasized my growing exasperation with Leonard, my hard-won conviction that my life would never improve if I didn't do something decisive, and the fact that, financially speaking, I could afford to take some time to figure things out (which I really hadn't known until I'd stopped at an ATM on my way to visit them).

Put that way, I thought it sounded pretty convincing. Apparently Bella and Joel agreed, because they both jumped off the couch, hugging and congratulating me as if I'd announced that I was pregnant (or something like that). Apparently, it had been clear to everyone else that I should've freed myself from Cavanaugh long ago, regardless of how many appendages I had to chew off. I guess they'd even told me this, quite explicitly, on several occasions. Now they just seemed to be relieved that I'd finally figured it out myself.

In the end though, Bella was far less interested in my job than she was in my date with April, which she grilled me about during our dinner at Pepper Sisters. I was happy to relive it all, but seeing Joel glaze over after the first twenty minutes, I tried to steer the conversation toward topics that I thought might interest him more—Turkish earthquakes, the influence of Harry Potter on fourth-graders, *chiles rellenos*. Bella perpetually found ways to drag us back to April though—my going out with anyone was such a novelty, she wasn't going to let the occasion pass without hearing all about it.

"So…did you get a goodnight kiss?" Bella asked when

Joel got up to use the bathroom.

"Uh, yeah, well…we fogged up the windows pretty good at one point."

"Second base?"

"Totally."

"Nice!" she grinned, somehow making me feel like my Mom had just congratulated me for touching April's boobs.

During the breaks in the interrogation, I did manage to get an update on their wedding plans, including the fact that one of Joel's friends was throwing them an engagement party in September. They were targeting June 24th for the wedding itself, and while they had found a promising caterer, they were still debating venues, music, and whether or not serving a vegetarian meal would unnecessarily antagonize certain carnivorous relatives. Despite the fact that Bella had clearly taken charge of the planning (Joel had more questions than I did), it was obvious that they were both really excited about getting married. I was actually beginning to look forward to it myself, even if Bella was already backpedaling on the idea of my wearing a "Maid of Honor" tiara.

Joel, an early-riser, threw in the towel around eleven that night, but Bella and I stayed up talking at their kitchen table (and finishing all of the ice cream in their freezer).

"So, do you have any idea what you're going to do with all of your free time?" Bella asked. "I mean, besides seeing April…"

"Not really…but it's sort of nice not to have anything planned for once. I like the idea of just having some space, you know?"

"Mm," Bella nodded, cleaning the last traces of chocolate off her spoon. "Just don't take *too* much space, okay?

You've always fared better with some structure."

"Yes, Ms. Marcellino," I laughed.

"Sorry…that came out wrong."

"That's okay…my third grade teacher wrote the same thing on my report card."

By 2:00 a.m., with all of the ice cream gone and Bella's yawns becoming more frequent and ferocious, I decided that it was time to head home. Still, Bella seemed surprised when I got up to leave.

"Wouldn't you rather crash here? You could be the very first person to sleep on our new pull-out."

"Well, maybe next time. I'm still so wide awake, I might as well just drive back now."

"Oh, *duh*…you probably want to go to Macrina in the morning…"

"You know, it hadn't occurred to me, but that's a really good idea."

"Uh-huh."

"But it is nice to have a reason to go home, you know?"

Bella followed me out to the car. We hugged once more in the dark of their driveway, Bella suddenly holding onto me as if she feared one of us might fall off a cliff. When she finally loosened her grip, she was smiling, but her dark eyes were glistening in the streetlight.

"What's the matter?" I panicked, at first assuming that I'd allowed my good mood to blind me to something horrible. It wouldn't have been the first time I'd been so oblivious.

"Nothing," she smiled, shaking her shaggy head. "It's just good to see you happy. It's been a while."

☙

The next few weeks were a beautiful blur. To my perpetual surprise, April was as enthusiastic about spending her every spare moment with me as I was with her. We returned to Neighbours for 80's night, attended a modern dance performance at the Behnke Center, and saw bands I'd never heard of at the Crocodile and the Showbox. It was all April's doing—once she realized how much I'd missed in my first decade in Seattle, she jumped at the opportunity to introduce me to her favorite things in the city. I enjoyed all of it, and I'm pretty sure that it wasn't *purely* because we were having sex between the cultural activities—April was also reawakening the parts of my brain that processed things like art, music, and literature…things that had once seemed important to me. I was realizing that maybe I wasn't quite the person I thought I'd become. Maybe I *did* like couscous after all. Or maybe I didn't. Either way, I had another chance to figure it out.

But the sex was definitely important too, not just because it was good to participate in it again (which it was), but also because April gave me a new perspective on it. April insisted that sex should always be *fun*, and she refused to be too serious about it. If I were to compare sex to dessert—and at the moment, I'm inclined to do so—I would describe sex with April as a strawberry sundae with hot fudge, whipped cream, and three cherries. By comparison, sex with my ex-girlfriend Christina had been more of a flourless chocolate gateau—really good for the first two bites, but ultimately too heavy. You'd still finish it, but you'd feel guilty afterwards.

I started spending more time than ever at Macrina Bakery, but I think that had as much to do with being unemployed as it did with dating April. In fact, our relationship made my Macrina visits more challenging, releasing April from what little sense of propriety she'd had before. Now, if I ordered French Toast, it was likely to arrive with an obscene drawing drizzled onto it. She'd also taken to calling me "Sexypants," which wouldn't have been quite so bad if everyone else at Macrina hadn't adopted the nickname as well. (*Hey Sexypants, how was the soup? Can I get you anything else, Sexypants?*) I got used to it all soon enough though, and eventually I kind of looked forward to the abuse. Life with April was like that a lot of the time—I'd never so enjoyed being uncomfortable.

When we weren't out on the town, we were usually at my place—we had it to ourselves, and my big-screen TV was better for movies. After our first date, when April had revealed that the passivity of movie-watching made her feel anxious and unproductive, I resolved to mentor her in the joys of inertness, eventually working her up to watching several movies in a row. Our best day in that regard was the rainy Tuesday we spent entirely on my couch, watching five DVDs in a twelve hour period, a feat made even more impressive by the fact that the list included the three-hour *Unbearable Lightness of Being* (April's choice) and the two-and-a-half hour *Brazil* (mine), and perhaps somewhat less impressive by the fact that the other three movies were *Kingpin*, *Liar Liar*, and *Summer School* (all at my insistence).

൙

After we'd been dating for a couple weeks, April declared that she wanted to cook me dinner. Finding a night when her roommates would both be out, we spent the evening at her apartment. I hadn't originally planned on sleeping there, but April was lying naked on top of me when she suggested it, and I've never been good at arguing with naked women.

"So I have tomorrow off from work if you feel like staying over," she'd said. "I could even make you some French Toast in the morning."

"Marry me?"

That night, April fell asleep almost immediately, her mouth slightly ajar, her left arm tossed casually across my chest. It had been a long time since I'd slept on a futon, let alone one as uncomfortable as April's, so I lay awake for a while, listening to her slow, even breaths. Sometime after I'd finally nodded off, I was startled by the sound of the apartment door closing—April had mentioned that Kate would be returning late from a gig. April herself slept on, undisturbed. Her alarm clock said that it was 3:17 a.m.

I groggily listened to the sounds of Kate shuffling around the apartment—the fridge opening, the toilet flushing, the water running. Then a light flicked on somewhere, brightening the gap under April's bedroom door, and I heard the steady *dum-dum-dum-dum* of stocking-footed steps in the hall. I was just starting to drift off again when the bedroom door opened and closed suddenly, releasing a blinding flash of hallway light.

When my eyes recovered, I realized that Kate was now in the dark room with us, standing just inside the door. At first I couldn't tell what she was doing, but after another moment, it became clear that she was undressing.

Given the clumsy and haphazard way in which Kate was stripping off articles of clothing and tossing them aside—her jacket, a sock, her shirt, the other sock, her pants—I guessed that she was just tipsy and had picked the wrong bedroom. I was torn as to whether I should speak up (likely waking April and scaring the crap out of Kate) or just pretend to be asleep and let her realize her own mistake. *She'll figure it out soon enough*, I thought, opting to play dead.

Once her eyes adjust, she'll realize.

But Kate showed no sign of realizing anything. Having peeled off every stitch of her clothing, she headed over to my side of the futon, the light from under the door outlining her naked shape. Just as Kate was bending down to grab for the covers, her breasts hanging a foot from my face, she finally saw me.

"Oh jeez!" she said, sounding surprised but perfectly sober. "Sorry, Garrett."

With that, she tiptoed quickly back to the door and went out, the hallway light briefly washing over her pale body. With all the commotion, I was certain that April would finally wake up, but she didn't even stir. She just lay there in the same position in which she'd fallen asleep, her open-mouthed breathing just on the pleasant side of a snore.

I lay awake a while longer trying to work out what had just happened. Maybe Kate was just tired? All of the bedroom doors did look very much alike. But it was her own apartment...how could she be that confused? My mind spinning with all of these different possibilities, I eventually drifted back to sleep.

❧

April was already out of bed when I woke the next morning. I found her in the kitchen, standing at the stove in a t-shirt and boxers. Her back was to me, and there was no sign of Kate.

"Hey...I was just going to come get you," she said when she heard me approach. "Breakfast is almost ready."

"Smells good." I said, sitting down at their kitchen table, a red-topped, chrome-trimmed monster that April had found at a flea market.

For a moment, we were both quiet, the sizzling of the

pan the only sound.

"So, something kind of strange happened last night," I finally said. "I think Kate almost got into bed with us."

"Oh no!" April giggled. "She must not have realized you were here!"

"Yeah, she seemed pretty surprised to see me."

"That's my fault—I should've left her a note. And I probably would've if *you* hadn't been distracting me."

I chuckled knowingly even though I wasn't quite getting the joke. I assumed that it was just my usual morning fog-headedness, but eventually I had to ask for clarification.

"So...how would a note have helped exactly?"

"Well, she wouldn't have tried to get into my bed if she knew you were here."

"But she might've otherwise?"

"Yeah—she sleeps in my bed sometimes."

"While you're in it?"

"Well, yeah...that's sort of the point. Sometimes she just doesn't like to sleep alone. Haven't you ever felt like that?"

"Sure...I guess."

"Why—does it *bother* you?" April teased, sitting down across the table from me.

"No...no, I just—"

"It's really no big deal," she said, now leaning across the table and, inexplicably, licking the tip of my nose. "Do you want two pieces, or three?"

"Two is good," I said.

With April back at the stove serving out our French Toast and scrambled eggs, I struggled to reconcile the seemingly mismatched pieces of information she'd given me. I found it remarkably difficult to focus with the cooling saliva-spot on my nose.

"She was completely naked," I added finally.

"Yeah…that's the way Kate sleeps."

"Ah," I nodded, capitulation masquerading as comprehension. In truth, the only thing that had become clear was that I wasn't getting any closer to solving the riddle, and that I probably wouldn't solve it even with twenty more questions. Even at the loneliest moments of my Cavanaugh career, I'd never once felt the impulse to sleep naked with Kevin Lanier, but I figured that maybe women were just wired differently in that respect.

Breakfast was good though, and as I ate, I started to feel more normal and less concerned about any strangeness in the night. It wasn't until an hour later, while April and I were cleaning up the breakfast dishes, that Kate finally emerged from her bedroom. She shuffled through the kitchen (in a bathrobe, thankfully) on her way to the shower.

"Morning," she said flatly, part greeting and part observation.

"Morning," we answered in cheerful unison.

With that, Kate went in the bathroom and closed the door.

‹∕›

I'd pretty much put the whole bed-sharing question out of my mind when it resurfaced a few mornings later at Macrina. I'd stopped in to have an apple tartlette, and since it was momentarily slow, April had joined me at the counter. She was telling me, in a kind of sleepy and meandering way, about the new work she'd done on her "Garbage Man" piece the day before—the latest bag of hallway trash she'd collected had contained a curious influx of Dinty Moore Beef Stew cans.

"There's probably no way for me to know for sure, but I really think he must be feeding it to his dog. I mean, how else could one guy go through seven cans of beef stew in two days? I'm nauseous just thinking about it."

"You're right—it's probably for the dog," I agreed, making a mental note to take out the garbage before April came over that night. I wasn't a Dinty Moore man myself, but my kitchen trash contained three empty Chef Boyardee cans that I didn't feel like explaining.

"I'll probably just end up including the dog in the piece," April went on. "I'd been thinking about it anyway, and the cans will give me a good place to start. Maybe I can even have him catching a Frisbee or something cool like that."

Throughout our conversation, April had periodically lapsed into little fits of neck rolls, which were often accompanied by an eyes-rolled-back, twitching-lid face that I found particularly disturbing. Finally I asked her about it, if only to make her stop for a moment.

"Is your neck bothering you?"

"Yeah, it's just a little stiff...I slept on it funny."

"You could use a new mattress," I suggested, recalling my night at her place. "Your futon isn't the most forgiving."

"Yeah, but I think the problem was mostly that Kate climbed into bed with me around two, and I ended up kind of hanging off the edge for the rest of the night."

"Oh..."

"I can't get too mad at her though—she's been a mess since she broke up with Sylvia."

"Sylvia?" I repeated dumbly, suddenly plunged back into the impenetrable mental fog of that first morning.

"She's a bartender at one of the clubs Kate's band plays

at."

"Oh…so Kate's…?"

"She's bi. You didn't know?"

"No."

"I mean, she *mostly* dates women, but she will mix in the occasional penis," April grinned. "It has been a while though…I think the last guy she hooked up with was actually right before we had our thing…what was his name… Cal? Carl?"

"Your thing?"

"Yeah, Kate and I had a very brief thing last year. I refer to it as my Lesbian Period, although it only lasted like three weeks, so I'm not sure it really qualifies as a 'period.' My Lesbian Interlude? My Lesbian Vacation?"

"Mm," I nodded, jamming the rest of the tartlette in my mouth. I also noticed that my ears were ringing with a sound not unlike a circular saw.

"Are you okay? You look a little freaked."

"Mm…fine," I mumbled through the mouthful of tartlette.

"It was really no big deal…"

"Mm-hm."

"I'm not even into women generally. Kate's the only one I've ever been attracted to."

"Sure," I gulped, forcing down a much-too-large hunk of tartlette, "she's an attractive woman." I was aiming for blithe, but I didn't quite make it.

"Really—you like her? If you're interested, I'm sure she'd be up for a three-way."

I'm not positive, but I think I might've blacked out for a moment. The next thing I knew, April was suddenly closer than she had been, with one hand on my arm and the other making reassuring swirls on my back. Her voice tiptoed between sympathy and laughter.

"Oh, Garrett, I'm sorry…did I scare you? I was so totally kidding…just breathe, okay? I'm sorry. Are you okay?"

"I'm fine," I said eventually. "It's fine."

"Too early in the morning for three-way jokes?"

"No, it's fine…I just had a piece of tartlette caught in my throat."

"Do you want some water?"

For rest of my visit at Macrina that morning, I was terrifyingly cheerful, doing my best to convince both April and myself of how utterly untroubled I was by everything I'd learned. Sure, I had some numbness and tingling in my extremities and my ears were still ringing so loudly that I had to shout to hear my own voice, but there was no conclusive proof that those symptoms had anything to do with finding out that my new girlfriend was regularly sharing a bed with her ex-girlfriend, who was regularly naked. No proof whatsoever.

When things started to pick up again at Macrina, April went back to work and I headed back to my apartment, where I found it harder to maintain the delusion that everything was hunky-dory. I ended up calling Bella, you know, just to check in, nothing much going on here, blah blah blah, but of course the whole story ended up spilling out. Bella offered her deeply philosophical perspective on it.

"I don't see the problem, Garrett—aren't guys supposed to like the idea of two women together? Isn't that a big male fantasy?"

"Well, it's not one of mine. Personally, the idea just makes me feel even more irrelevant than usual."

"I was kidding."

"Oh."

"But I still don't understand why you're quite so upset."

"Well, don't you think it's a little weird that she's sleeping with her ex-girlfriend?"

"Well, sure, that's a little unusual, but would you expect otherwise from April?"

"No, I guess not. But I mean, if I was still sharing a bed with Christina, don't you think April would have a problem with that?"

"Well, sure, that would definitely be weird."

"How is it any different?"

"Well, for one thing, you and Christina were never really *friends*, so there would only be one reason for you to be in bed together…"

"Okay."

"And for another thing, you and April are just very different. I mean, from the little I know of her, I'd believe that she can share a bed with somebody and have it be no big deal. For you though—and I mean this in the best possible way—*everything* is a big deal."

"Yeah. I know."

"I mean, are you actually worried that there's still something going on between them?"

"No…not really."

"Then what is it?"

"I don't know…"

"Speak, Garrett…"

"It's just, I know what it's like to get dumped…you know?"

"Okay…"

"And I know how, even when you're *not* really trying to get back together with the person, you still sort of *are* trying to get back together with them...you know?"

"So you think Kate wants to get back together with April?"

"Probably...I would anyway."

"But how do you even know who dumped who?"

"Well, I don't...but April's not the one climbing into Kate's bed."

"Okay, but April doesn't show any signs of wanting to get back together, does she? She did tell you it was nothing to worry about, right?"

"Yeah, that's what she says now, but what about when the novelty wears off and April starts to get bored with me? Kate's going to be there waiting, all naked and bisexual..."

"Well, I have to say, that's pretty paranoid, Garrett, and maybe sort of offensive. But if it's really bothering you, then you've got to talk to April about it. That's really all you can do."

"You're right...I should just talk to her."

"Maybe you could even bring it up during the three-way."

❧

I knew Bella was right, but I also knew there was very little chance that I would follow her advice. I'd detected a hint of annoyance in April's nose-licking declaration that her sleeping with Kate was "no big deal," the implication being that my even noticing it was slightly uncool. As much as the topic troubled me, the idea of raising it again and provoking a harsher reaction from April troubled me even more. When April and I were together, I just wanted to enjoy being with her—the idea of getting into a discussion that I already suspected wouldn't have a positive result had very little appeal.

So instead of talking to April, I worked extra hard at pushing the whole thing out of my mind. I willed myself oblivious to all the little things that otherwise might've fed my paranoia, like Kate casually giving April a backrub at the kitchen table, or the two of them randomly holding hands the day we all went to the aquarium, or even Kate barging into the bathroom to use the toilet while April was in the shower and then proceeding to carry on a fifteen minute conversation that I think was about bikini waxing, but which I couldn't completely understand without pressing my head right up against the door, which I wasn't about to do because really, why should I care what they were talking about anyway?

But of course I was a failure even at denial—the more I tried to ignore things, the more I noticed them. Finally one night, after what seemed like their 867th lip-kiss goodbye, which Kate punctuated with a playful double-handed squeeze of April's ass cheeks, I began to unravel. April and I were in my car, on our way to a movie, when it started.

"So you and Kate always kiss goodbye, huh?"

"Usually, yeah."

"That's nice."

"Yeah, I guess," April laughed.

"It's just not something you see all the time, not in America anyway. In Europe, maybe...they kiss all the time in Europe, although probably not on the lips. With them, I think it's more of a cheek thing. I've never even been clear on whether they actually make contact, or if it's just a kind of air-kiss, you know, but I'm pretty sure—"

"Garrett...?"

"Mm?"

"You can stop now, okay?"

"Okay."

"Seriously, you have nothing to worry about."

"Okay. Sorry."

I wouldn't say April was angry, but she wasn't joking either. I got the message loud and clear: if our relationship was to have any kind of a future, I would have to work much harder at hiding my feelings.

And after that slip, I did a pretty well for a while. April and I were still spending tons of time together, and we even drove up to visit Bella and Joel one Saturday, staying overnight on their pullout. Seeing how well April and Bella got along made me feel like my life was really starting to come together, even if I still hadn't given any thought to the whole job thing.

But I won't claim that April's relationship with Kate never caused me any anxiety during this period. There were still times, like the night Kate invited herself out to a movie with us, when I'd feel my blood pressure rising, but I was now doing a better job of defusing myself, mostly through a combination of deep breathing, positive thinking, and setting Kate's hair on fire with my heat-vision.

When I'd first started seeing April, Kate and I really hadn't talked much, but on the Sunday night when Kate went to the movies with us, I somehow ended up sitting between the two women. Ten minutes before the show was supposed to start, April decided that she absolutely had to have some Junior Mints, no matter how long the stupid line was, which left me alone in the theater with Kate.

We just sat there for a minute or two, enveloped in a strangely first-date-ish kind of silence—I smiled, she smiled, and then we both stared up at the screen.

"So…how's your band?" I finally asked.

"Oh, it's fine," Kate shrugged. "Abe's kind of driving me crazy, but that's nothing new."

"Who's Abe?"

"He's our lead singer…he writes all the songs. It's really his band, you know, the rest of us are just supporting players in his little rock-opera life."

"Ah."

"He's really not a bad guy. It's just lately, I think he's started to believe too much of his own PR. I have trouble taking him as seriously as he takes himself…he just reminds me too much of my little brother."

"What's the band called again? Hernia?"

"You're close—it's Ulcer."

"Sorry."

"Oh, I didn't choose it, believe me. Actually, I think I'd prefer Hernia…"

"At least you could have surgery for that, right?"

"Right," she laughed. "I'll have to bring that up with Abe—he always loves my suggestions."

"And the music itself…it's like, hard rock?"

"Well, I usually say that we're three parts Smashing Pumpkins and one part Metallica. Honestly though, I think Abe only adds the Metallica because so many people have told him his stuff sounds like the Pumpkins…which it does."

"You don't like it?"

"It's fine. Sometimes it's a bit much for me, but it's paying the bills right now, so…"

"So you play."

"Exactly. My worst night with Ulcer is still better than my best day temping. I think about that every time I consider quitting, and Abe's ego suddenly seems much more manageable."

"Mm."

"And I'm really making it sound much worse than it is—we're building up a loyal little following, and the band itself is actually really tight. You guys should come see us sometime."

"Yeah…that would be cool."

"I haven't had have much luck convincing April to come on her own, probably because I'm constantly bitching about the guys, but…"

"Do you have any gigs coming up?"

"Sure, lots actually. This Friday, we're playing right around the corner at the Sit & Spin. Sort of a Labor Day kickoff, pre-Bumbershoot thing."

"At the laundromat?"

"Well, yeah, but they have a club in the back. You've never been?"

"No…that sounds cool though."

"Well, if you can talk April into going, I can get you on the guest list."

Until that conversation, it had never occurred to me that Kate and I could possibly have anything in common (besides April's futon). Kate had always seemed so confident and together, with her perfect hair and sculpted cheekbones, that I'd naturally assumed her life was free of the half-baked compromises and muddling uncertainty that defined my own. Now I realized that she was struggling with the same crap I'd dealt with at Cavanaugh, only her position was even more precarious because quitting Ulcer would mean going back to answering somebody's phones for a week, or a month, or a year. Knowing this, she no longer seemed nearly as intimidating; she actually seemed kind of cool.

By the time April came scampering back from the concession stand, the previews were already in progress, blasting away at such a deafening volume that all communication required that we lean over the armrest and take turns speaking directly into each other's ears.

"Did I miss anything good?" April whispered loudly, still a little breathless.

"Not really, no."

"I know you said that you didn't want anything, but I got you a Kit-Kat, in case of emergency."

"Thanks," I said, inexpressibly moved by this gesture. I'd really wanted a giant Kit Kat, but had been too embarrassed to admit it in front of Kate.

A moment later, I leaned over the armrest again, April bringing her ear to me.

"Kate was just telling me that her band's playing at the Sit & Spin on Friday. We should go see them."

April's eyes cranked open even wider than usual.

"Really—you'd be up for that?"

"Yeah, I think it'd be fun."

April leaned in and kissed me once on the lips, a loud, theatrical "Mmmwa!" that I felt sure everyone in the theater could hear, even over the blaring previews. As I leaned back into my seat, I glanced over at Kate, but she seemed not to have noticed.

❧

In the irrational optimism of that moment in the theater, I'd deemed the whole Kate issue officially resolved. I'd just assumed that, having taken a step in April's direction, she'd take a step in mine, and we'd meet in some mutually acceptable place where Kate spent less time in April's bed. But over the next several days, it became clear that all my little gesture had really accomplished was making Kate an even bigger part of my relationship with April.

I first noticed it on Wednesday of that week.

After three years in business suits and a few weeks of cycling through the same ill-fitting khakis and polos, I desperately needed some new clothes. April had offered to go shopping with me, filling Bella's former role as wardrobe adviser. But then just as we were leaving for the Bellevue Square Mall, April invited Kate to join us.

It happened so fast that I hardly had time to grumble childishly under my breath, let alone object. The next thing I knew, the three of us were piling into the Jetta and rolling across Lake Washington on the floating 520 bridge. By that time, the fact that April and Kate had elected to sit together in the back seat was really just a bonus, because it gave me the freedom to sulk and glower without consequences.

Although I'd never dared describe it this way to April, I'd envisioned this shopping trip as a step toward figuring out who I was going to be, post-Cavanaugh. I'd wanted April's help because she seemed to have a more interesting vision of me than I'd ever had of myself. I imagined that she could somehow see the "David" within my unopened box of Froot Loops, and that together, we could find the clothes that would bring this better "me" to the surface.

But of course, the Bellevue Square Mall doesn't sell magical clothing, a fact that I had to accept once we arrived. I'd set out on an admittedly quixotic quest to find a new and unique identity, and I ended up at Banana Republic. I tried on a bunch of different things, and when I could get April's attention, she would give me a quick thumbs-up or thumbs-down, but she was hopelessly distracted by Kate's presence. I couldn't fathom how two women could become so engrossed in a men's clothing store, but somehow they managed it.

Eventually, I had to let go of the idea that April would be at all helpful on this ill-fated expedition. I processed my disappointment the only way I knew how: by spending some quiet time in the changing room assessing my midsection flab: its volume, its consistency, its fish-belly hairlessness. I was really becoming engrossed in this examination when I was startled by three quick knocks on the changing-room door.

"Garrett? Is that you in there?"

"Kate?"

"Yeah, hey, you should try this on," she said, flipping a striped blue dress shirt over the door. "I found it on the sale rack. It was the only one, but I bet it'll fit."

"Uh, okay…thanks."

And strangely enough, Kate was right—not only did the shirt fit, but I really liked it. It was the perfect end to the trip: we'd spent another yet another evening with my girlfriend's ex-girlfriend, who had ultimately proved more helpful than April herself. Leaving the changing room, I blindly grabbed a stack of new khakis and polos off the shelf—basically larger versions of the ones I was already wearing—and hauled them up to the register. The saleswoman smiled as I dumped everything on the counter.

"Did you find everything you were looking for?"

"Not really, but…I think I've made my peace with it."

☙

I felt far less peaceful on Thursday after April called to cancel our plans in favor of a "girls' night" with Kate and April's friend Sam, in town unexpectedly from New York. I couldn't blame April for wanting to see Sam, who didn't come back to Seattle often, but I also couldn't help feeling that the whole "girls' night" concept was really just a thinly-veiled "no-Garrett night"; I was the only guy they might've invited along anyway. And though I had absolutely no proof, I suspected that Kate was somehow behind that idea.

The evening still might've been salvaged if I'd followed through with April's suggestion that I call Kevin Lanier. I really did want to reconnect with Kevin—I hadn't spoken to him since his in-flight call on the night of April's show—but given my growing unease about things with April, I had a hard time convincing myself to pick up the phone, especially since there was a 50-50 chance I'd be talking to Kevin on his cell phone from some hotel bar in Boise.

My own cell phone rang at 8:30. It wasn't April calling, as I momentarily hoped, but my friend Ed Zielinski, the one-man IT department for a Seattle law firm called Rodgers Bennett LLP. I'd gotten to know Ed while working on his firm's website during my first year at Cavanaugh. We'd kept in touch via e-mail, but I hadn't actually seen Ed since running into him at a Radiohead show over a year before.

Ed said he was calling to make sure that I wasn't "dead a hotel room somewhere." He'd e-mailed me about a new project, but had gotten back an outdated Out of Office message referencing my last Boston trip. Apparently Leonard hadn't contacted my old clients as we'd discussed, nor had anyone bothered to decommission my Cavanaugh mailbox.

I gave Ed the short version of my quitting story and apologized for not getting in touch. Ironically, the project he'd tried to e-mail me about—overhauling and web-enabling the firm's Practice Management System so employees could access it from anywhere—sounded like fun. It was the sort of job I'd always wished I had more of at Cavanaugh: challenging yet travel-free, working with somebody I actually liked. I wondered briefly: *If I'd known about Ed's project sooner, would I still have quit?* I didn't consider it long enough to reach a conclusion. My life with Cavanaugh already seemed a million miles away.

ℰℐ

I met April for dinner at Noodle Ranch before Kate's gig on Friday. I was probably a little subdued, having spent Thursday stewing in an unseemly jambalaya of dejection and bad television, but April was totally wired. After being up all night with Sam and Kate, she'd been drinking coffee all day…and April *never* drank coffee. The girls' Neighbours-to-Alki itinerary sounded suspiciously like our own all-nighter, but even if I'd wanted to point this out, I never could've gotten a word in.

"But really, it was so great to see Sam again—it had been way too long. We figured out that it had been almost a year, which is just unbelievable to me, but Kate and I are going to visit her in New York in a couple weeks, so that'll be good. She has this microscopic one-bedroom in the East Village, really just a studio with a big closet for the bed, but I think we'll probably end up staying with my brother in SoHo because he'd be totally pissed if I went all the way to New York and didn't spend some time with him. I'm really excited though—it's been eons since I actually left Washington. I think the last time must've been when I went to Guatemala with Megan. Oh, was it that, or…?"

If April hadn't paused, I never would've caught up with her. There was just so much information coming at me, and so much of it was extraneous, that I just tried to seize on the critical points when they surfaced. Even then, I wasn't always certain about what I'd heard. *Did she really just say that she was going to New York with Kate?*

"No, actually, it was when I drove to Vancouver with Melissa—that was definitely after Guatemala, but I never think of it because it's just Canada…"

"So, wait…you're going to New York?"

"Yeah, probably the week after next, assuming we can get cheap flights. Although we'll probably go regardless because that's really our only window. After that, Kate's band has some studio time booked, and I've got some stuff at the Academy…"

"But didn't Kate say that Ulcer has all these gigs coming up?"

"Well, I guess they've got a little break while they get ready to start recording. I think she said Abe needs time to get his 'creative juices' flowing or something."

"Oh."

"That phrase has always grossed me out—'creative juices.' I don't know why I even said it just then. I just always picture this… What's the matter? You've got a funny look…"

"Nothing…I mean, I just didn't know you were thinking of going away."

"Well, I wasn't…until Sam suggested it last night. Or I guess it was really this morning at breakfast that we talked about it."

"Ah."

"It'll be okay, Garrett, I promise…"

"Oh I know."

"I mean, obviously you'll miss me desperately, but I actually think it'll be really good for us. I mean, we've been pretty hot and heavy for a while now…it'd be good for both of us to get some space. And it'll give you some time to figure some things out, you know, maybe see some of your other friends."

"Sure."

"That's another awful phrase—hot and heavy. I always picture these two big sumo guys in diapers doing piggyback, all flabby and sweaty and jiggly. Why do I always picture that? And why do these awful things keep coming out of my mouth tonight?"

"I have no idea."

April's scattered state seemed to keep her from fully realizing how irked I was by this impromptu vacation with Kate. This was good in that I knew April would've disapproved of my reaction, but bad because it further annoyed me that April always seemed so oblivious. Why didn't it occur to her that inviting Kate on our shopping trip was annoying? Why didn't she realize that phrases like "girls' night" and "it'll be really good for us" were far more annoying than anything else that had come out of her mouth tonight?

But I did at least have an inkling that I was being irrational, and that, combined with the two drinks I had with dinner, kept me from cracking right there. Getting some food into April also seemed to moderate her caffeine high, gradually bringing her back to a more endearing level of hyperactivity. I tried to steer us toward safe topics, which meant that we talked a lot about cows, organic farming, and the pros and cons of trying to make soy products taste like meat. Toward the end of the meal though, April abruptly changed the subject.

"So did you see your friend Kevin last night?"

"Oh, no…I didn't end up calling him."

"Why not?"

"Oh, I just wasn't feeling energetic enough for an evening with Kevin. And I figured he was probably on the road anyway."

"So what did you end up doing?"

"Not much…I just watched some TV and went to bed early."

April nodded, a shadow falling across her normally impish features. It looked like disappointment, but I wasn't sure.

"I just needed a quiet night," I lied. "It was good to relax."

☙

It was a muggy night, and during the short walk over to the Sit & Spin, I literally started to sweat the prospect of facing Kate. I felt like we were locked in a silent tug-o-war, and with girls' night blossoming into a full week in New York, I was losing. The last thing I wanted to do now was see Kate and her stupid band, but I could think of no way to avoid it, short of faking an attack of food poisoning. I didn't think I could pull that off, but if I'd known how the night would play out, I might've tried.

I'd walked past the Sit & Spin's bright blue façade many times, but I'd never gone inside. Stepping in from the street, the washers and dryers were through a doorway to your right, and the café was off to the left, floored in a checkerboard of pink and black and furnished with a kitschy mishmash of tables, stools, and vinyl-trimmed booths scavenged from a dozen defunct diners. And as if the space wasn't already busy enough, there was a yard sale's worth of junk haphazardly mounted to the walls and the ceiling: upside-down tables and paper parasols, tacky lamps fitted with colored bulbs, board-game boards repurposed as wall-coverings, and endless lengths of snaking electrical conduit, employed for purely decorative purposes.

Ulcer had two shows at the Sit & Spin that night, and Kate had recommended that we attend the later one because the band played better after a warm-up set. April and I found Kate and her Ulcer-mates having a between-sets drink at a booth by the front windows. They were easy to spot because (at Abe's insistence) they all wore coordinating black outfits featuring leather pants. Maybe it was just my sour mood, but my first impression was that they looked more like stand-ins from *The Matrix* on a coffee break than they did a rock band.

I was not in the slightest bit surprised when Kate, who had paired the leather pants with a stretched-out black tank-top, hopped up out of her seat to hug April, but I almost jumped out of my skin when she then turned and hugged me as well.

"Thanks so much for coming," she said, the pungence of her first-set sweat filling my head for a disorienting moment. "The new shirt looks great on you, by the way."

"Thanks," I mumbled, bewildered by our collision. Kate's last comment was a reference to the fact that, despite how I was feeling about her, I'd worn the blue striped shirt she'd picked out for me. Apparently vanity conquers all.

April had already met everyone in the band, but for my sake, Kate introduced them all: Abe, the angstful lead singer with the artfully unkempt goatee; Andre, the ever-sunglassed Belgian lead guitarist; and John, the maybe-too-old-for-this drummer, a successful studio musician in the 80s who now played with Ulcer for kicks. Abe and Andre, ensconced at the far end of the booth, acknowledged us with barely detectable head-bobs, but John greeted me with a finger-crunching handshake and April with a paternal peck on the cheek.

Pulling up chairs, April and I chatted with John and Kate about the first set, which they felt had gone well, despite the fact that Abe had spontaneously decided to sing an entire song lying on his back, disconnecting Andre's amp in the process. I really didn't want to enjoy this conversation, but it was hard not to—John seemed like a cool, no-bullshit guy, and Kate was funny and lit up in a way that I'd never seen her. I actually found myself thinking, *Okay, maybe this won't be so bad.* And for the first time all night, I felt sort of normal and comfortable.

About ten minutes before Ulcer was supposed to go back onstage, Abe and Andre stepped outside for a smoke, and Kate and April went to the bathroom to adjust Kate's low-rise lace-up leather pants, which were slipping crackward in the back. Why this operation required two sets of hands, I wasn't certain, but I was thankful that at least I wouldn't have to witness it. This left me with John the drummer.

John was one of those thickset guys who looked like he could've been really strong or kind of fat, but who was probably a little of both. He'd lost a lot of his hair, and what remained, he'd dyed platinum and grown to his shoulders. His leathery face suggested age, but his blue eyes were lively and youthful (or at least unrepentant).

"So you're with April?" John rasped, rattling the ice in his empty glass.

"Yeah," I said, sliding my chair in a bit closer so I could hear him over the throbbing intermission music.

"She's a sweet girl. I didn't know she was into guys."

"Oh?"

"As long as I live, I will never forget the day I walked in on her and Katie makin' in the can."

"Oh...really?"

"Yeah, we were playing over at the old Vogue, two sets like tonight. When it was time to go back on stage, nobody could find Katie. So I went into the ladies' room, you know, to check under the stalls, but there they were, goin' at it against the sinks."

"Wow..."

"I think I startled them, barging in like that, but I was like, 'Hey, don't stop on my account,' you know? It was a beautiful thing. I mean, where's the camera when you need it, right?"

"Yeah...right."

"I gotta say, I was devastated when they broke up. Just before you came in, Katie was telling me that they're going to New York...I was hoping maybe they were getting back together, but I guess not, huh? Ah, well...another dream shattered."

"Mm."

"Well, I should probably head back there. Good to meet you, Gary," he said, slapping me on the back as he got up.

"Yeah...you too," I said, still wearing the smile I'd stapled to my face halfway through John's poignant tale of girl-on-girl action. I was still sitting there alone at the table when April finally returned from the bathroom. I must've looked positively deranged—I felt certain that if I even twitched, my head would explode.

"Hey, are you okay?" she asked, putting her hand on my shoulder.

"Hm? Oh, yeah...great," I said, "How're Kate's pants?"

"They're fine," she laughed. "Should we head back? I think they're about to start."

Ulcer soon took the stage in the Sit & Spin's basement-like back room, eliciting rowdy shouts and whistles from the crowd, much of which had obviously been drinking since the first set. Abe started the show with what he described as "a new song...something a little different for us," which I soon realized meant that he'd just ripped it off from Rage Against the Machine. Sources aside, Abe's songs' all struck me as excuses for him to prowl the stage shirtless, demonstrating how deep, dark, and misunderstood he was for a guy with such toned abs. The crowd ate it up though, going mosh-pit bonkers from the first note.

It all just made me want to vomit, but then I probably wasn't in the best place to assess Ulcer's musical merits given that I was unable to stop picturing the bass player making out with my girlfriend while the drummer snapped photos for his scrapbook. I could feel the guitar-and-bass bombast buzzing in my chest, but what I actually heard was John's raspy voice in my ear: *Okay girls, a little more tongue this time. Okay, perfect!* And as much as Abe obviously wanted everyone to look at him, I couldn't take my eyes off Kate, who paced the left side of the stage, bass slung low over her hips, her face curled into the requisite rock-sneer.

But even with all of that going through my head, I might've been okay if the crowd hadn't been so enthusiastic, constantly bumping and knocking me as they threw themselves around, hardly seeming to notice when I got frustrated enough to shove back. I just couldn't fathom how anyone could get so amped about such soulless dreck. I wondered, *Are they really that shallow, or are they just that drunk?*

And just as I was thinking this, I realized that April was giddily flinging herself around with them—blonde hair flying, her face flushed with ecstatic laughter. And while I was gaping at her, convicting her for her bad taste, she swung around and looked right at me. There was no time to wipe the disgust from my face—she saw it, and I saw her see it—and that quickly, all of my righteous certainty shriveled and melted. And unfortunately, she came right over to me.

"What's the matter?"

"Do you actually *like* this?" I snapped, more accusation than question, more defensive than anything.

April just shrugged, suggesting that she hadn't even considered the question.

"I just don't really like this," I said weakly.

"Well, you don't have to stay."

"I know," I said, feeling smaller by the second.

April shook her head and went back to dancing, leaving me trapped in the angry little square of floor I'd staked out for myself. I could see no way out of it—too embarrassed to drop my issues and dance (as I knew April wished I would), and too cowardly to leave. And the thing was, I knew that if this were our first date, I'd be dancing, just happy to be with her. But I couldn't find my way back to that state of mind. And so for the rest of Ulcer's set, I loitered there uncomfortably, watching April dance from a distance and hoping she would look in my direction. She never did.

Even after Ulcer's last encore, April didn't come looking for me. I made my way over to her and, sensing me there, she turned and smiled and put her arm around me.

"I'm going to go say goodbye to Kate. Do you want to meet me outside?"

"Okay."

I waited in the dark as the crowd trickled out past me. They didn't seem nearly so bad now. By the time April emerged, almost everyone had gone. She smiled, slipped her arm around my waist, and we started the walk back to her apartment. For a while we were both quiet. I felt lucky that things hadn't gone worse. That is, until she spoke.

"Please don't take this the wrong way, okay?"

"Okay."

"I think we need to stop sleeping together."

"Oh. Why?"

"I think it's warping your personality."

"Oh."

"I mean, I *really really* like you...you're a great, sweet guy. But I want to *keep* liking you, and I just don't think that that's going to happen if we keep up like this."

"I'm sorry," I said, sinking into myself, knowing she was right.

"Don't be sorry. I'm not sorry. Sometimes things just don't work out."

✌

Over the week until she left for New York, I talked to April at least once a day—sometimes I called her, and sometimes she called me. No matter how our conversations began though, they usually ended with me begging her to take me back. We'd only dated for six weeks, but I was already addicted, not just to April, but to the idea of being with someone. I'd been alone for three years, and the thought of returning to that solitary state was unbearable.

Saturday, 2:05 p.m.

"Again, I'm really sorry. I don't know what got into me."

"It's okay. I understand."

"I sort of wish I could go back and do the whole night over."

"Do you really think that would help?"

"Well, yeah...I think I could handle things better than I did. I think I could be more normal."

"I really don't think you could."

"Well I could *try* anyway."

"But I don't want you to *try*, Garrett."

"Oh."

"I was actually kind of glad that you freaked out. It wasn't pretty, but it was the first sort-of honest reaction I'd seen from you in a while. And like I said before, I was actually more bothered by the fact that you didn't call Kevin the other night than I was by anything else. I really want to be your friend, but I don't think it's healthy for me to be your *only* friend, especially if I'm your girlfriend too."

"So if I got some more friends, then...?"

"If you got some more friends, I think you'd be a lot happier."

Monday, 9:37 p.m.

"But everything was fine until she almost got into bed with us, right? It was great, wasn't it?"

"Yeah, it was...it was great."

"So what if we tried *not* letting her sleep in your bed for a while, just so we could see?"

"But that's just part of who I am, Garrett. What good would it do for me to pretend to be some other way for a while?"

"It would give us a chance to see if that's the *only* problem."

"So what if it is? You can bury parts of yourself for a while, but they always come back. People do that all the time—they try to become the person who they *think* the other person wants them to be, and then six months or six years later, they realize how unhappy they are being this other person, and it's all over. Same result, it just takes longer."

"What if I bought Kate some nice flannel pajamas? What if we just started with that? L.L. Bean has some really nice ones…"

"I really think you need to get over the idea that my relationship with Kate is the reason we broke up. Kate was actually really bummed when I told her."

"She was?"

"Yeah—she really liked you."

"Oh."

"I mean, if this had *anything* to do with Kate, it was more related to the fact that you're uncomfortable with the idea of being attracted to two people at the same time. You're just not ready to accept the idea that you can be in a relationship with someone while also being attracted to someone else—it's just too much for you."

"So wait…you're *admitting* that you're still attracted to Kate?"

"No, I'm saying *you* were attracted to Kate, and it freaked you out. And really, I think she was probably a little attracted to you too."

"I…I don't know what to say to that…"

"I wouldn't expect you to."

"Okay…I definitely can't talk about this anymore right now…"

"Okay, well, call me tomorrow."

❧

I was caught in the powerful coils of a giant boa constrictor. I struggled for a while, but with my every exhale, the coils tightened, guaranteeing that each breath would be shallower than the last. I was getting hazier, slowly losing my will to resist. Eventually, the fight went out of me completely, and when I did finally black out, it was nothing but merciful.

The night I gave up, I remember getting off the phone with April and tossing the phone aside, thinking, *Well, I won't be needing this.* And I just sat there on my couch, staring into space for what must've been an hour, numb and drifting in the silence of my apartment. I had exhausted my capacity for emotion and argument, and now I was just blank, as unthinking as the couch on which I sat.

I awoke hours later, still on the couch: head slumped awkwardly to one side, mouth open and drooling, all the lights in my apartment ablaze.

And then, after a week in which I'd lost all interest in food, I realized that I was *hungry.*

5

Fight or Flight

It started slowly. I had a Ding Dong, just to silence my stomach and get me through the night. Actually, I had *two* Ding Dongs, because that's how they come.

In the morning, I had two more Ding Dongs with a glass of milk—a hearty, balanced breakfast. Then around eleven, I made a peanut butter & jelly sandwich, followed by a bowl of Froot Loops (the perfect post-April self-pity food) and an entire sleeve of Fig Newtons (age indeterminate). Mid-afternoon, I had the second sleeve of Newtons with the last of the milk (good to finish things up). For dinner, I ordered a pizza, which I dispatched over several hours on the couch.

Within a few days, I had completely discarded the conventional three-meal eating system, adopting an alchemic, self-medicating approach to food. Everything I ate was a response to (or an attempt to counteract) the last thing I'd eaten. I'd start with something snacky like Pringles or Doritos, which would drive me toward something desserty like Double-Stuf Oreos. After the Oreos, with my mouth coated in black cookie-muck, I might go for a few American Cheese slices. As a palette-cleanser, I'd pop open a jar of dill pickles, and then chase everything down with a Fresca, because somehow, diet soda washes away all gastronomic sins.

I didn't spend *all* my time eating though—I also watched a lot of television. Tripping through movies and sitcoms and music videos, I flitted away from the things that depressed me and lingered on the things that didn't. I avoided talk shows and game shows (too much desperation), and surfed toward *Friends* and *Seinfeld* and anything featuring Bill Murray or John Cusack. By this delicate technique did I regulate my mood.

That is, until I ran out of food.

I knew that my supplies were dwindling, but I was still unprepared for the moment when it arrived. Reaching into the fridge for the final two-pack of Ding Dongs, I found only an empty box. Several minutes of desperate rummaging ensued: *Didn't I see an old Chips Ahoy bag in the cabinet?* (A mirage.) *Or some Ben & Jerry's in the freezer?* (The iced-over ends of three pints, inedible even by my standards.) *Or maybe a half-jar of hot fudge in the fridge?* (Hardened into an impregnable brown epoxy.)

Eventually, I just had to accept that it was all gone.

Of course I recognized what was happening. Three years earlier, Christina's birthday dumping had sent me into a similar funk. That time, I'd gained 13 pounds, maxed-out my Visa on the 65"television that now filled my living room, and I'd only escaped the all-consuming food-and-TV vortex by accepting Leonard's job offer. In my wounded state, Cavanaugh had sounded perfect: I could make some money while keeping myself very, very busy.

I knew I could do that again. With one call to Leonard, I could be on a plane to Dallas or Boise, instantly too busy for wallowing and overindulgence. And yet the prospect of returning to my life at Cavanaugh—or even of hunting for a better job—was still more depressing than the thought of gaining another 13 pounds.

Bella called at around 11:00 a.m. By then, I'd dragged myself back to the safety of the couch, but I was discovering that TV was far less charming without packaged foods.

"So…how're you holding up?" she asked.

"Echh…I ran out of Ding Dongs. And everything else I guess."

"When was the last time you left the apartment?"

"I'm not sure…I think I met the pizza guy downstairs last night?"

"I don't think that counts."

"No, probably not."

"You should get out for some air, even if you just go to the supermarket. Consider it practice for next weekend."

"Next weekend?"

"The engagement party? You're still coming, right?"

"Oh…yeah, definitely," I said, finally rousing myself from my malaise. "And I will get to the store later…I'm just being lazy. It's the one thing I'm really good at these days."

"Have you had any more thoughts about the whole job thing?"

"Yeah, I've thought about it, but…I don't know. I just feel like I haven't figured anything out yet, you know?"

"Mm."

"I mean, I could go get some new job, but I'd probably end up just as miserable as I was before. I need to get some perspective…figure out what I really want to do with my life."

"Ding Dongs sound *much* easier."

"Exactly."

❧

My secret fear, which I couldn't share with Bella, was that going back to work while I was still alone would seal my fate as a bachelor. Not that I saw any alternatives—I'd stopped wishing for April to take me back, and I couldn't imagine meeting someone new in my condition—but I just wasn't ready to admit defeat, to give up the shreds of romantic hope that had inspired me to quit Cavanaugh in the first place. If I just held out a little longer, I thought, maybe everything would miraculously fall into place.

I took Bella's advice and headed out to QFC, but in hindsight, even this might not have been the best idea. While everybody knows that you shouldn't go grocery shopping when you're hungry, I would also submit that you shouldn't go when you're depressed and dreading your best friend's engagement party (*Pop Tarts, Nutter Butters, Double Stufs*), especially when said party is being hosted by her fiancé's co-workers (*Ruffles, Cheetos, Doritos, Smartfood*), thus guaranteeing that you won't know another soul in attendance (*Ho Hos, Twinkies, Ding Dongs, Powdered Donettes*).

I'd actually been looking forward to the event when April and I were still together, but on the drive home from QFC that day, I could only envision it as a nightmarish gauntlet of happy couples dragging me through the same degrading conversation again and again. *Oh, so you're unemployed? And single? And fat? That's great!*

ભ્જ

Standardized testing has suggested that I'm a reasonably intelligent person, but you'd never know it watching me haul groceries up to my apartment. I'm always convinced that I can—while supporting a full bag in each arm—dig the keys out of my pocket, blindly isolate the correct one (I have several that I can't discard until I remember what they're for), unlock my door, and finally shove it open without dumping everything on the floor.

Of course it never works, and upon returning from my QFC junk food run, I had trouble even locating my keys. Thus, I was still fumbling though my pockets—wobbling on one leg, bags pressed precariously between me and the door—when my new neighbor Clay came up the stairs. And despite my best efforts to become invisible, Clay saw me and loped right over, a crooked half-smile on his face.

"Let me give you a hand there," he said, deftly slipping both bags out of my arms.

"Uh, okay. I'm just trying to find my—oh…there they are."

As always, my keys were right where they should've been—I'd just missed them the first four times I'd checked that pocket. I turned to take the bags back from Clay, but he showed no sign of giving them up.

"After you," he smiled.

"Oh…okay. Thanks."

Leading Clay inside, I was suddenly aware of just how disastrous my place had become: the collapsing stack of pizza boxes in the entry, the crusty dishes and takeout containers barnacling every horizontal surface, the clots of unclean laundry collecting at the edges of it all. Apparently, some kind of feral shut-in had been squatting in my apartment.

"Do you have more to bring up?" Clay asked, casually elbowing aside my counter clutter to make space for the bags.

"Oh, no—I can get them."

"I'll help. It'll go faster."

As Clay and I headed back down to the car, I searched my mind for friendly conversation-starters, something neighborly to compensate for our awkward first encounter on the night of April's show. Looking back, there were so many innocuous things I could've asked—*How are you liking the apartment? Are you from Seattle originally?*—and yet, after a week in social quarantine, the question that came flying out of my mouth was, "So why'd you shave your head?"

Clay just laughed. "Why—you don't like it?"

"No, I do…it's just, you know, I actually considered shaving my own head once, but I was worried that it would look too much like a bowling ball, you know?"

"Uh-huh…"

"I mean, not that *yours* looks like a bowling ball, because you've got the sort of head that looks *good* shaved…I just think I have the wrong kind of head."

"Well, you never know until you try," Clay grinned, putting a hand on my shoulder. "I've got the trimmers whenever you're ready."

"Good to know," I said, glad to abandon the topic, even if I hadn't really gotten an answer.

At the car though, it was Clay's turn to pose an uncomfortable question. Seeing all the chips, soda, and other bad-for-you snacks filling my trunk, he obviously thought it couldn't *all* be for one person.

"Having a party?" he asked.

"Uh, well…"

Clay gave me a puzzled smile.

I knew that the simplest answer was "yes." A party, albeit for nine-year-olds, was a perfectly plausible explanation for my shameful haul. But in a shocking move that would irrevocably alter my relationship with Clay, I decided to tell him the truth. Having failed at friendly, I could at least be honest.

"Actually, no," I admitted. "Believe it or not, all this crap is for me."

"*Really.*"

"Yeah, I quit my job last month, and then my girlfriend dumped me, and since then I've spent a lot of time stuffing my face in front of the TV. I don't usually eat *quite* this poorly, but crap is the only thing that appeals to me right now."

"What was your job?" Clay asked, with what seemed like genuine interest.

"I was an IT consultant."

"And why'd you quit?"

"Well, eventually it was just making me miserable. I was always traveling and working these ridiculous hours and getting stuck with all of the ugliest projects. But then, it also sort of conflicted with my first date with April, so…"

"The one who dumped you?"

"Yeah. So as you might imagine, I've spent some time questioning that decision."

"Are you looking for a new job?"

"Not really. I mean, I will have to go back to work eventually, but I need more time to figure things out. And, you know, to eat all this stuff."

On the way back upstairs, I asked Clay if he worked. I phrased the question this way because I'd heard the steady *tssk-tssk-tssk* of what sounded like a Miles Davis CD hissing out under his apartment door at all hours.

"I'm teaching a few Philosophy classes at UW while I work on my dissertation."

"You're getting a PhD in Philosophy?"

"Well, that's the idea. I should finish this spring."

"And then what will you do?" I asked, having only the

loosest grasp of what went on in the Philosophy department. For the moment, I was picturing Clay, bald and toga-clad, orating in UW's Red Square.

"Well, a lot of people teach, but…I haven't decided yet." And with a grin he added, "I guess I need some time to think too."

As we carried the last of the groceries into my apartment, I began to worry that perhaps I'd shared too much (stuffing my face, etc.), and that Clay would now begin avoiding me in the halls. Before he went back to his own place though, he asked if I had any plans for dinner.

"Uh, no…not really."

"I was thinking of going down to Mama's Mexican, if you feel like joining me," he said. "I've been craving enchiladas for days…I think tonight's the night."

"Okay…sure. Any particular time?"

"Oh, whenever. I'll be writing all afternoon, so why don't you just knock when you get hungry?"

&

I would've preferred to settle on a specific time, but I also didn't feel like explaining to Clay that my new eating system had made hunger a sensation I no longer experienced. Instead, I resolved to go snackless for the rest of the afternoon, which would be no small feat, given that my cupboards were now bursting with empty calories. Naturally, I failed—there was a minor Smartfood outbreak at 2:30 p.m., followed by a Category 5 Twizzler Incident an hour later—but I was proud of myself for even trying.

I finally knocked on Clay's door at 6:30. I still wasn't hungry, but I could at least remember what it felt like.

"Hey Garrett," he said, waving me inside. "Just let me turn off my computer and I'll be ready to go."

Clay's apartment was smaller than mine—a studio rather than a one-bedroom—but it almost felt larger because it was so empty. There was no couch and no television…no furniture at all, really, besides the makeshift desk—a closet door laid across milk crates—where his laptop sat. The wall behind this desk was lined with more milk crates that had been stacked into bookshelves, while a demoralized beanbag chair slouched into the back corner by the window, encircled by a dozen splayed paperbacks.

I sensed that something important was missing, but it took me a moment to pinpoint it.

"Do you have a *bed*, Clay?"

"Oh, I've got an air mattress rolled up with my climbing gear," he said, nodding toward the closet, whose conspicuous doorlessness revealed a neon collection of parkas, packs, and ropes. A pair of ice axes hung on the wall beside the closet—storage doubling as décor.

"You sleep on an air mattress?"

"Yeah, I might end up buying a futon, but the Therm-a-Rest is fine for now. When I came back from Alaska this summer, I actually had trouble adjusting to a regular mattress."

"What were you doing in Alaska?"

"I did a Denali expedition with some friends, and then we spent a few weeks in the Wrangells. It was pretty amazing."

"Wow. So, have you ever climbed Mount Rainier?"

"Sure. I've also hiked all the way around it, which was actually much harder."

I knew that people climbed Rainier every day, but I was still awed by the revelation that Clay had stood on the summit of that giant ice bomb. From the plane on my way back from Chicago, the peak had looked unfit for humans, a place where you'd definitely need axes to anchor you, to keep you from being blown out into space. The image inspired a goofy, fourth-grade question that I couldn't help asking.

"Weren't you scared?"

Clay just laughed. "Sure, all the time. But that's half the fun, right?"

೧

I quizzed Clay about his "scary" climbing experiences on the walk to the restaurant, but when we stepped through the door at Mama's Mexican, I froze, unable to speak.

It was Kate.

She should've been in New York with April, but here she was—standing six feet from me, laughing with one of the waitresses.

I should explain that, while I hadn't *seen* Kate since Ulcer's fateful Sit & Spin gig two weeks before, she'd never really left my thoughts.

By day, she was the topic of my frequent, imagined debates with April, in which I dismantled her cockamamie theory that I harbored some kind of suppressed attraction to Kate. I varied my arguments from one daydream to the next, but I always included a declaration about how unfazed I would be if "Kate walked in here naked right now." At which point, Kate always *did* walk in naked (usually on her way to the shower, since the debates took place in April's kitchen), and April and I celebrated my undeniable unfazedness by sharing a heaping platter of French Toast (obviously a side-effect of my going cold-turkey off Macrina).

But on the night before this Mama's Mexican trip, I'd had a dream that seemed to overturn all of my debate victories. I'd dreamt that I was in the women's bathroom at the Sit & Spin, making out with Kate against the sinks. April was around somewhere too, her voice echoing from one of the stalls as she belted her way through a medley of Violent Femmes classics—"Prove My Love," "Please Do Not Go," "Add It Up"—that left me worried she knew what Kate and I were doing (though not quite worried enough to stop).

And so, when confronted with the real, flesh-and-blood Kate, all of the dream's confusing emotions came flooding back and I had to remind myself that we hadn't *actually* spent the previous night attached at the mouth. Either way, I didn't want to face her—particularly if April was lurking nearby—so I began to retreat quietly, the way one might flee a snoozing grizzly. But of course I backed directly into Clay, driving him into the door with a thud.

"Whoa!" he chuckled. "Hold on there…"

"Oh, sorry, Clay," I whispered. "I think I think I forgot my—"

But before I could remember whatever I might've forgotten—my dignity, perhaps?—Kate turned and looked right at us.

"Hey…Garrett!"

"Oh, hi Kate…I didn't realize… I mean, I thought…"

"What's that?"

"I mean…what are you doing here?"

"Picking up takeout for the band…?"

"No, I mean, shouldn't you be…weren't you going…?"

"Oh, right—New York! Well, naturally Abe moved up our studio time so I couldn't go. I just heard from April though, and she and Sam are having a blast."

"Oh good," I said, probably sounding too relieved. "I mean, I'm glad she went…"

"But how're *you* doing? I've actually been meaning to call you…"

"*Really?*"

"Well, you know, April asked me to check in while she was away…"

"Oh, right. Well, I'm good, you know…I'm fine."

"Yeah?" Kate smiled, sympathetic but unconvinced.

"Yeah, definitely. Oh, and this is my neighbor Clay," I said, remembering that he was still trapped behind me. "Clay, this is Kate. She's, uh…she's in a band."

"Nice to meet you, Clay," Kate laughed. "Don't let me hold you guys up though." And with a maternal rub of my shoulder, she added, "Take care of yourself, Garrett, okay?"

"Okay. You too."

As we followed the waitress back to our table in the Elvis Room, I chewed over Kate's parting comment. *Take care of yourself, Garrett, okay?* Her tone, while sincere, clearly implied that I *hadn't* been taking care of myself so far. This irked me a little—*who was she to say how I was doing?*—until I looked down and realized that I was still wearing my slippers, which had been a Christmas gift from my grandmother when I was twelve. Yes, they were rather shoe-like slippers—fully enclosed, with rubber soles—but they were also green suede, trimmed with white piping. Not exactly appropriate for a night out, even in the Elvis Room.

I felt Clay studying me as I read the menu, my heart still thudding from the encounter with Kate.

"Are you all right?" he asked eventually.

"Hm? Oh yeah…I'm fine. I was just kinda surprised to see Kate."

"And who is she exactly?"

"Uh, well, she's my ex-girlfriend's roommate."

"Ah," Clay nodded. "You did seem a *tad* uneasy."

"Kate's actually really cool, it's just, I'm sure she's heard every pathetic detail of the breakup, which I definitely could've handled better. Plus, she was present for my grand job-quitting announcement, which just makes me cringe now."

"Why? Do you actually wish you *hadn't* quit?"

"No, I guess not. I mean, I really should've quit ages ago, but…the whole thing just sort of seems ridiculous now, given how quickly things fell apart with April."

"Well, even if it didn't work out the way you hoped, I was impressed that you did it. Most people wouldn't have even tried."

"I think most people would call it flaky," I said, thinking of my father, whom I still hadn't told.

"Yeah, probably. But it definitely took some courage, and if you keep thinking that way, I bet you'll be just fine. I'll be really interested to see what you do next."

"Well, if history is any guide, I'll probably just fall asleep in front of the TV…"

"See? *Fascinating…*"

"Which you're always welcome to come over and watch, by the way, since I noticed you don't have a TV yourself. Why is that?"

"Oh, well, you know, I went through this phase where I considered myself very deep and intellectual, and so I kind of looked down on TV, and anyone who would watch it really."

"As you should…"

"But honestly, the more I work on this dissertation, the more I feel the need to watch *The Simpsons*."

"Well, that's something I can help you with. Maybe the

only thing."

ↀ

Clay did come over to watch TV that night, and each of the next few nights as well. Whenever he finished writing or grading papers, Clay would knock on my door and we'd watch *The Simpson* or *Friends* and pick through my doomsday supply of snack foods.

Left to his own dietary devices, Clay ate like he was training for something—lots of lean protein and leafy vegetables—but he seemed to relish the novelty of junk food at my place, studying ingredients and nutrition facts with an almost academic vigor, lingering over a single Twinkie or a handful of Cheetos for what seemed like hours. And while I knew Clay intended no harm with his investigations, they did start to make me self-conscious about scarfing a whole sleeve of cookies in one sitting, at least while he was present.

"Which would you guess has more fat per ounce," he asked one night. "Doritos or Ho Hos?"

"I would never guess, because nothing good can come from such questions."

"It's actually the Doritos. Surprising, huh?"

"I guess. Are you secretly writing your dissertation about my awful diet?"

"Sorry," Clay smiled, getting up to return the food to the kitchen. "I can get a little carried away…"

"What *are* you writing about anyway?"

"My dissertation? I guess it's sort of about the intrinsic value of insentient beings."

We both paused while I worked out his meaning.

"See, that still sounds like me…" I finally said.

"I'm writing about things like trees and mountains and rivers. I think maybe you're confusing *insentient* with *inert*."

"Ah…right."

Being around Clay pushed the "work" issue back to the forefront of my mind, which is to say that I now daydreamed about careers that he might deem cool and/or courageous. I quickly narrowed the choices down to "aerial firefighter" and "high school English teacher"—HBO had the movies *Always* and *Dead Poets Society* in heavy rotation that week— but given my difficulties with motor vehicles, I knew that nobody would survive my flight training.

Teaching, on the other hand, had sentimental appeal as one of my never-realized undergraduate career plans. I also liked the fact that it would be a total departure from my IT career (something I saw as brave), and that the additional schooling required would represent a 1-2 year deferral of any real decisions about my life. To my mind, teaching's only real drawback was its predictability—it was exactly the kind of thing people always considered when they became dissatisfied with their careers.

I ran the idea by Clay one night, just to gauge his reaction.

"So you don't want to continue with the technology stuff?" he asked.

"I could, I guess. I did like aspects of it, but…it was also just something I fell into. Nothing I ever set out to do."

"Have you ever worked with kids?"

"No…although, I do have a friend who teaches up in Bellingham, and he seems to love it," I said, pretending that Joel's elementary school experience had any relevance here.

"You know, I think they have programs where you can observe in a classroom and get a feel for what it's really like. You should check that out."

"Maybe I will," I said, thinking it a truly awful suggestion. *Why would I risk talking myself out of my one-and-only career idea before I even got started?*

"Teaching can be very rewarding though," Clay offered belatedly, a small compensation for shitting all over my dreams.

"But you're not sure that you want to keep doing it yourself?"

"Oh, the teaching isn't the problem—it's all the bureaucracy and the departmental politics that drive me crazy. I just don't know if I want to subject myself to that."

"I wouldn't have thought that politics would be an issue in the Philosophy department."

"It's the same everywhere. The Philosophy profs just have the loftiest reasons for why they deserve the big office."

"So what else would you do then?"

"Well, for the moment, I'll probably just get a job at REI. I need a bunch of new gear—a pack, a tent, some boots, a bike—and that way I could get it all with the employee discount."

"I see."

"What's the matter?"

"So basically, you're going to take your PhD and work in retail?"

"Yeah, for a while," Clay grinned. "Does that trouble you?"

"Not really…I was just wondering if they'd hire me too."

❧

At around four on Friday afternoon, I went across the hall to see Clay. I wasn't in the habit of barging in on his writing time, but socialization seemed like my best hope of avoiding a third consecutive *Law & Order* rerun. As it turned out though, Clay was leaving to meet a friend at the climbing center.

"You could come along," he offered. "Have you ever done any climbing?"

"Uh, no," I laughed. "I guess I always figured there were less dangerous ways to embarrass myself."

"Oh, it's not that dangerous. You'd be roped-up the whole time."

"But you don't dispute the fact that I would embarrass myself?"

"Well, that's always up to you."

"Uh-huh."

"Come on, it'll be fun. And the couch will still be here when you get back."

I started to formulate a smartass response—*at least I own a couch?*—but I knew Clay was right: if I didn't go with him, I would spend the evening alone in front of the TV, and I couldn't handle any more alone-time. And really, how bad could climbing be? With any luck, I might even throw out my back and be bedridden for Bella's engagement party, which was coming up the very next night.

"Okay, fine." I said. "Just let me change."

❧

Clay seemed to know everyone at the climbing center, so while he caught up with a few people, I drifted among the gym's towering faux-rock faces, eventually stopping to watch one particularly graceful climber creep spider-like toward the ceiling.

"So what do you think of the place?" Clay asked, coming up beside me.

"Well, it's definitely *cool*," I said, speaking for the kid in me who still saw an elaborate simulation of nature as better than the real thing. "But…it looks really *high*," I added, on behalf of the Liability Waiver-signing adult who was beginning to wonder if one more *Law & Order* really would've been the end of the world.

I soon met Clay's climbing partner "Stash" (aka Andrew Stachnik), an Anthropology grad student with a patchy beard who was both incredibly friendly and incredibly enthusiastic about my first attempt at climbing. By this time, I was planning to bail on the whole idea—I'd started to feel dizzy every time I looked up—but Stash had me cinched into a harness before I could even say *injury, paralysis, and death.*

"You should know that I have the upper-body strength of a nine-year-old girl," I said as Stash tied me into the rope that led up the 40′ wall, through the anchor at the top, and then back down to Clay's harness.

"Well, that's okay," Stash explained, "because your legs should be doing the real work. Just use your arms to hug that wall."

"And you're sure you can hold me?" I said to Clay. "I'm pretty heavy."

"No problem. I'll be taking up the slack as you go, so you'll never have far to fall."

"If you say so."

Reluctantly, I hauled myself up onto the first set of holds and started to climb.

I knew that I was out of shape, but I still couldn't believe how heavy and awkward my body felt, as if my beloved sofa was somehow still attached to my backside, pulling me earthward. My forearms trembled as I clung to the oddly shaped holds, and the higher I went, the harder I fought the sensation that I was about to slip backward off the wall.

There was no way I was going all the way to the top—

from the first step, I was just seeking the optimal face-saving elevation at which to give up. *Am I high enough yet?* I could hear Clay and Stash casually chit-chatting below me, but I wasn't listening to their words so much as waiting for a chance to interrupt. *Okay guys, I think that's far enough for today.* But whenever I did pause and look down at them— the unnerving perspective causing my stomach to slide up into my throat—Stash would just clap encouragingly and call up, "You're kicking *ass*, man! Hug that wall!"

And so I kept climbing, slower and slower, until I finally hit a dead end. I was about halfway up the wall and in an uncomfortable position: supporting myself on the toes of my right foot, while gripping a narrow shoulder-level hold with my left hand. I couldn't even find a place to rest my left leg, which dangled uselessly, and the next hold above me sat six inches beyond the reach of my right hand.

My only option seemed to be a lunge toward that next hold. I was hanging there, weighing my chances of success (3%) against the possibilities of lifetime paralysis (6%) or wetting my pants (91%), when I finally asked myself, *What the hell am I doing here? Have I completely lost my mind? I need to get down, now!*

But just as I was about to declare my cowardice, I heard Stash ask Clay, "So how's your girlfriend doing?" My head swiveled to look down at Clay, who saw me and now seemed hesitant to answer.

"You have a *girlfriend*?" I gasped, completely forgetting where I was.

"Uh, yeah. Is that okay?"

"*What* girlfriend? You never told me you had a girl-friend."

"Well…you never asked."

"But why haven't I seen her around? Does she actually *know* that she's your girlfriend?"

Honestly, this was just the shock talking, but when mixed with my preexisting acrophobic agitation, it came out as hostility. It also came out much louder than I'd intended, drawing the attention of the woman climbing to my left.

"Maybe we should wait until you're on the ground to talk about this," Clay smiled.

"Okay, so let me down."

"Don't you want to finish the climb? You're doing so well…"

"No, I just want to get down. The height is freaking me out, and I'm stuck anyway."

"You just need to swap your feet." Clay suggested. "Get your left foot onto the hold that your right one is on. Then you can step up with your right and keep going."

"I'd rather just come down."

"Just give it a try for me."

I looked to my new pal Stash, hoping that he would intervene—surely, this treatment must be against some kind of international climber's code?—but he did the opposite.

"It's all you, man," he clapped. "You got it."

Exasperated, I peered down at my right foot, wedged onto a hold too narrow to accommodate anything else. Knowing I couldn't support myself on one arm, I used my left foot to nudge the right off its hold, and then executed a frantic *step-grab-step* up to the next level. It wasn't pretty—I felt Clay tighten the rope as I wobbled through this maneuver—but I did it.

"There you go!" Clay said. "Now, really hug the wall."

"You guys keep telling me that, but how the hell do I hug a fricking wall???"

"Just bring your body in closer and get your weight over your feet. You're just making it harder for yourself, sticking your butt out like that."

My inclination, upon hearing Clay's advice, was to throw my shoe at him. Since this seemed impractical, I flattened myself to the wall and felt the tension drain from my arms, allowing me to take another step up.

"That's it. You've got it now."

I still felt fat and out of shape, but I no longer felt like I was about to die. So I kept climbing, actually beginning to enjoy myself, jazzed by the fact of doing something I'd *never* imagined myself being able to do. And with this strange new confidence animating me, I momentarily forgot all about Clay, Stash, and the ground below. I drove myself toward the top of the wall, certain now that I would get there...right up until I fell.

I just moved too fast, and my right foot slipped with such suddenness that I completely lost my grip. For a split second, I was free of everything, thirty feet over the floor. But before I could even process it all, the rope snapped tight and I was scrambling back onto the wall.

"You all right?" Clay called when it was all over.

"Yeah...I'm fine."

"You want to come down?"

"No...I just want to finish."

Back on the ground a few minutes later, Clay and Stash both slapped me on the back. Stash in particular was very excited.

"Nice job, man—how do you feel?"

"Like I'm going to vomit."

"Do you want to give it another shot, since you're already roped-up?"

"No. I'm good, thanks."

ᏂᏂ

Much later, in the car on the way home, I finally got to ask Clay about his mysterious girlfriend, whose name I learned was Shannon.

"She's been doing fieldwork in Venezuela for the last nine months," Clay explained. She's contributing to this nutritional study of an indigenous group there. Stash is actually working on it too—he's going down when she comes back in May."

"So...do you talk to her on the phone?"

"No, she's way out in the forest. Someone usually brings them mail every couple weeks, so we write letters."

"Wow. And you're okay with this arrangement?"

"Well, I have to be. The only way I could even get her to go out with me was to promise that I wouldn't hassle her about leaving."

"How long were you together before she left?"

"About eight months."

"So she's already been gone longer than you were together...you guys must be pretty serious."

"I am, anyway. We'll see if she is when she gets back."

I was mortified that, with all the hours I'd spent with Clay that week, I hadn't heard about Shannon. In my defense though, Clay hadn't volunteered any information, and there was no photographic evidence of Shannon in his apartment. My hindsight impression was that Clay had been trying not to think too much about her while she was so unreachable.

I was awed by the idea that this couple had planned to spend more time apart than I'd ever spent *with* someone. It was a situation that I couldn't imagine being in. If they were as serious as Clay seemed to be, how could they possibly decide to be separated so long? To me, the two concepts seemed utterly incompatible.

Regardless, something about Clay's story made me realize that I couldn't continue the way I'd been going. As much as I wanted to be in a relationship, I couldn't force it, and waiting was getting me nowhere.

"I think I need to get myself back to work," I announced, *à propos* of nothing.

"Yeah?"

"Yeah, I thought time off would be a good thing, but… working is good for me; it gives me structure. I think more clearly when I'm working."

"Would you go back to consulting?"

"I don't know…maybe. I really have no idea."

℧

On Saturday afternoon, having shoehorned myself into one of my old Cavanaugh suits, I headed north for Bella's engagement party. While I'd accepted the idea that I had to go back to work, I was still feeling a little somber about it. Quitting Cavanaugh hadn't proved to be the life-changing decision I'd hoped it might. In fact, I was seriously thinking about calling Leonard, who apparently hadn't replaced me or even assigned anyone to my accounts. I had some hope that I could negotiate a better situation with him this time, perhaps a guarantee of less travel, and more control over my own slate of projects. The work itself still interested me— like the project Ed Zielinski had called me about—if I could just find a better way to do it.

And then, before the impulse could leave, and before I could summon all the reasons not to do it, I pulled off I-5 into a rest area and dialed my phone.

But I didn't call Leonard—I called Ed.

"Hey, I was wondering…that project you called me about. Would you consider hiring me to do it? Like, on my own?"

Ten miles after that, having gotten the thumbs-up from Ed, I pulled over again and called Kevin Lanier, who had been talking about leaving Cavanaugh since the day I met him. I explained the situation—that I had one big project that could keep us busy while we drummed up more work—did he want to come in with me?

"Definitely. Let's do it, Spanky."

"Really? Just like that?"

"Yeah, it's about fucking time. Ingrid will be so relieved."

In hindsight, going out on my own seemed like an obvious choice. I'd fantasized about it plenty of times, but the practicalities always seemed overwhelming. I'd never seriously considered stealing Cavanaugh clients, many of whom had personal connections to Leonard, but if he was going to leave them hanging, why not?

❧

I'd intended to keep my news quiet until after Bella and Joel's party—I was scheduled to sleep on their pullout that night—but Bella sniffed it out the moment she saw me.

"Hey, you made it!" she said.

"Of course I did. Wild, rabid horses could not have kept me away."

"Yeah okay, whatever. What's up?"

"What do you mean?"

"I mean, you look like the cat who ate the canary. And a whole case of Ding Dongs."

6

Spastic in Seattle

And so, by the end of September, I was working again, and getting a major ego-boost from remembering that I was skilled at something beyond food- and TV-consumption. Kevin needed a few weeks to wrap things up at Cavanaugh, so I started on the Rodgers Bennett project without him, reporting to their posh Union Square offices every day and working side-by-side with their rumpled, one-man IT department, Ed Zielinski.

It would be impossible to list all the things I enjoyed about Ed, but if pressed to choose a defining attribute, it would be his uncanny ability to wear dress clothes without ever appearing dressed up...or even tidy, for that matter. Ed's oversized oxfords and chinos were so distressed, it looked like he'd rolled his bony body all the way to work. I also knew for a fact that his necktie—a 1970s striped fiasco that he wore every single day—had never been completely untied; Ed just loosened the knot and hung it on his doorknob before leaving work each night.

Ed's office was a windowless, L-shaped space that he'd claimed purely because it adjoined the server room. Once a storage area for extra furniture, it still housed a battered collection of chairs, file cabinets, and desks, one of which became mine. Secluded in this dim, crowded place, we'd put on some Radiohead or Morphine and code for hours at a stretch, only venturing into the daylight of the main office for food, bathroom breaks, and meetings.

Ed and I met frequently with the firm's new "Technology Committee"—a Noah's Ark assemblage of attorneys, accountants, and other staff charged with shaping the new system's functionality. People attended our meetings for different reasons—some had been drafted, some had a genuine interest in the project, and one in particular—tax attorney/know-it-all Paul Harbin—had a genuine interest in the sound of his own voice. As maddening as Paul could be though, he was unquestionably some kind of conversational superhero, able to transform any productive discussion into a monologue about Alan Greenspan, El Niño, or non-dairy creamer in twenty words or less.

But the committee member who most intrigued me was attorney Corinne Fletcher. Obviously a draftee, Corinne rarely spoke in our meetings, but her pained expressions at Paul's blather almost made up for having to hear him in the first place. Whenever Paul said something inane, off-topic, or inappropriate—this happened roughly three times per meeting—I watched for Corinne's reaction: a subtle wince, a ripple of nausea, or maybe a veiled eye-roll.

Corinne was also absolutely striking, which was probably why I'd noticed her in the first place. She possessed a challenging, Picasso-like beauty, the kind that could engender discord. Yes, she had long blonde hair and sea-blue eyes, but some might say that her skin was too pale, that her nose was too prominent for her mouth, or that her graceful neck was too long. She also seemed chronically weary, on most days looking like she could've used another two hours' sleep, her makeup never quite concealing the puffy darkness beneath her eyes.

Because Corinne was so singular, I honestly never expected to interact with her directly. On one occasion though, when Paul had hijacked our meeting and was lecturing us all on his foolproof plan for retiring at 47, I noticed Corinne staring into space with a wide-eyed expression of abject hopelessness. I was still watching her—probably smirking to myself—when she glanced over unexpectedly and our eyes met. It was too late to look away, so I just smiled and shrugged at Paul's ramblings. Corinne smiled wanly back and, slowly raising a finger-pistol to her temple, blew her imaginary brains out.

For a while, this pantomime suicide was the sum-total of our relationship. Corinne, like the rest of the draftees, soon found excuses to miss our meetings, and I was unsuccessful at orchestrating an accidental encounter with her elsewhere. In my travels around the office though, I did notice a few things about her:

1. She didn't seem to be particularly close to anyone at RB. She usually ate lunch at her desk, not seeming to belong to any of the little office cliques.

2. She was probably just a few years older than me, but in the eminently competent, self-assured way that she dealt with the other attorneys, she seemed *way* more adult than I'd ever felt. I could fake it briefly, but Corinne was the real thing.

3. Despite this adultness, she often had what appeared to be a Blue Razz Blow-Pop tucked in her cheek. She'd occasionally brandish it to emphasize a point, but mostly she kept it planted in her

mouth, the exposed stick twitching in nervous opposition to her tongue, which was perpetually a startling shade of magic-marker blue.

ꙮ

As the project intensified, I spent less time watching for Corinne and more time cloistered in Ed's office, sometimes not even emerging until mid-afternoon. On one such Thursday, Ed and I worked straight through lunch—unheard of for me—trying to resolve a thorny record-duplication problem. We finally got things under control around three, at which point I headed to the kitchenette for a celebratory soda.

Given the silence of the hallway as I approached, I assumed that the kitchenette was empty. Still, I probably wouldn't have been *quite* so startled to see Corinne there, leaning meditatively by the coffee maker, if I hadn't ambled into the room singing "I Wanna Dance With Somebody" in a silly, Bee-Geesian falsetto.

"Oh, hey—" I choked, stopping in my tracks.

"Hey," she said, unfurling a weary smile. "Sorry...I was just enjoying the quiet in here."

"And then I barged in with my little Whitney Houston tribute."

"Is that what it was?"

"No."

"I didn't think so."

"I'm Garrett, by the way. I don't think we've ever been introduced."

"Corinne. Nice to meet you."

"You too," I said, noticing that something she was wearing—maybe her shampoo, maybe her moisturizer—had a peachy scent to it.

"How's your project coming along?" she asked.

"Oh, I haven't a clue—I quit going to those meetings *weeks* ago."

Corinne laughed, an involuntary little giggle that lit her sleepy expression in a surprisingly girlish way. It was so charming that I immediately wanted to see it again, but she squelched that possibility with a measured sip of her coffee.

"It's actually going really well," I continued. "Ed and I make a pretty good team."

"So did you study computer science in college?"

"No, I actually majored in English at UW."

"Oh—me too. What year did you graduate?"

"'91."

"Ah…so you're just a youngster then. I was '88. I wonder if we were ever in any of the same classes?"

"Oh, I doubt it," I said, certain that I would've remembered Corinne. "But we must've had some of the same professors."

"Did you ever have Sam Martinson for anything?"

"He taught Shakespeare, right? Kind of good-looking, but kind of a lech?"

Corinne just nodded, a languid eye-roll. I was quickly discovering that the eye-roll, in all its variations, was Corinne's most-used facial expression.

"Yeah, I had him sophomore year," I said. "He was all over the women in our class. And his whole message seemed to be that everything in Shakespeare is some kind of obscene pun."

"That's definitely him," Corinne nodded.

"I think he might've even been *dating* someone in my class…that's what somebody told me anyway. Although he was so over-the-top, it's hard to imagine anyone falling for his whole sensitive poet-scholar shtick."

"Well...you'd be surprised."

"I guess..."

Corinne arched one eyebrow at me and took another sip of her coffee.

"Oh," I said, finally getting it and now feeling like an idiot. "*Oh.*"

"It was brief," she said. "It ended when I walked in on Mr. Poet-Scholar dating another girl in his office."

"Wow. I'm sorry."

Corinne shrugged, smiling faintly. "I was young and stupid, and I had a thing for older men. I got over it eventually."

I nodded, trying to appear as if I understood.

"Older men, I mean. I can still be pretty stupid sometimes."

Throughout our meandering little conversation, I kept expecting Corinne to realize that she had better things to do than talking to a pudgy IT consultant like myself. This never seemed to dawn on her though, and she stayed right there, leaning comfortably against the counter and occasionally sipping her coffee.

I couldn't help wondering why she felt the need to wear so much makeup. We're not talking Tammy Faye here— Corinne's makeup was always tasteful, and from a distance, you might not even notice it. Up close though, you could see that there was a fine layer of something covering her entire face. You might *think* that you were seeing skin, but you really weren't.

It was almost as if she regarded this mask as part of her business uniform, as obligatory and impersonal as her stone-grey suit and her slim black heels. Standing face-to-face with Corinne, I found myself imagining what it might be like to take a warm, damp cloth and, inch by inch, gently wipe it all away.

❧

On Friday morning, I made a series of excuses to escape Ed's office, hoping to run into Corinne again. After my fifth trip to the bathroom though, I began to suspect that she just wasn't around—her office light was on, but papers had been piling up on her chair all day.

Just before lunch, I decided to ask Ed about her.

"So, do you know Corinne Fletcher?"

"Sure," Ed nodded, not even glancing away from his monitor, fingers still clattering over his keyboard.

"So, she isn't like, *married* or anything, is she?"

Ed's clattering stopped, and he turned and looked right at me.

"I don't think so. Why—are you thinking of asking her out?"

"No. Probably not. I was just curious."

"But you like her?"

"Well, sure I *like* her...who wouldn't?"

"I don't know," Ed shrugged.

"I just meant that she's gorgeous. I mean, *I* think she is anyway..."

"But you're not going to ask her out?"

"No, that's not really my M.O., you know?"

"No."

"Well, for one thing, she's way too attractive. And for another thing, I hardly know her. I usually get to know somebody pretty well before asking them out. We spend a lot of casual time together, getting comfortable, and then, at the very moment when she can no longer conceive of me as anything other than a friend, I make some kind of awkward move."

Ed nodded thoughtfully. "Does that actually work?"

"No. Well...not so far anyway."

&

I finally saw Corinne later that afternoon. Ed had sent me to the storeroom to search for a missing SCSI cable, and when I emerged, Corinne was coming down the hallway toward me. We were the only ones in the corridor, but she didn't even seem to notice my presence, her eyes glassy and unfocused.

"Corinne...hey. How's it going?"

"Oh...hey, Garrett. Sorry...I guess I'm a little out of it."

"Everything okay?"

"Oh, yeah...just a busy morning, end of the week."

"Mm."

"But what's up with you?" she asked, rousing herself a bit. "What have you and Mr. Ed got going on today?"

"Oh, just some printing problems, a few access control issues..."

As I spoke, Corinne's gaze began to drift downward and I thought, *Oh God...I'm boring her.* But then she reached out and casually plucked a static-charged packing-peanut off my lapel.

"Oh, look at that," I said, "I was just digging through a box of those things. I thought I got rid of them all."

"You have one in your hair too," she grinned. "Turn around."

"Oh...thanks."

"Here," she chuckled, attempting to place the two clinging foam curls in my hand. They clung to each other, they clung to her sleeve, they clung to everything but me.

Eventually she pressed them into my palm and closed my fingers around them.

"There," she said, with a kind of bemused satisfaction.

I stared down at my hand, feeling suddenly marble-mouthed. "Thanks," was all I managed to get out.

"Well, have a good weekend, Garrett," she said, continuing down the hall.

"Okay, yeah…you too."

Watching Corinne drift off down the corridor, I was reminded of that woman I'd passed on the front steps of my building, the one who had stopped and asked if I was okay. In particular, I remembered the saturating regret that I'd felt afterwards, the utter certainty that I'd made a mistake in letting her disappear. Corinne wasn't vanishing completely, but I still felt like another opportunity had just slipped past me.

And the feeling only got worse back in Ed's office, that initial taste of regret blossoming into a sour, sinking nausea. Ed was asking me a question, something about VBScript syntax, but I couldn't focus on what he was saying. Eventually, I had to excuse myself.

"Can you hold on for a minute, Ed? I'll be right back."

I double-timed it down the hall toward Corinne's office, the whole time telling myself, *I can do this. She's definitely going to say no, but at least I will have asked. It'll be embarrassing, but I'll recover eventually.*

Corinne's door was open. She sat at her computer, its blue light reflecting off the oblong lenses of the glasses that she wore occasionally.

"Hi," I said from the doorway.

"Oh…hey Garrett."

"Are you busy?"

"Not really. What's up?"

"Well, I was just wondering...I don't know if you'd have any interest in this or not, but I was just wondering if maybe you'd be interested in getting some coffee, or a drink sometime, you know? Maybe even tonight? Or whenever. If you want to that is."

Corinne just watched me, a curious smile creeping across her face.

"Well," she said, removing her glasses with some difficulty, "I'm actually supposed to go to this wedding tonight."

"Oh, well, I certainly understand," I said, finally able to relax. I'd been fully prepared for this type of response, so it was actually a relief when it came.

"I don't even *want* to go, but..."

"I understand completely," I said, trying to make this the easiest rejection of her life. This was the part I was a real pro at, the only part of the whole dating process with which I was totally comfortable.

"Although," Corinne continued, "if you were feeling up to it, you could come with me."

I just stared at her stupidly; this wasn't in the script.

"I said that I was bringing a guest," she explained, "but I don't actually have a date."

"I see," I murmured.

"It's a far cry from coffee, but...I'm sure they'll have coffee at the wedding..."

"Honestly, I don't even drink coffee. I just knew that you did."

"Well, I'm sure they'll serve other things as well."

"Probably," I said, wondering why the word "YES" hadn't come out of my mouth yet.

"So what do you think?"

"Well, sure, but I wouldn't want to intrude..."

"Oh God, *please intrude*. I was just sitting here calculating how much liquor it was going to take to get me through the evening. You'd probably be saving me from severe alcohol poisoning by coming along."

"Okay. Sure."

"Well...good. I think the ceremony is at six, but not being a real churchy person myself, I was planning to skip straight to the reception. If that's okay with you."

After we'd worked out the details—she was going home to make herself "presentable," and I would pick her up at seven—I slipped back to Ed's office and sat down in front of my computer. Ed didn't look away from his screen, but after a moment, he spoke.

"So...what did she say?"

∽

I'd driven past Corinne's high-rise on Vine Street countless times, but I'd never been inside. With its marble lobby and navy-blazered concierge, the place was intimidating, especially compared to the Retrograde. And when I stepped off the elevator on the seventh floor, it was obvious that this was *not* the sort of building where someone would leave a broken TV or toaster oven outside their door for six months. The hallway was immaculate and church-quiet, and Corinne's oaken door made a deep, satisfying sound when knocked. As attached as I was to my building, I was starting to see the appeal of a more modern structure.

When Corinne answered the door, I learned what she'd meant by "presentable." The suit she'd worn to the office was gone, replaced by a long, silky slip-dress. It was the kind of garment that very few humans could even wear, and on Corinne it actually looked *good*.

"Wow. You look...*wow*..."

"Thanks. You look sharp, as always."

"Pffff..."

"Let me get my sweater, and we can go," she said, all signs of her afternoon weariness having vanished. *Perhaps she's just nocturnal*, I thought.

Once in the car though, Corinne became quieter. I'd felt a little self-conscious about chauffeuring her anywhere in my Jetta, but she actually seemed too preoccupied to notice its rattling dilapidation. She just gazed out the window, occasionally shifting in her seat or adjusting the drape of her dress. After a few minutes of silence, I spoke.

"So, in case it comes up, whose wedding am I attending?"

"Oh right...I should probably explain that. It's my friend Jill from law school. She's marrying this guy Jeremy, who she works with at Cabot & Miller."

"Is that where they met?"

"Yeah, although I doubt Jill will be there much longer. She desperately wants kids, and once she starts having them, I can't see her going back."

"Never?"

"No...I think, for Jill, law school will have been the world's most expensive dating service. But who am I to say that it wasn't worth it, right? I mean, ten years ago, she would've gladly paid a hundred grand to meet her husband-to-be."

"You don't exactly sound enthused. Do you not like Jeremy?"

"Oh, he's fine...whatever. Honestly, I've just been dreading this night. Knowing Jill, it's going to be a real scene, and I'm not big on crowds. I'm just praying she skips the whole bouquet-tossing torture…it's such a humiliating little tradition."

"*Who will be next?*"

"Right—because once *they* get married, they're desperate to get *you* married too. It's like they've joined a cult or something. That was why I told Jill that I was bringing someone—so she wouldn't try to fix me up. I mean, am I required to get married just because she did?"

"Not as far as I know."

"My friend Maureen has been with this guy for years… they live next door to each other. They're great friends, but they don't, like, *own* each other. And she doesn't have to ask his permission to go out with me for the night, you know?"

"Sure."

"Sorry. We're not even there yet, and already I'm ranting."

"Oh, it doesn't bother me," I said. "Good call on skipping the ceremony though. That could've been ugly."

"It's just been a long week," Corinne said. "Put a martini in my hand, and I promise I'll be a lot more fun."

თ

The reception, held at a hotel near the convention center, was in full swing when we arrived—the DJ had the music blaring, and already lots of people were dancing. It was two weeks before Halloween, and the ballroom had been decorated accordingly: black and orange tablecloths with flickering jack-o-lantern centerpieces. The wait staff were all in costume—witches and vampires and werewolves shuffled through the crowd carrying platters of champagne and hors d'oeuvres.

Corinne and I had been seated with her law-school classmates, Marissa and Paige, and the three of them spent some time catching up. I couldn't hear much over the music, so I just smiled and tried to appear less out-of-place than I felt. Watching Corinne, it was hard to believe that I was actually on a date with her. It was just such a strange turn of events, and I still hardly knew anything about her.

Corinne eventually interrupted her conversation to get herself another drink, which left me smiling across her empty seat at Marissa and Paige. Marissa said something, but I didn't understand her over the music, so I slid over into Corinne's chair.

"I asked if you and Corinne have been dating long?"

"Actually, this is our first date," I said.

Marissa smiled, and transmitted the information to Paige.

"Brave man," Paige shouted across Marissa.

☙

After dinner, which Corinne only poked at, I noticed the DJ conferring with Jill at the head table. Then there was some discussion among the bridesmaids, and eventually one of them produced the bouquet from under her chair. Corinne, absorbed in Paige's rant about her latest ex-boyfriend, hadn't seen any of this, but I felt certain that she'd want to know.

"I'm sorry, ladies," I said, standing up and leaning into their little huddle, "Could I borrow Corinne for just *one* minute?"

Corinne watched me, perplexed, as I lifted her out of her seat.

"Just follow me," I said, taking her hand.

I led Corinne across the crowded ballroom, dodging through the checkerboard of tables and skirting the dance floor. Once we'd reached the quiet of the hallway, I pulled her around the corner and safely out of sight.

"What's up?" Corinne asked, eyeing me with a suspicious half-smile.

"Just listen," I said.

Back in the ballroom, the music faded and the DJ's voice erupted through the microphone. *Okay, right now I'd like to get all of the single ladies out on the dance-floor...*

Corinne's eyes widened, and her jaw dropped.

"Oh...you are the *best!*" she gasped, punching me in the shoulder hard enough that it actually hurt. "But where can we hide? We definitely won't be safe here."

"I saw a lounge back by the lobby."

"Right—let's go before they set the dogs on us."

❧

"Do you see much of Marissa and Paige?" I asked once we were settled in the lounge, where it was finally quiet enough to have a real conversation.

"Not as much lately. I spend more time with my friend Maureen these days.

"She's the one with the neighbor-boyfriend?"

"Right. She was at Rodgers Bennett when I started, but now she's chief counsel for a medical software company in Bellevue. Which, I have to admit, is starting to sound pretty appealing. She's got her own little realm...nobody breathing down her neck."

"Have you ever looked around for something like that?"

"I haven't quite found the motivation yet...maybe after the New Year. Or maybe I'll end up doing something completely different. Sometimes I can't believe that this is really what I do for a living."

"How did you end up going to law school? Was there something in particular that inspired you?"

"Oh God...I don't even remember...it seems so long ago now..."

"There must've been something that put the idea in your head though..."

"I don't know...I guess it just seemed like a good job. Decent pay, no heavy lifting. Something where you could actually use your brain once in a while."

"Did you know somebody who was a lawyer?"

"Not really. I mean, there was the guy who represented my mother in the divorce, but he was a less-than-inspiring character. I *did* watch a lot of *LA Law* when I was an under-grad though..."

"There you go—that's something."

"*LA Law* is not exactly a divine calling."

"No, but for very similar reasons, I always wanted to be Batman. I just never followed through on it."

"Batman, huh? Why not Superman or Spider-Man? Those guys had the best powers."

"I just couldn't identify with them. Adam West was such a *real* Batman...he wasn't all rippling muscles, just lots of cool gadgets. It was much easier to imagine myself with gadgets than with muscles."

"So is that why you got into computers?"

"Well, I never thought of it that way, but I bet you're right."

"And you do have a lot of black in your wardrobe..."

"Yes...I *am* Batman, aren't I?"

"I went through a big Wonder Woman phase when I was seven. Flying around the house in my invisible jet, blocking bullets with my bracelets."

"That jet was pretty cool. Except, you could still see *her* in it...I never quite got that."

"Yeah, it sort of defeats the purpose, doesn't it."

We paused to ponder this for a moment.

"So have you found that being a lawyer is exactly like *LA Law*?"

"Pretty much, yeah. In fact, I was thinking that very thing this afternoon just before I nodded off at my desk."

"You did look pretty tired this afternoon."

"So is that why you asked me out for coffee—because you thought I needed some?"

"No...it was just the first thing that came to mind."

"But *you* don't drink coffee."

"No."

"You're kind of a goofball, aren't you."

"Do you have a problem with goofballs?"

"Not at all. I just don't know many."

ↁ

When Corinne and I finally returned to the table, we found Marissa sitting alone, poking dispiritedly at a cube of wedding cake.

"Where did you two disappear to?" she asked. "You missed the bouquet and the garter!"

"Oh well," Corinne shrugged.

"Paige caught the bouquet," Marissa went on. "She's over there now with the guy who caught the garter."

"Well...bully for her," Corinne smiled. "Something for her resume."

Buoyed by our conversation in the lounge (and another round of drinks), I somehow convinced Corinne to dance with me. This was obviously a poor decision on her part—as April discovered, I am physically dangerous on the dance floor—but I behaved myself for a while, mirroring Corinne's polite little hokey-pokey. It was only when the

DJ played Elvis Costello's "Accidents Will Happen" that my enthusiasm finally overwhelmed my dignity. Possessed by some lost, spastic member of the Temptations, I uncorked some whirling, hip-shaking, arm-waving choreography that I really had no business attempting. And yes, Corinne did turn beet-red and back away slightly, but she also smiled through most of it (if only from embarrassment), and I didn't fall down or remove any clothing. It could've been much worse.

ତ୍ୱ

It was almost eleven when Corinne and I finally left the reception. The evening seemed to have gone pretty well, and I thought I'd detected a legitimate spark between us, but Corinne's arsenal of halfway expressions made it hard to say anything for sure.

We were both quiet as we walked back to the car—Corinne seemingly lost in the steady *tock tock tock* of her heels on the sidewalk, and me resigning myself to the fact that the our date was ending. But then, just as we reached the Jetta, Corinne uttered the words that never fail to set my heart racing.

"Are you hungry at all?"

"Oh, I can *always* eat."

"I thought I was going to like that fish at the reception, but once it was in front of me, I just couldn't deal with it."

"So you aren't completely exhausted?"

"I probably should be, but at this point, my body-clock is so screwed up that I'm just starting to wake up."

"Why is that?"

"That's an excellent question. My doctor has a variety of theories, but at this point, I've decided that I'm just not a very good sleeper."

Corinne wanted breakfast food, so we headed to a diner in Queen Anne. She asked me about my partner Kevin, who I'd mentioned would be joining me at RB on Monday. I told her about Kevin's turbulent relationship with Ingrid, and Ingrid's relief that our new venture would mean less travel for him. Meanwhile, Kevin had already scheduled a November trip to Connecticut, doing some systems work for another former Cavanaugh client.

"I'm glad that Kevin is bringing in business, but I'm even more glad that I won't be there when he tells Ingrid. I hate to say it, but I don't think she'll ever stop him from traveling—he seems to like it too much."

"And who knows—if she ever did stop him, she might find that he drives her crazy, being home all the time."

"Yeah…I suppose. That's a heartwarming take on it."

"I write for Hallmark in my spare time," Corinne smiled.

"Any other hobbies I should know about? Stomping out wildflowers maybe?"

"That would require too much time outdoors. Though I did take up tennis recently."

"Because you like to hit things?"

"Well, yeah…plus I needed to get some exercise. When I finally quit smoking six months ago, I sort of made tennis part of my personal rehab program."

"Were the Blow-Pops part of that too?"

"Yeah. My mother is particularly horrified by those. I swear she'd rather I went back to cigarettes."

"Where do you play?"

"The Lakeside Tennis Club? It's kind of obnoxious… lots of old people with too much money. But they set up matches for you, and they've got some indoor courts, so…"

"I've actually been there—my old boss Leonard used to be a member. I'm an atrocious tennis player myself."

"Oh I stink too," Corinne said. "I've been taking all kinds of lessons, but I don't seem to be getting any better. It's kept my interest though, which is something."

ల

"Well, thanks for inviting me along," I said, when I'd stopped the Jetta in front of Corinne's building. "I had a great time."

"My pleasure," she nodded. "I'm glad you came."

"We should do this again sometime. I mean, not necessarily another *wedding*, but...something."

Corinne was quiet for a moment, smiling one of her faint half-smiles. "I had a feeling you were going to say that."

"Yeah?"

"You're sure you want to get into this?"

"Yeah...definitely. Why not?"

Corinne just shook her head.

"I mean, if you don't *want* to..."

"No...I had a good time," she said.

"Okay..."

"I'm busy tomorrow, but I'm free on Sunday. Do you want to try some tennis?"

"Sure."

"Well, call me on Sunday then. Say, around noon?"

"Okay."

With that, Corinne leaned over and kissed me, a quick kiss that lingered just slightly, like that last taste of something sweet that stays on your tongue longer than you expect.

"Goodnight," she said, slipping out of the car.

7

Illegal Briefs

As instructed, I called Corinne at noon on Sunday. It was obvious that I'd woken her, but she tried to claim otherwise.

"No, really...I was just trying to motivate myself to get out of bed. Give me an hour and I'll be ready, okay?"

Ninety minutes later, I was watching Corinne bumble around her condo in search of her left sneaker. Once the dissident footwear was located, her racquet was missing, and then her keys, and then the water bottle she'd just filled. Fog-headed as she was, she also seemed to have no idea just how devastating she looked in her trim white tennis dress, her hair tied back in a perfect golden ponytail.

"Okay," she sighed, "I think I'm finally ready."

From the moment she'd answered the door, something about Corinne had looked different, but it wasn't until we were leaving that I realized what it was. Her skin had the soft dullness of a fresh scrubbing, and there was an unfamiliar flush in her cheeks.

"What is it?" she asked, catching me staring. "Do you I have something on my face?"

"I just realized that I've never seen you without makeup."

"Do I need some? I don't usually wear any for tennis..."

"No, not at all...you actually look younger. I mean, not that you looked *older*, but…"

"Uh-huh."

"I mean, I just like seeing your face."

Corinne started to emerge from her stupor once we were on the court, becoming more present with each forehand and backhand. She obviously took her lessons seriously, her exaggerated strokes seemingly built from a series of still images: feet, hips, racquet, follow-through. I, on the other hand, flailed at the ball as if it were an angry wasp, each shot a new and unique affront to the game. Trying to forget how ridiculous I must look, I just focused on getting the ball back over the net, hoping my spastic cluelessness wouldn't irritate Corinne.

Quite to the contrary, Corinne was so absorbed in her own form that she seemed unaware of the absurdity that I was perpetrating. When the ball caught my racquet handle and popped straight up in the air, Corinne acted as if I'd hit a legitimate lob, laboriously setting herself up for an overhead put-away (which she then duffed into the net). When another of my mis-hits landed short, she ran it down like a drop shot, as if it had been a matter of strategy rather than incompetence.

Once I realized that Corinne wasn't going to get frustrated with me, and that she even seemed to be *into* our ugly little match, I really started to enjoy myself. And despite the differences in our technique, we proved to be good competition for each other—after nine games, Corinne was up 5-4. I'd have to hold serve in the tenth game to stay in the set.

Ultimately, my underwear proved to be my greatest weakness. Knowing that Corinne's club had an old-fashioned "tennis whites" dress code, I'd gone out on Saturday and bought a new Nike ensemble—white shirt, white shorts, white sneakers and socks. Clay had given me considerable shit about spending so much (*"I couldn't afford to go out with this Corinne woman even once."*), but I really should've purchased one more thing: a pair of white boxers. Getting dressed on Sunday, I'd discovered that all of the boxers that I owned, with their vibrant colors and patterns, showed quite clearly through my shorts.

At the last minute, I'd resorted to the only white underwear I possessed, some 1987-vintage briefs that were so hopelessly stretched out that they were constantly slipping down my ass inside my high-tech shorts. The longer rallies were brutal—with each step, my skivvies would slip a little further until they were wadded up around my thighs. Between points, I'd reach into my shorts (as discreetly as possible) and haul everything back up to the proper elevation.

Corinne was oblivious to my underwear struggles for most of the match, but in that critical tenth game, we played a point that went on so long that I actually had to reach back and yank my briefs up while on the run. In my haste, I yanked so hard that the lifeless waistband came right up out of my shorts.

Corinne, positioned perfectly at the net, had an unobstructed view of this maneuver. When I did manage to swat the ball back toward her, she just stood there, stunned.

"Sorry," I said, turning away and attempting to restore order without flashing her. "I'm just having a little issue here..."

"Did you just give yourself a *wedgie?*" she asked, blinking in disbelief.

"Yeah...sorry. My underwear keeps slipping."

"I thought you were running funny...but I figured that

was just how you ran. Need any help?"

"I've got it, thanks."

The next few points were short, but inevitably, we got into another marathon rally and I felt things slipping away. It was a fantastic point—easily the longest of our match—and even with my underwear wadding up and threatening to slip into view, I was racing all over, retrieving balls that I never would've expected to reach. I was feeling pretty proud of myself until I glanced up and saw Corinne smile as she gently stroked another ball toward the far court. It wasn't that I'd morphed into Michael Chang—Corinne was just keeping me in the point and making me run as much as possible.

Recognizing this, I sprinted toward the ball, waving my racquet and bellowing like a berserker. I whacked the thing back as hard as I could, thinking it would shoot down the sideline and crash into the fence. Instead, I ended up blasting the ball directly at Corinne, who hit the deck to avoid being beaned. I raced over to her crumpled form, apologizing with every step.

"ImsorryImsorryImsorryImsorry!"

For a second, I thought maybe she'd hurt herself, but then I realized that her shoulders were twitching with laughter rather than tears.

"Are you okay?"

"I'm fine," she smiled, as she sat up. "I probably deserved that."

"Yeah, you did. Exploiting your opponent's underwear is unsportsmanlike."

"Why don't you just take those things off?"

"I'd love to, but these stupid shorts are basically see-through."

"And...?"

"Well, uh...I just figured that would be unfairly distracting to *you*."

"Of course."

"Believe it or not, that shot stayed in. Although I have no idea what the score is now."

"Oh, I think I've had enough anyway. Why don't we just call it a draw and get something to eat? My morning coffee is eating a hole in my stomach."

∾

During our post-match meal (late lunch for me, breakfast for Corinne), I learned that Corinne had grown up in Kirkland, and that her parents, after several tumultuous back-and-forth years, had split permanently when she was in junior high. Corinne and her sister had stayed in Kirkland with their mother, and Corinne's father had moved to California with his girlfriend. Her father had remarried almost immediately, and her mother had done the same a few years later.

"So is your Dad still with that same woman?"

"Oh *God* no—he's on his fourth marriage at this point."

"Oh...wow."

"Dad's a charming guy," Corinne shrugged. "I've told him that this one has to stick though—he can't afford another ex-wife."

"Well...that's one way to look at it I guess."

"I'm guessing your parents stayed together?"

I hesitated for a second over this one, but since what Corinne had said was technically true, I saw no reason to taint a promising afternoon with too much reality.

"Well, my Dad's just not that charming," I said finally. "Unless you're into laconic guys who smell like bait."

☙

Walking back to Corinne's building later, I noticed that she was wearing one of her halfway expressions, as if she were trying to decide whether or not to smile.

"What're you thinking about?" I asked.

"Oh...just my friend Maureen. I saw her yesterday."

"And how's she doing?"

"She's fine. I was telling her about the wedding and how you'd gone with me. She just about died when I said that I was seeing you again today."

"Oh yeah?"

"I think she assumed I'd given up on men. But I told her, 'He's the first guy I've met in while that I could maybe stand to be around on a regular basis.'" With this, Corinne glanced up at me, searching my face for just a second before looking down again.

"Well, I'm honored...I think?"

She grinned, hooking her arm around mine as we walked. "It's a rigorous screening process, but I'm glad to say that you made the cut."

"Although I have no idea *how*..."

"Well, for one thing, you made me laugh," she said, briefly meeting my eye again.

In Corinne's glance, and in the way she pulled closer to me as we walked, I sensed a chance to stretch our date out a little longer.

"You know, *American Beauty* is playing at the Uptown," I suggested. "I think we could probably make the 4:30 show if you're interested."

"Actually, I was thinking about just going back to my place."

"Oh, okay. I mean, we could just *rent* something, if

you—"

Corinne pulled us both to a stop on the sidewalk and kissed me, a kiss that started out emphatic but then softened into something sweeter. Within a few seconds, I'd forgotten where I was and what I'd been saying.

"I don't want to rent a movie," she whispered, resting her warm forehead against mine.

"Me neither."

"Good."

☙

Maybe I shouldn't have been so surprised. I was learning that Corinne, despite presenting the appearance of apathy, was not a casual person. She valued her alone-time too much to waste it with someone she wasn't sure about; if she didn't already like me, we wouldn't have been sharing the sidewalk at that moment.

Corinne didn't tiptoe around things either—if she wanted to have sex, she was going to have sex. She abandoned herself to it, as if this were the last time that anyone would be allowed to have sex, ever. I tried to adopt the same attitude, but with mixed results. My one real misstep was joking about one awkward position that we'd ended up in. It was a comment that April might've appreciated, but Corinne just raised a skeptical eyebrow.

"So is it safe to speak now?" I asked, much later.

"If you *must*."

"I mean, I wouldn't want to disturb you or anything..."

"Well I'm sorry, but you broke my concentration."

"You seemed to recover."

"Yeah, once you finally stopped cracking jokes. For future reference, if you don't have anything dirty to say, don't say it at all."

"Speaking of which, what the hell was that thing you kept doing with the extra tennis balls today?"

"What...?!?"

"You know, where you'd like tuck it up under your skirt?"

"Well, that dress doesn't have pockets."

"And then if you missed a serve or something, you'd just reach down and *voilà*...extra ball. That was wild."

"Everybody does that."

"One more reason for me to take up tennis I guess."

"You know, you aren't much like anyone else I've dated."

"Oh, well you're *exactly* like everyone I've ever dated. My life has just been a blur of statuesque blonde lawyers."

"Echhh...don't remind me. I have a ton of work that I really don't want to do tonight."

"Then don't."

"I have to. I've put it off too long already."

"Well, then get your naked butt out of my bed."

"Ah, excuse me, but this is my bed?"

"Okay, okay...just give me a minute."

ço

Corinne and I saw a lot of each other over the next few weeks, regularly having dinner after work and playing tennis on the weekends. Being around Corinne, I started to feel like a different person—a more spontaneous and less inhibited version of myself. While April's unpredictability had kept me on my heels, I got to enjoy being the instigator with Corinne. And little by little, I felt like I was luring her out of the solitary existence into which she'd settled.

My sense was that Corinne regarded me as an exchange student from some sunnier reality—amusingly unacculturated, but also naïve. This was fine with me, because I thought she was a little crazy too. She'd had some uniquely twisted experiences that seemed to have warped her view of all relationships, and I saw it as my duty to liberate her from these delusions, to show her that two people could be together without the need for lying, betrayal, or restraining orders.

I knew that Corinne's parents' marriage figured prominently in her romantic worldview, but much of their history remained hazy to me. I was learning that when Corinne didn't want to talk about something, she walled-off the topic with boredom—the more sensitive the topic, the more bored she looked. Mentioning Corinne's father often elicited the glassiest of responses.

I was also learning that Corinne was probably never going to spend the night at my apartment (or invite me to stay at hers). I understood the reasoning—with her propensity for insomnia, sharing a bed just made things more difficult—but that didn't keep me from always hoping that *this* would be the night she'd finally stay over.

Of course Bella was curious about Corinne from the beginning, so she was calling and e-mailing me daily for updates. Bella was anxious to meet Corinne, but I knew I had to stall her. Dinner with Bella and Joel was as close to a "meet the family" situation as you got with me, and I couldn't put Corinne under that kind of pressure just yet.

"Are you afraid I'm going to embarrass you or something?" Bella asked at one point.

"Well, you *do* have a knack for pulling out these stories. Like the Kelly Mitchell story you saw fit to recount that night with Christina…"

"Oh come on—that's not embarrassing…"

"Not for *you* anyway."

"Well, if you think that's embarrassing, then I don't think I have *any* stories to tell."

"That's actually a good way of thinking about it. If you work on that idea for a while, maybe we can schedule something for December...say, 2001 or 2002?"

"You do realize that I'm just going to show up down there at some point."

"Yeah, I know."

ເ⁄ɔ

Once Kevin joined us at Rodgers Bennett, claiming the last desk in Ed Zielinski's crowded office, we really turned a corner on the project. Kevin was a skilled developer, but he proved even more valuable as a bullshitter, taking over the Technology Committee meetings and using every ounce of his charisma to deflect their barrage of last-minute changes and additions into a spec for the *next* revision of the system.

Under different circumstances, I would've happily extended my stay at RB, but Kevin and I both had new projects starting after Thanksgiving. On Kevin's final day at Cavanaugh, Leonard had confided—quite giddily, I guess—that he was retiring and selling the company to a larger firm. To me, this explained a few things—Leonard's office décor fixation, the hiring of a receptionist we never needed, and the fact that he'd never bothered to reassign my accounts. More than anything, the news motivated us to pursue all of our favorite Cavanaugh clients (which, for me, meant the ones in Seattle).

By November 1st, we had Rodgers Bennett's new practice management system built, and we'd started bringing in live data for testing. Having just imported the employee records, I clicked through them to verify that the data had come across corruption-free. *Addison, Baker, Bennett...*

I knew Corinne's information was in there too, but despite my curiosity, I was planning to skip past her record. *Caldwell, Crawford, Denny…* Yes, she was mysterious, but really, would learning her social security number or federal tax withholding tell me anything? *Driscoll, Duvall, Erwin…* But then again, if that's all it was, did it even matter? *Evans, Farmer…* I closed my eyes and clicked.

But then, well, I opened them: *Fletcher, Corinne.*

As expected, the information was pretty mundane—there was no mention of a criminal record, or a dependent minor living in Sacramento. In fact, Corinne's employee record yielded only two new tidbits about her:

1. Her middle initial was "M."

2. She was turning 34 on Friday.

☙

I was disappointed that Corinne hadn't mentioned her birthday, but I wasn't exactly shocked. Still, as one day after another passed without Corinne making a single reference to ever having been born, I felt a kind of depression settling onto me. I'd never lost my childhood enthusiasm for birthdays, and I just wished that Corinne and I could celebrate hers together, the way I'd always imagined most couples did.

Then it occurred to me that we still *could* celebrate, whether Corinne cooperated or not. I could take her out for a nice dinner and maybe even a play—she claimed to like theater, but rarely went—and maybe making plans would even nudge her out of her silence.

Midmorning on Thursday, I found Corinne in her office.

"*You* want to see a play?" she said, clearly skeptical.

"Well, yeah. I mean, I'm not *completely* uncultured. I

thought we could see what's playing at the Intiman or the Seattle Rep...unless you already have plans?"

"No...that sounds good actually."

 භ

When Friday finally arrived, Corinne and I had dinner at the Dahlia Lounge—by many accounts Seattle's finest restaurant, and by all accounts its most romantic, the room's soothing red-walled dimness practically demanding that you lower your voice, lean in closer, and make lots of eye-contact. The food couldn't have been better, but as the meal progressed from beef tartare and scallops to seared yellowfin and braised pork, I felt the depression descending again, along with the realization that Corinne really wasn't going to say anything, ever.

By the time the waiter had cleared our plates, scraping the tablecloth clean the way they do in the fanciest restaurants, I'd given up. I told myself that we were still having a good time, and that was really all that mattered, but it wasn't working.

"Are you interested in dessert?" I asked, already knowing the answer—Corinne never ordered dessert.

But Corinne paused, her expression thoughtful. "Maybe I should have *something*," she said. "It's actually my birthday today."

Hearing those words made me so happy, I just wanted to leap across the table and kiss Corinne. Instead, I just grinned...like, a really big grin that, judging from Corinne's worried expression, probably bordered on the weird and disturbing.

"What...? What did I say?"

"Nothing, sorry. It's just, I sorta knew. And actually, I got you something."

I hadn't originally planned on getting Corinne a gift, but I'd had a last-minute idea that was just too good to ignore.

"Happy Birthday," I said, slipping the slim box out of my jacket and setting it on the table between us. Corinne just looked at me, dumbfounded.

"But…how did you know?"

"Oh, it's in the system that we've been working on. I saw it the other day, and I've been waiting for you to mention it…"

"Oh. Well, I just didn't want to make a big deal out of it."

"I figured maybe it was something like that."

"But you got me a gift anyway?" she said, almost to herself.

"It's nothing. Go ahead and open it…if you want."

"Maybe later? I just feel a little weird here in the restaurant."

"Whatever you like. You're the birthday girl."

As Corinne was tucking the box into her bag, I saw a flash of panic in her expression.

"They aren't going to, like, *sing* to me now, are they?"

Corinne barely touched her dessert, an ass-kicking pear tart with caramel sauce that I ended up finishing for her. I couldn't *really* enjoy it though, because I sensed that my gift hadn't had the intended effect. Corinne seemed distracted, and in the car on the way to the theater, she became so quiet that I finally had to acknowledge that something was amiss.

"Are you okay?" I asked.

"I'm fine."

"Are you upset about the gift? It's really nothing…"

"No, it's fine. I'm just not a big fan of surprises."

"Oh."

"The whole dinner thing, and the play...it all just kind of feels weird to me now. A little creepy or something."

"Well, I certainly didn't mean to—"

"I mean, we've only been seeing each other for a few weeks, and you're, like, digging through my personal information and making these plans...I just wish you hadn't done it."

"I'm sorry. I just thought it would be nice..."

"It just makes me wonder if you're a little too into this."

"What does that mean?"

"Honestly, you can be a little intense sometimes..."

"Oh."

"You're just always *pushing*...let's do this, let's do that. I mean, did it ever occur to you that maybe there was a *reason* I hadn't mentioned my birthday?"

"I didn't think it would be a big deal...and I guess I just thought you'd come around..."

"Come around?"

"I thought that you'd have a good time...despite whatever issues..."

"Right. *You* invade my privacy, but I'm the one with issues."

"No, I just meant—"

"I mean, *excuse me* if I'm not the kind of person who throws fucking parties for herself. I'm just not into the standard birthday bullshit, okay?"

"Okay."

"You know what? I don't want to go to this fucking play. Can you just take me home?"

"I'm sorry."

"Just take me home, okay?"

Corinne's demand rang in the car all the way back to her building. She got out without a word, slamming the door so hard that I heard little rust-bits tinkling down inside it. I wanted to run after her, but I knew that with Corinne, I'd just be making things worse.

Back at the Retrograde, I snuck into my apartment, being careful not to alert Clay to my presence. Leaving the lights off, I flopped onto the couch and lay there in the dark, vibrating with disappointment. The evening had started so well, and somehow I'd fucked it up.

I'd started to drift off when then the phone rang. It was so loud, I knew the cordless had to be nearby; I fumbled for it in the dark. It was Corinne, her voice considerably softened now.

"Hey, it's me."

"Hi."

"I'm sorry I lost it on you there. You didn't deserve that."

"No, you were totally right—I shouldn't have been messing around in your personal information. I'm really sorry."

"I've just had some bad experiences...I think I'm a little gun-shy."

"That's perfectly understandable."

"But I have to say, Garrett...you *suck* at fighting."

"What?"

"I completely unloaded on you and you just sat there and took it."

"Oh. Well..."

"I mean, that might be a good thing. If you were any better at it, we probably wouldn't be talking now."

"Well, there are plenty of other things that I suck at if you want to go through the list..."

"Maybe another time."

"Okay."

"I did eventually open my gift."

"Oh yeah?"

"Actually, first I threw it in the trash, but then later I went back and opened it."

"And?"

"I love it. Where did you find it?"

"A comic shop in the U District. Believe it or not, they actually had a few different Wonder Woman watches. I think they said that one was from 1977."

"It's very cool. I'm going to wear it to work tomorrow."

"Were you actually able to get it around your wrist? The strap was probably made for a seven-year-old."

"It fits perfectly. When I first saw the little box though, I thought you'd bought me something really expensive."

"But you were just going to throw it in the trash?"

"Well, that was mostly a gesture. I was pretty pissed-off, but…"

"I'm really sorry."

"Are you prepared to prove it?" she asked.

"Absolutely."

"Okay, I'm coming over."

❧

I think that any description I might offer of what happened when Corinne arrived at my apartment would be purely gratuitous. What I will say is that we reconciled our differences, twice actually. By about eleven though, neither of us felt capable of further reconciliation, so we just lazed in the semidarkness of my bedroom, talking quietly about nothing. *When did it start raining?* Corinne lay on her side, her face smudged against a pillow, the street light from my windows throwing a rain-pocked veil over the soft curves of her skin—the swell of her hip, the acute angle of her shoulder, her breasts slumped sideways, one against the other.

I could see that Corinne was fading, her words getting fewer and her blinks lengthening until eventually her eyes stayed closed. For a while, I just lay there listening to her breathe and thinking how implausible her earlier anger now seemed. Finally she stirred a little, adjusting her pillow and slipping her feet under the bedcovers.

"I'm just going to stay here tonight," she murmured.

"Do you want a t-shirt or something?"

"No...I'm fine."

"Okay. Goodnight," I said, pulling the covers up over her.

"G'night," she said, eyes already closed.

Corinne's lids didn't even twitch when, ten minutes later, I clicked on my bedside lamp. I read for an hour or so, periodically gazing over at Corinne's sleeping face. I felt like we'd taken a big step that night, negotiating a potentially fatal blowout and becoming closer in the process.

And with Corinne breathing beside me, my own apartment suddenly felt different...alive somehow. No longer just a big locker for me and my junk, it finally felt like *home*. And I realized that this was what I'd been wanting all along, the thing that I'd been seeking since that day with Dana Burns. I'd thought I was looking for a girlfriend, but this was really it—this feeling of home with somebody, the feeling that I could just stay in this room for the rest of my life and die a happy man.

Maybe this doesn't seem like a big revelation, but at that moment, I was possessed by an almost unbearable need to share it with someone. For just a second, I thought about sneaking out to the living room and calling Bella, or going across the hall to see if Clay was awake. But then I came to my senses, realizing that I'd have to be insane to get out of that bed, for any reason.

8

Where Parallel
Lines Intersect

But the night of Corinne's birthday didn't prove to be the Great Leap Forward that I'd hoped it might. If anything, the next few weeks represented more of a Faltering Half-Step Backward, with both of us getting busier work-wise as Thanksgiving approached. It was more than just work though—Corinne hadn't stayed over again, and even when we were together, I sensed her shifting in and out of focus. She said she just wasn't sleeping well, but I found little comfort in that explanation.

Since Corinne was spending Thanksgiving at her mother's in Kirkland—"Believe me, you *don't* want to be there," was the closest she came to inviting me—I drove up to Bella's, taking Clay with me, since he wasn't going home either. Corinne and I planned to spend Friday together though, and after a blurry few weeks, I was really looking forward to it. When my phone rang just before ten that morning, I assumed it was Corinne calling to say she was on her way over, but it was Kevin.

"So Ingrid and I got in a *huge* fight last night."

This seemed like an odd thing to call about—frankly, their fights weren't uncommon—but there was a strange excitement in Kevin's voice, so I played along.

"What happened?"

"Well, we were driving back from Thanksgiving at her parents, and she mentioned that her brother Jake is coming home from the Navy for a few days, and that her family is planning to celebrate Christmas early so he can be there."

"Okay..."

"Well, bad boyfriend that I am, I had yet to mention that my Hartford trip, which I'd originally advertised as a few days, had sort of expanded into a two-week thing...and thus I wouldn't be around for that celebration."

"Oh no...so she freaked out?"

"Oh yeah, she threw the kitchen sink at me...*I don't know what we're doing together, you're never going to change, you only ever think about yourself, you're such an asshole...*"

"So what happened?"

"I asked her to marry me."

"You asked her to *marry* you?"

"Yeah, right there in the car. Well, I pulled over first, which Ingrid hardly noticed because she was still laying into me. But then I slipped the ring out of my pocket, and she was speechless."

"And you just happened to have an engagement ring in your pocket?"

"Well, I'd bought it for Christmas, but I've been so fucking terrified of losing the thing that I've been carrying it around with me ever since."

"And she said yes?"

"Oh yeah. She was crying, I was crying...it was a beautiful thing."

"Wow, that's great Kevin—congratulations."

"Thanks. We haven't picked the day yet, but Ingrid wants to do it while her brother is home, so..."

"Oh. So *soon* then, huh?"

"Yeah, well, I figure it's been long enough already, and if she wants to have her brother there, we might as well do it now. Which means that I have a *huge* favor to ask…"

"Oh, okay…"

For a second, I thought Kevin might ask me to be his Best Man—a weird idea, given that he had many closer friends—but the true nature of this favor washed over me with a wave of nausea just before he spoke the words.

"I need you to go to Hartford in my place…on Sunday."

"Oh, right…"

"I mean, some of the work can wait until after the honeymoon, but there's some final Y2K work that obviously can't wait."

"Sure…"

"I really hate asking you to do this, Spanky, but this is one time I absolutely cannot fuck up with Ingrid. And you definitely wouldn't need to get us a wedding gift. In fact, I think Ingrid would probably sleep with you if you played your cards right…"

"No, it's fine," I said, too preoccupied to even register Kevin's joke. "Just e-mail me everything you've got on the work."

"Do you want me to call them and explain?"

"No, I'll take care of it—you've got a wedding to plan."

"You're sure?"

"Yeah. And tell Ingrid I'm really happy for you guys, okay? I'll talk to you tomorrow."

Hanging up with Kevin, I sat on the couch for a while, turning it all over in my mind. I'd been looking forward to reconnecting with Corinne, and the last thing I wanted to do now was make myself disappear. I kept thinking, *If I just had another month…* I just wished that I could give Corinne more time to become attached to me before giving her such a good opportunity to forget about me.

℘

I was still sitting there, phone in hand, when Corinne arrived for tennis.

"New outfit?" she asked, smirking at my boxers-and-undershirt condition.

"Oh…I got interrupted. Kevin called. He and Ingrid are getting married…like, next week."

"Well, that's psychotic. Which sounds about right for them."

"Mm," I murmured, unable to stop chewing my lower lip.

"What's the matter?"

"Well, Kevin was supposed to go to Hartford on Sunday. Now it looks like I'll have to have to go instead."

"Wow…so he's just going to blow off his trip? How long was he supposed to be there?"

"Two weeks."

"Oh. Well, at least it's not *that* long, right?"

"Right," I nodded, trying to seem as unfazed as Corinne.

"Do you not like this client or something?"

"No, they're fine…I just didn't feel like getting on a plane right now, you know?"

Corinne nodded sympathetically, seeming to accept this explanation.

Then I had a miraculous thought. Or, I had a thought that seemed miraculous until I said it out loud.

"Hey, do you want to come with me?"

Corinne snorted with laughter.

"Hmm. Connecticut in December," she said, scrunching her nose. "I think I'll pass, but if you get any clients in the Caribbean, let me know."

ↄ

I should've enjoyed that weekend more than I did. After a week of misty cold blech in Seattle, the sun had finally come out. Corinne was in a playful mood, making merciless fun of me as she kicked my butt all over the tennis court. "Personally, I'd recommend hitting the ball with the *strings*," she called across the net. "But please, feel free to keep hacking at it with the frame." On another day, I might've responded with a lewd comment, but I was so preoccupied with my imminent departure that I just smiled stupidly and prepared to lose another point.

Corinne slept at my place on Saturday night, but not even that pleasant surprise could bring me out of my distracted funk. Long after she'd fallen asleep, I was still wide awake, trying to think my way out of this trip. I knew that Corinne was right—two weeks wasn't a big deal—but understanding it intellectually did nothing to dissipate my panic.

Eventually I just got out of bed and took my laptop out to the living room so I could analyze everything Kevin had e-mailed me in more detail. And when I really looked at it, I thought I could squeeze everything into one week. Yes, I might have to work 16-hour days while I was there, but it would get me home by next Saturday.

"That sounds hellish," Corinne said, when I told her my plan the next morning at breakfast.

"Oh, I've done it before. I mean, it's not like I was going to do anything *fun* with my free time anyway."

Corinne nodded and took a long, thoughtful sip from her mug.

"This isn't about *us*, is it?"

Her tone was casual, but I knew that my answer was important. I shoveled in a big crunching mouthful of cereal and pretended I hadn't understood.

"Hm?"

"I mean, you aren't killing yourself to get back here because of *me*, are you?"

"No, I just don't want to be there for two weeks. And as it turns out, it's not necessary."

She just nodded, sipping her coffee.

"I mean, seriously," I said, "have you ever been to Connecticut in December?"

✌

I departed for Hartford in a less-than-peaceful state of mind. Part of me still wondered if I should've canceled the whole thing, while the rest of me wondered if I should've gone for the full two weeks, just to show Corinne that my reluctance wasn't all about her (even though it was). It seemed likely that I was making a big mistake—I just wasn't sure which one.

I was once again connecting through O'Hare, which was mobbed with post-Thanksgiving travelers. It had been four months since I'd been there with Dana Burns, but I almost felt like I'd stepped off the plane into that very same day. It was as if, with its perpetual bustle, the place achieved a reassuring kind of datelessness, a continuous deja-vu. Walking down the bright, skylit concourse, I felt my mood lifting, and every time I turned my head, I expected to see Dana waiting by one of the gates, reading a paperback with her feet kicked up on her overstuffed messenger-bag.

Feeling daydreamy, I allowed myself to be carried along within the weaving stream of travelers, paying just enough attention to keep from getting trampled. Glancing up to check a gate number, my eye caught on a familiar face in the oncoming crowd. No, it wasn't Dana—this woman was smaller, with short brown hair. I definitely knew her, but from where? As she got closer, I studied her face, a memory beginning to surface. Had I gone to high school with her? Her outfit—a dark sweater over a pair of baggy khakis—didn't help place her.

When the woman and I were six feet apart, she glanced over at me, probably because she'd felt me staring. That was all it took though—in that instant of eye contact, I finally realized who she was, and I smiled. Her own expression remained defensively blank, but then there was a little flicker of something—her eyes widening—and she stopped, forcing several oncoming travelers to swerve around her at the last second.

"Hey..." she said with a slow smile. "What are *you* doing here?"

"I'm on my way to Hartford," I said. "What about you?"

"I'm actually on my way home."

"To Seattle?"

"Yeah, back to the Retrograde," she said.

"Wait—you *live* there?"

"Well...yeah."

"I live there too," I said.

"I know."

"But I've never seen you...I mean, except that one time—"

Since we'd stopped in the middle of a busy walkway, we were already being bumped and knocked by other travelers as they dodged around us, but at that moment, some guy rolled his 500-pound steamer-trunk into my left Achilles, buckling my whole leg and nearly sending me onto my ass. I recovered as gracefully as I could, which is to say: staggering backwards and howling in pain, arms flailing to keep from falling.

"Oh God...are you all right?" the woman asked. "Maybe we should get out of the flow of traffic?"

"That's probably a good idea."

As we made our halting way through the crowd, it occurred to me that I still didn't know her name.

"I'm Garrett, by the way." I said, once we'd safely reached the edge of the concourse. "Garrett Anderson."

"Meryl Larson," she smiled, revealing a dimple in her left cheek.

"It's nice to finally meet you for real," I said, suddenly noticing that my heart was racing—my encounter with the steamer trunk had been surprisingly aerobic.

"Yeah, and it's good to see you looking slightly less despondent."

"Right," I winced, recalling my melodramatic performance on the steps of the Retrograde. "I guess I was feeling a little sorry for myself that day."

"And today?"

"Well...you can't feel sorry for yourself *all* the time, right? You have to pace yourself."

It had been more than a year since she'd stopped me on the front steps of my building—our building, apparently—and although I thought I'd forgotten what she looked like, I realized now that the details had been there all along, tucked into some corner of my memory.

She was a compact person—maybe 5'3"—with a pretty, soft-featured face and cider-brown eyes. Her dark hair was cut in a loose bob, a little tousled from fiddling with it as she did, periodically raking her fingers back though it. Her black sweater was of that casual, gape-necked sort that looked like the collar had been torn off, thus exposing the neck of a white t-shirt underneath. Below the hem of her baggy khakis, she wore bright red running shoes, and like me, she had a nylon laptop case hanging from one shoulder.

"So why have I only seen you that one time?" I asked, amazed that I was finally going to get the answer to this question.

"Well, I haven't been around much. In the last year, I've probably spent a total of ten weeks in the US, so..."

"Ah...and those probably weren't the same weeks I was in Seattle."

"You travel a lot?"

"Yeah...or, I did. I'm an IT consultant...what about you?"

"Management consulting. I work for HRK International?"

"Oh, sure—they're based here in Chicago, right?"

"Yeah, I spent a few days at the main office early this week, and then I had Thanksgiving with relatives here. Before that though, I was in Japan for about three months. Now I'm finally headed back to Seattle."

"Just as I'm leaving..."

"Right. So are you going to be in Hartford for a while then?"

"No, I should be back in a week. That's what I told my girlfriend anyway."

"Well, I'll be around for a few months. We should have lunch when you get back."

"Sure, yeah...that'd be great."

"Or we could even get brunch at Macrina—I think I

saw you in there once."

"You did?"

"Yeah, I was getting a coffee to go, and I think you were sitting at the counter. I would've said hello, but I was in a hurry, and you didn't look up the whole time I was in line."

"That sounds like me. I get very focused when I'm eating."

۞

I walked away from this encounter in a state of almost religious mystification, convinced that O'Hare was some kind of Bermuda Triangle-type place unbound by the laws of probability. For over a year, Meryl and I had lived in the same building, crossing paths only once. Then when we did finally meet again, it was in an airport 2,000 miles away, a place awash in God-knows-how-many other people.

The rest of my journey passed without incident though, and despite being flat-out busy from the moment I landed in Hartford, my strange path-crossing with Meryl was often in the back of my mind. Every time I replayed our conversation though—whether I was sitting in a meeting, or waiting for a server to reboot—I had to wince at the fact that I had involuntarily pulled Dana Burns's "ham sandwich" trick, mentioning my significant other in a situation that didn't really call for it. Seriously, did it matter to Meryl how long I'd told my *girlfriend* I'd be gone? The words had just come out of my mouth, surprising even me. It must've been a guilty reflex of some kind—if I hadn't been thinking about sending improper signals, I wouldn't have been so anxious to stifle them.

I probably wouldn't have spent so much time thinking about Meryl if I'd had more success connecting with Corinne. She refused to use her work e-mail for personal things, and we seemed destined to miss each other on the phone: I'd call her office and get voice-mail, and then she'd call my cell after I'd gone to sleep. This would be frustrating under normal circumstances, but the day after I arrived in Hartford, all hell broke loose in Seattle. I'd heard something about protests being expected at the WTO conference that week, but I wasn't prepared for what actually happened: violence, vandalism, tear gas, and rubber bullets…much of it in the vicinity of Corinne's office.

After leaving messages on all of Corinne's various machines, I finally did get one e-mail from her saying that everything was fine—the firm had, where possible, dispersed the staff to less-exciting locales. She had been working from a client's office in Redmond and sleeping at her mother's house in Kirkland, though she didn't include a number for either place. I was getting the feeling that, riots or not, Corinne was making herself purposely unreachable.

On Wednesday night, possessed by the need to talk to *someone*, I called my sister in Arizona. As a rule, Karen and I never talked at "normal" times. Once while she was living in California, she'd called me at 11:00 p.m. on a Saturday, eventually revealing that she was at a party—she'd gotten bored and snuck into someone's bedroom. I often called her when I was traveling, one time talking to her from my cell phone in San Francisco while waiting for a tow truck.

Sitting in my hotel room, I dialed Karen's number.

"Hello?"

"Karen…it's Garrett."

"You know, I used to have a little brother named Garrett, but he moved to the Pacific Northwest to look for Bigfoot or something."

"Actually, I'm in Hartford at the moment."

"That's awfully close to Portland, my friend. Are you going to visit?"

"Not this trip. I did spend a weekend with them when I was in Boston this summer though."

"How did that go?"

"Oh, fine. I saw more of Sheila than I did of Dad, but that's nothing new. Have you talked to him recently?"

"He called yesterday, actually, to remind me that it was time to get my oil changed."

"Was he right?"

"Of course. He still can't carry on a normal conversation, but he has automotive ESP."

"Mm."

"So what's in Hartford?"

"A client."

"So you're still doing the traveling salesman thing?"

"I'm a *consultant*, dear. If anything, I'm more of a traveling technology prostitute. But actually, I quit my original job..."

"Is that a good thing?"

"It was at the time."

"Congratulations! So what are you doing in Hartford?"

"Consulting again, but now I'm my own pimp. I started my own company, me and another guy."

"Cool. So are you guys working on that whole Y2K thing?"

"Here and there."

"Do you think I should be worried about it? One of our neighbors here has been stockpiling bottled water and canned goods, and he's starting to freak me out."

"I wouldn't worry too much. You have a gun, right?"

"Of course."

"You should be all set then."

Whenever I got on the phone with Karen, I wondered why I didn't call more often. We weren't incredibly close, but that seemed mostly like a matter of circumstances—we'd never spent much time in the same place. I had the sense that, given the opportunity, we *could* be close, but until then, we would remain interested spectators to each other's lives.

"So, other than the survivalist neighbor, how do you like Jerome?"

"Oh, it's fantastic. Owen and I both wish we'd come a long time ago."

"So you're finding a market for your work?"

"Yeah, it's selling pretty well, especially given how sleepy Jerome is. We have a little gallery attached to the studio, so we've got my paintings and some of Owen's stained glass."

"Sounds nice."

"So when are you going to come down and visit us?"

"I don't know...I'd kind of resolved to stay-put for a little while."

"Well, I hate to tell you this, but if you ended up in Hartford, you failed."

"Yeah, I know. This was kind of unavoidable."

"Do you have Christmas plans? You could come down then."

"Yeah, I'm still trying to figure out the Christmas thing. I actually just started seeing somebody, so…I'm still trying to gauge how that's all going…"

"Well, you're welcome to bring her if you feel like coming to the desert for Christmas."

Karen's invitation certainly had some appeal. It had been over a year since I'd seen my sister, but I also knew that she'd probably want me to stay the whole week, and that the chances of getting Corinne to accompany me were slim, even if it was warm there.

"So how long have you been living in Seattle now?" Karen asked later.

"About twelve years I think."

"And no sign of Bigfoot yet?"

"What is it with the Bigfoot stuff tonight?"

"Well, I always thought that was why you picked UW— you were completely obsessed with Bigfoot when you were a little kid."

"I wouldn't call it *obsessed*."

"Well, you read every book ever written on the subject. And then one time you tried to tell me that you'd seen him in downtown Portland."

"Yeah, yeah, yeah...I was like *five*."

"No, you were like *twelve*. I remember, because it was the year that I—"

"Well, whatever...but that's definitely not the reason I picked UW. Actually, I think I was inspired by your saying that you liked Seattle."

"What!?! I never said that."

"You did too! About a year after you left, you sent me a postcard with a picture of the troll under the Fremont Bridge. You wrote something about Seattle being a really cool place. I still have it somewhere—I can show it to you."

"Wow—I must've been *really* stoned when I wrote that."

"What...?"

"Garrett, I hated Seattle. Why do you think I left?"

"You leave everyplace."

"Yeah, but I left Seattle *fast*—I was only there like a month."

"Well, apparently you liked it the day you wrote that postcard."

"As I said, I was probably high. That place was such a bummer that I had to stay stoned the whole time just to keep from killing myself."

"Christ, it's not *that* bad."

"If you like rain, it's heaven."

"It really doesn't rain that much…that's really overstated."

"Well, all I know is that I was there in January, and it took a month in California before I stopped feeling cold and damp."

❧

My return-trip through O'Hare was less magical than my two previous visits. For obscure air-traffic reasons, my flight was delayed an hour on the tarmac in Hartford, forcing me to sprint between concourses to make my connection in Chicago. By the time I landed at Sea-Tac that night, I was drained and disheveled, badly in need of sleep and a shower. Slouching out through the jetway, my only thoughts were of catching a cab back to the city and going to bed.

To my utter surprise though, Corinne was waiting for me at the gate.

She stood at a slight distance—arms crossed, half-smiling. After just a week apart, I was overwhelmed all over again by her beauty. It seemed unfathomable that this goddess could be waiting for *me*. And in that moment, all of the week's nagging doubts and frustrations suddenly seemed insignificant.

"Hey," she said, obviously trying not to smile too much.

"Hey…you didn't have to pick me up. Though I'm glad you did."

"Well...don't get used to it."

As much as she tried to be blasé about it, I could tell that Corinne was happy to see me. We drove back to the city in her silver BMW—it was actually the first time I'd been in her car, which, although more than a year old, still smelled brand new.

"So, if you have this beautiful driving machine just sitting in that garage, why are we always riding around in my rattle-trap?"

"I don't like to drive that much."

"Yes, but I could drive the BMW."

"No offense, Garrett, but you're a shitty driver."

"That's true."

"If you scrape a curb with this car, it does like $1,000 damage. I think that's actually the minimum service charge at the BMW dealer."

"Yeah, I've been meaning to get that wheel replaced on the Jetta."

From Sea-Tac, Corinne took me straight to dinner at the Dahlia Lounge. As far as I could tell, her choice of restaurants wasn't symbolic. She seemed to have forgotten Dahlia's role in the birthday disaster, and I certainly wasn't going to remind her.

"So did you end up going to the wedding?" I asked at one point.

"Yeah, Kevin and Ingrid harassed me until I caved. But it was actually nice—really small, and really short."

"Did you catch the bouquet?"

"Sadly, there was no bouquet toss. It was pretty barebones. I think Kevin and Ingrid were just about getting on with the honeymoon."

"So did they actually end up going to Bali?"

"Yeah, I think they were leaving first thing this morning. Oh, and Kevin introduced me to your old boss Leonard."

"Leonard was there?"

"Yeah, he was asking where you were. When I told him you were in Hartford, he looked kind of confused, and he was like, 'Is he visiting family?' And I said, no, he's working. And then he made this semi-charming, semi-lecherous comment about how he couldn't believe that you'd go to Hartford and leave me here..."

"Hey, I tried to get you to come..."

"So then he gave me his phone number."

"I wouldn't put it past him."

"He's a actually decent-looking guy for his age."

"He's a good tennis player too—you should call him."

"Maybe I will," she said with a wry half-smile.

The only thing I would've changed about that evening was my energy level—Corinne was in great spirits, but I was simply too tired to appreciate it. By the end of dinner, I felt myself starting to drift. I gagged down one desperate espresso with dessert, but it had no discernible effect—I just needed to sleep.

I don't even remember what happened when Corinne and I finally made it back to my apartment. After unlocking the door, the next thing I remember is waking up at around three to go to the bathroom. Corinne was still there, snoring gently beside me, wearing one of my undershirts. It was hard to reconcile this woman who'd greeted me at Sea-Tac with the one who'd seemed so indifferent to my departure. Just for a second, I wondered if maybe I should start traveling more often.

જી

Corinne and I slept late on Sunday, not emerging from

my apartment until sometime that afternoon. As we were coming down the stairs to the Retrograde's so-called lobby, I saw Meryl Larson coming in the front door with the Sunday paper tucked under her arm.

She'd been on my mind the whole week that I was gone, but Meryl had fallen completely off my radar after Corinne's surprise welcome at Sea-Tac. Seeing Meryl now, I felt inexplicably panicked—I actually had to fight the impulse to grab Corinne's hand and run back upstairs.

"Hey," Meryl smiled when she saw us. "You made it back." Her black pea-coat glistened with tiny droplets of water—apparently it was raining.

"Yeah...just yesterday," I said, feeling Corinne's gaze on me but not daring to look.

"Hi, I'm Meryl," she said, turning to Corinne. "I live upstairs."

"I ran into Meryl on my way through O'Hare," I added, as if that explained everything.

"Oh. Nice to meet you—I'm Corinne." Standing face to face, Corinne seemed to tower over Meryl.

"You guys heading out to lunch?"

"To a movie, actually," I said.

"Oh, well don't let me keep you. Nice to meet you, Corinne."

"You too."

Out on the sidewalk, neither Corinne nor I said anything for a block or so. I wondered how long I could hold my breath before I passed out. A minute or two? I wasn't even sure why I felt so uncomfortable.

"She's cute," Corinne finally pronounced, her matter-of-fact tone suggesting that she actually meant, *'She's small and non-threatening—don't you agree?'*

"Hm? Oh, yeah, she seems nice," I nodded, dancing away from the topic of cuteness.

"So you ran into her at O'Hare?"

"Yeah, on my way to Hartford. Strange, huh?"

"Do you know what she does?"

"Management consulting. She said she was sort of on her way back from Japan."

Corinne nodded thoughtfully. "And did you bump into any *other* women I should know about?"

She sounded like she was joking, but I had to check her expression to be absolutely sure.

"Don't look so nervous," she laughed, hooking her arm through mine. "I was just yanking your chain, but you're making me wonder..."

"I wasn't nervous; I was just considering my answer."

"Well, maybe you'd like to consult an attorney?"

"I don't think I can afford one."

"Well, this is so easy, I won't charge you...the correct answer here is *No*."

"Okay, so let me give it a shot...*No, I don't want to tell you about the other women*. Did I get that right?"

"Close enough."

We were fifteen minutes early for the movie, and as we sat in the silent semidarkness of the theater, Corinne put her hand onto my knee, her fingertips absently tracing the texture of my khakis. After a moment, I set my hand on top of hers, feeling its warmth under my fingers and palm. I knew this hadn't been what she'd intended—Corinne wasn't a hand-holder—but she didn't pull away either.

In the twenty-four hours I'd been home, Corinne seemed to have begun looking at me differently, quite literally. Where before she was all cool glances and sarcastic rolling eyes, she now seemed to look *at* me, as if she'd only just discovered that I was actually there, that I was more than a mere voice in her head. She never *said* that she'd missed me, but it sure seemed like she had.

9

Neighbors

On Monday afternoon, I went across the hall to visit Clay. I'd said a quick hello to him over the weekend, but we hadn't really talked since my return from Hartford. When I found Clay, he was squatting on the edge of his defeated beanbag, his expression wide-eyed and blank, a kind of frozen panic. As I entered, he glanced up at me with without turning his head.

"Hey," I said, taking a seat on the floor.

"Hey," he murmured.

"What's up? You look kind of freaked."

"Shannon called."

"She *called*? Like, on the telephone?"

"She went into town on their supply-run so she could call me."

"So...how is she?"

"She sounded okay, I guess. I didn't actually get to talk to her though. I was at school...she left a message."

"Is there someplace you can call her back?"

"No, they weren't staying...she only had a few minutes before the helicopter was leaving. It's like a half-day in each direction, so...she sounded pretty disappointed."

"I'm sorry, Clay."

Clay's eyes fell shut. With his right hand, he palmed the smooth dome of his skull.

"I thought I was doing okay with this whole long-distance thing, but...I couldn't believe it when I heard her voice on the machine. Just for a second, I thought maybe she was calling to say she was coming back early."

Seeing Clay like this was unnerving. Normally, nothing flustered him, and I think in some small way, I'd begun to count on that, on his imperturbable placidity. I did have an idea of what he was going through though—the frustration of distance—and I wished I could help.

"Have you ever considered going to visit her?" I asked.

"In Venezuela?" For the first time, Clay turned and looked right at me.

"Your quarter must be ending soon, right?"

"Classes are over," he said. "I'm just grading papers at this point, but...I doubt I could afford it."

"Well, your neighbor does have an obscene number of frequent-flyer miles. He could probably wangle you a ticket somehow."

"Really?"

"Sure."

Clay held my gaze for a moment and then glanced away again, his right leg starting to bounce up and down, as if this nervous motion were somehow integral to his thought process.

"Well, I'd definitely have to talk to Tim about it."

"Who's Tim?"

"Shannon's research advisor at UW. He's actually a friend of mine—we climb together sometimes."

"Well, talk to him then!"

☙

By Tuesday morning, Clay had the go-ahead from both Shannon's advisor *and* Shannon herself. By some kind of telephone-to-radio-to-tin-can linkup, Tim had gotten a message to Shannon, asking if she was ready for some R&R in Caracas with Clay. The answer had come back quickly: *Yes, please.* And after some back-and-forth with my travel agent, I got Clay a plane ticket, departing in just over a week. There were too many restrictions to use my frequent-flyer miles, so I bought the ticket myself and let Clay believe that I'd gotten it for nothing, just glad to be able to do something for him.

Clay was at school when I finalized the tickets, so I slipped the itinerary under his door and went home to do some work. I'd just gotten settled in the recliner—feet up, cold Pepsi in hand, warm computer on my lap—when there was a knock at my door.

"It's open!" I yelled, reluctant to move now that I was comfortable.

The door opened, and Meryl Larson's face poked inside. "Hello?"

"Oh, hey—sorry," I said, now struggling to propel myself up out of the chair without spilling my drink into my laptop. "I thought you were Clay."

Meryl took a half-step inside. "Clay?"

"My neighbor across the hall."

"Oh," she nodded, glancing uneasily around my cluttered entryway. She appeared to be wearing the same sweater and red running sneakers that I'd seen in Chicago, this time with jeans and the wool coat from Sunday.

"So...what's up?" I asked.

"Well, I had the day off, so I thought I'd see if you wanted to get lunch at Macrina later?"

"Uh...sure."

"If today's not good, we can do it another time..."

"No, it's fine. Today's good."

&

Meryl had errands to run, but she came back around one o'clock and we walked down to Macrina together. I have to admit that I was anxious about lunch, partly because I wasn't sure what to expect from Meryl, but mostly because I knew *exactly* what to expect from April.

I'd made my sheepish return to Macrina a month before. April had been so happy to see me gloom-free that she scrambled out from behind the counter and flung herself into my arms, staggering me right back out the door. So things were back to normal with us—whatever that was—which was why I felt confident that, in her good-natured way, April would manage to humiliate me in front of Meryl.

Sure enough, when Meryl and I came through the door, April was there at the counter, elbowing Noreen aside so that she could wait on us herself.

"Hey Garrett," April said, eyeballing Meryl.

"Hi, April. How are you?"

"I'm just swell," she grinned. "So...what're we having today?"

I guess I should've been thankful for April's professionalism while taking our order—she only made cartoonish winking faces at me when she *thought* Meryl wasn't looking. April wasn't always right of course, but...it could've been worse.

Meryl and I took our sandwiches to a table by the front windows. As we were getting settled—Meryl adjusting her chair, twisting open her Perrier—I was seized by the strangeness of the situation. I wondered, *Who is this woman, and what in the world are we going to talk about?* Meryl's face seemed both familiar and utterly foreign. *Were her cheeks always so…cherubic? She has almost no earlobes whatsoever— shouldn't I have noticed that before?*

Meryl happened to glance up at me while I was in the throes of this crisis; she just smiled self-consciously and looked away.

"So…did you get your errands done?" I asked, forcing myself back to normality.

"Oh, yeah…I had to renew my license, get my eyes checked…all that stuff that builds up when you're away. Do you have the day off too, or…?"

"No, just working at home. I mean, I don't have an office, so unless I'm visiting a client, I'm always at home. My friend Kevin and I started our own consulting business recently, so it's just the two of us."

"That sounds great. How's it going?"

"So far, so good. We'll see if it lasts I guess."

Meryl and I both took bites of our sandwiches and turned to look out Macrina's front windows. Outside, it was grey and misting, as it seemed to have been every day since I'd returned from Hartford. I wasn't a fan of winter in Maine, but sometimes Seattle's mild monotony wore on me.

For the next few minutes, Meryl quizzed me about Corinne—how we'd met, how long we'd been together, what she did for a living.

"My fiancé was a lawyer too," Meryl offered at one point.

"You're *engaged*?" I coughed through a mouthful of ciabatta.

"No, he's my *ex*-fiancé," she smiled, conjuring her left-cheek dimple. "We broke up almost two years ago. Although, if he'd *stayed* a lawyer, we might be married now."

Meryl explained that her fiancé Wade had been ambivalent about law, and for the years he'd practiced at his father's firm, he'd worked as little as possible, directing most of his energy into plotting their next overseas vacation. Then he took a position on a friend's congressional campaign, discovering a passion that Meryl supported even as his part-time involvement became an all-consuming thing. But when he started getting excited about running for the state legislature himself, she knew it was over.

"I couldn't ask him to give it up, but that just wasn't the kind of life I wanted, seeing each other at fund-raisers and all that."

"How long had you been together?"

"Six years, and I think we were engaged for three of them. We kept pushing back the date for one reason or another. I probably should've seen that as a sign."

"Did he end up running for office?"

"Oh yeah. He won...Wade Mullins?"

"The name sounds familiar."

"He's your state senator."

"That's probably why it's familiar."

"I was in Japan for the election, so I didn't even vote. He's a good guy though."

Meryl told me that she'd begun learning Japanese when she was six—her first grade teacher, Ms. Takaki, had taught language classes at her home. Meryl's eventual fluency had gotten her a research job in HRK's Seattle office, but it wasn't until after she and Wade split that she'd started spending most of her time in Japan. She'd been promoted to the management team for her next project, assisting with the merger of two companies—one in Seattle, and another in Osaka—that manufactured digital camera components. She was starting the groundwork in Seattle now, and would head back to Japan in the spring, staying for at least six months.

"Wow...congratulations. That sounds big."

"Thanks. Yeah, I'm still sort of digesting it. I just found out when I was in Chicago."

"I can't even imagine learning Japanese," I said, trying to ignore the fact that April was now pretending to moon me from across the room. "I took four years of French in high school, and the only thing I can remember is *Zût, il neige! Je va à la plage.*"

"You mean, je *vais* à la plage," Meryl corrected.

"Oh...right. See, I can't even remember that much."

"Well, close enough. Wade was forever confusing his French tenses and genders, but people still understood him just fine."

"Are you still in touch with him at all?"

"Wade? Not in a while, but mostly because I've been away. I think you could say we're friends at this point though."

My next question seemed natural enough, but for some reason, I had trouble getting it out of my throat.

"So, are you seeing anybody now?" I asked.

"Oh...no, I'm in a sort of not-dating period at the moment. I'm away so much that it wouldn't really be fair. If I had somebody waiting for me, I'd always be half-here, half-there...and after being with Wade for so long, it's been kind of a relief to just be *me* for a while, you know? I mean, I'm certainly not feeling desperate to dive back into a relationship just yet."

"Mm," I nodded, understanding this sentiment only in

that I'd heard other people say such things.

"Is it hard for you and Corinne, with your traveling?"

"Well, I don't actually travel much now. With my last company though, Cavanaugh Associates, I was all over the place. That was basically a three-year 'not-dating period' for me, except I didn't realize it until it had already happened."

"So when did you leave Cavanaugh?"

"End of July. That was when I finally realized that I *was* desperate to dive back into a relationship, and that if I didn't so something drastic, it wasn't going to happen."

Meryl nodded thoughtfully, her expression becoming a little distant.

"I mean, I've certainly felt twinges of that from time to time, that it would be nice... And I don't plan to do the overseas stuff forever. At some point, I *would* like to stop renting and buy a place of my own, you know? As it is, I do miss my family when I'm away."

"So they're in the area?"

"Yeah, my parents are in Snohomish, where I grew up. A couple of my brothers are there too with their families. How about you?"

"I have an older sister who lives in Arizona, but we're from Portland, Maine originally."

"How did you end up in Seattle?" Meryl asked, taking a bite of her sandwich.

"I'm looking for Bigfoot," I said, as matter-of-factly as I could.

Meryl giggled, covering her mouth to keep from spraying sandwich onto the table.

"I just discovered that that's what my sister thought anyway. I was a little Bigfoot-obsessed as a kid...apparently I got a little weird for a while there."

Meryl asked me more about Karen and what she did in Arizona, and I explained as best I could given that I hadn't actually visited her there yet. Meryl's next question, offhand as it might've been, was a little harder.

"So how do your parents feel about you living so far from home?"

I guess the question wasn't difficult so much as it forced me to make a decision. And for whatever reason, looking back into Meryl's cider-brown eyes and recalling our very first meeting on the steps of the Retrograde, I felt moved to tell her the truth.

"Well, it's hard to say what my father feels about *any-thing*," I said. "But if my mother was still alive, she'd probably drag me back to Portland by my ear."

"Oh, I'm so sorry," she said. "I didn't realize…"

"No, not at all…it was a really long time ago," I said. "I was eleven."

"Was she sick, or…"

"No, it was a car accident. She was just coming home from the grocery store, but it had been snowing…"

"Wow…I can't imagine dealing with that at that age. Or now, for that matter…"

"Honestly, I'm not sure that I did deal with it. Unless you count wandering around Portland telling total strangers that I'd been raised by a Bigfoot family. Do you know—is that one of the standard stages of grief?"

"I don't know," Meryl said, finally smiling a little. "Maybe it should be."

When Meryl got up to use the restroom, I sensed April trying to catch my eye. I pretended not to notice, but it didn't matter—April scurried over and crash-landed in Meryl's chair, grinning devilishly. An arc of dirty-blonde hair that had escaped her ponytail dangled alongside her face.

"So," April said, folding her hands on the table, "she's cute."

"Oh, no—we're not...I mean, we're just neighbors."

"She lives in your building? How convenient!"

"I'm seeing somebody else altogether actually."

"That guy Clay?"

"Uh, no...I, uhh—"

"Come on, don't be embarrassed—I think it's great that you're seeing somebody. I'd be worried if you *weren't*."

"Uh-huh."

"And now that we're just friends, we get to talk about these things. Ooh—she's coming back. Good luck!"

April crept back to the counter, an exaggerated tiptoe.

"You're popular here," Meryl observed as she sat back down.

"Yeah, I'm kind of a regular. That, and...April and I kind of dated. Briefly."

"*Really.*"

"Yeah. And she's intent on being buddies at this point. Today she seems convinced that you and I are an item."

"*What?*"

"That's what she was harassing me about while you were in the bathroom."

"And why would she think that?"

"Well, it probably has something to do with the fact that I've still never brought Corinne here. It just seemed like it would be too weird, eating with my current girlfriend while my last girlfriend waits on us."

As I said this, April whooshed by with a tray of hot drinks, discreetly sticking her tongue out at me as she passed.

"Yeah," Meryl smiled. "I guess there are plenty of other

places to eat."

As Meryl and I ascended the Retrograde's front steps after lunch, I was already feeling disappointed that she'd be leaving the country in a few months. I had the sense that, if not for the temporal and geographic obstacles, we could become good friends...but also that said friendship could prove complicated. Given that I still hadn't decided what to tell Corinne about lunch, maybe Meryl's departure wouldn't be an entirely bad thing.

"This was fun," I said when we'd reached the second-floor landing. "I'm glad you stopped by."

"Yeah, me too."

"Hopefully it won't be another year before we run into each other again."

"Well, I'll be around for a while, so don't be a stranger," she said. "And you'll have to introduce me to your friend Clay—maybe the three of us can do something."

❧

A few hours later, Clay found the itinerary I'd slipped under his door and came over to see me, jubilant about his trip. He and Shannon were going to spend two weeks together, meeting in Caracas and then traveling in Venezuela. Although I'd never had much interest in going to South America, some small part of me wished that I could be there—a mosquito on Clay's bald head perhaps—for that moment when he and Shannon saw each other for the first time after so many months. I could only imagine how powerful such a reunion might be.

❧

I called Bella on Wednesday. I was anxious to tell her about Corinne surprising me at the airport, but doing so had a consequence I probably should've foreseen.

"So does this mean I can finally meet her?"

"Uhhh…"

"What exactly is the problem here, Garrett?"

"Well…I just don't know how Corinne will react."

"Okay, whatever. I don't want to meet your stupid girl-friend anyway. I mean, I *did* ask you to be my Maid of Honor, causing much teeth-gnashing in my family, but that's okay…no biggie."

"All right, I'll ask her."

"Oh good!"

"When the right moment presents itself."

"Fine. Just so long as it's sometime this millennium."

"Ha ha."

"Speaking of which, what are you doing for Christmas?"

"I'm going to stay in Seattle. My sister actually invited me to Arizona, but Corinne offered to cook me dinner on Christmas Eve…I think I'd rather just do that."

"What about Christmas Day?"

"Corinne might come by if she gets back early from her mother's."

"Well, we're just going to Joel's parents' house—you're welcome to come with us. I hate to think of you sitting by yourself all day."

I had to agree that spending Christmas Day alone sounded strange, but I thought I'd feel even stranger at Joel's parents' house. Bella and I were close, but it wasn't my family—I would have to get my own life eventually.

"I'll be fine," I said. "I'll rent some movies. I always liked Christmas Eve better anyway."

"Okay, well…whatever you like. How was your Hartford trip, by the way?"

"Oh…I'm just glad it's over. But actually, something interesting did happen on the way out there. I had a layover in Chicago, and I ran into this woman Meryl who lives in my building."

"Wow. That's freaky."

"Yeah, and even weirder, I didn't even know that she lived in my building until I ran into her in Chicago. About a year ago, we'd talked briefly on the front steps of the building, but then I'd never seen her again, so I'd just assumed that she was visiting someone else."

"Wait—this isn't *the* woman, is it?"

Instantly my face felt hot and tingly—I hadn't remembered telling Bella (or anyone else) about The Woman on the Steps.

"So I guess I told you that story then?"

"Oh God…you were moaning about it the whole night. Don't you remember—you'd just gotten back and we went out for sushi? You were all bummed-out and complaining about how you should've stopped and talked to her?"

"That's starting to ring a bell…"

"You were drinking *heavily*…"

"Yeah…I sort of remember that now…vaguely."

"So this Meryl was *the* woman? And you talked to her?"

"Yeah. I had lunch with her yesterday."

"So what's she like?"

I'd only meant to mention Meryl in passing, but I now saw little choice but to answer Bella's questions honestly. I'd lost control of my own story, forfeiting the ability to shape it as I saw fit. And once we got through the basic information, Bella got to the question I knew she'd been waiting to ask the whole time.

"So, do you like her?"

"Yeah, sure. She seems cool."

"But I mean, are you attracted to her?"

"Well..."

"I seem to recall your saying, *If I ever see her again, I'm just going to ask her to marry me.*"

"Oh Lord...did I actually say that?"

"Just before you lost consciousness on my living-room floor."

"Right. Well, she seems cool, and she's definitely attractive...maybe if we'd met at a different time, there might be something there, but...as it is, I'm not even sure I'll see her again."

"Did you tell Corinne about her?"

"Corinne actually met her the other day."

"But you didn't tell her the whole story."

"Well, I'm not *completely* insane. I wasn't even going to tell you the whole story...except I already did."

❧

It was sunny and sixty degrees in Seattle that weekend—unheard of for December. Inspired by the springlike air that night, I talked Corinne into walking up Queen Anne Hill. She wasn't big on walking as an activity, but she indulged me.

"It'll be good exercise," she shrugged. "Especially since you didn't give me much of a workout on the court today."

Queen Anne is a tree-laced neighborhood draped over a steep hill at the northern edge of Downtown Seattle. The higher you go, climbing the various staircases built into the slope, the quieter and more expensive it becomes. In the upper altitudes, the apartment and condo complexes thin, giving way to imposing residences in a mishmash of architectural styles, from the very traditional to the most outrageous and gaudy stucco-and-glass contemporary you can imagine.

From the top of the hill, you can look down over the whole city, feeling like you're eye-level with the Space Needle and the unkempt stand of high-rises beyond it.

In the hill's sleepy upper-reaches, we came across a house that was under construction. The platform of the first floor was in place, terraced off the side of the hill, but the walls were still just suggested, outlined in two-by-fours. Corinne and I sat down on a pair of upended plastic buckets and looked down over everything, afforded a perfect view of the city through the house's open walls, and up at the sky through the nonexistent ceiling. In the dark, it was hard to tell if somebody was in the process of building this house in mid-December, or if the structure had been abandoned in this incomplete form.

"Wouldn't it be great to live up here?" I whispered, leaning back to see the smattering of stars above. After weeks of overcast, the sky was finally clear.

"You mean, like, in a house?"

"Well, yeah. I mean, assuming you could afford one."

"I don't know…houses seem like a lot of work. I mean, I kind of like the fact that I don't ever have to worry about replacing the roof or trimming the shrubbery."

"Yeah…you're probably right."

"Well don't let me talk you out of it so easily. Maybe you like trimming shrubbery."

"I think I was presuming that, if you had the money to live up here; you'd be able to hire someone to handle all the shrubbery-related activity."

"I guess that's probably true."

"It's just an amazing view. Bella and I used to walk up here, when she still lived in Seattle."

"Where did she move to again?"

"Bellingham. She's really bugging to meet you actually."

"Oh yeah?"

"Yeah, she keeps threatening to just show up down here sometime."

"Well...maybe I should just meet her then, before she does something drastic."

"Really?"

"Sure. It'll be interesting to meet someone from your home planet."

10
(Instrumental)

"You cannot let me have more than two drinks," Corinne said gravely. "I need to keep my wits about me tonight."

It was Thursday, and Corinne and I were on our way to Rodgers Bennett's non-denominational Holiday Party at the Union Square Hotel.

"Thanks so much for doing this," she said, already looking frazzled. "I just feel like if I go alone, I'll never get out of there alive."

Despite what Corinne might've believed, I was delighted that she had invited me. The fact that she thought I could somehow help her get through the evening made me feel semi-important, and not even the prospect of running into notorious spoken-word artist Paul Harbin could spoil that for me.

In the elevator on the way up from the parking garage, I had a thought.

"Do you have any plans for New Year's?" I asked.

"Uh, I don't think so..." she said, digging around for something in her purse.

"I was thinking it might be fun to get out of the city for the weekend. Have you ever been up to Victoria?"

"British Columbia?"

"Yeah, we could take the ferry up on New Year's Eve, stay a couple nights at a bed & breakfast...I've heard it's pretty at this time of year."

"How long does it take to get up there?"

"A few hours I think? I'd have to check."

"Let me think about it, okay? At the moment, I'm still feeling overwhelmed with tonight...I'm not sure I'm ready for the Millennium."

"Okay. Well, maybe I'll just look into it. I'm not even sure we could get a place so last-minute anyway."

❧

Corinne ended up enjoying the party more than either of us could've imagined. The first two martinis seemed to be the key—after that, she was talking with people she normally would've avoided. By the party's second hour, she'd discarded her two-drink limit and became so social that I actually lost track of her for a while.

By the time the party started to disintegrate at around eleven, everyone from Rodgers Bennett was pretty blitzed, partners and paralegals alike. Really, the only stone-sober people in the room were me and Ed Zielinski. Ed wasn't much of a drinker to start with, and I'd stopped after two beers thinking that Corinne might want to split at any moment.

I gave Corinne my arm on the way out to the car, mostly for the sake of balance. She was so foggy in fact that she actually fell asleep on the short ride back to her condo, only rousing herself when I stopped the Jetta in front of her building.

"Oh...are we there?"

"We're there."

"Suddenly I'm very tired."

"Well, you should probably get some sleep then. Shall I help you upstairs?"

"Okay."

As we were gliding upstairs in the elevator, Corinne collapsed gently against me, her eyes falling shut.

"You're a good guy, Garrett."

"Oh yeah?"

"You're the kind of guy that any girl would be proud to bring home to Mom."

"Okay, now I *know* you're trashed."

"See, you're observant too!"

സ

Clay had asked if he could watch a movie on my TV that night, so I wasn't surprised to find him stretched out on my couch when I got home from the party. What *did* surprise me was the fact that Meryl Larson was also reclined comfortably in my La-Z-Boy.

"Hey," Meryl waved as I came through the door.

"I hope you don't mind," Clay said, muting the television, "I invited Meryl to join me."

"Not at all. I guess I don't need to introduce you then," I said, sitting down beside Clay on the couch.

"I introduced myself," Meryl said. "I knocked on your door, and Clay answered."

"Did you guys watch a movie?"

"Yeah, we just finished."

"How was the party?" Clay asked.

"Oh, it was fine. Are you all packed for tomorrow?"

"I've been packed since Monday," Clay grinned.

"I'm so jealous," Meryl said. "I'd love to go to Venezuela."

We chatted like that for an hour, as if it were completely

normal for the three of us to be sitting in my living-room at midnight on a Thursday. The fact was, I'd only known Clay for two months, and Meryl for even less. It was getting so I hardly recognized my own life.

Eventually, Meryl stood up from the recliner and announced that she had to go to bed. To my surprise, she hugged Clay goodbye before she left, maternally admonishing him to keep himself safe. She waved goodbye to me as she was going out the door.

"You two became fast friends," I said once she was gone.

"Yeah, she seems great."

"So she just showed up here?"

"Yeah, I was just putting the movie in when she knocked."

"Did she say why?"

"No, but I didn't ask. But she mentioned you guys had a good lunch last week."

"Yeah…we did."

❧

I drove Clay to Sea-Tac early Friday morning. The sky was mostly grey, but dark slivers of Rainier's slopes were visible through the clouds along the southern horizon. It was the kind of thing that you could easily miss, but once you saw it, it was hard to look at anything else.

I live-parked the Jetta in the drop-off area and stood by as Clay hauled his pack out of the back seat. I knew it was irrational, but I was feeling a little panicked about his leaving.

"Is that it?" I asked. "You got everything?"

"I think so."

"Well, say hi to Shannon for me. And try not to bring back any parasites."

"Will do."

"At least we know nothing will come back in your hair," I said, surprising myself by giving his scalp a good-luck rub.

"You'll hardly notice I'm gone," he grinned, giving me a retaliatory hair-mussing and walking off into the terminal. "Bye, Garrett."

I took my time driving back to Seattle, visited again by the empty feeling I'd had after Bella had moved away. By any reasonable assessment, Seattle was my home, but at times it felt no more familiar than it had when I'd first arrived.

ॐ

"Hello, Corinne Fletcher."

"Hey, you made it to work."

"Barely."

"How're you feeling?"

"I've been better. I slept like the dead, but I'm still exhausted."

"You should've just stayed home."

"Probably. Half the office is out. And just so I know, did I say or do anything last night that I should be aware of? Like, did I tell off any of the partners or anything like that?"

"Not that I saw. But I doubt they'd remember anyway—Ed and I watched Bob Bennett fall asleep in his chair. Actually, he almost fell over backwards, but he woke up just in time."

"I guess I won't worry about it then."

ॐ

With Clay gone and Corinne under the weather, I was on my own for the rest of the day. I worked diligently for most of the afternoon, but by around 5:30, my focus had shifted to hunting for bed & breakfasts in Victoria, just in case Corinne agreed to go. As I'd expected, most places I called were full for New Year's, but I eventually found a small hotel downtown that had just had a cancellation. The room was a tad expensive, but after about four seconds of deliberation, I went ahead and booked it.

I tried watching some TV after that, but found that I was feeling way too antsy to give anything my full attention. What I really wanted was to get out of my apartment and be social, but short of driving up to Bellingham—vehicular suicide at that hour—there was nobody to be social *with*. Except perhaps Meryl Larson, and for whatever reason, I felt weird about knocking on her door, despite the fact that she'd apparently knocked on mine the night before.

At the next commercial break, I headed upstairs, emboldened by the belief that Meryl wouldn't be home on a Friday night anyway. When I rounded the corner onto Meryl's hall though, I caught sight of her narrow-shouldered shape, encumbered by an overfull laundry basket, lurching toward the building's back stairs.

Of course my first instinct was to flee—Meryl hadn't seen me yet, and if I was quiet, she'd never know I'd been there. My second idea—which seemed more promising— was to hurry back to my apartment, gather up a presentable selection of laundry, and race down to the basement, where I could "accidentally" run into Meryl. At any earlier point in my life, that's the option I would've gone with, but just as I was about to creep back downstairs, it occurred to me that *maybe* there was another way to handle this situation.

"Meryl...hey," I called out, trotting down the hall after her.

Meryl stopped, and with some effort, turned to look back at me.

"Oh, hey Garrett," she said, adjusting her grip on the

sagging basket.

"Here, let me help you with that..."

"Thanks," she said, gladly relinquishing the basket. "I really need to find a better way of getting this stuff down to the basement. Or just do my laundry more often."

"I have a bag that works pretty well," I said as we continued down the hall. "That way I can just cinch it up and kick it down the stairs if I want. Although, you should really make sure the super's wife isn't coming up the stairs when you do it."

"Oh no..." she laughed.

"Thankfully she's still pretty spry."

"Hold on—I'll get that," Meryl said, hustling ahead to the stairwell door and pushing it open with her backside.

"Thanks."

"So I assume you weren't coming up specifically to carry my laundry?"

"Actually, I was just bored," I said. "I came up to see if you were home."

"Where's Corinne tonight?"

"Still recovering from the party."

"Ah. Well, as you see, I have an electrifying evening planned, but you're welcome to join me. After this, I was going to order takeout from that Thai place down the street."

"Sounds good to me."

❦

Meryl's apartment was a clone of mine in its layout, but the dearth of dirty dishes and food-trash blurred the connection between them. While Meryl was in the kitchen calling in our order, I studied the photos that tiled her living room walls. There were scenes from France, Spain, and the Greek Islands, and a half-dozen other places that I didn't recognize. In one shot, a towering bronze Buddha sat atop a tree-covered hill. Another shot showed a curving beach lined with colorful fishing skiffs and overhung by a cloud of flapping gulls.

As beautiful as the scenes were, I found myself lingering longest over the photos in which Meryl herself appeared. I scrutinized her expressions, her posture, and her varying hair-lengths, as if these tiny clues could reveal something more profound about her. One such photo showed Meryl sitting in the grass beside a stone-edged pool with a sculpture at its center. Meryl was smiling at the camera, but not in the full-volume way you'd usually smile for a snapshot. This was a more private expression, a look that communicated something subtler that perhaps only the photographer would understand.

And so I imagined myself on the other side of the camera, receiving Meryl's smile directly. As I watched her through the lens, checking the light and the focus, the gentlest of breezes ruffled her hair. *Ready?*

"That one was taken at the Rodin museum in Paris," Meryl said, suddenly beside me.

"Oh…really?" I gulped, not daring to look back at her.

"The gardens there are just gorgeous."

"What about this one?" I asked, randomly selecting the big bronze Buddha—anything to shift the attention away from the original photo.

"Oh, that's in Hong Kong. That's a beautiful spot too, but the photo doesn't really do it justice—it was kind of overcast that day."

Kicking off her sneakers, Meryl sat down on the couch and pulled her feet up underneath her. It was a uniquely feminine sitting-posture, I thought. I could remember my sister Karen sitting that way, book in hand, when she was about fifteen.

"You've really been all over," I said, settling into an armchair across from Meryl. "The closest I've come to leaving North America is the French pavilion at Epcot."

"Really? Have you not wanted to go, or...?"

"I guess the opportunity just hasn't presented itself. I mean, I suppose I could go by myself, but...the ironic thing is that my mother was always saying how important travel was, to expose yourself to other cultures and all that. But I don't think that Rochester and Houston were the kind of horizon-expanding destinations that Mom had in mind."

"What was she like?" Meryl asked, her voice quieter.

"My mother?"

"Yeah. I mean, if you don't mind..."

"No, not at all..."

I told Meryl that my mother was an intense, opinionated woman who was, above all, passionate about being a parent. She'd taught us to read before we started school, and later harassed our teachers with her insights on teaching fractions or whatever else we happened to be studying. I told Meryl how it seemed like Mom and Karen and I were always together—Dad was usually on the boat, or fixing the boat—and how, at the time anyway, it never struck me as odd that our mother was our best friend, or that we might be hers.

Not that Dad was completely absent—he just stayed in the background, always in bed before the rest of us, and always gone when we woke. He was also, as Mom described him, "verbally frugal," communicating mostly through his actions. I told Meryl about coming home from school one afternoon and discovering all of the fallen leaves from our yard raked into one gigantic pile, a pyramid of old lobster pots stacked beside it. There was no sign of Dad, but I was sure he was watching from the house when I climbed the pots and jumped.

Much later, I wondered if Dad's reticence was actually just shyness, obscured by the fact that he was built like a bear. He'd been lobstering since he was a teenager, and he had few close friends. My guess was that he never expected to get married, at least not until the day Mom arrived to buy lobsters for her family's restaurant. She'd moved back home after getting her Master's at BU, and somehow this tiny woman—she was barely over five feet tall—had lured him out of his solitary existence. Having a family was un-doubtedly her idea, but it didn't really matter—by then, he would've done anything for her.

When she died, he seemed to go into shock. I don't think he had any idea what to do with his own grief, let alone ours. Maybe he thought that getting married again two years later would help. Sheila was nice enough—she worked at the marina, and Dad had known her forever. She loved him, and he certainly needed someone. My sister wouldn't accept it though—she and Dad had a huge blow-out—and for the last year that Karen lived at home, I don't think they exchanged a dozen words. As soon as she could, Karen moved out.

"Where did she go?" Meryl asked.

"Everywhere…all over the western US. She used to send me postcards, often blank…I'd just get this postcard from Durango or Eugene and I'd know she'd moved again. Until I got to college, that was pretty much the extent of our communication."

"You really must've missed her," Meryl said after a moment. "You lost your mother, and then you lost your sister."

It was a simple truth, but one that nobody else had thought to look for. There had always been concern about how I'd fare without my mother—I'd heard my aunts whispering about it at the funeral—but nobody had even blinked at Karen's departure. Meryl seemed to grasp it intuitively though, and I actually had to fight to keep from welling up a little. Not out of sadness or grief—it was something more like gratitude.

"Yeah," I said, when I could speak without my voice breaking. "I definitely missed her."

"Do your sister and your father talk at all now?"

"Oh yeah, she's over all that. She probably calls more than I do, actually...but I wouldn't say they're close. None of us are all that close, really."

"That's kind of sad."

"Well, I think Mom was the one who held us all together, and when she died, it was like somebody had cut the ropes and set us all adrift. In my better moods, I think maybe it's good for us, having to find our own way without her telling us what to do."

Meryl and I relocated to her kitchen table when our food arrived. Although I'd never thought of my family's history as uplifting, I felt lighter for having conveyed some of it to Meryl. Maybe it was just that, relieved of the effort I usually made to avoid the topic, I could relax a little.

I asked Meryl about growing up in Snohomish, a small town about thirty miles north of Seattle. I'd never been there, but I'd always been curious about the place. Settled in the 19th century, the town was ancient by Washington standards. Meryl explained that her parents were both from there, and that her father, now retired, had for 30 years worked as an engineer at Boeing's facility in nearby Everett.

"It was a good place to grow up, but I can't really imagine living there now. I think I've just become more of a city person."

"Do you still have friends there?"

"I certainly know tons of people there, but nobody I really hang out with. My best friend from high school, Tracy, she lives in Issaquah now with her husband and their two-year-old son Ethan. I visit her whenever I can…when I'm *here*, that is, which hasn't been much lately."

After we'd finished eating, I got up to use the bathroom. Passing Meryl's bedroom door, I caught a glimpse of an acoustic guitar on a stand. Meryl was at the sink rinsing her plate when I got back to the kitchen.

"So, you play guitar?" I asked, sitting down at the table.

"Oh, just barely," Meryl said, loading her plate into the dishwasher. "I took it up in college, but I've only played sporadically since."

"I'd love to hear you play sometime."

"Oh, I'm not sure you would," Meryl said. "Are you all set with your plate?"

We moved back to the living room and talked for a while with the TV on. I was really enjoying myself, but soon began to worry that I was overstaying my welcome. Meryl eventually got up to refill her drink, and I decided that I'd make my exit when she came back. To my surprise though, Meryl returned with the guitar in her hand.

"All right," she said, stopping in the doorway. "I'll play *one* song, but there's no way I'm doing any singing. You'll just have to use your imagination."

"Okay," I said, stunned that I'd convinced her to play at all.

Meryl settled on the couch, and after a check of the guitar's tuning, she set her fingers and began to play.

I recognized the song immediately, its familiar first chords climbing in steady succession as Meryl popped the woody sounds from the strings. At the top of this ascent, it glided for a bar, Meryl strumming with the soft tips of her fingers, merely preparing to climb again, spiraling lazily upward. I'd probably listened to the song a hundred times before, but it wasn't until Meryl's lyric-less performance that I heard how the chords followed the blackbird of its title, climbing and twisting in the air before falling back, level by level, to its beginning.

As Meryl played, I was able to watch her in an unhurried way, noticing things I might not have otherwise—the unadorned boyishness of her hands, the ever-so-slight protuberance of her upper lip. She didn't seem nervous until her one little fumble—the strings buzzed angrily as she missed a fingering and Meryl winced, flushing crimson. She recovered though, playing on without pause, eyes self-consciously fixed on the fretboard.

I found myself so moved by it all that by the time she'd finished, strumming away the song's final chord, it was all I could do to keep from getting up and hugging her. When she was done, Meryl slumped slightly and let out a sigh of relief.

"I'm still kind of learning it," she said, scrunching her nose in dissatisfaction.

"It sounded great to me. I've always loved that song."

"I'm surprised you could recognize it without the melody," she said, setting the guitar aside, and tucking a curve of chestnut hair behind her ear.

"Well, I played trombone in high school marching

band, and we *never* had the melody. Actually, it's too bad I left my trombone in Maine because I can still do a mean rendition of The Pointer Sisters' *I'm So Excited*."

"Oh yeah?" Meryl said, finally smiling again.

"Yeah, but of course it's only the bass line. And I have to do *this* the whole time…"

Springing up out of my chair, I marched across Meryl's living room, violently swinging an invisible trombone from side-to-side.

"I can also do *The Heat is On*," I said, "but again…"

"Not the melody?"

"I can demonstrate if you like?"

"Maybe another time."

11

Truth Hits Everybody

Saturday, December 18th was the big day, the day when the two most important women in my life would finally meet. Having overcome my worries that Bella would uncork some fatally embarrassing story, or that Corinne would freak out under the pressure, I was getting excited about introducing them to each other.

Corinne and I played tennis that afternoon, and for the first time in weeks, I actually won a few games. Corinne still beat me handily of course, but I walked away from the match pleased with my efforts.

"It was a little more competitive out there today," I observed in the car on the way back from the club.

"You thinking of joining the pro tour now?"

"I'd consider it. Although they do travel an awful lot."

"I find it remarkable that you're actually able to gloat over a loss. To a girl, no less."

It had only been two days since I'd gone to the holiday party with Corinne, but it felt longer somehow. As I drove along, basking in the glow of my defeat, I realized how much I'd missed her deadpan banter and wry half-smiles. Corinne hadn't asked what I'd done Friday night, so I'd decided not to mention my evening with Meryl. However, this seemed like an opportune moment to mention the other thing I'd done that day.

"So I called some places in Victoria to see if they had any vacancies for New Year's."

"Oh?"

"I didn't expect to find anything so late, but actually, a nice little hotel downtown had just had a cancellation for Friday and Saturday. So I booked it."

Corinne had been gazing out the window, but now she turned and looked at me.

"You booked it?" she said, not exactly angry, but not far from it.

"Well, yeah...just in case we decided to go. Otherwise we can just cancel."

Corinne nodded, shifting her gaze back out the car window.

"But if we *did* go," I continued, "there are two different ferries on Friday morning that would work…"

"Isn't Victoria where that Algerian terrorist was? That guy they just caught with the trunk full of explosives?"

"Well, yeah…but I think he was actually headed to Seattle to blow up the Space Needle or something. If you're worried about terrorists, it's probably way safer up there. I doubt anybody would bother blowing up Canada."

"I don't know…" she said eventually, "It just sounds kind of complicated for New Year's…taking Friday off from work, getting up there and back. The idea of going away just sounds overwhelming at this point."

"Right. Okay, well...I'll just cancel it then."

I'd been prepared for some resistance, but this swift defeat left me at a momentary loss. I was so stunned, in fact, that I didn't notice Corinne still simmering beside me. That is, until she spoke, snapping the silence.

"So are you going to sulk for the rest of the day now?"

"Hm? No—I mean, I'm not *sulking*...I'm just...disappointed."

"Well, I'm *sorry*, but I just don't feel like going away. I mean, is that okay? Do I get a say in this?"

Corinne was already so agitated that I was speechless. I felt like a backhoe operator who, with one wrong plunge of the shovel, hits a gas line and blows the roof somebody's house.

"Of course you have a say. Like I said, I'll just cancel the reservation—it's no big deal."

"I just feel like you're always *pushing* with this stuff. I *never* really expressed any interest in this trip, but you just kept bringing it up, and I end up feeling guilty for not wanting to go."

"Well, I just wanted to do something fun for New Year's...and I guess I figured that if I didn't suggest something, we probably wouldn't do anything."

"But we don't *always* have to do something, do we? I mean, I spend more time with you than I ever have with anybody, but you act all wounded if I want a night off."

"Again, I was just disappointed," I said, now becoming frustrated. "But I think you're blowing this *way* out of proportion. You really have to stop seeing everything I do as part of some evil plan to control your life. All I did was make a hotel reservation...it's not like I registered us for fucking *china*."

"No," Corinne admitted after a pause.

"I thought it sounded like fun, but if you don't want to go, that's totally fine. I'll just go some other time. Maybe I'll go up with Clay when he gets back."

"Well, I wasn't saying that I'd *never* want to go..."

"Okay, well...whatever. Let's just forget I even mentioned it, okay?"

We were both quiet for another minute, but the mood in the car was considerably less charged now, cooler air sweeping in behind the thunderstorm. Corinne was the one who eventually spoke.

"You said 'fucking'," she grinned, looking straight ahead.

"Yeah...I know."

"I don't think I've ever heard you use the f-word before."

"Well..."

"So maybe I'm a teensy bit on-edge about tonight," Corinne offered.

"Why?"

"Oh, it's just the new people thing. You know, I feel like I'm auditioning."

"You shouldn't worry—just be yourself and everything will be fine."

☙

My prediction held true for most of our evening with Bella and Joel. Bella had at one time considered law school, so over dinner at The Pink Door she peppered Corinne with questions about work, which Corinne seemed happy enough to answer. Listening to the women talk, I got the feeling that they appreciated each other's bluntness—neither was the type to mince words—and all in all, they got along better than I could've hoped.

"I'm so glad Garrett finally suggested we do this," Bella said as the waiter was clearing away our entrees.

"I suggested this? I seem to remember you threatening me."

"Oh, it wasn't a threat," Bella said, mostly to Corinne.

"I just explained that if he didn't introduce me to you soon, I was just going to come down sometime—probably without warning—and introduce myself. At that point, Garrett wisely suggested that we have dinner."

"And how is that different from a threat?" I asked.

"Well, call it what you like—I did what I had to do. I mean, you'd been talking about her nonstop for the last two months..."

"Well, that's not really—"

"And *then* when you told me that you'd turned down a chance to spend Christmas with your sister, I knew the situation was getting serious," Bella grinned. "You gave me no choice."

I'd been cringing since Bella's "talking nonstop" comment, and by the time she started in about Christmas, I was wishing that I had a MUTE button that would make *her* stop talking. I could only imagine the thoughts that must be filling Corinne's suspicious mind, and how long it would take me to undo the damage.

At this point, I was hesitant to even look in Corinne's direction, but I knew I had to say something, particularly since I'd never even mentioned Karen's invitation to Corinne.

"My sister wanted me to come to Arizona," I said, as off-handedly as possible. "But you know, she's always trying to get me to come wherever *she's* living at the moment—she's never visited Seattle since I've been here."

I forced myself to look up and meet Corinne's gaze, if only for a second. I'd expected hostility, but Corinne was just watching me with one of her indecipherable in-between expressions. She wasn't quite smiling, but her eyes projected a certain warmth...or was it just weariness? After a beat,

Corinne picked up my conversational thread so casually that it made one wonder if there had really been a pause at all.

"Oh, my father's always been the same way," she said. "He's always inviting me and my sister out to Florida, but he'd *never* come here to see us. I've started to wonder if there are warrants he's avoiding here."

Bella and Joel laughed, blissfully unaware of the mine-field we'd just skirted.

The conversation continued amiably through dessert—Corinne even asked Bella about her wedding plans—but I was just wondering when the other shoe would drop. I knew that Corinne couldn't ignore the implication in Bella's comment—that I'd stayed in Seattle for Christmas specifi-cally because of her. This was exactly the kind of relation-ship-pressure that Corinne hated most, which was exactly the reason I'd never mentioned Arizona to her in the first place. Recalling the fight we'd had on her birthday—*It just makes me wonder if you're a little too into this*—I had to re-gard Corinne's seeming indifference at dinner as an act put on for Bella and Joel's benefit. I would hear about it eventu-ally; it was just a question of when.

It had become a cold, windy night by the time we began the short walk from the restaurant back to my apartment. We made our way down First Ave, Bella and Joel walking just far enough ahead of us that we could only hear snippets of their conversation. Corinne was very quiet, and I thought maybe this was it—the reaction had finally come.

After a block of complete silence, I decided to take Corinne's hand, figuring that this would inspire a reac-tion. But instead of glaring at me or batting my hand away, Corinne just gave me a sleepy half-smile, as if I'd roused her from a dream. What's more, she actually moved closer to me, hooking her arm around mine as we walked.

I was mystified. This was unusually affectionate for Corinne, even on a good day. Could it be that she really wasn't mad? No, I decided, she's not letting me off the hook here—she's just waiting for Bella and Joel to leave. Once they're out of earshot, she'll let me have it.

But again, even after Bella and Joel headed home, the axe didn't fall. Corinne and I sat on the couch watching TV for a half-hour, and she didn't say a word. I waited breathlessly for her to start in on me. *So you talk about me nonstop?* But she just sat there, cozied warmly against me, her breaths so deep and regular that I thought she might be asleep. I just wished she would say something and get it over with.

When I couldn't stand the suspense any longer, I decided to kiss her. If Corinne was even slightly peeved, then a lingering let's-get-it-on type kiss would surely unleash the torrent of expletives she was obviously bottling up, right? *What is with you? I can't believe you... You're so... You're such a...* But once again, my plan failed—Corinne kissed back, with unusual ardor actually. A few minutes later, we were staggering back to the bedroom, joined at the mouth and pulling each other's clothes off as if one of us was going off to war the next day.

That's when I realized that Corinne wasn't going to flip out on me after all, that maybe we'd actually had some kind of breakthrough. Maybe something about our fight that afternoon, or even meeting Bella and Joel, had finally made her realize that there was nothing to fear here. Maybe this day had been exactly what we'd needed.

Later, as we lay silently in my darkened bedroom, I decided that I should just enjoy this moment—Corinne's skin smooth and warm against mine, the peachy scent of her hair—rather than trying to analyze or explain it.

"Thanks for going tonight."

"No problem," Corinne said softly, sounding as if she'd already started to drift.

"I'm glad you finally got to meet Bella."

"Yeah...she seems nice..."

A dozen breaths later, Corinne was asleep.

☙

Corinne awoke with a cold on Sunday, and between that and work, we didn't see each other for a few days. This made for some quiet times at the Retrograde, given that Kevin and Clay were still out of the country (and for reasons mysterious even to me, I wouldn't give myself permission to call Meryl). I stayed busy, working away on an online ticketing system for a club in Pioneer Square, but it almost felt like I was traveling again, minus the hotels and airports.

By Thursday afternoon though, I felt like I'd exhausted the benefits of quiet contemplation. I called Corinne at the office, and for the briefest of moments, my release from solitary seemed imminent: yes, she was feeling better, but no, she wasn't available.

"I'm actually meeting Maureen for dinner tonight," she said. "She and Robert are going to Aruba for Christmas, so I want to see her before she leaves. But we're still on for tomorrow, right? I'm cooking you Christmas Eve dinner?"

"Yeah...right."

"Why don't you give me a call around noontime, just to make sure I've gotten my ass out of bed?"

"I can do that."

Our conversation was over so quickly, I really didn't know what to make of it. Had Corinne just blown me off?

She'd been elusive all week, my calls going straight to voicemail, and I had wondered if there was more to it than her cold. In the end though, I wasn't certain I *wanted* to figure it out; I just knew that I wasn't going to spend yet another night alone.

∞

I invited Meryl down for pizza and Thursday-night TV, but we actually talked more than we watched, Meryl sitting cross-legged on my couch while I reclined in the La-Z-Boy. *Friends* was a rerun, but one that Meryl had never seen.

"Wow," Meryl said at one point, "it must be cold in that studio."

"Oh, Rachel? She's always like that."

"You'd think somebody would tell her."

"You would think. Although, I've started to wonder if it's intentional."

"Seriously?"

"Well, yeah, I mean, it's not like the show's *live*, right? If they didn't want us to see Rachel's nipples, we wouldn't see them. And yet there they are, week after week. I'd say her nipples make cameos in 37% of the episodes."

"And you can say this authoritatively because you've seen every single episode of *Friends* ever aired?"

"Well...yeah."

"Really? I was sort of joking."

I shrugged. "I was TV-deprived as a child. Maybe I'm still making up for lost time."

"Did your Mom ration your viewing?"

"No, she just refused to have a TV, no matter how much I begged. She said that I'd just waste all my time in front of it and, as always, she was right."

"So when did you get your first TV then?"

"About a year after Mom died, Dad just went out and bought himself one. No explanation or fanfare—we got home from school, and it was sitting in the living room."

"You must've been psyched."

"*I* was, but my sister wasn't. She tore into Dad, saying it was an insult to Mom's memory and all that. I think she actually scared him too—for a couple weeks, nobody went near the thing, and in the end, I was the only one who really ever watched."

"Your father never did?"

"Not really. I think he'd just been hoping to catch a Red Sox game now and then, but the reception was usually so lousy that he just gave up and went back to the radio."

"Did you ever think maybe he got the TV for you? Because you'd wanted one?"

"Well…"

I'm probably an idiot for never having put this together, but in my own defense, I was only twelve when it all happened. I honestly thought Dad had bought the TV for the Sox games. In fact, I'd always felt like I was getting away with something by watching it—he'd never given me permission, and I definitely had to sneak it when Karen wasn't around. But Meryl's suggestion made sense—it was just the kind of odd gesture Dad would make, seeing me struggling but feeling ill-equipped to help. And if Dad had bought the TV for himself, it would've disappeared after Karen's hissy-fit. For him, it wouldn't have been worth the abuse.

"I mean, obviously I don't *know*," Meryl added, when I didn't answer right away. "It was just a thought."

"No, you're probably right. He just never said anything…"

My last sentence hung in the air for what seemed like

forever before a Mountain Dew commercial came to my rescue, filling the space with its bombast. Meryl and I both watched as if interested.

"So how's Corinne?" Meryl asked a little later.

"Oh, she's good. She's out with her friend Maureen tonight."

"What did you get her for Christmas?"

"Do you want to see?"

"Sure."

Hustling off to my bedroom, I dug the little box out of my sock drawer and brought it back to Meryl.

"Wow," she whispered as she opened the box. "They're beautiful."

I'd searched long and hard for a gift that would satisfy my desire to give Corinne something meaningful without sending her into a claustrophobic conniption because it was too expensive. These freshwater pearls, which I'd stumbled upon at a cramped little jewelry store on Pike Street, seemed like otherworldly pebbles, each of them uniquely oblong and touched with a golden iridescence. Strung together—three narrow strands with a simple clasp—something about them seemed to echo Corinne's own idiosyncratic beauty.

"She's going to love that," Meryl said. "You did good."

"Thanks."

"That's one thing I definitely miss about being in a relationship—exchanging gifts with someone at Christmas."

"Yeah?"

"Yeah, there's just something different about it when you spend so much time with somebody, and you know them so well that you're the best person in the world to choose a gift for them. Maybe that sounds goofy, but...Wade and I we were really in sync like that for a while. I think that was probably the happiest I've ever been…having someone know what you're thinking without even having to say it. Your lives just sort of start to flow together, you know?"

I considered telling Meryl the truth: that in many ways, Corinne was just as elusive and unknown to me as she had been before we'd started dating. That I felt like she'd been dodging me all week, and I didn't know why. But at that moment, the truth seemed like such a downer that even *I* didn't want to hear it.

"Yeah, definitely," I said.

"I think that's one reason I was so hesitant to start dating again after Wade. I just couldn't bear the thought of starting over and going through all that getting-to-know-you stuff with someone else…investing myself in another relationship that might not go anywhere."

We stuck to lighter topics for the rest of the evening: Hydrox vs. Nabisco and Double Stuf vs. Single Stuf; the "we" on Meryl's answering machine, added to appease her mother, who'd never stopped worrying about Meryl living alone in the big city; and the clashing cast of characters on Meryl's current project, and her recurring dream of locking them all in a room, flipping off the lights, and running away.

The later it got, the more I found myself wishing that Meryl didn't have to go home, that we could just keep talking until we couldn't hold our eyes open any longer. But when *ER* ended at eleven, Meryl stood up from the couch and stretched.

"Well…thanks for inviting me over," she said, drifting toward the door. "And if I don't see you, have a great Christmas."

"Yeah, you too," I said, trailing after her. "Do you want

to take any of the pizza?"

"Oh...no, that's okay. I'm heading to Snohomish to-morrow, so..."

"Okay."

For a long moment, Meryl and I stood by the door, star-ing down at our shoes. I can't say what was going through Meryl's mind, but I was trying to think of something to detain her there, even just a few minutes longer.

"All right," Meryl finally said, pulling the door open de-cisively. "I'll see you later?"

"Okay."

"All right. Have a good night."

With that, she slipped off down the hall. I clicked the door closed behind Meryl, but lingered there, listening to her footsteps softening into the distance.

Slouching back to the living room, I beached myself on the couch where Meryl had been sitting all night. The eleven o'clock news was on—live footage of a house-fire on Capitol Hill—but I muted it, still hearing Meryl's voice from ear-lier in the evening. *having someone know exactly what you're thinking* I wondered if Corinne was home yet, and if I'd even crossed her mind all night. *Your lives just sort of start to flow together.*

જી

I was still in that same position on the couch when, twenty minutes later, I again heard footsteps in the hall. I didn't pay much attention to them until they stopped out-side my door, followed by three quick knocks.

As soon as I saw Meryl, I knew something was wrong.

"Hey Garrett," she said, her voice unsteady. "Do you think you could give me a jump-start? My car seems to be dead...I must've left the stupid dome light on or something."

"Sure, but…what's wrong?"

"Well…my brother called earlier…he left a message. Apparently my father had a heart attack, and they took him to the hospital in Everett."

"Oh…"

"I tried calling home but there was no answer, and when I called the hospital, they said they didn't know if he'd arrived yet. And then my fucking car wouldn't start, so I don't know if he's alive or…"

"I'll drive you," I said, snatching my keys off their hook.

"No, you don't have to…if we can just—"

"Really, it'll be faster. Come on."

The Jetta, as if to declare its readiness, started with a roar. For most of the drive, Meryl stared straight ahead, her blind eyes fixed on the road ahead of us. Occasionally, she'd just start talking, mid-thought.

"He's never had a single problem with his heart before…"

"Do you want to try the hospital again? I have my cell…"

"No, I just want to get there. I just wish Mark had left more information. I mean, was he *conscious*, or…"

Meryl suddenly turned to face out the side window. She barely made a sound, but I sensed the quivering change in her breathing. When she turned back, her face was damp, her eyes shining in the oncoming headlights.

☙

February 5, 1981. I hadn't even gone to the hospital after my mother's accident. Elena Anderson had been dead for almost two hours by the time my grandmother had come to take me out of school. When my sister finally explained it all to me, I realized that I'd been playing dodge ball at the moment of my mother's death. This revelation had destroyed me, the knowledge that I'd been playing this foolish game, so blithely unaware. Shouldn't I have sensed it somehow? As Meryl and I drove up I-5 toward Everett, I wondered if she was now having similar thoughts about our evening together.

I went to the funeral home for Mom's wake, a place of such permeating ickyness that even the carpets and chair-cushions seemed embalmed. I refused to enter the room though, afraid of what she might look like, afraid that I'd never be able to unremember that image of her. I sat on a wooden bench out in the hall, listening to the murmuring and intermittent sobs. People came out and tried to coax me inside. They assured me that my mother just looked like she was sleeping, but I didn't buy it.

More than anything, I remember the weather the day it happened. Grey and bitingly cold, it had started snowing early—maybe nine o'clock that morning. The week before, we'd had back-to-back Nor'easters, twin blizzards drop-ping so much snow on Portland that it was piled up ev-erywhere—on roofs, on sidewalks, on cars—and there was just nowhere to put any more. On top of all that, the new snow seemed insignificant, just a fresh coat to whiten every-thing up. I'd been distracted all day at school, watching the snow fall out the window and itching to get home and work on the igloo I'd begun to carve into the snow-mounds that edged our driveway.

In later years, it was always the weather that brought me back to that day. Whenever the snow started to pile up, the world closing in, I'd feel that same tightening in my chest. I didn't always realize why immediately. It didn't matter if it was even February—it was just that kind of day that would do it, the kind of day that we never have in Seattle. Or in

Jerome, Arizona.

享

When Meryl and I finally arrived, the Everett ER seemed half-closed—one scruffy guy dozed in the waiting area, while a janitor shepherded a wobbling floor-polisher across the tiles. Given the urgency of our trip, the quiet was unnerving. Meryl stood in silence, her arms crossed tightly, as the receptionist keyed Mr. Larson's name into the computer.

"He went straight upstairs," the woman finally pronounced. "West Elevator to the third floor, follow the signs to Cardiology."

"Can you tell me anything about his condition?"

"I don't have that information, ma'am. The nurse at the desk will give you an update."

Meryl and I flew upstairs only to find the Cardiology desk deserted. As the quiet seconds ticked by, Meryl's composure began to crumble, tears running freely down her cheeks.

"Where *is* everybody?"

A nurse appeared at the far end of the corridor, and I started down the hall toward her.

"Excuse me, can you help us? They told us downstairs that Carl Larson had been brought up here?"

"What was the name again?"

Before I had a chance to repeat it, there was another voice. I turned to see that a fortyish guy with a salt-and-pepper beard had come around the corner behind us.

"Meryl, over here."

"Mark...where is he? Is he okay?"

"He's down the hall. They just brought him back from the angioplasty."

"Is he okay?"

"They're saying he should be fine. He's tired, but..."

"But he's going to be okay? He's not going to die?"

"He'll be fine, Meryl," Mark smiled. "He's not going anywhere."

That was it for Meryl. She crumpled against her brother, sobbing with relief. Everything that she'd been struggling to hold in came out now. Mark practically had to hold her up, to keep her from falling right onto the floor.

"Hey...it's okay. He's fine."

I really didn't want to cry in front of Meryl and her brother, but the longer I stood there watching Meryl weeping into her brother's chest, the more I felt it rising within me. Just when I thought I couldn't hold it off any longer, Mark glanced up at me and smiled with utter casualness, as if meeting me at a party.

"Hey, I'm Mark," he said quietly, reaching his hand around Meryl's small, shuddering form.

"Garrett," was all I managed to say.

"Where is he?" Meryl sniffled, smudging tears from each cheek. "I want to see him."

"Down this way," Mark said.

I trailed Meryl and her brother down the hall, but when Mark pushed open the door of Mr. Larson's room, I knew I couldn't go inside. Instead, I ducked into the men's room across the hall and closed myself into a stall.

I was just so glad that he was alive, this man I'd never met, and yet all I felt was a knife in my chest. It was a familiar feeling, this overwhelming, unreasoned sorrow. Suddenly, I was 11 again, limp in my grandmother's arms. I couldn't even say why I was crying—because he was okay, or because he might've died? Because someday he *would* die, because someday we would *all* die? I might've been crying for my mother, gone almost twenty years but perpetually on my mind, or even for my father, who I finally realized had lost even more than I had.

I don't know how long I was in there. When I was in the throes of it, I heard someone come in and then go back out. And then later, when it had mostly passed and I was just sitting with my head slumped against the stall, I heard the door creak open again.

"Garrett? Are you in here?" Meryl called.

"Yeah. Out in a sec."

"Okay. Take your time."

Meryl was waiting in the hall for me. I knew I looked bad, but before I could utter a word of explanation, Meryl hugged me. I was surprised that there was so much strength in her small form. Even more, I was surprised at how much I'd needed it. We stayed like that for a while, the two of us holding onto each other in the empty hallway, rocking gently.

"How's your Dad?" I asked.

"He asked me to get him a cheeseburger."

We both laughed.

"How about you?" she asked. "Are you okay?"

"I'm fine. I'm just relieved."

"I think I'm going to stay here tonight," she said eventually. "Will you be okay driving back alone?"

"Yeah, I'll be fine."

"You're sure?"

"Totally. Don't worry about it."

"Thanks for the ride."

"Anytime."

☙

On the drive back to Seattle, my thoughts swirled from Meryl to my mother and then to Corinne, who seemed to have been fading into the distance since Sunday. *I'm probably just expecting too much*, I told myself. *We've only been together for eleven weeks.* But I also had the sense that time wasn't the real issue here. *Your lives just sort of start to flow together.* That Corinne and I could be together for eleven years and I might still feel just as alone as I did now.

I decided that I needed to talk to Corinne, to tell her how I really felt: that none of us could say how long we'd be here, that life was too short for this kind of distance. I was still convinced that, deep down, Corinne really wanted to let me in…I just wasn't sure she'd want to do it at 2:00 a.m.

But I dug out my cell and dialed Corinne's number anyway, knowing I'd lose my nerve by morning. She answered, her voice quiet and unsurprised, as if she'd been waiting for my call.

"Hello?"

"Hey, it's me. Can I come over?"

"Sure."

"I'll be there in fifteen minutes."

At the time, I interpreted Corinne's willingness to see me as a sign that I was doing the right thing. She answered the door in her bathrobe.

"Sorry about the hour," I said.

"Oh, I was up anyway," she shrugged.

We settled in the living room, dawdling in small-talk about Corinne's evening with Maureen while I tried to muster the courage to say what I'd come to say. I'd imagined that it would be effortless, that the right words would just come flowing out. But faced with her now, I was scared, and I didn't know how to begin.

Finally there was a pause, and I knew it was time. Corinne was watching me with such warmth that I'd lost my desire to confront her, wishing I could just linger in the bathwater of her gaze, but I also knew that she was waiting for me to explain this visit. And so, with my eyes on the floor, I began.

"So...you remember Meryl, from my building?"

"Mm."

"Well, her father had a heart attack tonight. That's actually where I'm coming from now...I drove her to the hospital up in Everett."

"Oh. Is he okay, or...?"

"Apparently he's going to be fine, but we really weren't sure for a while. And it just got me thinking about how none of us know how long we're going to be here..."

"Mm."

"I mean, I've never expected my life to be perfect, but I also don't want to end up thinking that it might've been better if only I'd done something differently. And right now, I feel like this—you and me—is one of those situations where I could do better."

Corinne had been listening quietly, looking down at her folded hands, but now she looked up at me as if this was the first thing that had surprised her all night.

"Why would you think that?"

"Because I haven't been honest with you. I've hidden my feelings because I was afraid of scaring you off. But I don't want to do that anymore...I *can't* do it anymore. I can't expect you to open yourself up to me if I'm not doing it myself."

Corinne just nodded, looking down at her hands again.

"I really like you," I said, "and I think this could really

be something if we gave it a chance, but there's this distance between us. And I know I'm probably freaking you out right now, but...I think, at some point, you have to let *somebody* in, you know? And I'm really not a bad guy."

"I know," she murmured, still not looking at me.

"But right now, I'm never sure where we stand. Sometimes it seems like I'm your best friend, and other times it seems like I hardly know you. And I'm not saying that we need to be together every minute of every day...I just need to know that I'm not alone. But most of the time, even sometimes when we're together, I still feel like I am."

Corinne nodded, eyes still lowered.

"So...what would you say you want, exactly?" she asked.

"I'd just like to be part of your life. We're so separate right now—you have *your* place and *your* stuff and *your* time, and I have mine. We go out on dates, and then we go our separate ways, and we don't really share anything. I'm not talking about moving in together or anything...I'd just like our lives to start flowing together a little more."

Corinne nodded.

"I mean, I know I'm being really impatient here, so I'm not asking for it to happen all at once...but I would like to feel like we're headed in that direction."

Corinne nodded, preparing to say something. When she did finally speak, her voice was halting, unsteady in a way that it had never been.

"I know...I mean, I *knew* that that's what you wanted. And, over the past few days, I guess I've been trying to figure out if I could give you that. Which is amazing to me, because at one time, I wouldn't have even considered it. And that's actually why I wanted to talk to Maureen tonight. It's been on my mind so much, especially since Saturday.

Meeting your friends, I knew...I knew I couldn't just keep ignoring it."

"Oh."

"I know *you're* ready for this stuff," she continued, "but I'm still not sure if that's even what I want. I mean, I just don't know *what* I want."

"From me?"

"From my life. I mean, I know you want to get married someday—"

"Well..."

"That's okay, Garrett. I'm not saying that's a bad thing, but I just don't know if I could do that...ever."

"Really?"

"It's really hard for me to imagine. Honestly, I don't know if I'd ever want someone else around all the time. I mean, I really like having my own space...my own place."

"So it's not just marriage then...you wouldn't even want to live with somebody?"

"Probably not...but I can't really say right now. And I don't know if it's fair to either of us to keep you waiting while I figure it out. I mean, I worry that being with you might actually keep me from figuring it out."

Even so delicately couched in I-don't-knows, Corinne's words chilled me. I'd arrived thinking that I was the one with something to say, but that impression was changing.

"Why would I keep you from figuring it out?"

"Because I like you, Garrett, and I want you to be happy. And I think there's a chance that, in the end, I might try to give you what you want, even if I wasn't sure it was the right thing...for me, for both of us. And I think there's really a good chance that I'd just screw it up."

"So you'd rather be alone than risk screwing up?"

"No. Well…it's not my life I'm worried about—I don't want to screw up *yours*. I can't accept that responsibility."

"But I'm responsible for my own life; I'm the only one who can screw it up."

Corinne shook her head. "I'm not so sure about that," she said. "I mean, if I said, 'Let's get married, right now. Let's fly to Vegas and get married.' What would you say?"

"Well, I don't know. I guess—"

"Oh come on, Garrett. You *know* you'd be calling the airline before I even got the words out. And that's not because I'm such a catch—that's just who you are, where you're at right now. And in some ways that's great…really. But you're *so* ready for a serious relationship, you're actually kind of dangerous right now. And I can't bear the thought that, with one bad decision, I might waste a year, or even five years of your life."

For a while, I argued weakly that I wasn't talking about marriage, blah blah blah. Corinne listened, but even I knew that I wasn't making much sense. I was just bewildered by where we'd ended up, and that I'd somehow led us here.

Corinne had seen, perhaps from the very beginning, what I wouldn't fully admit to myself. She knew that, no matter what I might say, I would be forever holding out for her to come around. I always believed that she'd eventually give in, that she'd see that the thing I wanted—a serious, intimate relationship—was only right and natural. I'd decided that her fears were merely a side-effect of past relationship trauma, something that she could—and *should*—get over. But in truth, maybe I was the one who had something to get over.

I felt like I'd gotten nowhere. I felt like a child.

12

The Sound of
One Hand Clapping

Before I left that night, Corinne tried to convince me that I should still come over for Christmas Eve dinner. As mature and considerate as her offer might've been, I was pretty sure I'd rather set myself on fire than spend the holiday with the latest person to dump me (though I phrased it more gently for Corinne).

The one thing I did want to do on Christmas Eve was call my father. I'd talked to him on Thanksgiving, but our conversation had been so perfunctory and unremarkable that I could hardly remember what we'd discussed. And really, it seemed like most of our exchanges were like that—brief, bi-monthly check-ins in which neither of us said anything of consequence. For years, I'd been okay with this, even grateful for the simplicity of it. But after one night in the Everett ER, it just seemed sad. Maybe even tragic.

Dad answered, his voice muffled by the way he always held the phone, with the mouthpiece angled back toward his neck. And from that first clipped "hello," I could see him in our kitchen, a bear of a man in a stained t-shirt and jeans, tethered uneasily to the rotary phone he would never bother to replace.

"Hey Dad—it's Garrett."

"Hey boss."

"I just wanted to call and wish you guys a Merry Christmas."

"Merry Christmas. Your sister just called too."

"Oh yeah?"

"She said you had a hot date tonight," he said, a tiny smile curling into his words.

"Oh, right. Yeah, I guess I mentioned that to her."

"How's the car running?"

"Oh, it's fine I guess. It's running."

"Did you get that exhaust squared away?" Dad asked, jogging my memory of what we'd discussed on Thanksgiving.

"No, I haven't had a chance yet."

"They can ticket you if it's too loud."

"Right. Well, maybe next week…things are looking a little less crazy then."

"Good."

I should've figured out exactly what I wanted to say before calling Dad. My messy and amorphous hospital-night emotions were simply no match for Dad's ability to redirect all conversations toward automotive maintenance. Plus, I knew the clock was running—never a fan of the telephone, Dad would only talk for so long, at which point he'd either wrap things up or, if he sensed you really weren't finished, he'd hand you off to Sheila so you could tell her whatever was so important.

"Actually, it's a good thing my car is running," I said. "I had to drive a friend to the hospital last night. Her father had a heart attack, and her car wouldn't start."

"Dead battery?"

"Uh, probably…I guess."

"You've got jumper cables though," Dad said, more statement than question.

"Yeah, we just didn't have time to mess with it. Thankfully, it seems like her father's going to be okay though."

"Good. Good."

That second "good" was a clear sign that I was losing him. He was preparing to wrap things up, that is, unless I could find a way to reengage him.

"Hey, I've been wondering...do you remember that very first TV we got?"

"The Zenith," he said, another question without a question mark.

"Yeah, the Zenith. Do you still have it?"

"It's out in the garage."

"Does it still work?"

"Sure it does. Sometimes I put it on when I'm out there."

"Any luck getting the Sox on it?"

"Well, we've got cable now, so..."

"Oh, right. Well, that's good."

"Yeah."

"I always loved that TV," I added, in a truly bizarre and desperate attempt at expressing my gratitude for something that Dad may or may not have done for me almost 20 years before.

"You want it or something?"

"No...I've got one here."

"Oh."

"I was just thinking, maybe the next time I come out, maybe we could watch a Sox game. Like, together. Or even go to one."

"Sure."

"Great. That'd be fun."

And then after a pause, Dad added, only half-joking, "You know they don't play in the winter though, right boss?"

"Yeah, Dad…I know."

&

I passed Christmas Day on the couch, sliding through a stack of DVDs and replaying my last conversation with Corinne. *You're actually kind of dangerous right now.* I knew she was right, but I also felt powerless to do anything about it.

The phone rang a few times, but I never budged to answer it. By Sunday, I was at least checking the Caller ID before letting the machine pick up. The only call I even considered answering was from *Larson Carl, Snohomish WA.* I hovered over the answering machine while Meryl left her message.

Hi Garrett, it's Meryl. I just wanted to let you know that we brought Dad home today and he's doing well. I'm going stay here in Snohomish tonight, but I'll stop by when I get back to Seattle. Thanks again for the other night. I hope you had a good Christmas and that Corinne liked her gift. Okay, bye.

Maybe I was just hitting a blood-sugar low, but standing there, listening to Meryl's voice being recorded, I felt a little out-of-body. Even as it was happening, it already seemed to be in the past. Was Meryl really on the other end of the phone, or was I just listening to a recording from days ago?

&

I was still on the couch when Meryl knocked on Monday night. Being the first interactive, three-dimensional human that I'd confronted in a few days, it was a little overwhelming seeing her.

"Hey Garrett!" she said, her cheerfulness almost blinding.

"Hey."

"How are you? Are you busy?"

"No, not at all," I said, realizing that I'd come to the door wearing the white tennis shorts I'd bought for Corinne's club. "Sorry...come on in."

Meryl followed me back toward the living room, where I reassumed my horizontal position on the couch. Meryl leaned in the doorway, arms crossed casually in front of her.

"So how's your Dad doing?" I asked.

"He's doing well," Meryl smiled. "A little grumpy, but... everybody's pretty relieved."

"That's great."

"So how've you been?" she asked. "What've you been doing?"

"Oh...you know, just hanging out."

"How was your Christmas?"

"Quiet."

"Did you not shave today?" Meryl asked, squinting down at me in amusement.

"Oh, yeah...I guess I forgot."

Meryl nodded, accepting this explanation. In truth, I hadn't shaved since Thursday—my facial hair is just so blonde and pre-adolescent patchy, it's barely visible for the first week.

"Did Corinne like her necklace?"

"Uh, well...I never got a chance to give it to her. Actually, we broke up."

"You *broke up*?"

"Yeah, we broke up."

"When did this happen?"

Meryl didn't alter her arms-crossed posture in the door-way, but her shoulders stiffened and her cheerful expression was replaced by what I would describe as a look of nausea. She glanced around the room, as if scanning for clues she'd missed.

"It was Thursday night. Although, I guess it was techni-cally Friday morning by then, but..."

"Thursday night? You mean after you left Everett?"

"Yeah, I stopped at Corinne's on the way home."

"But what happened?"

"Well, honestly, things hadn't been great between us. I mean, they weren't horrible, but...I'd kind of gotten the feel-ing she'd been avoiding me all week. So on the way home that night, I was thinking about a lot of stuff—life and death, my parents, some of that stuff you'd said about rela-tionships—and I decided I should confront Corinne, you know, get it all out in the open. So I got myself all fired-up to do the whole making-my-stand gesture, but it just didn't go the way I'd planned. Basically, I discovered that I'd de-luded myself, once again, into thinking that there was really something there when there wasn't."

"What did I say exactly?" Meryl asked uneasily. "You said that you were thinking about something that I said about relationships...?"

"Oh, well...you were just talking about how great it was when your lives started to flow together and all that, and I was just thinking how I've been wanting that for so long, but that Corinne and I just didn't seem to be getting there. I thought I should talk to her about it."

Meryl nodded, looking down at the floor.

"It had been building for a while though," I said. "We

were always looking for different things...I was just in denial about it. It's probably good that it didn't drag on any longer."

Meryl chewed her lip, her eyes lowered and dark. Then suddenly she looked up at me again.

"So where did you go for Christmas?"

"I just hung out here. I know it sounds depressing, but it was fine. I actually could've visited some friends up in Bellingham, but I just wasn't in the mood."

"Is Clay back yet?"

"He comes back January 2nd."

"How about your partner there...Kevin?"

"I think he might've gotten back from his honeymoon over the weekend, but I haven't talked to him yet."

"Have you talked to *anyone*?"

"No, but I really haven't felt like it. Would you like some Honey Nut Cheerios? I was thinking of having some."

"All right," Meryl finally said, waving me off the couch. "Come upstairs with me."

"Okay. Why?"

"I was just about to make myself some dinner—you can help."

I didn't really want to go anywhere, but Meryl was insistent and I lacked the resolve to resist. She put me to work slicing vegetables for a salad while she boiled water for pasta and heated some sauce from the freezer. I hadn't felt hungry when we started, but once the food was there under my nose, I realized that I was.

While we were eating, Meryl explained how her father had ended up at the hospital that night. It had begun when Mr. Larson and Meryl's brother Mark came back from getting a Christmas tree.

"I guess they were taking the tree down off the car when my brother noticed that Dad was just *running* with sweat. Mark asked him if he was feeling okay, and Dad was like, 'I'm fine...just a little light-headed. And I seem to be having some chest-pain.'"

"Just a little chest-pain."

"Yeah, right. Dad kept insisting it was indigestion, but Mom just called 911. And I guess Dad didn't even want to see the paramedics at first, but when he finally let them check him over they said, 'Sir, you're having a heart attack. You need to come with us *now*.' And at that point, I guess he finally believed it."

"Wow."

"We're really going to have to watch him though. Two hours after we brought him home on Sunday, I caught him trying to haul that stupid Christmas tree into the house by himself."

"The day after Christmas?"

"Exactly—who cares about the damn tree! But he's a stubborn guy...we actually ended up putting the tree up anyway."

"I could help you install some webcams so you can keep tabs on him from Japan."

"That would be perfect! Though I'd also need some kind of intercom system so I could just break in and say, *Dad, put the firewood down and back away!* Or even better: *Dad, that is the most unflattering pair of chinos I've ever seen.*"

"I'm sure we could arrange that."

"There are just so many things I'd like to say to him...if I were in another country, and he couldn't talk back."

As Meryl and I were laughing about this, I realized that it had been days since I'd smiled. During my Christmas couch-coma, I'd watched a half-dozen comedies without even cracking a grin. *Maybe this is what I need*, I thought. *Screw relationships—I just need more friends.*

 es

Meryl dropped by every night that week after work, sometimes staying for an hour, sometimes staying longer. I sensed that she was keeping an eye on me, making sure that I didn't slip back into my self-pitying couchatonia. I wasn't feeling quite as despondent as I had in the days after the breakup—mostly, I was just numb—but I still wasn't feeling particularly talkative either. At least once every day, I resolved to call Bella and tell her what had happened with Corinne, but I always found some new way to avoid it.

On Thursday afternoon, Meryl called me from her office and asked if I'd go computer shopping with her that night—she wanted to get her parents using e-mail so it would be easier to keep in touch when she went back to Japan. She came directly from work, still dressed for the office in a coffee-brown pantsuit and chunky-heeled ankle-boots. I'd become so accustomed to seeing her in sweaters and rumpled khakis that this OfficeWear seemed like a costume, like she was playing a "businessperson" in a TV commercial.

"So you don't wear the red sneakers to the office?" I asked.

"I wish," Meryl sighed, dropping herself onto my couch and sinking into her suit-jacket.

"You okay? You look a little...fried."

"Oh, I'm fine. I just spent the afternoon refereeing a spat between two of the morons on my project team. That's definitely my least favorite part of this new position, managing these other personalities, trying to keep everything moving without damaging anyone's ego. I swear, they're like children, but children playing with millions of dollars of someone else's money."

"We can do the computer thing another night if you want," I suggested. "It's not like I've got a busy schedule."

"No, I still want to go—I just need a moment to collect myself."

We took Meryl's car (with its new battery) to Compu-Haus in Bellevue. Out on the road, I realized that, aside from a two-block walk to the video store, this was my first time out of the Retrograde since Christmas Eve. I wondered momentarily if Meryl had planned it that way, if this trip was just part of her plan to keep me occupied.

"So what did you do today?" she asked at one point.

"Mostly I worked. And I napped on and off."

"You mean you fell asleep with the computer on your lap?"

"Pretty much."

"Have you heard from Corinne at all?"

"No, and honestly, I don't expect to. I mean, we didn't really leave anything unsettled...we're just in very different places, and now we know it."

"Well...whenever you're feeling up to it, there are plenty of single women at HRK that I can introduce you to."

I'd certainly never forgotten Meryl's Declaration of Not-Dating, but there was still something depressing about her offering to set me up with other women. Not that I wanted to date *anyone* at that moment, but did she have to make her lack of interest so obvious?

"Oh, well...I'm actually thinking of jumping on that 'not-dating' bandwagon of yours. Is there any paperwork I need to fill out to join officially?"

Meryl smiled without looking over at me. It was hard to

tell if she was amused or embarrassed.

"No," she said finally. "There's no paperwork."

❧

I finally heard from Kevin on New Year's Eve. Back from their honeymoon in Bali, he and Ingrid wanted me and Corinne to go out with them that night. Perhaps because of his own back-and-forth history with Ingrid, Kevin didn't take the news of our breakup too seriously.

"Hang in there, Spanky—she'll come to her senses soon enough."

"Honestly, I don't think she ever lost her senses—that was just me."

"All the more reason you should come out with us tonight then. You sound like you could use a few drinks."

"That's okay—I think I'm just going to take it easy."

"Okay, well...if you finish wallowing before midnight, call me on my cell. Otherwise, I'll talk to you on Monday."

I spent Friday channel-surfing through the rest of the world's Millennium festivities. It's embarrassing to admit that, beyond loading software patches for clients, this was the first time I'd given the larger Y2K computer issue much serious thought. People had often asked me what I thought would happen at midnight on the 31st, and I'd always laughed and told them not to worry, that the problem had become totally overblown in the public's imagination.

But really, what the hell did I know about power grids and nuclear reactors and air traffic control systems? I built cutesy web apps for a living. And thinking about the Y2K consultants I'd known at Cavanaugh did nothing to increase my confidence: I'd once watched Walter Rubens back his green Geo Metro right over a small traffic island, completely beaching the little car, its tiny donut-wheels spinning ineffectually in the air.

So as I watched Australia's transfixing celebrations—some kind of firelit aboriginal dancing with stilts—I started to think that maybe all hell *would* break loose at midnight. Maybe the country's infrastructure would fail, and the financial systems would go haywire. *Whatever,* I thought. *Bring it on.*

Meryl's company was hosting a Millennium Extravaganza at one of the hotels downtown that night. On her way out, she tried to convince me to go with her, but I played the immovable object.

"It might actually be fun," she said. "They've got an 18-piece jazz band, and open bar all night. We wouldn't even have to stay for the whole thing—we can just take off if you aren't having a good time."

"I appreciate the offer, but trust me, I'd be absolutely no fun."

"Okay. Well, if you change your mind, it's at the Roosevelt."

When I was finally alone, I had to chuckle at the fact that, after pressing Corinne so hard to make New Year's plans, I'd ended up fighting to spend the night by myself.

Deciding that I'd had enough culture, I switched over to MTV and watched No Doubt celebrate midnight on the East Coast by covering REM's "It's The End of the World As We Know It (And I Feel Fine)." The fact that Gwen Stefani sang the whole song wearing braces on her teeth suggested to me that, despite the lyrics, she was hedging her bets.

Around 10:30, I was starting to doze off on the couch when there were three quick knocks on my door. It was Meryl, her hair flattened and damp, with a devious grin on her face.

"What're you doing back so early?"

"Well, you can only have *so* much fun in one night, so...I decided to come back here. But I didn't return empty-handed," she said, producing a fat-bottomed bottle of champagne from behind her back. "I stole it on my way out of the party."

"Seriously?"

"No, they actually gave it to me. But only because I said I had to get home to check on my sick father."

"He'd be so proud," I said, heading back to the living room. "Come on in."

"Where would I find clean glasses?" Meryl said, taking the champagne to the kitchen.

"Mm...I might only have mugs right now. I keep forgetting to start the dishwasher."

"Well, mugs it is then. Unless you think we should wait until midnight to open the champagne?"

"Nah—if the world ends, it would just go to waste."

"Good thinking."

When she emerged from the kitchen, Meryl plopped herself down beside me on the couch and poured us each a brimming mug of champagne.

"Cheers," she said, thunking her mug heavily against mine.

"Cheers."

I know very little about champagne, but it was obvious from the first taste that this was special, otherworldly stuff. Delicately fizzy and fruity, it seemed to evaporate from your tongue, leaving your mouth both sweetened and perfectly refreshed. Each sip was like a full day at some kind of magical mouth-spa. I felt my mood lifting almost immediately.

"Not bad, huh?" Meryl said, as I was draining my first

mugful.

"It's…delightful," I said.

"*Delightful?*" Meryl giggled.

"I'm sorry, but that's just the only way to describe it. I'm absolutely *delighted* to be drinking this."

"I heard someone at the party say it's like, $200 a bottle," Meryl said.

"Well…clearly, it's worth every penny. You want another mug?"

"Definitely."

As we were finishing the bottle, Meryl and I watched the sad remains of Seattle's millennial celebrations on TV. The rest of the world's cities were having their most spectacular events ever, but our mayor, amid fears of explosive-toting Algerian terrorists and WTO-like civil unrest, had canceled Seattle's planned festivities and cordoned-off Seattle Center. All that remained were five minutes of fireworks launched from the Space Needle.

"Wouldn't it be funny," I wondered aloud, "if after canceling everything and bringing in all this security, the fireworks guys accidentally blew up the Space Needle?"

"At this point, it wouldn't surprise me," Meryl giggled.

"You know, we could probably see these fireworks for real if we went up on the roof."

"It's cold out," Meryl said, scrunching her nose. "And kind of drizzling."

When the big moment finally arrived, the end of the 20th century, Meryl and I were still slumped beside each other on the couch. A few seconds into the New Year, Meryl raised one hand and held it in the air, palm facing me. I gave her a puzzled look.

"High-five," she said. "The world didn't end."

ↅↄ

On New Year's Day, I finally called Bella to update her on everything that had happened over the last week. She was as sympathetic as ever, but also true to form, she recovered quickly. By the end of the conversation it was as if Corinne had never existed.

"So, it sounds like you've been spending a lot of time with this Meryl woman. Anything going on there?"

"No...we're really just friends."

"You said she was there with you last night though?"

"Yeah. We split a bottle of champagne and high-fived at midnight."

"And I presume you're not using 'high five' as a euphemism..."

"Not at all. Actually, the other day, she offered to set me up with one of her co-workers."

"Are you going to take her up on it?"

"No...I really think I need a break from the whole dating thing. Corinne was right—I'm a menace."

"I think you're probably overreacting there, but..."

"Well, in any case, I'm not even vaguely interested in dating right now, and I don't think I will be for quite a while."

Bella just laughed.

13

The Flood

In January, Clay returned, glowing from his trip. After all of the recent upheaval in my life, I was happy to have both of my guy-friends back: Kevin, by his very nature, curbed my tendency toward taking myself too seriously, while Clay's even, rational presence seemed to keep my most hysterical inclinations in check.

Clay, Meryl, and I also started spending a lot of time together. None of it was earth-shattering stuff—eating together, going to movies, and even grocery shopping together—but for the first time in ages, I felt peaceful... satisfied... even happy. I also felt more plugged-in than I had in a while, confident that if I slipped in the shower and died, someone would notice before I started to stink.

With Clay often ice-climbing on the weekends, Meryl and I also spent some time alone. Our relationship was hard to categorize—we were still getting to know each other, but we also enjoyed an unusual closeness that, without our awful trip to Everett Medical Center, would've taken much longer to develop. Despite this connection though, Meryl and I rarely made physical contact, always maintaining a six-inch buffer if we shared the couch, and carefully stepping around each other if we passed in my narrow kitchen.

It was almost as if, after our hug at the hospital, we were both wary of every little collision.

I'd be lying if I said that I wasn't attracted to Meryl—I always had been, and sometimes I even imagined that she also harbored some small attraction to me. But I was finally beginning to understand that I didn't need to act on this attraction just because it was there. In fact, *not* acting on it—just letting it crackle between us—could be enjoyable in itself.

So how long did it take me to get over this warm-and-fuzzy, happy-we're-friends crap and start wishing that Meryl and I could be something more? Two months as described above, spending day after day in Meryl's general proximity; two nights in my apartment, described next; and ten seconds in the Larson's damp Snohomish basement, described thereafter.

Why did it take me that long? Partly because I'd accepted Corinne's pronouncement that I'd become "kind of dangerous." I'd resolved to ignore the relationship-obsessed part of my brain for a while, an act made easier by the fact that Meryl was about to leave the country. Plus, Meryl had declared that she was in a "not-dating period," and after my Festival of Denial with Corinne, I was inclined to take Meryl at her word. I'd never been so full of romantic swagger that I'd believe I could attract a woman against her wishes.

❧

At the end of February, Seattle was struck by a rainstorm that blew unrelentingly for two days, causing minor flooding in certain areas of the city. One such area was Meryl's apartment.

During the storm's first night, rain puddled on the Retrograde's flat, ill-maintained roof, eventually finding weaknesses in the flashing where two sections of the brick building met. Unfortunately for Meryl, this joint ran directly above her apartment, and sometime after she'd fallen asleep, the light fixture above her bed started to drip rainwater befouled with plaster and who-knows-what-else. She'd awoken to wet, musty sheets.

Meryl called around 2:00 a.m. to ask if she could sleep on my couch. She arrived wearing sweatpants and a t-shirt.

"Thanks again," she said, adjusting the blankets I'd dug out for her. "I would've slept on my own couch, but it's even worse than the bed. I counted five different leaks up there."

"What did the Super say about it?"

"Put buckets under the leaks and don't turn on the bedroom light."

"That was his entire solution?"

"Until it stops raining anyway."

I was wide awake by the time I got back to bed, but I didn't mind—for a while, I just lay in the dark listening to the wind and rain. At certain moments, when the building would creak and groan in a certain way, it felt like Meryl and I were out at sea, riding out a storm in the hold of some rickety old ship.

I awoke smiling the next morning, but the feeling only lasted until I emerged from my bedroom: Meryl was gone, her blankets folded neatly on the coffee table. I sank, disappointed, onto the couch and read the note she'd left:

Garrett,
Thanks for the use of your sofa. If this weather keeps
up, I suspect I'll be back on it tonight.
Off to work,
M.

All day, I rooted for the storm. Screw the low-lying areas, I thought—just give me one more night of foul weather, another shot at waking up with Meryl still in my apartment.

Meryl, Clay, and I watched a movie at my place that night, the wind gusting menacingly outside. The rain was fading, but it didn't matter—with Meryl's bedroom light still impersonating a shower nozzle, she had already decided to spend another night with me. I'd never thought I'd be so grateful that Clay didn't own a couch.

ᴄ⁄ᴐ

Meryl was still asleep when I got up on Saturday. She lay on her right side, facing into the couch, but with her left arm reaching defiantly out in the opposite direction, as if feeling for something on the coffee table. By the time I got out of the shower though, she was sitting up, rolling her head gingerly from side to side.

"Hey," she said quietly.

"Hey," I said, dropping myself into the recliner. "You sleep okay?"

"Yeah, fine. Is that *more* rain I'm hearing?"

"No, just dripping—the rain seems to have stopped."

"Thank God."

Meryl and I stayed like that for a long moment, drifting in the morning quiet. Water gurgled through the building's drainpipes and tapped on windowsills, but we just sat there, still as sponges on the ocean floor. Meryl sighed but didn't move, just hunched there on the couch, the blanket still covering her legs.

I think that's when it started. In that moment, I found myself wishing that Meryl and I could just sit there indefinitely, drifting sideways through that sleepy Saturday morning. And yet I also knew that the moment would pass, that its finiteness was part of its perfection.

"Do you feel like some pancakes?" I finally asked.

"Sure."

"Shall I start some coffee too?"

"You have *coffee*?"

"I always keep some around. You know, for all my guests."

I'd offered pancakes partly because I knew they would take time to prepare, and I wanted to draw this morning out as long as possible. While I clunked around in the kitchen, Meryl lounged in the recliner, flipping through a copy of *The Seattle Weekly* that had been on my coffee table for the last month. Butter melted itself across the nonstick surface of my frying pan. The newspaper rustled in Meryl's hands. For the first time in days, the sun shone.

Even after we'd sat down to eat, we didn't talk much—just brief exchanges between mouthfuls, our forks clinking against our plates.

"I should probably go look for a new couch today," she said.

"How about the mattress—is that salvageable?"

"Probably not. Maybe I'll go over to that place in Bellevue and look...they seemed to have a lot of stuff."

"I could go with you, if you want some help."

"Sure. That'd be great."

I still didn't fully realize that Meryl Larson had hypnotized me. All I knew was that I'd do just about anything as long as it was with her. Which is probably why, on Sunday, I found myself offering to clean her parents' basement. In my defense, my original suggestion had been that we go to a matinee at Pacific Place.

"Oh, I'd love to," Meryl said, "but I should really go out

to Snohomish today. My parents' basement flooded in the storm, and all of this old furniture and stuff got soaked. My Dad wants to get it out before it starts to mildew, and I'm just worried that he'll try to do it all himself."

"Well, I'm not doing anything today...I could help."

"Oh...well, it's really nice of you to offer, but believe me, this is not how you want to spend your Sunday. It'll be really messy, and I'll probably be there all day."

"Well, it'll go that much faster with an extra pair of hands, right?"

"Well..."

"Come on...if I don't go with you, I'll just sit on the couch all day. It'd be good for me to get off my butt."

"Well, if that's what you want to do. I warn you though, you're going to get wet, and probably smelly..."

"Trust me, you don't know wet and smelly until you've spent a day on my father's lobster boat. When the wind is right, I can smell it from here."

It was a bright day, warm for February, and as we headed up I-5 toward Snohomish in Meryl's Honda, I felt quietly giddy at having contrived to spend the afternoon with her. Crossing the short trestle bridge over the Snohomish River was like sliding backwards a hundred years. With its worn, red-brick storefronts and grand old homes, Snohomish felt very different from the sprawling, new-construction suburbs that surrounded Seattle. Meryl's parents lived in a weary Victorian on the edge of the historic district. As we rolled up the driveway, Mr. Larson stepped out onto the porch and waved.

If I hadn't known otherwise, I would never have guessed that this man was just a month past a heart attack. Standing there on the porch, round and ruddy-cheeked, Mr. Larson looked more vigorous than I felt. Bald on top with trim grey hair all the way around, he wore a red flannel shirt and beige corduroys that were thinning at the knees.

"Hey Dad," Meryl said, giving him a hug. "This is my friend Garrett."

"Nice to meet you," I said, shaking his hand.

"I've wanted to thank you for recommending the computer that Meryl bought us," he said. "It's remarkable—when I was at Boeing, a system that powerful would've required its own *room*."

"Yes, and that tidbit was fascinating the first twenty times I heard it," Meryl added. "Where's Mom?"

"At the market. She should be back soon."

Meryl's father led us down the narrow stairs to the house's stone-walled basement, its sour humidity intensifying with each step. The place was packed with the accumulated detritus of several generations of Larsons—old rugs and furniture, toys and sports equipment, musty books and partial sets of china in disintegrating boxes. Since Meryl wouldn't let him lift anything, Mr. Larson settled for triage: sifting through the items and telling us where to take them—up to the attic, out to the porch for airing, or directly to the dump.

Most of the furniture was too big for one person to handle, so Meryl and I would each grab an end and baby-step our way up the steep basement stairs. It was hard work that required Meryl and I to be in unusually close proximity to each other, occasionally bumping as we navigated the crowded basement, our hands often reaching for the same holds as we lifted a waterlogged armchair or ottoman. After two months of such deliberate not-touching, these little collisions were surprising at first—each one eliciting a *sorry* or *excuse me*—but we got used to the contact soon enough. In fact, I found that the more we broke down the physical barrier that had existed between us, the further I found myself *wanting* to break it down, a desire that soon became a serious distraction for me.

After hauling an antique love-seat up three flights from the basement to the also-crowded attic, Meryl and I paused for a moment in the basement. We stood, sweating and winded, surveying what was left to haul. Mr. Larson was out on the porch unrolling the rugs that had gotten soaked, so for the moment, we were alone.

"I bet you regret having volunteered for this *now*," Meryl said.

"Not at all," I said. "This is certainly more fun than staying Seattle by myself."

"I find that hard to believe."

"Why...aren't you having fun?"

"Well, I *have* to be here."

"Oh come on..."

"Okay, maybe it's a *little* fun," she said. "Like, 5% fun, and 95% something else."

Standing there in the glow of Meryl's indulgent smile, and with the sharp, sweet scent of her exertion in my nose, something happened. I felt myself hooking my arm around her narrow shoulders and tugging her to me. I felt her body warm against mine, her arms reaching around to my back now, her smooth, soft face brushing mine, our mouths finding each other.

This didn't actually happen—Meryl and I remained where we stood, with twelve inches of musty air between us—but I came so shiveringly close to acting on my daydream that I finally saw what was going on. Despite my intention to remain romanceless and satisfied with friend-ship, all of the time that we had spent together had finally taken its toll. I'd been feeling it all weekend, but I just hadn't recognized it until now: I'd fallen in love with Meryl Larson.

"So what's next?" I asked, clapping my hands together as if anxious to get back to work. In truth, I was just trying to snap myself out of this dangerous reverie.

"Do you want to try the armchair?"

"Mm...how about something smaller for this trip? Give me time to recover from that little couchy thing."

"I believe it's called a love seat," Meryl laughed. "But if you want something small, you could just grab one of those boxes."

We didn't have much left to do, but the work became harder for me because I was also struggling against this new distraction. Up until this point in our relationship, I'd done my best to ignore Meryl's body, to pretend that she existed purely from the neck up. Now, I was suddenly aware of how good Meryl looked in her jeans and fitted black turtleneck, its sleeves pushed to her elbows. After a while, even Meryl's lobeless ears were distracting me.

By the time Meryl and I hauled the last rug out to the porch, my head was spinning. The cool air felt good on my face though, and it brought me (mostly) back to my senses.

"I can't believe we got all that stuff moved," Meryl said as we were driving a final load to the dump. "I really appre-ciate the help."

"No problem."

"My mother invited us to stay for dinner, but we don't have to if you'd rather get home. You probably had other things that you wanted to get done today."

"Not really. I'm happy to stay."

At dinner, the four of us sat clustered around one end of table that could've seated another eight people. In keeping with Mr. Larson's new dietary regime, Meryl's mother had prepared a heart-friendly feast: grilled salmon with roasted baby potatoes, carrots, and greens. It was all delicious, and on any other day, I would've gone back for seconds, but my stomach had been a little off ever since that moment in the basement with Meryl.

"So Meryl told me what you do, Garrett," Mrs. Larson said, "but I've already forgotten."

"I do computer stuff…I'm an IT consultant."

"Oh yes—you ran into each other at the airport."

"That's right," I said, returned to that strange moment at O'Hare, seeing that first blank look on Meryl's face, the recognition spreading slowly through her expression. Already, it seemed like something that had happened to two strangers.

"So, you do a lot of traveling as well?" Mrs. Larson asked.

"Not anymore. I kind of burned out on that, so I'm trying to stay local these days."

"Now there's an intriguing idea," Mrs. Larson said, turning innocently to Meryl.

Meryl just shook her head.

"My wife doesn't approve of Meryl having a career," Mr. Larson said mildly.

"You both know that's not it—I just wish she didn't have to be away for so long."

"You could always visit me, Mom."

"I know," Mrs. Larson said, nodding with resignation. "But maybe you could work on her, Garrett? Talk to her about the virtues of staying home?"

"I could try," I said, meeting Meryl's eye for an instant, "but as much as I'd rather she stay, I don't think I'd have much luck."

I felt Meryl look over at me again, but I didn't look back.

"You're probably right," Mrs. Larson sighed, "But that's never stopped me from trying."

I was a mess on the ride back to Seattle. It had been a confusing day—one minute I was recognizing the nature of my feelings for Meryl, and the next, I was being reminded of the hopelessness of it all. Perhaps this was just my fate, I thought, to be surrounded by female friends, but to remain a bachelor. *Utterly Fucked*, the Garrett Anderson story.

"So, when are you leaving?" I finally asked. As I heard the words coming out, I realized how out-of-the-blue the question must've seemed to Meryl.

"For Japan?"

"Yeah."

"Well, I don't have a firm date yet, but…probably mid-April."

I nodded, counting weeks in my head. *Six weeks, maybe seven?*

"It seems like your Mom really doesn't like your traveling," I observed.

"No, she doesn't really like any of us to go away…"

"It *is* a pretty long trip though."

"Yeah…but my promotion and this project sort of came as a package deal, so I can't really complain. I am a little worried about my Dad though."

"He seems like he's in good shape. He's really bounced back quickly."

"I hope so. At least this time I'll be able to e-mail them.

Provided they remember how to use the computer."

"Well, just have them call me if they have trouble. I'm pretty good at tech support."

"That's really nice of you to offer, but if I give them your number, my mother *will* call you. She's not shy that way—she'll be calling just to chat."

"That's okay," I said.

"Seriously? That wouldn't bother you?"

"Not at all."

That last bit—suggesting that Meryl give her parents my number—was my masochistic streak stepping forward. What better way to torture myself in Meryl's absence than by talking to her mother on the phone?

‹›

I got back to my apartment around ten o'clock and flopped onto the couch. A few minutes later, Clay knocked and pushed open the not-quite-latched door.

"Hey," he said, "what happened to you?"

"Hm?"

"Where were you all day?"

"I went to Snohomish with Meryl. Her parents' basement flooded, and we were...moving stuff."

"Oh, I see. So this is just Garrett *mooning*?"

"Mooning?"

"You know...pining, yearning, longing."

I just looked at Clay, dumbstruck. My instinct was to deny it, but I could tell from his stupid grin that there would be no point.

"Is it really that obvious?" I asked.

"Well...to *me* anyway."

"Do you think she knows?"

"It's hard to say...she's not quite as transparent as you

are."

I considered taking offense at this remark, but I knew he was right.

"So what're you going to do?" Clay asked.

"Nothing. There's nothing I *can* do."

"Why do you say that?"

"Well, it's not like I can just ask her on a date. I mean, she told me explicitly that she can't even think about relationships right now. Plus, she's leaving the country in seven weeks and won't be back until like, October. Besides which, I shouldn't even be thinking about any of this in the first place because I'm mentally unfit to be making these kinds of decisions."

"And why are you mentally unfit?" Clay asked, apparently amused by my misery.

"I'm unfit because, as I sit here right now, part of me is already feeling like this is *it*, you know, like, Meryl's the one. Which, I mean...what is wrong with me? Every woman I've ever dated, at some point I've thought, *'Maybe she's the one.'* It's pathetic, really. Corinne had it right—I'm dangerous, and until I can go into a relationship with a clear, rational head, I shouldn't even be dating."

"Okay, but what if Meryl slips away because you're too busy trying to figure out how to be rational? Honestly, I think you *have* to go into every relationship thinking that it might be the one, because that's the only way you'll be open enough to recognize it when it is. And in the end, I think it's as much about willingness as anything. People fall in love because they *want* to be in love—because they're ready and willing—and because the other person will let them."

"But that's the thing—Meryl doesn't want to be in love right now...she's said as much."

"Well, maybe that's what she said before, but people's feelings about these things can change pretty quickly."

"But that's exactly the kind of thinking that got me in trouble with Corinne…and most everyone else I've dated."

"Well, all I'm saying is, if you feel so strongly about Meryl, I think it's worth a shot."

"Really?"

"What if this is the one time you're *supposed* to go charging in uninvited? I mean, the fact that it was the wrong approach for all of those other relationships doesn't necessarily mean that it's the wrong approach for this one, does it? Maybe all those past failures were just preparing you for this."

I knew Clay was feeding me my own propaganda, but it was working. Maybe my open-to-everything, this-could-be-it attitude was the one thing I had going for me. At the very least, Clay's perspective was less depressing than the one I'd taken.

"So what would you suggest I do?" I asked.

"Well, you could go talk to her."

"And say what? *Hi Meryl, while we were moving furniture, I realized that I want to spend the rest of my life with you?* I think that would probably just freak her out."

"Why? You've been spending tons of time together, and she obviously likes you."

"Sure, she likes me as a friend, but that's a far cry from romantic attraction. Trust me—I have some experience with this."

"Okay…but if you don't talk to her, what else can you do?"

"I don't know…wait? Do it at a time when it didn't seem quite so out of the blue."

"And when would that be?"

"Well...right after she declares her undying love for *me*...I think I'd feel pretty comfortable at that point."

"How about after she starts dating somebody else? Would that work for you?"

"I just don't want things to get all weird between us. If she's not interested and I go bringing up the whole romantic thing, it'll just make her uncomfortable and probably sour our whole friendship, which is the last thing that I want. I think I'd rather never have sex again than lose Meryl as a friend."

"Uh-huh."

"I mean, of course my first choice would be to still have sex, but..."

"I get the idea."

"I'm just saying that, if I'm going to do this, I want to try to figure out where I stand with her...to see if she actually seems interested before I go doing anything drastic."

"You mean like talking to her?"

"Exactly."

14

Here Comes Your Man

My plan to study Meryl for clues about her feelings seemed like a good one until I realized that I had no idea what I was looking for. If we watched a movie together and she sat beside me on the couch instead of taking the recliner, did that mean she was ready for a relationship? If I offered her an Oreo and she declined, was she telling me to back off? Much of the time, my grand plan degenerated into me gazing longingly in Meryl's direction and moaning about the situation to Clay, who didn't want to hear it.

But then, in the second week of March, Meryl mentioned that her friend Tracy was coming to Seattle for a visit.

"If you're around, I was thinking maybe the three of us could have dinner?"

"Monday night? Sure, yeah. I have a meeting that afternoon, but I should be back."

"Tracy has to pick up Ethan at her mother-in-law's afterwards, so we'd have to eat pretty early—5:30 or so. Does that sound okay?"

Given that I had a 4:00 p.m. meeting in Bellevue, I had no business accepting Meryl's invitation, but there was also no way I was going to decline. The fact that Meryl wanted me—and apparently not Clay—to meet her best friend had to mean something, right? Sure, I'd have to make good time coming back to Belltown, but it was doable...in a helicopter.

Of course my meeting ran long, so I didn't leave Bellevue until just after five, at which point the traffic going back to Seattle was already hideous. I tried stealing some of Kevin Lanier's tailgate-and-weave driving maneuvers, but not being as slick as Kevin, they only resulted in several horn-honking near-misses and me swearing sailor-like at every car, traffic light, and pedestrian who dared get in my way.

Stopped at one particularly busy light, I noticed that the souped-up Honda Civic across from me was signaling left and already twitching over the stop line—the driver clearly planned to make his left turn in front of me, whether I liked it or not. In my addled state, I was determined not to let him succeed.

When the light turned green, I gave it everything the Jetta had into the intersection, hoping to menace the Civic into respecting my right-of-way. As expected, the Honda also raced out and started into his turn—tires chirping, soup-can exhaust blatting—but the driver didn't even seem to notice me until I was almost on top of him.

That's when I panicked, cutting sharply to the left to avoid the Civic but also putting myself directly in the path of the pickup coming behind him. Seeing no other options, I cut the wheel even harder to the left, *nearly* executing a full left turn onto the cross-street. I say "nearly" because I did make a brief excursion onto the sidewalk—thankfully, it was deserted—in the process sideswiping an impressively immobile light-pole.

I stopped the car and sat with my head on the steering

wheel. When my limbs stopped quivering, I dug out my cell phone and called Meryl.

"Hello?"

"Hi Meryl, it's Garrett."

"Hey, are you still coming?"

"Well, I'm trying, but I'm running a little late. I just thought I'd call in case you guys wanted to go without me."

"How long will you be?"

"Probably another fifteen minutes."

"Oh, that's fine—don't worry about it. As it turns out, Tracy doesn't have to pick up Ethan, so...no rush."

"Oh. Perfect. Well, I'll see you in a bit then."

I stepped out of the car to inspect the damage, my knees still wobbling with adrenaline. The Jetta's right side was scraped and dented all the way from the front wheel to the back door. The light pole had also removed my passenger-side mirror, which I found shattered on the sidewalk. As I collected the pieces, it occurred to me that maybe all my psychic self-torture over Meryl was beginning to manifest itself physically. This did not seem like a good development, for me or my long-suffering car.

I made it back to the Retrograde just before six and, after a stop at my apartment to change clothes, went up to Meryl's apartment. She and Tracy were sitting in the kitchen when I arrived.

"We were thinking of going to the Santa Fe Café," Meryl said after the introductions had been made. "Sound okay?"

"Sure."

"Do you want to drive, or should I?"

"Oh, you can drive," I said, "I feel like I've been in the car all day."

☙

Kevin and I had a client meeting in Kirkland a few days later. He was waiting in front of his building when I pulled up, his grin slipping away as the Jetta approached. When I finally stopped in front of him, he seemed loath to touch the smashed-in door handle, instead gesturing that I should roll down the window.

"Jesus Christ, Spanky, what happened to your car?"

"Oh...I had a close call the other day."

"WHAT?" he shouted back, unable to hear me over the speedboat gurgle of my unmuffled motor. The trip over the curb seemed to have further damaged the exhaust.

"I HAD A CLOSE CALL!"

"DOES THIS DOOR OPEN?"

"JUST PULL REAL HARD!"

"Jesus."

"Sorry."

"I hate to break it to you, man," Kevin said, slamming the door shut (it caught on the second try), "but once you hit something, it's no longer a close call. At that point, it's just an accident."

"Well, I just meant that I didn't hit any other cars—the light-pole did all that."

"Did the light-pole modify your exhaust system as well?"

"No, I think that was the curb."

"What the hell were you doing?"

"Well, I was running late, and this guy cut me off, so..."

"What were you late for?"

"Oh, nothing really. I was just meeting this woman who lives in my building."

"You had a *date*?"

"No, it wasn't really a date, it was just..."

I'd never even mentioned Meryl to Kevin before, but

during our ride to Kirkland, I outlined the whole situation for him. Not surprisingly, he had an opinion on the matter.

"I really think you're killing yourself with all this hanging-out stuff. The more time you two spend watching TV with baldy there, the more you're reinforcing the whole 'friend' vibe."

"I think Clay would actually agree with you on that."

"You need to change the dynamic. If you want her to start seeing you as a boyfriend, then take her on a date. I mean, you don't have to call it a date, but you need to get out and do something, just the two of you, alone in some totally new environment."

"Okay, but...how do I manage that?"

"I don't know...maybe get two tickets to a concert she'd like and tell her that a client gave them to you. Because the tickets just fell into your lap, it's not a date, but you still get your night out."

"That's an intriguing idea."

"It's not intriguing, Spanky, it's fucking *brilliant*."

"And I should definitely take relationship advice from you, right? Because you slept *where* last night?"

"Right beside my beautiful wife, thank you very much."

"Oh...really?"

"I was only in the motel for one night."

∽

I let Kevin do most of the talking at our meeting. While everyone else debated server-side versus client-side scripting, I was thinking about how to make Kevin's idea work, trying to remember if Meryl had mentioned any upcoming shows she wanted to see. Over the next few days, I memorized her CD collection a few artists at a time and then fruitlessly scoured the web and *The Seattle Weekly* for concert listings.

I'd all but given up on finding an event when Meryl herself laid the perfect idea on my coffee table.

The three of us were sitting in my living room—Meryl and I on the couch, Clay in the recliner—and Meryl was flipping through the paper looking for movie times. Before she found the listings though, she paused to study an advertisement for a Van Gogh "Portraits" exhibition that was coming to the Seattle Art Museum.

"We should go to that," she said, tapping the ad with her finger. "I love Van Gogh."

Meryl moved on so quickly that I don't think Clay even heard her, hypnotized as he was by an eye-surgery video on TLC. It was just the sort of idea I'd been waiting for, but I also knew that Meryl's "we" probably included Clay. If I were to announce that a client had given me two tickets to this Van Gogh show, Meryl might just suggest that we get Clay a ticket too.

After doing a little more research though, I determined that the opening night of the Van Gogh exhibit on the 24th was a semi-exclusive event, a $250-a-ticket benefit for some scholarship fund. That, I figured, was my best bet, provided that I could actually get some tickets. Thankfully, I knew a guy who could help.

I called my old boss Leonard, who located the tickets in less than an hour—one of his countless business associates had purchased a pair but couldn't attend. So the story I told Meryl when I called her at work wasn't a *complete* lie: I said that Leonard had offered me the tickets because a friend couldn't go. I just left out the part about my calling Leonard first.

"That's the exhibit you wanted to see, right?"

"Yeah, definitely, but...you wouldn't rather take Clay?"

"Oh, uh...no, actually, I don't think Clay's a big Van Gogh fan."

"Oh, okay. Well, great...let's go then."

When I got off the phone, I put on Soul Coughing's *Irresistible Bliss* and danced around my living room like a fool. I had a good feeling about this night, like maybe it was the first step toward something important. Halfway through "Super Bon Bon"—the bass almost buzzing my speakers off their stands—I realized that Clay was looming in my living room doorway, watching me with his crooked grin. I just about jumped out of my skin when I saw him.

"*Jesusmother*—"

"Oh, don't stop—you looked like you were having fun!"

"You scared the shit out of me."

"You usually don't play the stereo quite that loud—I just came over to see what was up. What are we celebrating?"

"Well, my old boss found me two tickets to the opening of that Van Gogh exhibit that Meryl wants to go to."

"Just two? I don't get to come?"

"Nope. Oh, and if it comes up, you don't like Van Gogh."

"I see—now you're just trying to date her without her realizing?"

"Maybe so," I said, too happy to be troubled by Clay's sarcasm. "But if things go well, that might change."

⚬⌒⚬

When the misty Friday night of the Van Gogh opening arrived, I felt myself getting nervous, as if this really were my first date with Meryl. We'd agreed to meet in front of the museum, since Meryl had a late meeting and would be coming straight from the office. Hoping the exercise might settle my nerves, I walked to the museum, spotting Meryl waiting as I came up the sidewalk. Leaning by the bus shelter, she gazed toward The Lusty Lady across the street, whose flashing pink and black marquee declared "ALL CLOTHING, 100% OFF!"

"I think you need a completely different ticket to get in there," I said when Meryl didn't notice me beside her.

"Oh...hey. Sorry...I guess I was spacing."

"Something on your mind?"

"Oh, nothing important. Just all of the things I didn't get done today."

"Ah."

"But since it's officially the weekend, I guess I shouldn't be thinking about work, huh?"

"That's right," I said, "you should be thinking about more profound things, like...how did Seattle's biggest art museum end up across the street from its most famous peep show? Although, I suspect Van Gogh might've appreciated the arrangement."

"You're probably right," Meryl smiled.

Entering through the museum's glassy, vaulted lobby, Meryl checked our coats while I headed straight to the bar-cart to get us some wine. I was surprised by how right Kevin had been about changing the dynamic between us, how from the moment we'd arrived, islanded in a murmuring stream of well-dressed strangers, Meryl and I instinctively edged closer together. And by the time I reached the bottom of my second glass of wine, my earlier nervousness was a blurry memory.

The exhibit itself was in a quieter space on the second floor, up the museum's grand, tiered staircase. Meryl and I made our way through the rooms, orbiting each other closely, shifting places as the flow of the crowd required. As we paused before the painted faces of children, prostitutes, and the artist himself, one of us might whisper a comment, but mostly we communicated in glances, posture and proximity.

The longer we continued this dance, the more I found myself longing for some small physical connection. *What if I just took her hand? What could be so horrible about that?* But as tempted as I was, I resisted, aware that the two glasses of Zinfandel (with no dinner) were perhaps doing a too much of my thinking.

"I think this one is my favorite," Meryl said as we stood before a self-portrait from the end of Van Gogh's life. Flickeringly lit in nocturnal blues and greens, the image's effect was strangely peaceful, despite the fact that he'd painted it while in an asylum.

"It's so different from the others," she whispered, her face just inches from mine. "He looks more hesitant, a little frailer. For somebody who was so troubled, he must've known himself pretty well. It's like he painted it from the inside out."

As Meryl spoke, I found myself watching *her* face instead of Van Gogh's. When she'd finished speaking, Meryl glanced up at me, and the words came out of my mouth without a thought.

"You know, you have gorgeous eyes. Just spectacularly gorgeous."

Meryl looked back at me, mute, her aforementioned eyes frozen with what appeared to be panic. For some reason, I was undeterred by this reaction.

"That's actually what I remembered most from the first time I saw you, out on the steps that day—your eyes, and the fact that you were so nice to me."

Now Meryl looked away with a mild, mortified smile,

crimson rising through her face like some kind of cartoon thermometer.

"Sorry...I didn't mean to embarrass you."

"Oh, it's okay," she said, still not looking at me. "I'm easily embarrassed."

"Should I not have said that?"

"Uh, well...you just caught me off guard."

"Give me a couple glasses of wine, and you never know what I might say."

"Are you hungry?" Meryl was still blushing, but now smiling in a broad, comic way that begged me to go along with her abrupt subject change. "I could go for some real food." As she spoke, I felt Meryl's fingers lace themselves between mine, locking our hands together.

"I can always eat," I said.

All the way down that stone staircase, with Meryl leading me by the hand, I was glow-in-the-dark Garrett, grinning from ear to ear. The descent was like a long, slow victory walk, and all we needed was the celebratory music, maybe that big chorus from Beethoven's Ninth, or the bouncing jangle of The Pixies' "Here Comes Your Man." I couldn't decide which was more surprising—that I'd said what I'd said, or that Meryl hadn't freaked out. Part of me wished that I could just linger in that mini-triumph for the rest of the night.

As Meryl and I neared the bottom of the staircase, I noticed this guy down in the lobby watching us expectantly. I'd actually seen him earlier—we'd waited together momentarily during my first trip to the bar-cart. With his sharp-featured, broad-shouldered, Brooks-Brothers, former-second-string-quarterback good looks, he'd seemed really familiar, but I hadn't been able to place him. I started to put it together when I realized that he was looking at Meryl. Just before he called out, I figured out why I recognized him—he was Wade Mullins, my frigging state senator, and Meryl's ex-fiancé.

"Meryl...hey!"

"Oh God...Wade...hi."

While Meryl and Wade were doing the hug-hug kiss-kiss thing, Wade's female companion and I smiled uncomfortably at each other. She looked to be in her mid-thirties, and was blandly striking in a faux-blonde, grew-up-with-money, former-runner-up-homecoming-queen sort-of-way.

Wade eventually introduced the woman as "Cynthia," a non-committal description that I didn't think much about until Meryl introduced me as "*my friend* Garrett." I pretended to listen while Wade and Meryl were catching up, but I was really just trying to figure out why Meryl had felt the need to define our relationship so clearly. Was the prospect that we might be involved so horrible that she had to rule it out immediately?

Even worse, Meryl and Wade actually seemed happy to see each other, exchanging the obligatory you-look-greats with a genuineness that normally would've been touching, but which on this occasion just made me gag. The longer they chatted, the further my magical moment with Meryl seemed to slip away, until I began to wonder if it had even happened. When they started talking about getting together for lunch, I had to excuse myself.

I took as long as possible in the bathroom, and when I finally emerged, Meryl was just saying goodbye to Wade and Cynthia. I waved from a distance, relieved that I'd escaped the rest of the interaction.

"Sorry about that," Meryl said. "I really didn't expect to

run into *him* tonight."

"I actually saw him earlier, but I didn't recognize him. He looks different in person...*balder* maybe."

"Balder? Really?"

"I mean, obviously I know he's not *bald*, but he's like *all* forehead."

"Hm. He looks pretty much the same to me."

We had dinner at a gratingly colorful theme restaurant down the street from the museum. I'd never liked the place, but by then it didn't matter—the evening had already been ruined by the appearance of Senator Mullins. For about sixty seconds, I'd felt certain that Meryl and I were headed into unexplored territory, but now we were right back where we'd started. That tingling moment in front of Van Gogh now seemed irretrievable—Meryl behaved as if she didn't even recall it, and I was feeling too sober to put myself out there again.

"I bet they're engaged—that's probably why he wants to have lunch, to tell me. Did you happen to notice a diamond on her finger?"

"No, but I tend to miss those things."

"Yeah, I didn't get a chance to look either. I knew it wouldn't take him long though—he needs to have some-body around."

☙

"So how'd it go?" Clay asked when I got back to my apartment.

"Before or after we ran into her handsome ex-fiancé?"

"You ran into Wade Mullins?"

"Oh yeah—thrill of a lifetime. Then Meryl made a lunch date with him, which was also exciting. And *then* she spent the rest of the evening talking about Wade and the history of their relationship. I have to say, I can't freaking *wait* to hear about lunch."

"Okay, so you ran into her old boyfriend. Why is that the end of the world?"

"Well, Meryl and I had just had this great little moment, and then Senator Forehead appeared and *poof*—it was like it never happened. I'm starting to think that my approach to this situation has been fundamentally flawed."

"You think?"

"I thought that if Meryl and I couldn't be a couple, I'd still be happy being friends, but...now I'm not so sure."

"I believe your exact words were, 'I'd rather *never have sex again* than lose her as a friend.'"

"Yeah, well...I still think it might work if she agreed to be celibate too…"

"But at this point, what would be the harm in just talking to her? If you're already so miserable, could you really make things any worse?"

"Probably in some way that I have yet to imagine."

Clay shook his head. He was losing his patience with me, and I couldn't blame him.

"I know, I know," I said. "You're absolutely right; I have to deal with this somehow. I've been pussyfooting around for too long already."

"Hallelujah."

"I mean, this is why I quit Cavanaugh, right? Because I wanted to find somebody to be with. And what kind of attitude is that anyway: *I don't want to be in a relationship right now.* It's like winning the lottery, and saying *No thanks, I don't want to be wealthy right now.*"

"There you go!"

"But what do I do exactly? I mean, I know I have to talk

to her, but should I take her out to dinner or something?"

"Garrett, haven't you had enough meals with this woman yet? Just go upstairs and tell her how you feel."

"Wouldn't that be really weird though, just going up there and spilling my guts?"

"Could it be any weirder than the way you've been acting?"

"I guess not, but...I just can't go up there tonight. I'm not in the right frame of mind."

"Okay, Garrett. Whatever."

"I'll do it tomorrow though, I swear—we're supposed to have brunch anyway."

ৎৄ

I was prepared to endure some abuse from April when Meryl and I arrived at Macrina on Saturday. My explanation that Corinne and I had broken up only seemed to confirm April's suspicion that Corinne had never existed in the first place, whereas April had now seen Meryl and I together on several occasions. When she finally came over to take our order, April pulled up an empty chair and sat right down with us.

"Howdy neighbors," April grinned.

"Hi April," I said. "You remember Meryl?"

"Of course I do," she said, slugging me semi-playfully on the arm (ouch). "How could I forget your neighbor Meryl? Hey Meryl."

"Hello," Meryl laughed.

"Anyway, what can I get you guys?"

My intention was that, at some point that morning, I would lay my cards on the table and tell Meryl everything that I'd been feeling. But the thing was, I was having such a good time just hanging out with her that I had no desire to ruin the mood by launching into something so serious. With the previous night's urgency having passed, I just wanted to enjoy my favorite French Toast with my favorite companion and not think too much.

"You know, it wasn't until I got back to my apartment last night that I realized that I'd talked about Wade nonstop through our entire dinner. I felt awful."

"Wade? The name's not ringing a bell…"

"I almost came back down and apologized. You must've been bored to tears."

"It wasn't quite that bad."

"Well, it was nice of you to listen anyway. And you have my word that I won't mention him again today."

"What do I get if you slip?"

"I don't know," Meryl laughed, "what do you want?"

"Okay, how about this: if you slip, you have to play me another song on the guitar, and this time you have to sing."

"Oh God. Well, that would definitely motivate me."

"Hey, do you feel like seeing a movie this afternoon? I've been wanting to see *Wonder Boys*…I think it's playing over at Pacific Place."

"Sure, but I have to get my grocery shopping done first. I'm down to my last roll of toilet paper, and my cupboards are starting to look like, well…*yours*. Minus the Ding Dongs, of course."

"You know, we actually call them *Ring Dings* from where I come from."

"Very interesting. I always thought you just called them *dinner*."

"I'll go to the grocery store with you if you want."

"Okay. Are you actually going to do some shopping?"

"No, I just like the supermarket."

Since I'd now be spending the whole day with Meryl, I saw no reason to force the whole "feelings" conversation— I could just play it by ear and bring it up when the moment seemed right. Relieved of that pressure, I felt instantly lighter.

Which is probably why our whole trip to QFC was such an escalating spiral of silliness. It started with me sneaking items into Meryl's cart—a tin of Spam Lite, four cans of Redi-Whip, a package of adult diapers—all of which she re-shelved without a word. Then there was Meryl, in the Health & Beauty aisle, calling over to me, "Honey, did you already finish that new tube of Preparation H?" Followed by me turning the color of a tomato, allowing her to continue. "Would you rather try the suppositories this time?"

We were behaving like teenagers, but we also seemed to be finding our way back to where we'd been the night before, back to that slightly-more-than-friends place where I could tell Meryl how gorgeous her eyes were and it was sort of okay. In fact, things seemed to be moving so swiftly in that direction that I began to think that we wouldn't need to talk after all. Maybe she already knew what I was feeling, and maybe she was feeling something similar. Maybe things were on a course to work themselves out on their own.

Despite all our goofing around, we did eventually reach the end of Meryl's shopping list. Our cashier—a heavily pierced woman in magic-marker mascara—seemed to be fuming over something when we arrived. I smiled at her as she was pulling Meryl's cart over, but all she gave me back was a belligerent stare.

I did my best to distract Meryl while the cashier was unloading the cart, but even as I was talking, I could see Meryl watching out of the corner of her eye as each item was scanned: one gallon milk, one loaf wheat bread, six yogurts. So Meryl noticed immediately when the cashier grabbed the box of Ding Dongs that I'd hidden under the paper towels.

"Hey...those aren't mine," Meryl said, more play than protest.

"Oh, don't be embarrassed, hon," I said. "Everybody needs a Ding Dong now and then."

"I can't *believe* you snuck those by me," Meryl laughed. "What are you, twelve?"

I don't know what came over me. Maybe it was the tractor-beam power of Meryl's smile, her face just inches from mine, or maybe it was just the end result of all our flirtatious misbehavior in the aisles. Whatever the reason, I kissed her. I just leaned down and kissed her smiling mouth. Caught up in that moment, it seemed perfectly natural to me, but... apparently, not to Meryl.

She didn't move or pull away, but she didn't exactly participate either. It was like an *Unsolved Mysteries* reenactment of the time I'd kissed Bella that night on the beach, except of course Meryl and I were standing in the glaring daylight of the checkout line at QFC. As I withdrew, Meryl turned her face away, instantly red. I looked mostly at the floor, but glanced sheepishly up at the cashier to see how much she'd noticed. She was actually waiting for us, her expression one of utter boredom.

"Do you want the Ding Dongs or not?" she asked, still holding the box.

"I guess not," I said. "Sorry about that."

Meryl and I remained shoulder-to-shoulder through the rest of the checkout process, but we were completely silent for the first time all day. Watching the cashier wave one item after another over the scanner, I was already feeling nostalgic for the way we had been just a half-hour before. The cashier scanned a can of tuna, and I thought, "I remember when she put that in the cart. Things were so much better then, back before I'd *completely lost my mind*."

"I'm so sorry," I said, once we were outside. "I shouldn't have done that...it was a stupid, stupid thing."

"It's okay," Meryl said, urging the rattling cart across the asphalt toward her car. "It's just where I'm leaving so soon, I don't think it would be a good idea, you know?"

"You're absolutely right—I was way out of line."

"I mean, it's as much my fault, I know. We've gotten really close, and...that's partly why I don't think it would be a good idea. Our friendship means a lot to me, and where I've got less than two weeks left in Seattle, I don't want things to get all weird between us."

"Absolutely," I nodded as Meryl was unlocking the trunk to her car. But then I actually heard what Meryl had said. "Wait...less than two weeks? When are you leaving?"

"Well, I was originally supposed to leave on the 17th, but as it turns out, I have to be there sooner, so...now I'm leaving a week from Monday."

"Oh..."

"It just came together yesterday...I hadn't gotten a chance to tell you."

"I see."

"Please just promise me that things aren't going to get weird between us," she said, looking directly at me for the first time since the kiss. "I really don't want that to happen."

"No, it won't get weird...I promise. Of course it won't."

But even as I was saying this, I was plotting ways to avoid Meryl for the next nine days. It wasn't that I was angry or even hurt—I was just embarrassed...horribly, horribly embarrassed. I figured we could probably resume our old rapport someday, but it would be a while before I could look at her without re-experiencing my checkout-line mortification. The fact that she was leaving for six months suddenly seemed like a blessing.

Of course, I still had to spend the rest of the day with her. In the name of proving that things weren't going to get weird, I hauled her groceries up to the third floor, helped her put them away, and even went to the movies with her that afternoon. The whole day though, I felt like I'd left my body and was watching an understudy play the role of Garrett Anderson.

For a stand-in, he was reasonably convincing, but something was off—his laugh was a little too manic, and he had the timing of an overseas phone call. But then again, Meryl's performance wasn't entirely believable either—she talked too much, mostly about work, filling every little silence in a way that just wasn't like her. One had the sense that this entire production was being enacted by second-stringers.

❧

Sunday granted me a small reprieve—Meryl spent the day in Snohomish (and this time, I didn't offer to go along). When Bella called that afternoon, I almost didn't answer, but I decided that I should just get it over with and tell her the whole story.

"I'm sorry, Garrett," she said. "I wish there was something I could do."

"Well...at least I finally know."

"Know what?"

"That we just weren't in the same place after all. I mean, she even told me that she didn't want a relationship, but I somehow convinced myself that she'd change her mind. It's like a sickness with me. Heck, I even made the same mistake with you, right?"

"Well..."

"I just keep throwing myself off that same cliff and then running back up and throwing myself off again. At this point, it's just getting old."

15

The Fugitive

I just avoided Meryl for the next few days—given that she was leaving so soon, I saw no reason to torture myself. I also knew that if I was forced to look Meryl in the eye, she'd see how disappointed I was. Having her pity me, I thought, was the only way that I might feel worse than I already did. And for the time being anyway, I didn't want to see Clay either—I didn't even want to *sense* that he had thoughts on the Meryl debacle—what I should've done, what I should do now, blah fucking blah.

Of course avoiding both Meryl and Clay meant spending a lot of time away from the Retrograde, something that didn't come naturally to me. For the first couple days of that week, I worked in my apartment until about four, and then I took my laptop down to the new Starbucks on First Ave. I'd never understood who would go to Starbucks when Macrina Bakery was right down the street, but I soon found out—fugitives like myself, and tourists.

When I'd had enough of Starbucks (a scruffy fugitive-type with his own laptop appeared to be on the verge of striking up a conversation), I headed over to the Cinerama and slipped into an early movie. Finally around ten o'clock, I snuck home under the cover of darkness, relieved that

Clay was playing his stereo loud enough to mask the sounds of my return. Inside, my answering machine was flashing with two hang-up calls, and Meryl's number was the only one in the Caller ID.

On Wednesday, Kevin was supposed to come to my apartment around five to discuss some new projects, but I e-mailed him and suggested that we meet at the Belltown Pub instead (right beside the Starbucks—I was working my way down First Ave). I explained that I just needed to get out of my apartment for a while, to get some air. That afternoon, I packed up my computer and went down to the pub early to avoid running into Meryl on her way home from work.

I waved to Kevin as he came through the door. He ambled over to the table, hands pocketed, with an eyebrow-raised smirk on his face.

"What's up, Spanks?"

"Not much. How'd it go today?"

"Fine. I think they're all set for a while. I'll shoot them an invoice tomorrow."

"You want a beer or something?"

"Sure."

We made work-related small talk for a few minutes, but the whole time, Kevin watched me with a kind of suspicious curiosity, his expression reminiscent of the one my sister had worn the day I'd told her about seeing Bigfoot in downtown Portland.

"So why are we here, Spanky?" Kevin finally asked.

"Well, I've outlined the projects we've got on deck so we can go through them—"

"No, I know that. I mean, why are we *here*?"

"Oh, I don't know. I just needed to get out...I've been in the apartment all day."

"Uh-huh. Is that your final answer?"

"I think so..."

"I've just never known you to be the cabin-fever type. And you've never particularly liked bars."

"Well, I just don't want to be at my apartment right now...because I'm avoiding Meryl."

"The woman you told me about? What happened?"

"Nothing really. That's the problem I guess—it's just become painfully clear that it's not going to work out, so I'm avoiding her until she leaves town on Monday."

After Kevin and I wrapped up our work-talk, we ordered some food. It was good to have a comrade after two nights of hiding-out on my own.

"So how are things with Ingrid?" I asked at one point, realizing that Kevin hadn't mentioned her.

"Well, let's see...she's *pregnant*. That's something I guess."

"She's *pregnant*?"

"Yup."

"Intentionally?"

"Sort of."

"Well that's great—congratulations! How do you feel?"

"Good...I think. Although I'm having real trouble seeing myself as some poor individual's father."

"Oh, you'll be a great Dad, Kevin."

"You might be the only one who thinks so."

"Well, I didn't say that you'd be *responsible*, but that kid will have a lot of fun."

Kevin and I stayed at the pub until around eight, when Ingrid called. I heard Kevin tell her that we were "celebrating the good news," but his pained grin suggested that she wasn't buying it.

Packing up my stuff, I slunk back to the Retrograde,

sticking close to the buildings and peering around corners before proceeding. In the end though, my stealth was all for naught—Clay and Meryl were sitting in my living room, watching my TV, when I got home.

I was annoyed—neither of them had asked if they could watch my TV, and on top of that, they both seemed awfully cheerful. I'd also hoped that, after two days of conspicuous absences and unreturned phone calls, they'd deduce that I was avoiding them and give me some space.

"Hey," Clay called as I came through the door.

"I hope you don't mind," Meryl said, "we broke in to watch your TV."

"That's fine," I said evenly, hanging up my coat and trying not to betray my annoyance.

"Did you have a late meeting or something?" Meryl asked.

"Yeah...Kevin and I had to talk about some things, and then we had dinner."

I really didn't want to join them in the living room, but there was no way of avoiding it. Since Meryl had taken the recliner, I sat down on the couch beside Clay, keeping my eyes fixed on the TV. They seemed to be watching *Die Hard* on cable, and although this was a bizarre choice for the two of them, I wasn't going to give them the satisfaction of asking about it. On the next commercial, Meryl swiveled around in the recliner and looked at me.

"So Clay and I were saying that we should do something fun this weekend, since it'll be my last one here for a while. I suggested that we go up to Victoria for a night. You'd mentioned wanting to go there, right?"

"But you're leaving Monday, right? Don't you have to pack and all that?"

"Yeah, but I'm pretty much done."

"Well, I should probably check with Kevin. He mentioned that he might need a hand this weekend...server upgrades that we can't do during business hours."

"Oh. Okay."

"I'll let you know though."

"Okay. Well...it was just an idea."

Meryl went home when *Die Hard* ended, but Clay remained planted on my couch.

"So, what was that all about?" he asked.

"What?"

"Come on, Garrett...even in the realm of fake excuses, that one wasn't very convincing. You never work weekends."

"Well...*this weekend* I might have to, okay?"

"She told me what happened at QFC."

"Oh."

"She also said you promised things wouldn't get weird between you two."

"Well, I figure that if I don't actually see her, things are far less likely to get weird."

Clay just looked at me.

"I don't understand," I said. "What do you want me to do?"

"Get over yourself and come to Victoria with us."

"I just don't know if I can handle that right now...it'd just be too uncomfortable."

"Isn't this the same woman that you were just talking about, saying how wonderful she was and how important her friendship was to you? Do you remember that?"

"Yeah."

"Well, now she's leaving for six months. Is this how you want her to remember you the whole time she's in Japan—

sulking like a little kid?"

"No."

"Well, then just do this. Come to Victoria with us, have a good time for one more weekend, and then for the next six months, you can sulk to your heart's content."

യ

On Saturday morning, the three of us headed for Tsaw-wassen, British Columbia, where we would get the car-ferry to Victoria. I'd finally given up feeling awkward around Meryl, and now I was just bummed-out: bummed that Meryl was leaving, bummed that things hadn't worked out between us, and bummed that I'd fouled things up by even trying.

The ferry ride was a pleasant surprise. It was sunny if not exactly warm, so we sat out on the deck, absorbing the fresh air and change of scenery. As we rumbled along, weaving amongst the evergreen-encrusted islands that clotted the waters between mainland BC and Vancouver Island, I felt the heaviness of the last week lifting.

Victoria was just as beautiful as I'd heard—like a turn-of-the-last-century British port that had been miniaturized, sanitized, and dropped on the Canadian coast. The whole city seemed to be overflowing with flowers—pots hanging from light-poles, window boxes erupting from hotels and restaurants, and clusters springing from every balcony. It was a very comfortable place, wrapped around a placid little harbor that looked too clean for anything more serious than sailboats. Arriving in Victoria, I immediately regretted the fact that it had taken me so many years to get there.

Around two o'clock, we checked into our hotel, a quaint four-story place downtown with a peripheral view of the water. Since the weather was so good, Meryl suggested that we go for a walk, remembering a quiet beach nearby from a previous visit. We parked Meryl's car on a sleepy, house-lined street and followed a path through the trees and out to the water.

The wind had kicked up, discouraging conversation, so we worked our way down the rugged beach quietly, together but separate, moving gradually toward a rocky promontory that could've been the end of everything, or merely a corner to another stretch of beach. Each of us picked along at a different pace, with Clay in particular venturing further and further from us, mounting the outcroppings that extended into the cold, sloshing water.

Eventually, I realized that I'd completely lost sight of Clay. I couldn't imagine that he'd made it to the corner already, but there was nowhere else for him to have gone, except into the ocean. Meryl was nearby—sitting cross-legged on a big rock, facing out toward the water—so I made my way over and sat down beside her.

"Hey," I said. "Did you see where Clay went?"

Meryl squinted over at me, a wincing smile. "Actually, Clay left."

"Back to the hotel?"

"No...back to Seattle."

"He's going back to *Seattle*? Right now?"

"Yeah," she nodded, still with that uneasy smile.

"Why? Why would he do that?"

"Well...because that was sort of the plan?"

"What plan?"

"Well, from the way you were acting, I knew you wouldn't come all the way up here if it was just the two of us, so...Clay said he'd make sure that you got here, and then he'd take the ferry back to Seattle."

"But why?"

"Because I wanted to talk to you."

"About what?"

"About a guy. Somebody I've kind of been seeing."

"You've been *seeing* somebody?" I hadn't meant to sound angry, but it had sort of come out that way.

"Kind of."

"Who?" I asked, wondering how she'd possibly had the time.

"Just this guy...somebody I met a few months ago," she said, looking out toward the water. "Actually, I met him at the airport."

"Oh," I murmured, finally catching on. "That guy."

"I liked him right away...we just kind of clicked, you know, and I felt really comfortable around him. And at the time, he was seeing somebody else, which was actually great as far as I was concerned, because I didn't feel like I could really be in a relationship anyway, and it kind of took the pressure off."

"Uh-huh."

"But the more I got to know this guy, the more I liked him. He's just this big *heart*, you know, and I loved that about him. He's just completely unable to hide what he's feeling, no matter how hard he tries. And more than that, he can't help but act on what he's feeling, even if it's an incredibly bad idea at the time."

"Mm."

"And I mean, *that's* the kind of person that I want in my life, you know? It's not always convenient, but it's *real*, and it's rare. And despite the fact that supposedly I didn't want a relationship, I found myself thinking up ways to spend time with him. And I kept saying to myself, 'I'm *sooo* glad that he's with somebody, because otherwise I'd be really con-flicted about this.' I mean, at the time, it seemed like the perfect situation—I didn't want a relationship, and he was already in one, so we could just hang out without things getting too complicated. I didn't have to worry about where it might go."

"Uh-huh."

"But then he *broke up* with the woman he'd been seeing, which left me in a really weird spot. I started thinking things I really didn't want to be thinking. I kept telling myself that there was no way I could start a relationship when I was about to leave the country, but...I was also kind of slipping into it, little by little. And *then*, just when I was most con-fused about everything, the jerk went and kissed me. At the grocery store, if you can believe that."

"Oh, I'd believe it," I said, staring down at my hands.

"And when it happened, I just panicked. I was so surprised, and I'd so thoroughly convinced myself that I couldn't let this happen, that I shot him down. The practi-cal, career-minded part of me took over, saying, it's not a good idea. But almost right away, I felt wrong about it...I knew I'd made a mistake. Seeing the look on your face—"

"His face…"

"Right. But at that point, I still didn't know what to say. I was still so turned-around, I didn't think there was any-thing I could do. But then once I had time to think about it, I realized that there *was* something I could do. All along, I'd been listening to this voice in my head saying, *You can't do this now, you need to concentrate on work, wait until you get back from Japan.* But I suddenly realized, that's not *my* voice. I thought: why *can't* I do this now? Why should I wait? And all at once, I felt like such an incredible jerk for letting my stupid job get in the way, the very thing that I'd so resented Wade for doing. I never in a million years thought that I'd become that kind of person, but somehow...I had. And I wasn't even *liking* my job that much."

"Mm."

"So...anyway. This guy..."

"Yeah."

"I didn't mean to do it, but...I think I kind of hurt his feelings, and I want to find a way to let him know that I really do care about him, and that if he's willing to wait, I'll definitely make it up to him. Any ideas about how I might do that?"

"I don't know..." I mumbled, awash in embarrassment.

"I mean, I did have *one* thought..."

And then she kissed me. She took my face in her hands and kissed me squarely on the lips. I won't claim that, aesthetically speaking, it was the most perfect kiss in human history—between the onshore breeze and the emotion of the moment, there was some eye-watering and even a little nose-running. Despite all that though, it was undoubtedly the most explosively wonderful I'd ever felt in my thirty years on planet Earth.

As much as I'd hoped for it and fantasized about it, in the end, I was completely overwhelmed by the fact that Meryl felt the same way that I did. For the first time, it wasn't just me pining after someone who was ambivalent to my existence. Finally, I was truly in sync with someone else. Sitting there with Meryl, her face warm against mine, I could only wonder what I'd ever done to deserve such an honor.

"That might do the trick," I said when I was able to speak again.

"Yeah?"

"I'm really sorry, Meryl...I—"

"Let's not beat ourselves up too much, okay? This isn't an exact science."

After a while, we got up and headed back down the beach, walking hand-in-hand now and bumping into each other regularly as we negotiated the gritty sand.

"So," I said eventually, "I was wondering, if you're not busy tonight, if maybe you'd want to have dinner with me?"

"I don't know...that's awfully forward of you."

"I don't mess around, you know? I'm just a direct, to-the-point kind-of-guy."

"Well, I guess I could, especially since the only other guy I knew here ditched me back on the beach."

"I have to say, I'm still a little flabbergasted by that."

"Me too actually. It was all I could do to keep from laughing. That's why I was facing the water—so I wouldn't have to watch him when he made his break."

"And you actually *planned* that?"

"Well, the taking off part was all Clay's idea. I just want-ed him to come along and then maybe leave us alone for a while. But he thought that this would be better...or at least more fun for him. He was pretty excited about it actually."

ༀ

That night, eighteen months after we'd first met on the front steps of the Retrograde, and thirty-six hours before she was to board a flight to Japan, Meryl and I went on our first official date. We had dinner at a funky, wood-paneled fish house called Pescatore's, and afterward, we strolled around Victoria's sheltered inner harbor, eventually stopping on a bench facing the marina. Holding Meryl's hand on my lap and watching the wavering reflections of streetlights on the water, I found myself unable to stop smiling.

"So," Meryl said, nudging me with her leg, "I guess you can stop trying to convince April that we're just neighbors."

"To be honest, I wasn't trying *that* hard."

"But now, if she doesn't see me for six months, she'll probably be pretty confused."

"That's an excellent point. Maybe you should consider canceling your trip—you know, for April's sake."

"I think she'll manage."

"Sorry. I had to give it a shot."

"You could just come visit me over there."

"You wouldn't mind that?"

"I think I just invited you."

"That would be great. Of course I don't speak any Japanese, so I'd probably have to hire an interpreter or something."

"I can probably recommend somebody."

Meryl and I hardly slept that night, but not for the reason you might think. For most of the night, we just lay there in the dark, sometimes talking, sometimes not. It was just so amazing to have her there beside me that I didn't want to miss a second of it. I knew it wasn't possible, but I wished that I could just stay awake until she had to leave.

16
Arrivals & Departures
04.03.2000

Despite my hopes for a last-minute change of heart, Meryl didn't cancel her trip. It struck me as a rather cruel reversal that I, having rejected a life of perpetual motion in hopes of finding someone, was now being left behind. Yes, she was coming back, but that wasn't much of a consolation as we drove to Sea-Tac. There's something irrevocable about air travel—once you're on that plane, you're going *somewhere*, and there's no guarantee that you'll ever return to where you started. Airline jargon aside, all flights are really one-way.

Once she'd checked her luggage, Meryl and I sat down near her gate. I hate all goodbyes—there's just no way to do them right—but I knew that this one would be harder than most. I had months of backlogged feelings, and in the end, I'd have 25 words or less in which to express them. It was a no-win situation.

Eventually though, the moment came—Meryl's row was called for boarding. We just sat looking at each other for a long moment.

"I'm really going to miss you," I said, standing up and hugging her to me.

"Me too."

"I just don't feel like I've had time to say everything I

wanted to say, you know? There's all this stuff that wants to come out, but...I'll think of it all in the car on the way home."

"There'll be time. I promise."

"If you say so," I said, now looking directly into Meryl's cider-brown eyes. And then, before I even realized what was happening, I said it: "I love you."

Once the words were out, I realized that this was really all I'd wanted to say. The real obstacle hadn't been time; it had been whether or not I'd dare tell Meryl what I was actually feeling. And just as she had in the checkout line at QFC, Meryl turned her face away. But after a beat she turned back to me.

"I love you too," she whispered, pulling me closer and resting her head against me.

We stayed like that for a while, locked together just as we'd been that night at Everett Medical Center.

"Okay," Meryl said eventually, "I have to go before I start to cry."

"Stay safe, okay?" I said, reluctantly loosening my grip.

"I will."

"I love you," I said.

"You said that already," she smiled.

"I know. I can't seem to stop."

When Meryl finally hustled off toward the gate, I could only watch her go, tears rolling down my face as she disappeared into the jetway. The perpetual hubbub of airport life swirled around me, unaffected.

Sitting down by Meryl's gate, I thought about my old life with Cavanaugh Associates, and in particular, that day with Dana Burns. I'd felt certain that if I had someone like Dana in my life, I would never feel bad again, or at least not